ECLIPSE
OF THE
SON

BY

CARON HARRISON

Published by

Caron Harrison
Ballabunt Croft
Cooil Road
BRADDAN
Isle of Man
IM4 2AQ

Copyright © 2002 Caron Harrison

All rights reserved. No part of this publication may be reproduced, stored in a retrieval system, or transmitted in any form or by any means, electronic, mechanical, photocopying, recording or otherwise, without prior permission in writing from Caron Harrison

Caron Harrison has asserted her moral right to be identified as the author of this work.
All the characters in this book are fictitious, and any resemblance to actual persons, living or dead, is purely coincidental.

ISBN 0 9531155 2 6

Designed and produced by
The Short Run Book Company Ltd,
St Stephen's House,
Arthur Road
WINDSOR,
Berkshire, SL4 1RY

Also by Caron Harrison

The 'Cider and Schnapps' Novels

Shades of Grey

Divided Loyalties

Acknowledgements

My heartfelt thanks must go to my long-suffering husband, Nigel, and my daughters, Bryony and Erica, for their helpful comments and patience over the years, also to all the friends and family who have encouraged me to persist in self-publishing. My thanks are also due to Hildegard Becker for her hospitality and providing me with insights into the German way of life. Finally I must mention our dog, Bonny, whose daily walks over the past fourteen years have proved inspirational.

ONE

Gustav Halstrup slammed the newspaper onto the table in disgust, setting his empty coffee cup rattling. So the murdering traitor was free because his son, Siegfried, the movement's brightest star, had turned his coat too! Never would he have expected it of Siegfried. He was the last person, the very last person to squeal on his comrades, even on his own mother and stepfather, for the sake of the father he had hated since the day he was born. It was simply not possible!

Gustav took off his glasses and gazed up Berlin's bustling Kurfürstendamm towards the Kaiser-Wilhelm-Gedächtniskirche. The morning traffic was at a standstill. A large van delivering to one of the exclusive furriers had scraped the side of a florist's van whilst trying to park and was now projecting out into the traffic. The two drivers were loudly haranguing each other until the arrival of a police car swiftly cut short the argument. Ignoring the fracas, Gustav signalled to his usual waiter for more coffee. He had more important things on his mind than Berlin's traffic problems. As a theatre actor he was usually on stage during the evening television and radio news reports. He relied instead on the morning paper to keep him thoroughly informed about the progress of Karl Driesler's trial. Siegfried's testimony, confirming Karl's account of events, had shocked him to the core. Each morning since he had risen early to buy a paper and read for himself the full and horrific details.

The waiter arrived with the coffee. Young but experienced, he knew the café's regular customers and fussed over the famous actor.

"Your top-up, Herr Halstrup. Can I get you anything else?"

The actor was usually quite affable, but today the waiter's question was answered by a curt shake of the head, a head that sprouted grey and brown curly hair. It was not so much Gustav Halstrup's looks that had gained him fame, the waiter reflected, more his dynamism, strength of character and, when needed, his charm. The latter was distinctly lacking today. He poured fresh coffee then retreated gracefully as the actor waved him briskly away.

Gustav donned his wire-rimmed glasses again, picked up the paper and continued reading the final résumé of the Dortmund-based trial that had gripped the country's attention for so long.

The defendant, Karl Driesler, had finally been acquitted of the murder of the Free Democratic Party politician Josef Garisch on the grounds that a guilty verdict would have been unsafe. There was no denying Driesler was holding the gun when it fired, but the judges had accepted the defence's claims that Garisch's own German Shepherd dog attacking the defendant had possibly caused the gun to fire. Taking into account other mitigating circumstances they had heard during the trial, the judges deemed Driesler had also served sufficient of his current sentence for grievous bodily harm to his son, and allowed him to walk out of court a free man.

The newspaper took every opportunity to remind its readers of the neo-Nazi slant to the story. The defendant claimed that the politician was a former SS officer with current neo-Nazi contacts, who included Driesler's son, Siegfried, as well as Garisch's son, Wolfgang. To begin with, Siegfried Driesler and Wolfgang Garisch had stated that the defendant had pulled the gun on Garisch senior. Then, in an extraordinary about-turn before the trial began, Wolfgang Garisch and Siegfried Driesler had both agreed with the defendant that Josef Garisch had pulled the gun on Karl Driesler first and that Driesler had snatched it off him in self-defence.

Unlike the general public and the judges, however, Gustav had known Karl and Siegfried Driesler, as well as the murdered politician, personally. Sipping his coffee he thought back eighteen years to his trip to England in 1950 when he had first met the former prisoner of war and his wayward illegitimate son. Gustav had found the six-year-old Siegfried a lost soul crying out for guidance, only knowing he hated the father who had been a traitor to Nazism. Gustav remembered with fondness the way the little boy had responded to his instruction in duplicity; instruction that had blossomed further than he would have dreamed possible, until Siegfried Driesler had become one of the neo-Nazis' most accomplished assassins. Gustav had felt immensely proud of that boy, keeping track of his progress and involvement in the higher echelons of the movement, although never meeting up with him personally. Secrecy and security were paramount and Gustav's high profile as an actor restricted his movements. Much as he had wanted to meet Siegfried again, the young man's activities were too dangerous to be associated with, as Josef Garisch had found to his cost.

But now Siegfried was a traitor himself.

Deep in thought Gustav let the paper fall to the table. A moment later he was dragged from his ruminations by a shadow falling across it and he looked up to see his flat-mate and fellow-actor, Christian Bracht, reading over his shoulder.

"Been here long?" Christian Bracht asked breezily. "You seem to be getting up earlier and earlier these days." He pulled out a chair and sat down close to Gustav so he could continue reading the newspaper. The waiter had spotted the new arrival and was already threading his way through the tables, bringing a fresh cup of coffee and a bread roll for the young man he suspected was Gustav Halstrup's lover.

"Yes, it's the spring air and lighter mornings. I can't sleep in any more," Gustav replied just as breezily, all anger immediately buried deep inside. He had kept his interest in the trial and connection with the Driesler family secret from Christian, who had no idea about Gustav's neo-Nazi involvement. He reached in his jacket for his cigarettes and lit one, not bothering to offer one to his young lover until after Christian had drunk his first cup of coffee.

Christian Bracht pointed to the paragraph detailing the murdered politician's former identity. "Makes you wonder, doesn't it? These politicians could be anybody. It's incredible that a former SS officer could be elected to the *Landesrat!*"

"Yes, but nobody knew what he was. They weren't voting for a Nazi," Gustav countered.

"Of course not. But the fact they didn't know is what makes it so shocking. Perhaps the authorities will check out all our politicians even more thoroughly now. Maybe find a few more skeletons in cupboards," Christian laughed, breaking open his roll and spreading it thickly with butter. "This Driesler chap did us all a big favour, by the look of things. He deserves to have got off."

"Absolutely. We can't have Nazis getting their feet back in the door," Gustav agreed.

"It just goes to show, you can never be sure who these Nazis are." Christian took a large bite out of the roll, blissfully unaware of his lover's mendacity.

"So it would seem." Gustav drew deeply on his cigarette then stubbed it out in the cut-glass ashtray. He then picked up the newspaper, folded it and deftly changed the subject. "How long do you reckon this play will run for?"

Christian was only too happy to accept the change. The stage was always a preferable subject to politics. "Six weeks at the most. Load of rubbish really. It's too way-out even for the hippies in the audience. 'Stockhausen on stage', as one of the reviews called it. They weren't wrong for once." He smiled at Gustav. "Still, they liked you, as usual."

"Hah! The reviewer's a friend. Owed me a favour." Fiddling with the cigarette butt, grinding it in its own ash, Gustav realised he must deal with the traitors. He came to an abrupt decision. "I've had enough, Christian. These plays are getting worse and worse. I need a break – some time out to re-assess my life. When this play closes I'm off."

"Off?" Christian sat in stunned incomprehension. "Off where?"

Gustav shrugged. "I've no idea yet. I've only just thought about it."

Christian put his hand on Gustav's. "But what about me? Us?"

Gustav shook off his partner's hand. They had always been careful in public not to display any affection towards each other. "Sorry. Call it a mid-life crisis if you like, but I've had enough. I'll leave Berlin. Pastures new and all that."

"But it doesn't make sense! You're well known here."

"All the more reason to get out. I'm getting stale here. It's all happening elsewhere ... in the West."

"I'll come too!"

Gustav looked Christian forcefully in the eye. "No! Nothing personal, but I'm going alone."

*

It was the end of yet another harrowing chapter in his life. His innermost fears had been laid bare to the world, his mental status put under the microscope, his character dissected and reassembled by the media into strange and unrecognisable forms. To be fair, for the most part they had been sympathetic once the full story came out, but his trial had brought him to the attention of those fanatics who still lurked in the shadows and who would now seek vengeance for his crime.

The departure lounge at Düsseldorf airport was almost deserted as Karl Driesler found a seat near the gate for the London Heathrow flight. A girl of about fourteen sat nearby, trying to read a book, but she kept nervously looking up at the people gathering in the area. Karl also felt nervous of those around him, half-expecting yet another reporter to lob awkward questions his way. A gaggle of passengers sauntered up, mostly businessmen in leather coats clutching briefcases and copies of *Frankfurter Allgemeine* or *The Times*, depending on nationality or inclination. Karl could have read either, but at the moment his concentration would not stretch beyond his own world and his newly regained freedom.

So much had happened in the last eight months, so many terrible things but also several miracles. He had killed a man, betrayed his wife, lost his mother and nearly died himself of complications from an old war wound. But in counterbalance to all that, he had been acquitted of the murder, while his illegitimate son, Siegfried, had joined the family fold at long last, having angrily shunned it all his life. And, as if that wasn't enough, Sophie, Siegfried's wife, was expecting a baby in the summer. Karl smiled at the news that was still sinking in. He was going to be a grandfather, and he was going home at last.

The girl sitting nearby smiled back and Karl realised she thought he was smiling at her. She looked rather lonely and uncertain. It was probably the first time she had flown alone, even flown at all, he thought. No. It was her return flight, he decided. She was English. He could tell by her clothing: faded jeans and hand-knitted mauve jumper. His own daughter, Sabina, had worn similar clothing at that age, but sported West German fashion now she lived over here in his childhood home.

His thoughts went back fifteen minutes to when he had kissed his daughter goodbye and shaken her boyfriend Wolf's hand. Siegfried had been there too, and leaving him so soon after their reconciliation had been particularly hard. Although he could still feel the pressure of Siegfried's hand on his back from their embrace he now felt totally cut off from them all, as if the prison door had slammed shut on him again.

He shuddered. A departure lounge was a bit like prison in some ways; you could not leave it until you had permission.

Stupid thought! As a distraction he looked over to the girl again. She seemed wary now, having smiled at a stranger, and Karl decided it was probably best to ignore her unless she got into difficulties with anything or anyone. Her long blonde curls and innocent face would make her a target for any lecherous types around, although the elderly lady just sitting down opposite him hardly fitted the bill. Her feathered hat and the cut of her suit proclaimed she was German. She glanced casually at him, as though doing a similar assessment of his nationality, and he thought she might find his English-tailored suit but Nordic appearance confusing. As he suspected, she peered at him harder, frowned then hurriedly picked up her hand baggage and moved further away to a safer distance.

His face had been splashed over the newspapers and on television as an alleged killer. Although acquitted, the verdict had left sufficient doubt in some people's minds to condemn him still as a murderer who had got off on a technicality. At least back in Britain his trial had not been reported except in his local paper, the *Hereford Times*. Over the years he had been living in England his name had featured in it several times. The locals all knew at least a part of his troubled history.

The past would never leave him, he realised, feeling the start of that familiar plunge into depression. The trial was yet another weight on the balance against him. Not only was he German and ex-SS, but now a murderer, albeit an acquitted one. On the face of it people might be right to judge him harshly, but they simply did not know all the facts.

The pit in his mind was deepening and he had to do something about it. During the war he had invoked his girlfriend Ilse's name to see him through the terrors, but after marrying Katherine in 1947 while still a prisoner of war of the British, it had been her name that had seen him through his dark hours. Breathing slowly and deeply he mentally repeated her name but, despite his mantra, his current fear burst through the mental barricade. Has she forgiven me?

Facing his wife again was going to be the hardest part of everything that had happened. Since his adultery with Ilse, Siegfried's mother, last August he and Katherine had had precious little time together. He had always been in custody and they had found conversation very difficult. Katherine's letters assured him she had forgiven him but he would soon be finding out if that were really true.

That night with Ilse had smitten his conscience far more than the killing of Josef Garisch. The latter event had been a blessing, a release from the shackles of the past, a wrapping up of history in brown paper and filing it away at last. But betraying Katherine was a guilt that would never die, and he must learn to live with it.

An announcement for the Heathrow flight came in German and Karl saw the teenage girl look up anxiously at the departures' board. She relaxed when the English translation followed and scooped up her shoulder bag, keen to be safely on the plane. Other passengers were gathering their belongings together but Karl felt a sudden reluctance to move. Here in the departure lounge he was in limbo, cushioned from the world outside like in prison. Now he had to face the world again, a free man.

The last thought unexpectedly made him smile. It was like his release from the POW camp all over again.

With that memory of happier times he picked up his raincoat and duty-free bag containing perfume for Katherine, and headed for the gate.

*

Sabina Driesler gave one last wave as she watched her father disappear through passport control on his way back to England and freedom proper. Wiping the tears from her eyes she tugged at her boyfriend's sleeve. "I need a coffee."

Wolfgang Garisch guessed she wanted to stay in the airport near her father as long as possible until his plane actually took off. "Me too."

Siegfried Driesler, Sabina's half-brother, was also at the airport to see his father off. He pretended to consult his watch, but he too was grateful for the chance to delay resuming his old life. "I'll join you. I could do with a bite to eat before driving to Sophie." He realised he might be unwelcome company for the pair of lovebirds. "Do you mind?"

Sabina looked up at Wolf. He seemed amenable. "Why not? I'm sure we could manage something to eat too," she said with a smile.

Wolf nodded his agreement, cast his eyes about for a sign to the restaurant then set off, hand in hand with Sabina. Siegfried followed the pair he had thrown together with the intention of turning Sabina into a Nazi in order to torment their father. He was still amazed at the totally unexpected results of his matchmaking, turning Wolf away from Nazism. Siegfried winced. His simple plot had proved devastating in the dramatic changes it had wrought to all their lives. Everything was so damned complicated now.

Düsseldorf airport's restaurant was not yet busy and they managed to find a table overlooking the taxiing aircraft. They quickly spotted what they thought was their father's plane waiting to load its complement of passengers. They gave their orders to the waitress and spent a few moments watching a Pan Am aircraft land. It was Wolf who finally put into words what was on all their minds.

"Well, I guess we're going to have to watch our backs from now on. Our former friends aren't going to forgive us."

Sabina reached for Wolf's hand. "The police know we're in danger. If anything happens to us they'll know who to blame."

"But they won't be able to prove it," Siegfried warned. "I ought to know. They never caught me!"

Sabina looked uncomfortable. She still could not get used to Siegfried being an ally, and reminders of his violent past did not help.

Wolf tried to reassure her. "We're safe for the moment. It's all too recent and high profile for them to risk anything now. Besides, we've smashed the local group. With my father – the man who claimed to be my father," he corrected himself caustically, "- dead, and Siegfried's stepfather fled, the Altenrieds and Sophie's parents all under surveillance, it doesn't leave anyone else in the upper echelons. There's a power vacuum here. They'll have to find someone to fill it. Until that happens I reckon we're safe."

"The trouble is, that might not be for long – unless I can convince them I'm still a part of it," Siegfried said.

"How do you expect to do that?" Sabina asked him, doubtful that his conniving could protect Wolf and herself.

"Shouldn't be too difficult. After all, deep down, you don't really believe I've changed, do you?" He was looking at Sabina as he spoke.

With his gaze upon her, Sabina did not know what to say. For years she had regarded him as an enemy, and a few moments ago he had admitted to multiple murders. Even though he had just saved their father from a probable life sentence, she still found it difficult to warm to him. She could not entirely trust him, as her father seemed to have done. She decided to challenge him.

"Have you changed?"

"What do you mean? You've seen I have!"

"You've told us you have, though I can't understand what made you change so suddenly."

A shadow flitted across Siegfried's face, a shadow he allowed them both to see. "Father understood. Ask him." He turned away to face the window. Outside an Air France jet was manoeuvring into its parking position.

"I'm asking *you*, Siegfried."

He swung back to face her, angry now, but keeping his voice restrained in such a public place. "I know you don't believe me, Sabina, and I'm not sure Wolf does either. But I *am* on your side now. It's just very difficult for me at the moment. For Wolf too. We've betrayed our families and friends. We're on our own. But I've still got a wife who's expecting our child. What am I to do? I've trodden very carefully with her up to now, but soon – today, probably – I'm going to have to discuss all this with her. You don't know Sophie like I do, but her total belief in Nazism is what drew me to her in the first place. She's a strong-willed woman and she's not going to bend to my wishes just because I ask her to." He turned abruptly back to the window.

Sabina felt Wolf's hand on hers and she looked at him. He shook his head gently, warning her to leave off interrogating Siegfried.

"We've both lost our parents," he said quietly. "I've lost the man who pretended to be my father," the bitterness still rang clearly in his voice, "and my mother won't speak to me now, let alone have me in the house." He nodded towards Siegfried's turned back. "He's in the same boat too. He can't see his mother or stepfather since they fled to South America, and the father he's only recently learned to love has just gone back to England. So don't be too hard on us."

She accepted his gentle reprimand. If she could understand Wolf's rejection of his former Nazi beliefs, then she should accept Siegfried's. But with Siegfried it was so much harder. He was a born liar and self-confessed murderer. As yet he had expressed no regrets about his former lifestyle. It would need more than just a public declaration in court to convince her of his sincerity.

Their food arrived, but Sabina could only pick at her cold meat salad. With her father's departure she now felt alone and vulnerable, despite Wolf's presence. They were both in danger from neo-Nazi reprisals. For all she knew it could be Siegfried who was still their agent. His about-turn could be a ruse to stay close to them. But why had Daddy found it so easy to accept Siegfried's change of heart? With all the celebrations and organizing needed after the trial there had not been a quiet moment when she could quiz him about Siegfried's turnaround. Now it would have to wait until she next went back to England.

"Not hungry?" Wolf asked, pointing at the hardly-touched food on her plate.

"No. You have it," she replied, passing it to him. She watched the aircraft outside as Wolf and Siegfried devoured their food. She noticed that the aircraft they reckoned was the Heathrow flight was leaving the terminal buildings and taxiing to the end of the runway. She pictured her father inside, eager to be off and flying back to his wife and sons and the life he had left behind eight months previously. Was he excited, nervous, anxious even? Had he really been unfaithful to her mother while staying with Ilse, as Siegfried had claimed? If so, had her mother forgiven him? Her mother's absence from the trial was notable, although of course it would have been difficult for her to leave the farm at such a critical time of year as lambing. What she would give to be a fly on the wall at their reunion, Sabina thought.

She watched his plane rise up into the distance, become a dot no bigger than a sparrow, then turned her attention back to the pair at the table. They had finished eating and Siegfried had paid the bill. She gathered up her handbag and rose with them from the table.

Siegfried shook Wolf by the hand. "Keep in touch and watch your backs!" he warned before turning to his half-sister. "Please trust me, Sabina," he begged, stooping to plant a kiss on her cheek.

Sabina checked herself from stepping back out of his embrace. In the courtroom, amidst the celebrations, it had been easier. Everyone was hugging and kissing everybody else. Here, having had time to reflect, it still felt like she was embracing the devil himself.

"I'll try."

"You'll have to if I'm going to be best man at your wedding."

Despite herself, she blushed. "You're a bit presumptive, aren't you?"

He grinned. "I've known Wolf too long not to know what he wants. You'll see!" With that he slapped Wolf on the back, buttoned up his jacket and headed for the exit.

"'Bye, Siegfried," Wolf called after him. "Good luck with Sophie!"

If he heard he did not react, but as he turned the corner by the doorway they saw his face set grim with the task ahead.

"God, it's a mess," Wolf muttered as he shepherded Sabina out of the restaurant towards the exit nearest the car park. Since his mother could not drive he had inherited his father's car. It was the only concession Frau Garisch had been willing to make to the son who had blown apart the lie she had worked so hard at maintaining for twenty-three years.

As they stepped outside a cold gust of wind whistled between the terminal building and the multi-storey car park, making them both clutch at their open jackets. They hurried into the lift to the third floor. Within its privacy Wolf felt bold enough to tackle a subject close to his heart. He stood behind Sabina, his arms around her breasts, drawing her towards him.

"Siegfried's right, you know. He does know my mind. I'd been thinking just the other day I don't like us being so far apart – you in Medebach, me in Dortmund. I won't know if you're safe or not. Now everything's over, I'd be much happier if you came to live with me. It'd be easier for you to get a job in Dortmund. Medebach's certainly not got much to offer."

The lift doors eased open and they spent a moment trying to orientate themselves to find the car. Sabina found the moment essential to take in what Wolf was suggesting.

"You mean live together?"

"Yes, why not? These are the swinging sixties, you know. People do it all the time."

"Yes, but the trouble is, my parents still live in the forties. I'm not sure they'd be very happy ..."

"Bina?"

"Yes?"

He grasped her by the shoulders, turning her towards him. He put his face down close to hers, their lips almost touching. "Will you marry me?"

Her answer was immediate as she raised herself slightly to kiss him full on the mouth. As they finally drew apart she murmured: "The sooner the better!"

*

The sight of her husband on the television news, with his arm linked through his father's and half-sister's, struggling through the crowds of reporters outside the court in Dortmund, had filled Sophie Driesler with dread. She remembered Siegfried saying something shortly after the car accident that had cut short their honeymoon. But with all the trauma of the operations on her legs, then the discovery she was pregnant, as well as Siegfried's preoccupation with the trial, she had not fully digested what he had been telling her. Now it was all too clear.

The small television set in her private hospital room provided all the evidence she needed as to just how far he had turned away from all they believed in, from what had brought them together in the first place. To publicly embrace his father he must have completely accepted Karl's anti-Nazi viewpoint, a feat so astounding as to seem impossible. Yet he had mentioned as much to her, couched in vague terms, she now realised, so as not to worry her unduly when faced with operations and a difficult pregnancy, which would be spent for the most part flat on her back. Her legs were held together now with metal plates, the flesh around the joining bones still open in places and awaiting skin grafts. It was going to be a long haul, the doctors telling her it was doubtful she would be up on her feet again much before the baby was born, some time in August.

Sophie laughed out loud at the thought of herself, hugely pregnant, trying to walk again. It was a joke! If it had been just the one leg damaged she might have been able to hobble around by now, but with both legs crushed what chance did she have? How was she going to cope with a new baby and Siegfried's betrayal too? Ever the dutiful husband, he had telephoned regularly during the trial to see how she was. Now the trial was over she could expect him to visit her again.

Duty. It was a word he seemed to have forgotten the meaning of. What about duty to his beliefs, his comrades in the party, all the people who daily put their freedom at risk working towards the greater goal? Her own life had been dedicated to following the path her parents had chosen. She had never questioned their purpose: to cleanse Germany of its filth and rebuild the Fatherland to its former glory, united and pure. The monstrosity of the Berlin Wall was a symbol of the enormity of the task, but it did not daunt their endeavours to establish Nazism again in a reunited and greater Germany.

Maybe her child would be a part of that Greater Germany; maybe she would have to wait for grandchildren before the time would come again. But come it would. With or without Siegfried's help.

Anger welled up inside her, her hands clenching with impotent rage the bedcovers by her sides. The news programme was over, replaced by a political discussion about the implications of the trial. She could not escape the wretched business. Losing her temper she reached for the call button. A smiling nurse hurried in a few moments later.

"Yes, Frau Driesler?"

"Could you change the channel for me, please? It's just politics. Awfully boring."

"Isn't it just!" The nurse stepped over and re-tuned the set to a nature programme about marine life in the Indian Ocean. A boldly patterned fish was swimming in and out of coral stalks. "I bet he's a beauty. I can't wait until we get colour televisions here, can you, Frau Driesler? Those tropical fish must be fabulous to look at."

"Yes, they are. I saw some on my honeymoon in the Caribbean." Sophie's voice trembled, warning the nurse of incipient tears.

Deftly she changed the conversational channel too. "You're scheduled for a visit from the obstetrician tomorrow morning, you know? Just to check all's well."

Sophie grimaced. "I could really do without being pregnant right now. It's just too much on top of everything else."

The nurse tried to console her. "At least the nausea's gone. You'll be feeling some movement soon. That'll be exciting." She straightened the bedcovers and sat Sophie forward before plumping up the pillows. "Now, is there anything else you want while I'm here?"

Just my husband back, Sophie thought bitterly. "Yes. Today's papers if they're still around. I'd like to read about the trial in more detail."

The nurse smiled. It was quite exciting being even remotely associated with a murder trial when Frau Driesler's husband was a star witness. The less she thought about Herr Driesler the better. Her lascivious thoughts might betray her, but she would have changed places with Frau Driesler any day, smashed legs or no smashed legs, to have that man for a husband. Those piercing grey eyes, that silky blond hair and those long, long legs ...

"Nurse Büchner. The newspapers?"

Hanna Büchner's head jerked up. "Oh, yes. Of course." It was impossible. The mere thought of Siegfried Driesler turned her into a drooling schoolgirl. "I'll just get them."

Sophie watched her leave the room. She knew the girl was besotted with Siegfried. Most girls who liked their men tall and blond were. But Siegfried was a handful – incredibly demanding and with an aggressive streak she had very quickly had to learn how to handle. Complete submission when demanded was the key to success. But was she to submit now? If he demanded she must renounce her Nazi aims and follow his traitorous way, could she refuse? And if she did refuse, what would he do?

Sophie had been told about Siegfried's ruthless reputation shortly before she first met him. It had been Gustav Halstrup in Berlin who had disclosed to her one day over dinner that the party's most accomplished and devious assassin was one Siegfried Driesler, based currently in Dortmund. Gustav had been very proud of the fact he had been one of the first to educate the six-year-old Siegfried in the art of deception.

It suddenly occurred to her that if Siegfried was so good at deception, maybe he had deceived the court and his father. Maybe she had misheard exactly what he had said to her shortly after the accident, when she had still been on painkillers and not really listening. Siegfried would never betray them all like that without good reason.

Footsteps in the corridor heralded the return of Nurse Büchner with the papers. Once she was gone, Sophie set about studying the reports of the trial, trying to find clues to Siegfried's behaviour. Was he really a traitor?

*

Katherine Driesler stood anxiously at the arrivals' gate, scanning the faces as they came through the doors. The flight from Düsseldorf had been announced and now it was only a matter of time before she saw Karl again. So much had happened since he was last home at the beginning of August. In those eight months she had sprouted grey hairs like mould on an apple. She was exhausted from worry, anger, and running the farm as best she could with their sons' help. On top of it all, lambing had only just finished and she was at her lowest ebb ever. Which was why her good friends and godparents, Donald and Gertie Murdoch, had told her to spend a few days in London alone with Karl upon his return. "Work can wait," they had said, handing her a cheque for fifty pounds. "It's what we'd put by as our contribution to Karl's legal expenses. But since that mystery benefactor came forward to foot the bill, we decided you both deserved a jolly good holiday."

Dear Donald and Gertie, Katherine thought, as yet another batch of passengers emerged at the gate, some searching eagerly for waiting friends or relatives, others marching purposefully off to find a taxi or catch the bus to London. The Murdochs had replaced the parents she had lost, becoming surrogate grandparents for Sabina, Richard and Paul. Without their love and support she would never have survived the last eight months. She had never told anyone else of Karl's infidelity, although Siegfried had known and she thought Sabina had suspected something, but Donald and Gertie had seen her pain, even though ignorant of its cause, and now wanted to make everything right for her and Karl again. But would it be?

Her heart thudded in her chest as a tall figure, clutching a suitcase with a raincoat draped over the top in one hand and a duty-free bag in the other, appeared amongst the arriving passengers. What struck Katherine immediately was how very pale Karl's face was. A prisoner's pallor. She had forgotten.

He was searching for her amongst the small crowd, spotting her quickly and hurrying past the barricade towards her. She did not move, felt rooted to the spot as he put down the case and carrier bag by his side and tentatively reached for her hands. She felt her own anxiety mirrored in him – strangers almost.

He had to speak loudly above the noise and bustle of the arrivals' hall. "A clean slate?"

So he knew how difficult this was for her. She could feel his thumbs gently rubbing hers and the old magic began to work once more. She smiled up at him. "A clean slate."

His arms were round her in an instant. Despite the crowds it was the first time since the events of last summer that they had really been alone together, without prison guards or hospital staff watching over them. They held each other, without speaking, feeling each other's body close until eventually they moved apart. Still without speaking, Katherine picked up Karl's raincoat and carrier bag, leaving him the suitcase. It was the same raincoat and suitcase Siegfried's mother had returned to her after Karl's arrest, when Ilse had gleefully boasted of her night with Karl. Katherine shuddered at the memory and tried to thrust it aside.

"We're getting a taxi into London," she told an amazed Karl. "Then we're staying at a decent hotel for a few days, seeing the sights ... and each other ... all courtesy of Donald and Gertie." She put a hand up to his white face. "Besides, you need to get some colour in your cheeks before the boys see you, or they'll think you're a ghost!"

"But what about the farm?" he protested.

"Richard, Paul and Werner can manage just fine between them." Werner Gimpel had been a prisoner of war with Karl, coming to work for them on the farm upon his release. "The boys have grown up so much while you've been away," she continued. "Richard coped almost single-handedly on the lambing night shifts. I'm very proud of him and you must be too." She might as well say this now, since the topic had cropped up. "He's got his own areas of responsibility now. He might not want to give them up, just because you're back."

He shrugged. "Fair enough." It seemed a lot had changed during his absence.

Once outside they hailed a taxi and were driven to the small but smart hotel in one of the back streets of Bayswater that Gertie Murdoch had booked for them. Here, Gertie had assured Katherine, they could feel totally anonymous, away from the glaring publicity of the last few months.

As they unpacked their suitcases into the wardrobe Karl remarked: "This was a good idea of the Murdochs. Trouble is, I've only got summer clothes!"

"I thought about that. I've brought you a jumper."

Karl laughed and pulled her into his arms. "You never ... er ..."

"... cease to amaze me?" Katherine suggested.

He grimaced. "Listen to me! I've been away so long I've almost forgotten how to speak English." He ran his fingers through her wavy auburn hair, found them lingering over the new streaks of grey. He drew her closer to him, resting his cheek on top of her head. "Why am I always so much trouble for you, Schatz?" He felt her go tense at the use of the endearment. Raising his head he saw her eyes were cast down towards the floor. "What's the matter?" She was drawing away from him, turning her back. "Katherine! What's wrong?"

Katherine sat down on the double bed. She had feared this would happen, had told herself not to let it. She licked her lips anxiously, then told herself to be honest with him. He would understand. She patted the bed beside her and he sat down, but not too closely, obviously aware of a serious problem.

"It's you calling me 'Schatz'. I can't ever forget that you used to call *her* that, before you met me. And now ..."

Karl knew exactly what she meant. On their night together last August Ilse had repeatedly called him by that term of endearment, just as she had first done during the war. "Go on," he gently urged.

She sniffed. "It's been a long time, Karl. So much has happened. It's difficult adjusting to having you back so suddenly and I still..."

She sniffed louder. "I still keep thinking of you with her, especially when you c-c-called me..." She broke down in tears.

Karl did not know what to say or do, whether he should try to comfort her or let her be. Fearing being pushed aside he sat quietly until her sobs subsided, then he offered her his handkerchief. She accepted it with a bashful smile, blew her nose loudly and wiped her eyes.

"I'm sorry. It's all been such a strain. I'll be all right." She handed him back the damp handkerchief. "Of course it's been a strain for you too, and now I'm not helping with my silly behaviour."

He put an arm across her shoulders. She did not flinch. "A clean slate, you said. Well let's make it a totally clean slate, like we'd only just met. Before we were married I could never take you out anywhere, to dances, films, restaurants or whatever. Let's do it all now, and get to know each other again. We'll take our time, no rush with anything, just enjoy ourselves."

She sniffed again but nodded. "And sleep a lot," she added. "I think I've got eight month's worth to catch up on." In case he got the wrong idea, she added: "Sleep, that is."

"It's all right, Sch- Treasure," he quickly corrected himself. "I understand. Now, we've got the whole afternoon ahead of us. What do you want to do?"

"You're the one who's just been released. What do *you* want to do?"

His response was immediate. "See some trees and walk on grass! Hyde Park?"

"You're on!"

They donned their raincoats as the cloudy sky suggested rain, then hurried out of their hotel, crossed the Bayswater Road and entered the park at Marlborough Gate. They walked hand in hand along the edge of The Long Water in gentle drizzle, admired the daffodils then sat down for a snack in the restaurant by the Serpentine. The rowing boats on the Serpentine were still laid up for the winter like rows of sleeping ducks, although the real ducks were very active in their nesting preparations. They continued walking along Rotten Row to Hyde Park Corner, stood outside the gates of Buckingham Palace for a while watching the guards, before

Katherine steered Karl towards the Ritz for afternoon tea – another of Gertie's ideas.

"You can't get much more different from prison than this!" Karl whispered as they entered the famous portals.

"Shhh!" Katherine chided light-heartedly, well accustomed to having a notorious husband. Taking charge she announced their reservation to the headwaiter. Their coats were taken and they were shown to a table.

When their tea arrived Karl raised his china cup and took a long swig. "Ah! A decent cup of tea! I'd forgotten how much I missed it."

"Spoken like a true Englishman," Katherine laughed.

Her words jolted him. At the moment he felt far from English. His recent experiences in Germany had left their mark. He had been and felt totally German for eight months, had just this morning been in Düsseldorf, still had German money in his pocket, his body if not his watch was still set to German time, an hour ahead. Now here he was in London, a strange and foreign place, with a wife who was treating him almost like a stranger.

"Did I say something wrong?"

Karl realised his cup was still mid-way to the saucer and put it down. "No. I'm just taking time to re-adjust to being back in England ... and free."

"Take all the time you need."

"You too." There was a long pause. Karl finished his tea and fruitcake. Katherine re-filled his cup, then pointed to the cake stand.

"Another cake? An éclair?"

"Thank you." She put one on each of their plates. He took a bite out of his, licked the cream off his lips, chewed thoughtfully, then said: "I wonder how Auer is."

"Who?"

"Auer. My cell-mate."

"Oh yes, of course. Auer."

"We got quite friendly eventually, after he tore up your first letter to me and flushed it down the pan. I told you about that, didn't I?"

"Yes."

"I expect they've put someone else in with him by now."

"I expect so." She pushed aside her unwanted éclair. "Karl. I don't want to hear about Auer. Tell me about Sabina and Wolf, your family, Siegfried even!"

About to take another bite, Karl put down his éclair. "Sorry. I wasn't thinking. Of course you're not interested in Auer." He glanced around the packed room. Large ladies in large hats were most prevalent, although there was a fair sprinkling of couples, mostly middle-aged like themselves. The young and trendy would not be seen dead in the Ritz, he supposed.

"Siegfried's going to have trouble with Sophie, I think," he told Katherine.

She cocked an eyebrow interrogatively. "What makes you say that?"

"Ah, of course. You've not met Sophie."

"I did briefly, if you remember. At your mother's funeral. Very attractive. A bit like Ilse really." She bit her lip. "Her looks, I mean."

"I know what you mean," he reassured her. "But I take it you don't know what she's like."

"Well, I've gathered she's wholly supportive of Siegfried's politics, if that's what you mean?"

"Yes. But whereas he's completely changed his opinion and has come to see sense, she is hardly likely to."

"Are you sure about that, Karl?"

"About what?"

She hesitated a moment. "That Siegfried's changed."

"Totally," he assured her. "He confided things to me that made me understand just what he'd been through. I was the first person he'd ever told and I understood because I had been through a similar ordeal. We didn't have to say much to each other, as there was such a ..." He found himself struggling for the right English words again. A word finally came to mind but he knew it was not the best one. "A connection between us. I knew we could see the truth in each other."

Katherine still looked sceptical. "So what was it that happened to him?"

A blob of cream on Karl's plate suddenly held a great attraction for him. He began to push it around the plate with a teaspoon.

"Karl?" She reached for his hand to hold it still. "Did you hear me? What happened to Siegfried?"

Apart from Siegfried, the only other people who knew the full extent of Karl's torture by Yugoslav partisans during the Second World War were his psychiatrist and Donald and Gertie's son, Robert. It was to Robert Murdoch Karl had first poured out his history in 1946, and it was Robert who had later repeated it to Katherine in 1947 to persuade her to help Karl recover from his mental breakdown. But Robert had later told Karl that he had kept certain facts from Katherine, and this incident was among them. It was still not something he wanted her to know about.

He looked Katherine in the eye at last, his decision made. "He wouldn't want you to know, nor anyone else. I'm his father, he told me and I understand."

She felt excluded, hurt even that Karl could not confide in her. She had heard horrific details of his past. What was so different about this? "Isn't it something I ought to know? Surely if it happened to you too ...?"

"No." He glanced at his watch. "Time we were off if we want to get tickets for a show."

Katherine had to let the matter rest, but her doubts about Siegfried remained.

TWO

Sophie heard the brisk footsteps approaching her door and guessed they were Siegfried's. The door opened and, sure enough, his head appeared followed by a bunch of deep purple tulips. Satisfied she was awake and decent he came in.

"Hello, stranger," she welcomed him, putting down the magazine she had been reading.

"Hello, my beauty." Siegfried replied, ignoring the implied reprimand. He knew she was not being serious as she tilted her chin up and pouted her lips. He sat down on the bed and kissed her long and hard, making up for all the days spent apart. She responded eagerly, clasping him to her, running her fingers through his short hair as though it had been months rather than two weeks since she last saw him. He broke off the kiss before they became too aroused, and saw the look of frustration on her face.

"I want you, Siegfried, and I want you right now," she whispered, but her voice acknowledged the improbability that her wish would be fulfilled.

"I want you too, Schatz, but we'll both have to be patient, won't we?" he told her, kissing her lightly on the tip of her nose as a sign of affection rather than desire. Needing a diversion he laid the flowers on the bedcover, noticing the cover of the magazine as he did so. "*Mother and Baby*, eh?" he remarked, flicking through the pages with apparent interest. "Starting to get into the swing of things are you, Liebling?"

"I thought I'd better. It'll give me something else to worry about, apart from my wretched legs."

"Worry about? Aren't you pleased? I thought you were."

"The more I think about trying to walk again, the more I wish I wasn't pregnant. It's all very well for you to get excited," she added petulantly, "but you're not the one who's lying here day in, day out."

"It'll get better. The doctor just told me you'll be able to sit in a wheelchair soon."

"Wonderful!" She glowered at him, her blue eyes burning deep with resentment at her plight.

Siegfried stroked a strand of blonde hair that had fallen over her left cheek before tucking it behind her ear. "I can see you're feeling low, Liebling." His fingers caressed the back of her neck but her response proved brusque.

"Hmph, that's an understatement! One thing's for sure. I'm not going to stay in our flat. Not if I'm in a wheelchair, with a baby to get in and out of the lift, and only the cellar room to dry nappies in." She grabbed the magazine from him and leafed through it rapidly until she found the article she wanted. "Reading this it says nappies need sunshine and fresh air to dry properly. Apparently the sun works on the stains and ..." She suddenly broke into a giggle, her mood lifted, as she saw instant boredom appear on his face. "It's a whole new world, having babies. There's a lot to learn."

He grinned back. "I can see that. I can also see you're enjoying it really. Or you will do once you're out of this wretched bed." He suddenly gripped her arm. "But you're right. I remember only too well my mother's torment with small children in a flat. I'll start looking for something." His hand moved down her arm, his grip lessening as it reached her hand, which he squeezed reassuringly. "But you won't be in a wheelchair, Liebling. You'll be up on your feet again well before it's born, I promise you."

She leaned against him and he knew it was going to be difficult introducing the subject of politics with Sophie in this frame of mind. They had not talked about his change of heart for a long time and then only briefly. He needed to know whether she supported his decision, had forgotten about it or simply not understood.

Comforted by his closeness and unaware of his dilemma, Sophie continued her train of thought. "We'll have to start thinking of some names."

She ran her manicured fingers over his equally immaculate ones. Clean nails were something his stepfather, Paul Zopf, had always insisted upon, and she knew Siegfried had taken everything Paul said to heart. But having lost his right arm in the war Paul needed frequent visits to a pretty young manicurist and Sophie suspected he had an ulterior motive. Had Siegfried taken that on board too? Had those immaculate, strong fingers caressed anyone else while she had been bedridden in hospital? She surprised herself by deciding they had not. She picked up his hand and brought it to her lips, her tongue giving his index finger a suggestive lick.

Reluctantly Siegfried abandoned any attempt to discuss the bigger issues that were weighing him down. Now was not the time. She was depressed enough without risking a major argument. Instead he joined in her game of gentle seduction, pressing his finger lightly between her lips into the moistness beyond. Then with a grin he suddenly withdrew it and returned to the matter in hand. "No hippie names like 'Blue' or ... er ... 'Sky'!" he laughed.

"As if I would!" Her mood had calmed and she squeezed his hand. "You know, having you here, I feel so much happier with the idea. I was beginning to get really depressed. But now ... I don't know. I think I'm quite looking forward to being a mother."

"That's great. You keep thinking positive thoughts instead of negative and you'll be running around far sooner." His words 'negative thoughts' reminded him of his conversation with Wolf and Sabina at the airport. Since the trial he had not had the chance to speak to Sophie's parents, who would now consider their son-in-law a traitor. He decided to put out some cautious feelers. "How are your parents? I don't suppose they'll ever forgive me and Wolf for informing on them."

"Too right they won't!" she berated him, then gave him an indulgent smile and dropped her voice right down. "But I think I can assure them when they visit me tonight that you were putting up a smokescreen to protect us." Her smile turned to a wicked grin. "After I saw you on television with your father I felt really angry with you," she confided. "You looked like you genuinely had turned your back on us. Of course, when you told me before the trial about your need to help your father, I was glad for you. He's a nice man despite his views on National Socialism. But I had assumed your apparent change of politics was only a show for the world at large. That's why I accepted it so readily. I didn't think you'd really turned traitor."

Her smile faded, as she went on to explain her recent doubts about him. "But on television you looked like you really had changed your views. It was clear your father certainly believed you had, and he wouldn't easily have been persuaded, I know! So I read the reports of the trial and really thought about everything you'd said, like 'you were doing it all for us'. I knew then, that what with Herr Garisch's murder and the trial and everything, it was inevitable some of us would get hurt. Denying involvement would have always left you open to suspicion, but admitting to it and clearing the air, so to speak, meant people could give you and Wolf a second chance and believe you had reformed. Brilliant tactics! But do you know what really convinced me?"

Dumbfounded by her reasoning, Siegfried could only shake his head.

"The fact that you didn't pass on all the names you knew, like the members in Berlin." Her voice was barely above a whisper now. "I know what you told me. As far as the police are concerned we've seen the light. But we know better, don't we, Liebling?"

So that was how she had rationalised it, Siegfried thought. Shut away in hospital with nothing to do but think, she had managed to make the situation fit her own ends. But with Sophie still a committed Nazi it meant he must now lead a double life. At least her parents should be back on his side. He just hoped the rest of his former colleagues were as easily persuaded that he and Wolf were not traitors, but masters of damage limitation.

Casually nodding in reply to Sophie's question, he steered the conversation away from dangerous territory. "Your parents have had problems with their neighbours after all this business, haven't they? Have they found a new home yet?"

"Yes. With no close neighbours this time. And they say they chose it with grandchildren in mind. No steps for pushchairs, a local duck pond and ice-cream parlour to visit, and a big tree in the garden to hang a swing from."

Her last words reminded Siegfried of a garden he had known long ago – in England. "The other grandparents' house also has a swing," he remarked.

Sophie looked confused. "How can that be? I thought they were living in an apartment in the middle of Montevideo."

"Not my mother's. My father's." He took a deep breath. "Look. It's all got very complicated recently, but I think we ought to show willing and visit my father some time."

The wicked grin flashed back to her face. "Part of the smokescreen?"

"If you like."

"I'll look forward to it. I like your father. He's like you."

"I'm like him, you mean."

"Pedant!" She snuggled against him. "Do you think if it's a boy, he'll turn out like you too?"

"God help him if he does!"

"But you're perfect," Sophie protested.

And a two-faced liar, Siegfried thought bitterly.

*

Opa was looking tired after the strains of the trial, Sabina thought as she hugged her grandfather on the doorstep of Haus Fichtenblick. Or maybe it was the celebrating afterwards! Whichever it was, he must have been watching out for their car and was at the door ready to greet them after their drive home from Düsseldorf. Sabina was amazed at how readily she had begun to think of the black and white house, standing on its own by the forest outside Medebach, as home. Perhaps because it was half-timbered like the Herefordshire farmhouse she had grown up in, or maybe because she loved the occupants dearly. Especially Opa, all alone since Oma's death last November, and missing her desperately.

Sabina moved aside to let Opa shake Wolf's hand as he always did. She was so glad Wolf was totally accepted here, despite everything that had happened in the last year. She crossed the threshold to find Tante Anna just emerging from the kitchen, wiping her floury hands on a towel.

"Did your father get away on time?" Anna asked her niece.

"Yes. He couldn't wait to get on that plane back to England, away from all the reporters. He'd had a bit too much of his homeland, I think."

"Hardly surprising really, when all he saw of it was through prison bars. Still, hopefully that's all behind him now."

Dieter Driesler, who had already disappeared to the cellar, came back clutching several bottles of Dortmunder. "A beer, Wolf?"

"Why not," Wolf agreed, knowing full well Sabina's grandfather needed a drinking companion. "I'll get some glasses."

He followed Dieter into the living room and went across to the ornately carved dresser, made by Dieter's father at the turn of the century. He took out four glasses, anticipating Sabina and Anna's participation. Sure enough Sabina was bringing her aunt through from the hall.

Dieter grunted, opened three bottles and divided the contents between the glasses. "Better get some more up before I sit down."

"Don't worry, Papa," Anna told him. "Wolf knows where they are." Trying to restrict her father's alcohol intake was a daily part of Anna's life these days. They all waited for Dieter to settle down in his favourite chair and raise his glass.

"*Prost*!" they chorused then drank from their glasses.

"Are you rushing back to Dortmund, Wolf, or can you stay for a meal?" Anna asked, knowing full well what his reply would be.

"Er, I'm in no rush. A meal would be great, thank you." Wolf turned to Sabina sitting next to him on the sofa and whispered: "Are you going to tell them, or shall I?"

"I'll do it." She cleared her throat and smiled at her aunt and grandfather. "We've got something to tell you." She paused a moment to look smugly at them. "While at the airport, we thought about our future together. Wolf asked me to marry him and I accepted!"

Anna let out a delighted squeal, put down her glass on the table in front of her and went over to hug both Sabina and Wolf. Dieter too was soon out of his chair, joining in with hugs and handshakes.

"Congratulations to the pair of you! That's wonderful news." He sat down again and raised his glass to them. "Sabina and Wolf! *Zum Wohl*!" As he took a swig of beer, his thoughts turned to his eldest son. "Does your father know, Bina?"

"No," she admitted. "This was after he'd gone. I suppose we ought to ask his permission really."

"A formality, I'm sure," her grandfather assured her. "But necessary, nevertheless. What time do you think he'll arrive home?"

"Quite late, I should think. Best wait till tomorrow. I don't want to overshadow his homecoming with our news."

"You're right," Anna agreed. "Let him and your mother have a little time just for themselves." She noticed Dieter heading for the door. "What are you up to, Papa?"

"There's a bottle of Sekt in the cellar. I'll put it in the fridge to have with our meal later. To celebrate properly."

"Good idea," she said, shrugging her shoulders at Sabina as if to say he had a good excuse this time.

While he was gone they finished their beers, picked up the glasses, empties and the unopened bottle, and went out to the kitchen. Dieter soon joined them with a large bottle of Sekt, which he thumped down on the table. Anna knew he would head back for the living room and the beer given half a chance, so forestalled him.

"Why don't you and Wolf go for a walk, Bina? I'm sure you've got plenty to think about with wedding plans and everything. Papa can walk with you as far as the sawmill to tell Stefan, Rudi and Uwe the news, can't you, Papa? Oh, and tell Rudi to bring Adele and the children over for supper."

Her father took the hint. "That's a good idea. I need to go down there anyway to sort out tomorrow's delivery with Rudi." He looked over Sabina's lightweight shoes. "Do you want to get changed before we go?"

"Yes. I won't be a moment." She ran upstairs to her room, changed into jeans, a warm jacket and walking boots then joined them outside on the track to the family-run sawmill.

They saw Anna's husband, Stefan, first. He was handing a delivery note to one of the lorry drivers when he caught sight of them picking their way round the stacks of logs awaiting barking. The sawmill was a noisy place so he pointed to the soundproofed office where, through the window, Dieter's second son, Rudi, could be seen talking on the telephone. By the time they all squeezed into the office, Rudi had finished his call. He and Stefan proved as thrilled as Anna and Dieter at the news.

"It's one bit of good news after another!" Rudi declared, kissing his niece on the cheek. "But I can't believe you're old enough to be getting engaged! I can still picture you as a chubby two-year-old on your first visit here."

Sabina giggled. "Now don't you go blurting out all my little mishaps to Wolf!"

Stefan was busy thumping Wolf heartily on the back. "Welcome to the clan! I'm sure you'll be as happy in it as I've been."

Dieter stood behind Sabina and placed his hands over her shoulders, staring at Rudi to catch his attention. "Bring Adele and the children round this evening. We're going to be celebrating again."

"Sure, Papa. We wouldn't miss it for the world."

"Where's Uwe?" Sabina asked, looking through into the sawmill for her eldest cousin.

"Gone with Peter Witter on a delivery," Stefan informed her. His stepson preferred customer liaison to the manual work of the sawmill, but the family was happy with that arrangement. Uwe had a gift for negotiating, which brought in good orders for the Driesler sawmill.

Sabina and Wolf stayed to chat for a few minutes then left the others to their work. The weather was fine enough to head off for a walk, although a few patches of late snow still lay in sheltered hollows. With his arm round her shoulders and her arm round his waist, they ambled off up one of the rutted tracks leading into the forest, their hips bumping together until Sabina hopped out of step and into the action of a three-legged race. She could feel the warmth of him through her jacket and snuggled closer against him. After a few minutes she pulled him to one side of the track towards a majestic old beech tree.

"I came across this last autumn, after Oma's funeral," she said, running her fingers over the silver-grey bark. Faintly visible were a heart and the initials KD and IB. "Karl Driesler and Ilse Brünninghaus." She turned to face him under the copper-budded canopy of branches, her boots scrunching the dried brown leaves and beech mast. "My father and Ilse used to come up here when they were courting. I didn't bring you up here before, as I couldn't bear to see it. But I think I'm getting over it now." Even though she had tried not to think of them together she could not deny their former relationship, and could even raise a joke about it now. "Perhaps Siegfried was even conceived up here!"

"Quite likely, I'd have thought," Wolf laughed, finding his thoughts unavoidably following a similar trail. He tugged her away from the tree. "Come on. I'm getting cold."

The track led them steadily uphill. As they rounded a bend the view opened up in front of them where the forest had been cleared some years previously. They stood side by side, arms linked, looking out over the surrounding hills and meadows down towards the little town of Medebach, where the grey spire and pinkish stone tower of St Peter and Paul's church dominated over the half-timbered houses.

"Will we be getting married there?" Wolf asked nodding towards the spire.

His words jolted Sabina, reminding her that Medebach was not her true home. She continued staring at the view but tightened her grip on his arm. "I've always pictured myself getting married in the church where I was christened – in Penchurch. I hadn't thought ..." Her voice faltered and she looked anxiously up at him.

"Of course," he reassured her. "All your friends and most of your family are in England. I've got nobody to invite except Siegfried. It makes far more sense to get married in England."

Her relief was immense. Until that moment she had almost forgotten her English roots, but was now aware how deeply they still grew in English soil. "Thank you, Schatz. But what about your mother? Shouldn't we at least invite her?"

He shook his head sadly. "No. She's made it perfectly clear I've ruined her life and she doesn't want to know me."

"But it might be just the excuse she needs to get back to you," Sabina protested. She could not envisage alienating herself from her own family like that. "Even if she doesn't want to make the journey to England, at least you would have asked her. It wouldn't be such a total break with her, would it?"

Wolf smiled at her childlike innocence, but then remembered she was only nineteen and had lived for eighteen of those years surrounded by a large and loving family who meant everything to her.

"We must try, Wolf," she persisted. "You can't just abandon her, even if she's abandoned you. She is your mother."

"Can I be sure? I always thought that man was my father until my mother let slip he wasn't." He laughed at her shocked expression. "No, she's my mother, all right." He sighed. "You're right. We should at least invite her."

Sabina gave him a hug. "Good."

"Family means everything to you, doesn't it? No matter what they've done, if they're family you still love them."

"You're speaking about Siegfried, of course."

"No. Actually I meant your father." She was silent and he thought he had offended her, was referring to Karl's supposed indiscretion with Ilse. "I'm sorry, Bina. I didn't mean to …"

"It's all right. No need to apologise. I was just thinking about him and Mummy, wondering how they were getting on. I know she's taken it very hard, but we saw them together that evening, Daddy and Ilse I mean, chatting away like old friends. Paul was off on one of his regular 'business' trips and of course Ilse felt lonely and wanted more than just companionship. I'm not trying to condone what happened, but if Ilse came on strong to Daddy, I can see it might have been difficult for him to resist."

Wolf thought back too to that evening in August last year at Paul and Ilse Zopf's home. He had indeed seen Ilse flirting with Karl over dinner. He gave an involuntary laugh and Sabina looked at him in surprise. "Sorry. I was thinking how restrained we youngsters have been with our sex lives, while it's the adults who can't control themselves!"

Sabina had to laugh too but then she grew serious again. She pulled him over to a fallen log and sat down facing the view over Medebach. "Do you mind, Schatz? I mean us. Up until now you've respected my wishes not to go too far, but now we're engaged and talking about living together, I'm getting the feeling you're …" She broke off in embarrassment.

He swivelled sideways so he was astride the log and held both her hands in his. "Of course I want you, Bina. I always have. But I'm prepared to wait until we're married, if that's what you really want and the day's not too far off!"

She felt herself blushing. "It's just that … well … I'm not sure I do want to wait. Everyone else seems to be having all the fun these days, and I feel quite old-fashioned not joining in just because of tradition. It doesn't seem such a big deal anymore, staying a virgin. Especially since I've found the man I love. You'll be the first, and the last, so why wait?"

"Why indeed!" he beamed. He leaned forwards and kissed her nose, then her cheek. His mouth settled near her ear, her long auburn hair tickling his nose as he whispered: "How about here, now, under the beech trees on a bed of leaves. What could be better?"

His sudden urgency took her by surprise, but rather than trying to resist she accepted it, felt it invading her own body. She shivered in excitement at the feel of his hands on the nape of her neck, felt her own physical response as his mouth closed on hers, and the overpowering need in her. He was right. This was the place, the time, with the beech wood's blessing and protection. In her mind's eye she saw again the carved heart and initials. It had been right for her father. It was right for her.

As Wolf led her by the hand to a discreet bower overshadowed by a lion-shaped rock, Sabina wished she had been wearing a skirt rather than jeans. Her apprehension mounted as Wolf began unbuttoning her jacket. Suppose somebody saw them! But when she lay down on the deep, dry bed of leaves which had gathered in the hollow, she realised they were invisible from the track. Looking up over Wolf's shoulder she noticed another heart and initials carved on the rock behind him. If her father knew of this spot, it must be safe, she thought with a smile.

Eagerly she turned her attention back to Wolf. He was nuzzling her earlobe as his shaking hands fumbled with her blouse, then her bra. He did not seem particularly expert, which she was pleased about. She had no idea what she was supposed to be doing, if anything, so lay placidly, returning his kisses, running her fingers through his hair and gasping occasionally as his fingers and tongue moved over ticklish areas of her body.

"OK?" he whispered.

"Yes," she murmured.

His still trembling hands moved to her jeans, undoing them and easing them over her hips with a confident, fluid motion. Her underwear was also deftly slid down, and before she knew it he was on top of her. It was all over and done with rather quicker than she had expected. She had enjoyed it, but not as much as she had hoped. Wolf seemed very pleased with himself, however. He lay beside her, picking leaves out of her tangled hair, a soppy grin on his face.

"What's it like being a woman at last?" he asked.

Sabina hesitated. "I hadn't thought of it like that. I suppose I am now, aren't I? A woman in love." She sat up and brushed a leaf off her jacket. Taking the hint he brushed her back clean for her. "Does it show?" she asked. "Do you think they'll guess what we've been up to?"

"No, of course not. Stop feeling guilty, Bina."

She giggled. "I can't help it when I keep seeing that." She pointed to the carving on the lion rock. "It's like he's here, watching me."

"Well that just goes to show you haven't done anything he hasn't. But if you're going to feel like this, the sooner we get married the better."

Sabina gazed up at the clouds scudding behind the lattice of silver-grey branches and felt the trees speaking to her, blessing her physical union with Wolf, telling her when to formally unite with him. "How about Midsummer's Day, or as close to it as can be arranged."

"Fine. Any particular reason?"

"It's the right day," she declared confidently.

*

The bright lights, hustle and bustle of a London still reeling from recent violent anti-Vietnam War demonstrations was intimidating to them both, but particularly to Karl. He felt ill at ease in the late evening crowds of Piccadilly Circus. Hyde Park had been pleasant with its fresh air and green leaves, but the warm, stale blast emerging from the entrance to Piccadilly tube station seemed threatening. They followed the signs for the Bakerloo line northbound, both too tired after the long day to talk much, and stood on the platform awaiting the rattling rails and rushing wind of an approaching train. In retrospect it had been a mistake to go out to a show on their first night together, but they had been keen to make the most of their visit to the capital.

"It's way past my bedtime," Karl yawned as they found a place to stand in the crowded train. "Lights out was at ten o'clock. And I'm an hour ahead still."

Katherine clutched at his coat as the train jolted on a set of points. "At least we can sleep in."

"With any luck." He was holding onto a strap with one hand and Katherine's shoulder with the other, as the straps were rather high for her to balance easily. The shaggy bearded man next to her, wearing a vibrant, Paisley-patterned shirt, seemed to make no effort to avoid bumping into her. Karl suddenly realised the man was stoned. He drew Katherine closer and turned slightly to put himself between her and the man, feeling more vulnerable than he had in prison. Perhaps it was because he had Katherine to protect now. At least it was only five stops to Paddington. He followed their progress on the wall map, breathing a sigh of relief when the doors slid open and they could ease their way out and up into the fresh air again.

"The hotel's only a few minutes' walk away," Katherine told him. "I just hope I can recognise the way in the dark."

"Lead on, Mac..."

"Macduff," Katherine reminded him, setting off south towards Sussex Gardens. Despite her fears she found their hotel without any hesitation. As they walked up the plushly carpeted stairs to their room her feet began to drag.

"Tired?" Karl asked as they reached their door.

She nodded, standing aside as he turned the key in the lock. She followed him in, put her handbag on the dressing table and took off her coat, hanging it carefully in the wardrobe. This was the moment she had been dreading; after eight months apart he would be bound to want to make love to her, but mental images of a gloating Ilse spoilt any chance of her welcoming such a prospect.

As she got into bed with Karl already lying there she felt truly ashamed of her feelings, but could do nothing about them. She lay down, turned out the bedside light and waited anxiously. She felt him raise himself on one elbow then his lips touched hers softly in a loving, but certainly not passionate, kiss.

"Goodnight, Schatz," he mumbled and was asleep a minute later.

Katherine felt the tension drain out of her. She had been frightened of her own husband's embrace, frightened she would not be able to respond to his advances. But she had gained a temporary reprieve. Despite her earlier tiredness she now felt unable to sleep. Here she was, lying beside Karl for the first time in months; a moment she should be relishing. She turned towards his sleeping form. By the light of the street-lamps she could make out his body. He lay on his side, left arm tucked under the pillow, right tucked into his chest, his knees, as ever, drawn up to keep his feet from projecting over the end of the bed. The familiar sight warmed her. She reached out her left hand and laid it gently on his shoulder, feeling its slow rise and fall as he breathed. She edged closer, rested her knees on his thighs and curled into his chest, moving his right arm so it draped over her. He stirred slightly, adjusted the position of his head, then lay still again.

Now she could hear his beating heart, feel the familiarity of his whole body through the fabric of his pyjamas and feel safe again, no longer alone and fending for herself. Tears pricked her eyelids. It would be all right again. It had to be!

She woke next morning to the feel of a bristly chin on her neck and a hand on her breast. Outside the roar of traffic was audible, while along the corridor a door banged. Karl stirred at the sound but did not seem to waken. Katherine tilted her head to try to see the time on her watch lying on the bedside table. It was seven-thirty. Late for her, even later for Karl, but not late for the world at large. She laid her head back on the pillow. There was no rush to get up except to answer the call of nature. Having thought of the idea, however, she could not dismiss it. Very carefully she eased herself from under Karl's arm and crept out of bed.

When she got back in she was aware of a difference in him. Bare flesh met her hand. His pyjamas were gone. As she registered the fact his eyes opened and creased into a smile. Without a word his fingers alighted on the top button of her nightdress and began to undo it. She lay there, allowing him to do what he wanted, raising herself so he could pull the nightdress over her head, wanting him more and more as his fingers gently caressed her skin. Suddenly she raised her arms and pulled his head down to hers. Their mouths met and she found herself consumed by passion. As desperate now as he was, Katherine grasped his firm buttocks in her urgency to accept him. All these months without him her body had secretly hungered for him. She tipped her head back to look up at him and his grey eyes met hers. For an instant she was taken back to their first ever union on the freezing farmhouse's kitchen floor. Now she was grateful for the soft, warm bed and the years of experience.

As they lay still again, she spoke in his ear, smiling to herself. "So much for taking things slowly at first!"

Hearing the smile in her voice, he raised his head off the pillow by her cheek so he could look down at her. He returned the smile. "You were a bit tense last night, weren't you? But you're all right now."

She nodded. After all those months he still knew her so well. Ilse's shadow was hopefully beginning to fade.

THREE

Sophie was so engrossed in the estate agent's leaflets Siegfried had left for her that she did not hear the nurse's knock nor was she aware of her entry. Gripping her attention was a chalet-style house, complete with balcony off the master bedroom. The house was compact without being cramped, was on the outskirts of a large village, adjacent to fields and woodland. It had a downstairs playroom/study, a large fitted kitchen with corner table and seating unit, as well as a reasonable sized dining room. It was quite new, the garden not planted up with much yet, so there would be room for a sandpit and swing. Best of all it was in the next village to where her parents were moving.

"That looks nice," a soft voice said in her ear.

Sophie jumped. "Oh!" She put a hand against her thudding chest. "You startled me. I was miles away." She held up the house details for Nurse Rolfes to read. "It is nice. I think it's the best I've seen so far. I'll tell my husband to go and have a look at it."

The nurse handed the paper back having glanced briefly through it. "I came in to tell you, you have a visitor, Frau Driesler. A Herr Halstrup. Shall I tell him he can come in?"

"Gustav!" Sophie exclaimed in delight. "Yes, of course. Just give me a moment to sort my hair out. Can you pass me my brush, please?"

Sophie wielded the hairbrush, straightened the bedclothes and awaited Gustav's arrival. He was taking a huge risk coming here. The police could well be monitoring her visitors after her denying having any neo-Nazi contacts. Gustav was high up in the Berlin hierarchy. It would be a disaster if he were uncovered.

A brief knock on the door heralded his entry. He entered clutching an enormous bouquet of spring flowers. Ever the ladies' man, Sophie thought, lifting her cheek to receive his kiss. "Gustav! How lovely to see you! And how kind of you. They're beautiful!"

She knew he lived with another actor, but she also knew he liked the ladies too. More like Tony Curtis than Charlton Heston in looks, his face appealed to many of his fans, but it was his charm that had captivated her. He was great fun to be with, and she trusted him absolutely.

"Sophie, my poor darling. What has that wicked Siegfried done to you?" He looked sympathetically at the outline of her legs under the raised bedclothes then pulled over the visitor's chair and sat down close to her side.

His theatrical expressions amused her, as she knew how much it was all put on. "Come off it, Gustav. You know he didn't do anything. Except get me pregnant. Did you know?" she added when she saw his shocked expression.

"No! I had no idea. News travels rather slowly since ..." He pulled a sour face but then instantly transformed it into a warm smile. "Well I never! I suppose I ought to say congratulations but it must make things a touch more awkward for you."

"It will do, once I get back on my feet, I think," she told him. "But I'm getting used to the idea."

Gustav immediately grew serious. "Sophie, darling. How are you going to look after a baby on your own?"

"On my own? But I won't be on my own." She had a sudden inkling of what he was driving at. "Are you talking about me and Siegfried?" He was looking rather oddly at her, wanting explanation she realised. "There's nothing wrong between us, in case you thought there might be, Gustav." She paused, choosing her words carefully. Despite having her own room, this was still a public place. Anyone could be listening outside the door. "Look," she said, picking up the new house details from the bedside table and waving them at him. "This is what we want to buy."

He frowned, as he understood what she meant. Despite Siegfried's very public rejection of National Socialism, they were still together. "Sophie, you must realise, I haven't seen Siegfried for a very long time. Has he changed a lot?"

"Not as much as you seem to think," she cautiously replied. "He's just the same as ever he was."

"Are you sure about that?"

She hesitated too long. "Yes. I think so."

"You *think* so," he repeated slowly, his voice suddenly menacing. His dark brown eyes bored into hers to read the truth. "I need to know," he added quietly.

She nodded. "I know," she whispered. "At first I thought one thing, now I think another. He's fine. Wolf's betrayal was the problem. Siegfried had to deal with it the safest way he could. He's still playing safe."

"I see."

They were speaking barely audibly. Gustav's face was close to hers, so close she could see the blocked pores at the side of his stubby nose.

"And what about Wolfgang Garisch? Do you think his betrayal of us is all a cover-up too?" he asked.

Sophie swallowed hard. She was finding Gustav's probing questions increasingly difficult to answer honestly. She liked Wolf – really liked him – but of his motives she was uncertain. "I don't know," she said. "I'm too cut off from things here." She knew he expected her to hazard an opinion. Licking her lips nervously she made her verdict. "I would like to say he and Siegfried are working together on this, but I do know his mother won't speak to him. As you must be aware, she's facing a possible jail sentence for aiding and abetting in her husband's false identity. Bearing that in mind, I would say he probably has turned his coat."

Gustav leaned even closer to her. "So if it's true of Wolfgang Garisch, why not of Siegfried Driesler too?" He allowed his words to sink in a moment before continuing: "Don't let your dreams of domestic bliss blind you, Sophie. I want to know if you have any doubts at all about him."

Now she dared not look into those eyes. "Of course, Gustav. You can be sure I'll contact you if – "

"No," he warned. "Too dangerous. I took far too big a risk coming here, but I had to speak to you myself. I knew I could trust you to give me an honest answer, couldn't I?" he demanded.

"Yes," she unhesitatingly replied, managing to look him in the eye. Duty was duty, even when it involved her own husband.

"Good. Wildfowl will contact you every so often, in case you do develop any doubts about him. Got that?"

"Wildfowl. Yes."

He pushed the chair back and stood up. "I must be away now," he said at normal speaking volume. "There's much to be organised. I don't know when I'll get to see you again, darling, but promise me you'll be up on your feet again soon."

"I promise," Sophie said, still somewhat subdued.

Gustav bent and kissed her lips before whispering seductively in her ear: "You're a clever girl, Sophie. We're proud of you. Don't you forget that."

His departure left her feeling chilled. He did not normally kiss her like that. She picked up the bouquet he had left on the bed, which consisted of red tulips, white narcissi and a very dark red, almost black, foliage plant. The floral colours only hinted at Nazi allegiance, but, nevertheless, she felt uncertain about keeping them in her room. Gustav should never have come.

*

Lane Head Farm had never looked more wonderful, Karl thought as he stepped out of the Land Rover onto the cobbled yard. He stood and surveyed the distant Black Mountains of Wales, taking a deep breath of fresh, spring air. It was heavy with the distinctive sour odour of sheep, but that made it all the more welcoming. Molly, the Border Collie, ran up to greet the occupants of the Land Rover, sniffing briefly at Richard, the driver, before breaking into rapturous whining as she encountered Katherine. She seemed not to have noticed Karl, but then ran around the side of the vehicle and stopped dead in her tracks. Recognising his smell she knew she had not seen him for a long time. Her greeting when it came was ecstatic, and Karl had trouble walking towards the farmhouse door with Molly leaping around his feet.

"All right, Molly, calm down now. Down!" he commanded as she tried to lick his face.

Richard laughed. "Your fan club awaits, Dad," he said, pointing to the open door. There stood Karl's youngest son, Paul, with a very white-haired Donald and Gertie Murdoch on one side, and Werner Gimpel's English wife, Vera, on the other. They all held between them a banner proclaiming the message: WELCOME HOME!

Unable to contain himself any longer, Paul dropped his section of the banner and rushed out to hug his father, while Molly whined and tried to get between them.

"I missed you, Dad," Paul said into his father's chest.

Karl was staggered how much his son, now almost fifteen, had grown since he last saw him at his hospital bedside last November. Although Katherine had been over to visit him in prison since then, the boys had stayed at home to run the farm and for Paul to concentrate on his schooling.

"I missed you too, Paul, but I'm very proud of you, helping out so much." He turned to Richard, nearly as tall as himself now. "You too, Richard. I'm very grateful. I'm sorry you had to leave school."

Not one for showing his emotions, Richard shrugged aside the compliment. "It means I get plenty of practice at driving. Werner's let me drive everywhere since my birthday. I've got my test soon," he added proudly. Leading his father to meet the others patiently waiting their turn, he noticed his mother getting luggage out of the Land Rover and went to help.

Gertie Murdoch, petite and rather frail these days, grasped Karl's hand in her claw-like one and found herself choked for words. Tears welled up in her eyes and she simply hugged him. Donald and Vera gushed their welcomes, interrupted by the popping of a champagne cork as Richard did the honours with a bottle in the kitchen. They all trooped in behind him, Gertie, Werner and Vera sitting themselves down around the kitchen table, while Donald occupied the rocking chair by the range. He stretched out his hands to warm in front of it, before accepting a glass of champagne from Richard.

As Karl stood with glass in hand, he turned to the Murdochs, the providers of the champagne. "I just want to say thank you for all your support, for this ..." he raised his glass, "and for our few days' break in London. I think I can truly say we needed it." He caught Katherine's eye and smiled. "But believe me, you don't know how much I mean it when I say how wonderful it is to be home. Thank you also for all your wonderful letters. They truly kept me going when I felt down."

There was a heartfelt silence broken suddenly by Paul, embarrassed by his father's speech. "We've cooked a special meal for this evening," he told his parents. "Roast lamb, 'cause we thought Dad wouldn't have had any lamb while he was in ... Germany."

"It's all right, Paul. You can say 'in prison'," Karl laughed. "We all know where I've been."

Paul grinned sheepishly. "I know, Dad, but I've got into the habit of saying it at school."

Karl understood Paul's predicament. "It can't have been easy for you having a jailbird for a father. Still, I'm home now and that's all that matters." Needing to lighten the mood again he looked around for Richard. "Where's that bottle? Donald's glass is half empty."

As Richard did the rounds with the remains of the second bottle he remembered something he had to tell his parents. "Sabina phoned three days ago. She didn't know you were staying in London and asked when you'd be back. She said she'd phone tonight."

Katherine was immediately concerned. "I hope everything's all right."

"She sounded fine on the phone. Quite bouncy, in fact," Richard reassured her. "She probably just wanted to check you didn't get hijacked by reporters on your way over, Dad."

They all laughed.

"You can thank your lucky stars the story was never so big over here," Donald said. "We had a bit of flack from the nationals after you were arrested, but after that nothing, apart from the local papers, of course, who've kept up with the story. That was partly why we wanted you and Katherine safely out of the way in London just at first, so you wouldn't get hounded. It seems to have worked, though now you're back and people round here get wind of it, it might stir things up again."

"I'm sure Mr Kellett wouldn't mind seeing your name dragged through the mud again," Richard said with youthful insight. Andrew Kellett had suffered the ignominy of having his fiancée, Katherine, snatched from him by a German prisoner of war. The two men had been enemies ever since, although Andrew's wife, Audrey, had always burned a flame for Karl.

"Mr Kellett can go to hell!" Paul declared vehemently.

"Paul! Language!" Katherine warned. "And I think you've had quite enough of that stuff," she added, removing the champagne bottle from his grasp. She lifted it to check its contents. Only a drop left. Putting it down on the battered but well scrubbed kitchen table she made her way over to Gertie.

"Thank you so much for making me stay in London a few days. It made it much easier than coming straight back here," she murmured into her godmother's ear. "We needed that time together."

"I thought you might, dear. You've been apart a long time, and so much has happened. I'm glad it did the trick."

Katherine had never told any of her family or friends about Karl's infidelity, but Sabina seemed to have guessed something was amiss, and may have discussed her fears with Gertie. Whatever the situation, Gertie was her usual considerate and tactful self when it came to delicate matters, although Katherine knew she loved a good gossip about people not so close to her heart. No one else in the village would have heard a whisper of suspicion about Karl. It would be dangerous indeed if Audrey Kellett thought Karl was up for grabs. Putting such thoughts firmly out of her mind, she glanced around the kitchen at the food preparations. Saucepans of prepared vegetables stood by the sink, and, judging by the rich smell of rosemary and lamb enveloping the kitchen, the roast was cooking well.

"What needs doing then, Gertie?"

Gertie raised her arthritic hands in refusal. "Vera and I have everything under control, dear. This is your party. You just go and freshen up after your journey while I get the boys to set the table."

While everyone finished their champagne then set about completing the domestic and farm chores, Katherine and Karl took their luggage upstairs to their room. As he stepped inside, Karl looked around. It was the same as ever. Katherine's favourite picture of a bluebell wood hung in pride of place over the double bed Karl had made. The old Edwardian wardrobe stood in the corner, weighed down by bags of material and sewing paraphernalia. The chintz-draped dressing table chosen by Katherine's mother still blocked the view from the small, draughty window. Setting the bags carefully on the carpet, Karl took Katherine into his arms and kissed her tenderly.

"It's good to be home. I never thought I'd be back here. Thank you ... for allowing me."

She felt incipient tears welling and tried to blink them away. "It wasn't easy," she told him honestly.

"I know. And I'm grateful." He noticed an escaping tear and wiped it away with his finger. "And I promise it'll never ..."

She put her fingers on his lips to silence him. "There's nothing more to be said, Karl. It never happened." His lips moved under her fingers as he kissed them, while his eyes gave her the promise she had not let him utter.

The moment was interrupted by Paul's voice calling up the stairs to them. "Can you bring the chair from your room down, Dad?"

They smiled at each other. It was good to be home!

The roast lamb was every bit as good as promised. Karl accepted second helpings pressed on him by Gertie who had never got out of the habit of trying to feed him up, ever since he had first come to work there as a prisoner of war back in the autumn of 1946. Almost twenty-two years ago, Karl thought incredulously, spooning more mint sauce onto his plate. And almost twenty-one years since their wedding day. Another four and it would be their silver wedding. They must find a way to celebrate the occasion in true style.

Donald and Werner were deep in discussion about the joys of retirement, although neither was fully retired. Even at eighty-two, Donald still had a few private patients who would only see him, while Werner, sixty-five last January, had delayed leaving Lane Head Farm because of Karl's absence. Donald was quizzing Werner about his plans now that Karl was home again.

"So is this it now, Werner? Are you finally going to hang up your pruning saw and billhook?"

"I would, Doctor, but I think I will still need them. Vera says I should take up gardening."

"But there's not enough in your little patch to keep you busy for long!" Donald reasoned.

"I know, that's the trouble."

"And I've got too much garden. Gertie's hands aren't so good now and she can't wield the secateurs like she used to. How about you coming and giving me some help for a few bob a week?"

As Karl listened to the conversations around him he realised how wonderfully familiar and so delightfully ordinary they were. Gertie was pressing Vera to help at the Women's Institute jumble sale, while Katherine was hearing all about Paul's latest female admirer at school. So different from anything he had heard in prison. Only Richard sat quietly, not part of a conversation. Their eyes met and they smiled in mutual recognition of being on the outside of things.

When the telephone suddenly rang in the hall, Karl was first out of his seat to answer it. When he returned he tapped Katherine on the shoulder and told her Sabina and Wolf wanted a word. His eyes glistened with excitement as he waited for Katherine to return. When she too returned, her face beaming, Karl stood by his chair and banged on the table with a spoon.

"Attention everybody. I have an important announcement to make. That was Bina on the phone. She wanted to welcome us home, then she put Wolf on to ask me something." He paused dramatically, making sure he had everybody's rapt attention. Satisfied all eyes and ears were on him, even Donald's slightly deaf ones, he announced: "He wanted our permission to marry Bina!"

As the cries of delight died down, Donald called out: "So what did you tell him?"

Karl grinned. "I told him they had my blessing, and I guess Katherine said the same. You've never met Wolf, I know, but he's a very responsible, sensible young man. He acted with great restraint throughout the whole recent business. Even when he thought I had shot his father, he never took it out on Bina. We'll be proud to have him as a son-in-law." He was saving the best bit till last. "And guess what? They want to get married this June, here in Penchurch!"

"That's a bit sudden, isn't it?" Richard could not help commenting.

"She's not pregnant, Richard, if that's what you're thinking!" Karl rebuked him with a laugh. "They just can't see the point in waiting a long time. They want to share Wolf's flat in Dortmund and didn't want to upset anyone by not being married first."

"Good for them," Gertie declared. "There's too much of this 'living together' lark going on these days. One thing leads to another, then the whole of society breaks down. It's no wonder there are so many drug addicts in London these days."

Katherine winced. Drugs were already a sore point where Wolf and Sabina were concerned. In the days when Siegfried had been intent on hurting his father, he had asked Wolf to get friendly with Sabina then supply her with reefers in the hope she would progress to harder drugs. But knowing her father's own devastating experience with drugs at Dachau, Sabina had been horrified when Karl had told her exactly what her 'herbal' cigarettes were. Despite that she had maintained her friendship with Wolf, and look where it had led to now, Katherine thought.

She quickly got Gertie back to the point. "Just think! It will be our big chance to get all Karl's family over here. Rudi's the only one who's ever visited us and that was simply ages ago. I wonder if we can get them all to come. Hopefully all the cousins will come too – Anna's three and Rudi's two. It'll be quite a feat of organisation!"

Karl thought of his father. "It's just what Papa needs. Something to take his mind off Mama's death. He's like I remember your father was when I first came here, Katherine. He can't really get down to work."

"Well he is seventy-two after all, isn't he?" Katherine objected.

"You know what I mean, though. He still likes to think he's in charge of the sawmill, but ..."

"... his heart's no longer in it," Donald finished for him.

"Exactly."

Donald looked across the table at his wife. "Well we've more than enough room to put people up, haven't we, dear?"

"But surely you'll be putting up Robert, Alice and the boys," Katherine interjected.

"Ah, yes, if they're invited, of course," Donald agreed.

"Of course they'll be invited! We look on them as family, just like you two."

Not wanting to be left out of things, Vera said somewhat hesitantly: "We could put a couple up."

Gertie rubbed her gnarled hands together in glee. "This is going to be some gathering!"

More interested in his belly than weddings, Paul was scraping together the last of the cauliflower and carrots out of the serving dishes and liberally applying congealing gravy. He was, however, aware enough to ask: "Will Siegfried be invited?"

There was a moment's silence, during which all eyes turned on Karl.

"Yes. He'll be invited." He could sense their doubts. "I know it's difficult for you to accept he's changed. After all, you've not seen him since Mama's funeral. But I have, and from what he told me, I *know* he no longer feels the way he used to about me. Ask Bina and Wolf. They're convinced."

"Well, it's their wedding, of course," Katherine conceded. "They must invite whoever they want."

Karl could see the doubt still in everyone's eyes. Siegfried was going to have a hard time of it if he did come to the wedding, he thought.

By the time pudding was over, coffees consumed and their guests departed, Karl did not feel he had made much headway in pleading Siegfried's case. If anything he had lost ground as all the old stories had been aired and exclaimed over afresh. It seemed Siegfried could not shake off his past so easily.

In the still of the evening he wandered out, alone at last, to the workshop, a place of sanctuary and retreat. He was pleased to find it tidy and more or less as he left it. Idly he took down a chisel from the rack on the wall, ran his thumb over the end and found it sharp. There were fresh wood-shavings in the waste barrel. Someone had been working on something recently, but all was neatly tidied away. He sat on the stool at the workbench, resting his elbows on its grooved and pitted surface and gazed out of the window at nothingness.

He was still there half an hour later when Katherine came out to find him.

"Happy?" she asked.

He nodded. "Happy."

*

The accountants for Zopf Construction had asked Siegfried for a meeting. He had put it off twice already because of the trial and then the need to find a proper house. But he had to turn his mind back to the business sooner or later and begin picking up the pieces. He arrived at his Dortmund head office at seven-thirty on the appointed morning to check that all the necessary documents had been assembled as instructed. His stepfather, Paul Zopf, had drummed the fear of God into his employees, but it still did not prevent the occasional slip-up. Paul was a perfectionist, Siegfried too. As he flicked through files, re-arranging the order of certain documents, making mental notes about others, he was reminded how dire the company's position was.

Since Paul's escape to Uruguay to avoid arrest for his neo-Nazi activities, his construction company had gone into free-fall. No new projects had been forthcoming once the news broke, while certain major supply companies were proving slow in fulfilling contractual obligations. Siegfried knew he had to take the bull by the horns and do it quickly, but it was going to be difficult without Paul's experience and former contacts.

Promptly at eight o'clock his secretary brought in a cup of coffee. He had inherited her from Paul as she was the senior woman and knew the ins and outs of the firm almost as well as Paul. Unusually for Paul's female employees, Birgitte Schiersmann was no raging beauty and never had been, but this was because she had been with the firm since Paul's father's time. She had joined during the late thirties' boom years, had seen it expand even more during the early war years, then survived the rubble and muddle of the post-war years. She was already working in a senior position when Paul joined the family business in 1953 after his release from prison for war crimes. She had looked on Siegfried as an upstart and usurper at first, but quickly recognised his determination to do his best for the firm, and had very soon mellowed to the point where she now treated him like the son she had never had.

"It's good to see you back at the helm, Herr Driesler," she told Siegfried, as she put the coffee tray on a small, marquetry-topped table beside his desk.

"Thank you, Frau Schiersmann. I can't say it's good to be back. I would far rather be by Sophie's side, but this mess," he waved at the documents covering his desk, "needs sorting out. Otherwise neither you nor I will get paid this month."

Birgitte Schiersmann raised her finely plucked eyebrows in horror. "That bad is it, sir?"

"Strictly between you and me, Frau Schiersmann, yes. We'd committed ourselves heavily on the new housing estate development, fully expecting to be offered it, and had held back on other work because of it. As you well know, as soon as Herr Zopf left for Uruguay we were ditched as likely contractors. Other smaller projects also fell by the wayside at the same time. We're making do now solely on work contracted before last November, with nothing in the pipeline. And the accountant, when he gets here, is going to tell me I've got to do something about it."

"Well if anyone can do anything, you can, sir," she told him warmly.

Siegfried looked with fresh eyes at the woman he had taken for granted for so long. "Thank you for your confidence, Frau Schiersmann. I can assure you I'll do my very best."

When she had gone, Siegfried sat back for a moment in the large leather chair, once Paul's, now his, and spared a thought for the rest of the company's employees. There were over a hundred on the payroll. Much of the actual building work was contracted out to specialist firms of plumbers, heating engineers and suchlike, but there was still a substantial number of labourers, site surveyors and office staff who would suffer if Zopf Construction went to the wall. Not to mention his mother and Paul Zopf, as well as Sophie and himself.

At eleven o'clock his assistant, Julius Nagel, appeared with Georg Huwald, the accountant. Both men were considerably older than Siegfried, and both barely hid their belief that at twenty-four he was far too young to be at the head of such a large firm. Siegfried shook Huwald by the hand, waving him to the chair opposite. Nagel sat adjacent to Huwald and waited for Frau Schiersmann to serve coffee then sit herself down to take notes of the meeting. With the pleasantries seen to, Siegfried got down to business.

"Thank you for your patience, Herr Huwald. I'm sure you appreciate the personal problems my family has been going through recently, hence the delay in our meeting. Rest assured, Herr Nagel here has been holding the fort and he has prepared this statement of finances to show you our current position." He nodded to Nagel, who was keen to have his voice heard.

Siegfried sat back into the soft black leather and watched both Nagel and Huwald as the former took them through the financial crisis and what measures he had taken so far to minimise losses.

He had to admit, Nagel gave a good account of his efforts and Huwald was obviously impressed too, but not enough, it seemed. As Nagel finished his résumé, Huwald took off his glasses, wiped them with his handkerchief and tucked them into his breast pocket.

"Thank you, Herr Nagel, for your very full report. You have highlighted the main problem areas, but I notice you didn't mention the capital reserves in the holding account. Can you explain what use will be made of them?"

Nagel glanced at Siegfried, who sat forward in his chair to intervene.

"That is family money. It's not to be used."

Huwald's puffy eyes narrowed. "If the account is registered to the company then it is company money. It can't be held back for private purposes."

Siegfried was well aware of that. He also knew that the interest from that money was the current source of funds sent to Paul and his mother in Uruguay.

"It has to be," he declared firmly. "That money cannot be touched."

"I'm sorry, Herr Driesler, but the way things are that money must be used to keep the business afloat. If you need family funds I suggest you sell off your property in Bavaria."

Siegfried took a deep breath to control his anger at the man's effrontery. "There is no need for that, Herr Huwald. You'll see that by the summer I'll have got this firm back on its feet. Panic selling is not necessary."

"If you're so sure, Herr Driesler, I'll defer to your judgement," Huwald said coldly. "But I want you both and the records to know," he added with a conspiratorial glance at Nagel, "that my advice is otherwise."

"Fine."

It seemed the meeting was over. Huwald carefully put his notes into his briefcase, snapped it shut and got to his feet. Pointedly he offered his hand first to Nagel.

"I wish you luck and good judgement. You're going to need it. Good day, Herr Nagel, Herr Driesler."

With his office empty once more, Siegfried contemplated the morning's events. Nagel and Huwald were plainly in league with each other. Nagel was a competent assistant but a threat, who would use his ability to overrule Siegfried whenever he could. If Paul had wanted Nagel to run the company on his departure he would have said so, but he had left Siegfried in charge. He was determined not to betray Paul's confidence in himself, but the decisions must be his.

"I'm doing this my way," Siegfried said through gritted teeth as he flicked the switch on the intercom to Frau Schiersmann. It crackled as she acknowledged his call. "Get me Herr Doktor Druck, head of Dortmund planning department, on the phone, please." He remembered recent attempts to contact other departments. "And don't let them fob you off with excuses this time!"

The fires of ambition were burning again. Siegfried was determined not to fail. There was always a solution to a problem.

FOUR

Christian Bracht drew up the blinds and looked out over the Berlin rooftops. The late morning sun sparkled in the waters of the River Spree and the traffic hummed like bees on honeysuckle. He felt happy because Gustav was back from his two-day trip away, wherever he had gone. Christian had feared Gustav would not return even to see the close of the play, despite what he had said. But sure enough he had turned up at the theatre in the nick of time to put on his make-up and get changed into costume for the evening performance. Afterwards he had breathed not one word about where he had been and Christian had not liked to press him to find out. It was enough that Gustav had returned.

He padded naked across the polished wood floor of the hallway, his bare feet leaving momentary damp imprints, and opened the door to the kitchenette. His heart sank at the mess in the sink, so while the coffee percolated and two eggs boiled, he washed up the several cups and plates Gustav had managed to use late last night. Gustav was fickle when it came to tidiness. Some days he could be the perfect housewife, other days he simply could not be bothered. Perhaps it depended on whether he was having a male or female day, Christian smiled to himself. His own tidiness was a standing joke amongst their friends, and maybe he was obsessive about it, but he did not mind clearing up after Gustav occasionally.

Drying two cups and saucers he put them on two trays, took one set off again to wipe the tray clean of coffee rings and honey smears, reset it and poured out the coffee. He was going to treat Gustav to breakfast in bed this morning as a welcome home surprise. He hoped the eggs were perfectly cooked. The rolls were yesterday's, but that could not be helped. Balancing a tray on each hand like a waiter he returned to the bedroom he shared with Gustav. He put his own tray down on the chest of drawers then called out softly: "Good morning!"

There was a stirring under the bedding. Gustav's dark head poked out, his eyes bleary and face creased. "What's this?" he muttered.

"Breakfast in bed."

"Why? We usually go to Hubner's."

"I fancied a change."

Gustav looked at him suspiciously, but sat up and rubbed the sleep out of his eyes, before accepting the tray onto his lap. Christian picked up his own tray and sat on the edge of the bed by Gustav, but his proximity met with immediate irritation from Gustav.

"Just because I go away without you, doesn't mean you have to fawn over me when I get back," he said cruelly. "I meant what I said. When this bloody play's over, I'm off. Alone." He picked up a teaspoon and cracked the top of his egg as if to demonstrate the breaking of their relationship. He had scooped out two mouthfuls before noticing Christian still sat motionless on the edge of the bed.

"Hey. Eat up. It'll go cold."

Christian flung the tray on the floor, showering the wall with coffee. The boiled egg disappeared under a chest of drawers, leaving a trail of yoke on the floorboards.

"You don't care, do you!" he shouted. "I mean nothing to you! All this time together and you think you can walk out and leave me. Well it doesn't work like that, Gustav. I love you – I can't live without you. If you go, I'll follow!"

Slowly Gustav put down his spoon and set the tray on the bedside table out of harm's way. "Now look here, Christian," he said reasonably. "I understand how you feel, but you can't expect me to feel the same as you. I'm not one for being tied down to any one person. Never have been. Besides I'm too old for you. Find someone younger."

Christian stood staring bleakly out of the window. The sun still shone on the Spree, but now he saw it through a sparkle of tears refracting the sun's rays like diamonds. The diamonds pierced his heart but he blinked them away. Quietly and with great dignity, he turned to the chest of drawers, rummaged in it for a clean pair of underpants and socks, then withdrew to the shower.

Finishing his breakfast, Gustav pondered on what Christian's behaviour meant. The sound of the shower stopped, an electric razor started up, then a few minutes later he heard the front door click. Gustav leaned back against the pillow with relief. That little scene seemed to be over.

He would have to move out, he decided. Christian could stay on in the flat, find another lover to share it with. A few weeks in a boarding house would serve his own purposes until he could leave for Dortmund. His recent excursion had revealed that all was far from well there, and he had been delegated to sort it out. By the time Christian returned he would have moved out. They would still see each other at the theatre each evening, but that was unavoidable. Their rift might even add a new dimension of tension to the otherwise banal play. But that would never do. It had to end its run as soon as possible.

The boarding house Gustav chose later that day was further out of the city than he had intended, but it made the break from Christian all the more effective. There was less chance of them meeting accidentally outside of the theatre. Gustav had already handed in his notice to the theatre company, so while Christian would be busy rehearsing the forthcoming play in the afternoons, Gustav was free to meet certain acquaintances and discuss strategy to rebuild the devastation wrought to their network in the Dortmund area by Wolfgang Garisch's treachery.

"We've lost all our top people there," Gustav was explaining over the lunchtime hubbub of a busy restaurant to three elderly, sober-suited office types. "Even the lesser ones have to keep a low profile now. You remember Sophie Wendt, now Driesler, who was here last year? Her parents ran the gauntlet of the police enquiry and came through with comparatively little trouble. But they're now marked as Nazi sympathisers. Fresh blood is needed."

"Talking of blood," one of his companions growled, "the traitors remain unpunished. What are they playing at over there? It's been nine months and Garisch's boy's still at large. Why haven't we sent a hit squad to deal with him and those Drieslers?"

"My dear friend," Gustav soothed. "That's exactly why I'm so keen to get over there myself. My recent foray was illuminating in that it showed me how little is left to work with. Everyone's under suspicion and dare not make a wrong move. As for Siegfried Driesler, we need to tread very carefully. I knew him as a boy and was immensely impressed both by his loyalty to us and by his supreme ability to throw people off the scent. I remain to be convinced he's no longer one of us. I've spoken to Sophie, his wife, and she herself is uncertain about his loyalties, but I know a way I can find out for sure. You must just be patient and give me time to make my own thorough assessment. You can be sure I'll make appropriate arrangements if and when necessary."

The corner they were sitting in was dark, but he could see the set of his companions' vengeful faces. They each nodded slightly in turn, giving their consent to his campaign of action.

"Don't take too long," the white–haired one told him. "We want results."

"Oh, you can be sure I'll get results," Gustav declared confidently.

*

A diamond solitaire adorned Sabina's ring finger. She stopped work every so often to admire its iridescent sparkles, then resumed her crosscheck of the sawmill's invoices against the ledger entries. Her Uncle Rudi had been only too willing to hand over many administrative tasks to her, and at least she was earning her keep and a little pocket money. But it would be good to find a proper job in Dortmund once she was married. It would make the whole business of work-permits and such-like unnecessary.

Despite the noise she did not mind the sawmill; in fact the smell of sawdust reminded her of the tool-shed at home and the times she had sat on a high stool watching her father carving one of the little figurines he was famous for. She had noticed quite a few similar ones dotted about Haus Fichtenblick, and had been told that all the Driesler males had made them over the generations. But why should it be just the men? She reckoned she had seen her father make enough to have a go herself. Perhaps she could persuade Opa to help her a bit. She could even make one for Wolf as a wedding present! Inspired by the idea she determined to approach Opa about it that evening.

"You sound happy!" a beaming Stefan told her as he came into the office.

"Sorry?"

"You were humming to yourself. A sure sign of happiness, but then we know the reason why, don't we? Here let me have another look at that ring."

He was indulging her, she knew, but she happily held out her hand for him to look.

"Very nice." He let go of her fingers. "So you're going to make us all visit England at long last, are you?"

She laughed excitedly. "Well, it's about time, isn't it? Fancy you lot never having been over. It's a disgrace!"

"Well, we're at a disadvantage, aren't we, not speaking English. Rudi had to take someone with him when he went to help that time your dad broke his leg."

"Yes. Gustav. I can't remember him, even though I named my teddy bear after him. They both had the same curly brown hair and brown eyes apparently, but I don't think Daddy liked him much."

"No, he wouldn't have," Stefan agreed, aware that Sabina did not know the full story behind Gustav's sudden fall from grace.

"Did you know him then?"

"I met him when Rudi and I went to Dortmund. He sort of latched onto us in the pub. We'd gone to get an English phrasebook for Rudi, among other things. Rudi was trying out a few phrases over a beer or two and Gustav helped him out with the pronunciation. When he heard why Rudi needed the book, he asked if he could go with him. So you see, we hardly knew him. We certainly didn't know he was ho-" He suddenly remembered Sabina was not supposed to know about Gustav.

"He was what?"

Stefan grimaced, then decided that she was quite old enough by now to be told. "That he was homosexual, or bisexual, or whatever the term is. He was the cause of your Aunty Sarah's divorce. Gustav ended up going off with her husband."

It was a truly enlightening moment for Sabina. She had not heard of such things before and did not know quite how to react. Stefan could see her perplexity.

"Perhaps I shouldn't have told you. I don't suppose your Aunty Sarah wanted many people to know. I shouldn't mention it, if I were you."

Sabina shook her head in puzzlement. "No. No. I won't."

"I think he did her a favour, though," Stefan added as an afterthought.

"Who? Gustav?"

"Yes. She married the wrong man for the wrong reasons. She was well rid of Perry."

His words sounded ominous to her. She looked anxiously up at him. "You don't think I'm marrying the wrong man, do you?"

"Good heavens, no!" he riposted. "Wolf's a fine young man." He paused to let his doubt trickle through to her. "It's just his situation now is so ..." The only word he could think of to use would surely frighten her, but he said it anyway. "... so dangerous."

She was frightened. He could see that clearly. He perched on the edge of the desk and put a hand on her shoulder. "I don't want to frighten you even more, but do you really think you should stay in Germany? Wouldn't it be safer if you and Wolf lived in England?"

Under his hand she shrugged and tried to sound unconcerned. "If they're going to get him, they'll get him anywhere. But it's been so long now and nothing's happened. Perhaps nothing will. Perhaps they're too frightened of being caught, now the police know all about them."

Stefan shook his head. "You don't know them, Bina. You didn't live through the war. They're ruthless and determined people who don't give up. I've been meaning to say something to you for ages, but didn't like to interfere. Now I have and I'm glad." His hand gripped her shoulder in warning. "Don't underestimate them, Bina."

She looked up at him. "Don't worry. We won't. Wolf's quite aware of the danger."

Stefan sighed. "I just wish there was more we could do to protect you, but ..."

Sabina smiled bravely. "We're all in danger. Me, Wolf, Daddy, Siegfried. The police know that, and that is our insurance. There's nothing more we can do."

Stefan managed a smile too. "Right. Life goes on, eh? And so does work. I'd better leave you to it, or Rudi will think you're shirking."

"Onkel Rudi?" she laughed. "You must be joking. He's the biggest softy on earth – after you!"

Alone once more with her ledgers, Sabina smiled in deep gratitude for the family she adored. For the first time ever she found herself thinking about what it would be like having children of her own. She saw her own brothers, Richard and Paul, as uncles like Rudi and Stefan who would play rough and tumble games with their nieces and nephews. It was a shame Wolf was an only child, but that made her own family all the more precious.

Then there was always Siegfried. She remembered with a start that Sophie was pregnant, that the next generation was already begun. She would be an aunt of sorts herself soon, her father a grandfather – to Siegfried's child. Unthinkable! Putting such novel thoughts out of her head, she concentrated once more on the ledgers.

When she returned to Haus Fichtenblick later that afternoon, she remembered her earlier thoughts about woodcarving. She sought out her grandfather and found him sitting by the tiled stove in the living room, engaged in the very activity she was interested in. At his feet was spread newspaper to catch the falling pieces of wood, which would later be used as kindling to light the stove.

"What's that you're carving, Opa?" she asked him brightly.

The knife in Dieter's hands continued slicing and shaping as he spoke. "A Saint Peter for Frau Baumgarten. She already has Saint Paul."

Sabina nodded. Medebach was predominantly Roman Catholic, although just over the state border, in Hessen, the population tended towards Protestantism. Brought up a Protestant, she nevertheless attended the Roman Catholic Church of St Peter and Paul in Medebach where the Driesler family had always worshipped. She found no trouble adapting to the services. She had studied Latin at her grammar school, and felt perfectly at home in the church where her grandparents had been married and her father christened.

"May I see?" she asked, holding out her hand to take the roughly carved figure.

Dieter handed it over, waiting patiently while she examined it closely.

"I was looking to see how you got the initial shape," Sabina explained. "I'd love to have a go myself. Would you show me, Opa?"

He looked surprised but pleased at her request. Her presence in the house eased some of his loneliness since Gisela's death. It would be good to share a skill with his granddaughter over the evenings. "Of course. Let's go out to the workshop and find you some tools and a nice piece of wood to start with. Come along."

She tagged along behind him, winking at Anna in the kitchen as they passed through on their way out to the yard.

Haus Fichtenblick was a long half-timbered house fronting the quiet road. At its end, and seemingly part of it, was a large barn with several storerooms. One of these was the workshop where larger woodworking projects were undertaken. Woodcarving, however, usually took place of a winter's evening indoors by the stove, and more often now that Opa spent less time at the sawmill. She followed him into the workshop and watched as he selected a handful of fine chisels, rasps, coping saw, knife and soft pencil.

"You choose a piece of wood from that shelf," he told her. "Not too large," he warned. "It's easier to start small. Look for a piece which suggests something to carve."

Sabina rummaged around and held up a beautifully grained piece. "This looks like feathers!"

"Let's start with a duck, then" her grandfather beamed.

And the next one will be a wolf for my Wolf, Sabina thought happily.

*

Katherine was consulting bookings for their guest accommodation. They had a few regulars who had come each year since Land Head Farm first offered bed and breakfast. More often than not, however, guests were just passing through the area and were directed up by the local postmistress or pub landlords. The sign at the bottom of the lane had generated custom too. The B and B business was very much a sideline for the farm, but it did seem to be a growing one. The farmhouse itself had only three bedrooms so Katherine had been pleased when Karl and Werner had suggested converting the old feed store and loft. Between them they had done all the work, including making the beds and other furniture, although the project had not been without mishap. Karl had fallen off a ladder while tiling the roof, and had broken his leg, resulting in Rudi's arrival with the demon Gustav to help out. She shook her head in remembered anger at Gustav's subsequent behaviour as she found the page for June bookings.

"That's a relief!" she said to herself. "The twenty-second's free." She took a red pen from the telephone table and drew a big cross over the entire weekend of Sabina's wedding. It was less than three months off and there seemed so much to organise.

"Not like our wedding!" she said to Karl later over lunch at the kitchen table. "Apart from booking the church and getting permission for us to marry and for you to have the weekend away from camp, there wasn't much to do. Everyone invited contributed a bit of food for the reception, Gertie organised the cake, and most of the guests were local. This time the German invasion is going to create quite a few headaches!"

Karl was pleased to hear her talking so freely about their wedding. He sensed she still had a few problems at times, coping with his fling with Ilse, but she was hiding it well. "I've counted up sixteen of them if they all come, Monika's husband too. Heaven knows how we'll find rooms for all of them."

Katherine grinned as she spread butter on a slice of bread. "The village is banding together in readiness offering rooms, so Gertie tells me. They can't wait to meet your lot. But Gertie suggested a large tent on their lawn could cope with most of the younger ones, as long as they don't mind all being in together. At least they'd have safety in numbers and wouldn't have to struggle with English. We'd just have to provide sleeping bags and camp beds."

"I'll mention it to them next time I write. See what they say." Karl reached for the water jug and filled up everyone's glasses. As usual Richard was intent on filling his stomach as fast as possible and was not a participant in conversation, but Karl decided he should join in the fun. "Are you going to be an usher, Richard?"

His head jerked up from his plate at the sound of his name. "What?"

"An usher. Are you going to be one?" Karl repeated.

"Does that mean I have to wear one of those silly suits and a top hat?" he demanded, his grey eyes showing extreme anxiety at such a prospect.

Katherine laughed. "I've no idea! It's up to Bina what she wants for everybody, I should think."

"Oh no!" Karl spluttered. "You're not catching me in an outfit like that. Nor Wolf, and especially not Siegfried!" He thought a moment. "I expect they'll want to wear their loden suits. It might be nice if my family all came with their traditional clothes – make Wolf feel more at ease getting married in a strange country."

"That's a nice thought," Katherine agreed. "But then you're speaking from experience, aren't you, Schatz?"

Karl smiled happily at her resumption at last of their pet name for each other. Ilse's shadow was definitely fading.

By the end of the meal their heads were reeling with the lists of things needing organising. Even Richard was starting to get into the swing of things. As he and his father set off down through the sheep meadows he began to think of his sister as a married woman.

"It's amazing how quickly people change, isn't it, Dad?" he said, closing the gate to the orchards carefully behind them to keep the sheep well away from the chemicals being used there. "A year ago Bina was still at school, and now look at her. Living in Germany and about to get married."

"I could say the same about you, Richard. A year ago you were still at school, and fully intending to take A' Levels. Now you're a full-time farm worker. Quite a difference!"

"I suppose so. But I'm not doing anything I haven't always intended doing anyway. A' Levels weren't really necessary, were they? In fact they would have been a waste of time, when I think about it. It's only because I did so well with O' Levels that I stayed on."

"Yes, but at least you'd have had the chance to go to college, if you'd wanted to."

"But I don't want to. I'm happy here."

They had reached the first orchard where the leaf buds on the James Grieves were beginning to open on twigs hanging limply in the still air. Karl and Richard strolled over to where their brown overalls and masks lay in a heap by the drums of pesticide and the tractor-driven crop-sprayer.

As they donned their protective gear, Karl asked: "So what plans do you have for the future of Lane Head Farm?"

Richard stopped with one leg in his overalls. "Me? Er ... none. Why should I?"

"I thought while I was ... away you would have started thinking about running the farm yourself."

Richard kept his eyes on his feet as he resumed donning his overalls. "Well, yes, um ... I did start to think of it as mine, but I didn't make any plans."

"How old are these trees we're spraying?" his father asked him suddenly.

Richard looked up, answering without hesitation. "Granddad planted them shortly before the war. So nearly thirty."

"So how long before they need replacing?"

This time Richard looked blank.

"You see? There's more to farming than doing the same thing you did last year," Karl told him. "You have to keep progressing, move with the times as tastes change and technology improves. Look at us with these masks and overalls. Your grandfather never bothered with such things, but I won't risk getting pesticides on us." His eyes shifted from his son's as he broached a taboo subject. "My time in Dachau showed me only too well what chemicals can do to a body. Everyone else round here thinks I'm over-cautious, but I'd rather not take the risk." He finished buttoning his overalls, picked up his gloves and facemask then smiled encouragingly at Richard. "When you get back to the house this evening, you go into the study and look up the life-span of apple trees."

"Yes, sir!" Richard bellowed, coming to attention. Then he grinned and relaxed again. "It's good to have you back, Dad."

"It's good to be back. I'm just grateful you all coped so well."

Richard thought he should disabuse his father of that idea. "Mum was pretty upset while you were away. She didn't say much, but we could see she was miserable."

"She missed me then," he stated, anxiously awaiting Richard's corroboration.

"You bet!"

Karl turned towards the tractor. At least Richard, and probably Paul too, had no inkling about Ilse. Katherine had spared him his sons' wrath. Hopefully no one else knew, except Siegfried of course.

As he climbed onto the tractor he saw a familiar dark blue Jaguar approaching along the valley road. Its occupant saw him over the low hedge and screeched to a halt. Karl had not yet donned his facemask and knew he had been recognised by his old adversary, Andrew Kellett, the heir to Froxley Grange. Karl glanced at Richard. He too had heard the car stop and had left the barrels of pesticide to wander over to the gateway to see who it was. Karl climbed down from the tractor and joined Richard as Kellett leant on the gate, intent on conversation.

"I heard they'd let you out of prison," Kellett began in his customary pompous manner. He was about the same age as Karl but was neither as fit nor as tall. He hated having to look up to the man he despised, and his hatred was audible. "I'm surprised you dare show your face back here."

Karl kept his cool. He was used to Kellet's provocations, even found them slightly pathetic. He felt sorry for the man who had been denied the wife he wanted, settling for the local man-hunter, Audrey, only to find she still hunted. Their elder son, Alex, had died the previous year of a heroin overdose, and Karl could not spontaneously be rude to the man.

"Why not? Everyone's been very understanding and welcomed me back."

"It's always been the way, hasn't it?" Kellett sneered. "You have all the women eating out of the palm of your hand, don't you, no matter how outrageously you behave. You only have to smile in their direction and they all come running, skirts raised ready –"

"That is not the case," Karl swiftly cut him short, knowing full well that Kellett was the one guilty of accepting women's favours.

Andrew Kellett was intent on mischief. He did not intend a full-scale argument here in front of Driesler's son, but at least he could give him food for thought. "A shame your wife's the same. You think you're the only man who's had her?"

Karl was acutely aware of Richard's presence, but could not walk away now. "What do you mean by that?"

"Just what I said," Kellett said with a smug smile. Having dropped his bombshell he turned his back and strolled jauntily to his car.

Karl, open-mouthed in astonishment, watched him drive off, but Richard angrily threw a rotten apple at the departing car. He turned to his father in protest.

"How dare he say things like that about Mum. It's not true! She's not seen anyone while you've been away – only Robert when they went over to visit you."

Karl's heart sank. Robert? Surely not! But how would Kellett have found out?

"Dad, don't believe him. He's only winding you up," Richard pleaded, seeing his father's distraught face.

Karl wanted to believe him, but Kellett had sounded just too smug for it to be a lie. Nevertheless he had to shrug it off for Richard's benefit. "You're right. It's just the sort of thing he would do. He's never forgiven me for marrying your Mum." He realised he was still holding his facemask and gloves. "Back to work!" he declared, slapping the gloves on his hand in lieu of Kellett's face.

That whole afternoon Kellett's words echoed in his mind. As he drove up and down the rows of fruit trees, the man's smug expression haunted him. He wasn't lying, but how on earth would he know if Katherine were seeing someone else, unless Audrey had heard wind of something and mentioned it to him? He stopped by the barrels for a refill, then switched off the tractor's engine and jumped down onto the grass by Richard who was already filling the pesticide reservoir.

"I've had enough," he told him. "Your turn now. How've you been getting on with the fencing?" While the sheep were out of the orchards, Richard was taking the opportunity to repair holes before the sheep found them and forced them wider.

"Not bad. I've done up to the second damson tree." He put down the empty barrel and screwed the cap carefully back on.

"Richard," his father said slowly.

Richard knew what was coming. He had seen his father thinking about what Mr Kellett had said. "Don't worry about it, Dad. Mum really missed you. She wouldn't see anyone else, I'm sure."

"How many times has Robert been here?"

"Dad! He's the last person she'd –"

"No, he's the first. He's closer to her than anyone else. And they had the opportunity when they came over to visit me in prison." He knew he should not be voicing his doubts about his wife to Richard like this, but he wanted information and Richard was the only one who might supply it. "How many times has he been here?"

Richard frowned. He really didn't want to go behind his mother's back like this. "Leave it, Dad," he snapped. "You're making a mountain out of a molehill."

"So what's the molehill? He has been here?"

"Yes, but with Alice and the boys at Christmas ..."

"And?"

"And on his visits to you. It's nothing! Mr Kellett's succeeded in winding you up. That's all it is."

Karl studied his son's face. Richard certainly believed what he had said to be true. But that didn't necessarily mean it was. Short of confronting Katherine or Robert there seemed little else he could do. He was certainly not going begging for details from Kellett.

The afternoon's work kept his hands busy but his mind raged. When he and Richard returned to the farmhouse at the end of the afternoon he heard Katherine on the telephone in the hall. As he stepped out of his boots by the back door he heard her final words.

"'Bye, Robert. Speak to you again soon."

Richard too heard the fateful words and saw the pain then anger in his father's face. They exchanged glances: Richard's pleading for clemency for his mother, Karl's a demand for his son not to interfere.

"Ah, there you are," Katherine said with a smile, oblivious of the undercurrents around her. "That was Robert doing his professional thing, calling to see how you were settling back in, Schatz. He would have phoned this evening but he and Alice are off out to dinner with friends."

"And did you give me a clean bill of health?" Karl asked caustically.

His tone was lost on Katherine. "Of course," she gaily replied. "I told him you'd been down to the pub and to market, and how understanding everyone had been. Robert said everyone must be used to excusing your little foibles by now!" she laughed.

"My whats?"

"Foibles." She sensed his unexpected irritation and quickly thought how to explain the word. "Weaknesses, peculiarities – I don't know! How would you explain it, Richard?"

"Peculiarities will do, Mum," Richard muttered, aware of a growing atmosphere in the kitchen. He wondered whether he ought to hang around but his father abruptly strode across the kitchen and disappeared into the study, closing the door behind him. At least he didn't slam it, Richard thought uneasily. He felt some explanation was due to his mother. "Mr Kellett stopped to welcome Dad home."

Katherine understood immediately. "Ah. I see. A bit of friction was there?"

Richard nodded but did not elaborate. With any luck the whole thing would blow over without any interference from him. His mother was adept at handling his father's strange moods.

FIVE

Karl sat at his desk, hands clasped as in prayer in front of his face. He was not praying. He had no god to pray to. But he needed to think.

He could hardly blame Katherine if she had looked elsewhere for affection after what he had done with Ilse. He had even written a letter to her from prison saying as much, in the darkest hours before Wolf and Siegfried's U-turns, when he had thought he would be locked up for life. If she had already sought solace in Robert then he could hardly complain. But why did it have to be Robert? Robert was his closest confidant, the friend he phoned when he needed to unburden himself. Robert knew everything about him, more even than Katherine knew. How could he trust him now?

It had to be Robert. There was nobody else Katherine would look at, and the telephone call just now seemed to confirm it. His call probably was partly professional, to see how his adopted patient was coping with freedom again, but was that now based on the need to adjust his own behaviour accordingly? How often did Robert telephone during the day when he knew only Katherine would be in the house?

His ruminations were interrupted by a gentle tap on the door. It opened cautiously and Katherine appeared holding a mug of tea.

"Alright, Schatz? Richard said Andrew Kellett had been doing his usual trick of provoking you." She put the mug down on the desk beside him and ruffled his hair.

Whatever had happened, it was not her fault. He must not blame her, Karl told himself. "Yes, I'm alright." He smiled at her and took a sip of tea.

She sensed he wanted to be alone with his thoughts so planted a kiss on his cheek and told him: "You finished early today. Dinner won't be ready for half an hour."

"OK. I'll catch up with some paperwork then." He pulled the pile of post towards him, but as soon as she was out of the study he ignored it.

Who could he talk to now if he didn't have Robert? Should he confide in Richard, who at least knew what was going on? Somehow he felt not. Richard was too young to understand the issues involved. Rudi? He was a possibility, although they had seen little of each other since the outbreak of the war, and long distance telephone calls were not ideal. Werner? Donald Murdoch? He had to talk to someone. He knew better now than to keep it all bottled up inside. But there was no one else Karl felt comfortable enough with – except Siegfried!

Over dinner he sensed Richard watching him, and he managed to maintain an air of normality. Katherine seemed not to notice anything wrong, while Paul was oblivious as usual to anything but the food on his plate. Inside, however, he was hurting and the food on his own plate seemed to have lost all its flavour. He had to force himself to eat it and refused second helpings.

Katherine was going out later that evening to a rehearsal of the Penchurch Players' latest production, J.B. Priestley's *An Inspector Calls*. She was playing the part of Sybil Birling, and her mind seemed to be fixed on getting dinner over with and cleared away before she went out. Karl kissed her dutifully goodbye as she hurried out to the Land Rover at seven o'clock. Paul and Richard had disappeared out to the work shed for an hour's carpentry, so he had the house to himself. He headed straight for the telephone in the hall.

*

The boxes of wedding presents still sat unopened in the spare bedroom of the flat. Periodically Siegfried looked in on the pile to remind himself of Sophie and of their wedding, which seemed so long ago. He had given Sophie a list of what was there and who sent it, so she could write to thank people, but he had no need of most of the items until Sophie came home from hospital. It would give her pleasure unpacking them all, he had decided. Besides, everything would need packing up again when they moved to the house. It would be pointless him doing anything now, alone. He shut the bedroom door and returned to the living room.

Although he had lived for several years alone in the flat, the few months Sophie had spent with him before their wedding had changed the feel of the place totally. Her presence was needed, the rooms felt empty without her, and he could not bear to spend a minute longer in the flat than necessary. He almost always ate out and did not linger in bed of a morning. There was too much to do for lying in, anyway. Currying favour with planning departments and building supplies merchants took almost all his time. That and visiting Sophie and looking round the houses she selected from the agents' details. Her favourite certainly appealed to him too. Now he just had to make sure the finances could cope. Part of the problem was the large legal bill he had settled for his father's defence. The honeymoon had been very expensive and he still had to see that sufficient funds found their way to his mother and Paul. He would need a considerable sum to commence purchasing the house, and on top of that there would be extra expenses for Sophie's treatment and the birth of the baby.

It was all starting to seem too much. He needed a break. He looked up at the wall clock. It was only five to eight. He decided to call Wolf. Reaching across to the telephone table, he put the instrument on his lap and dialled.

"It's Siegfried," he said into the receiver. "Are you busy?"

"No. Why?" came Wolf's voice down the line.

"I need some company. Any chance of you joining me for a drink?"

There was a pause, presumably while Wolf consulted his watch.

"OK. Our usual?"

"Great. See you there in ten minutes." Siegfried put the telephone back on its table, picked up his coat from the back of his armchair and glanced in the mirror. His blond hair was short enough to stay tidy, unlike many of his contemporaries these days. He looked a bit tired but still handsome, despite his broken nose. Checking his appearance was a habit his all too brief marriage had not altered. Eating on his own so much he attracted interested glances from women, and it had been four months since his honeymoon. He recognised he had acquired and retained his stepfather's cavalier attitude to women, although there was no denying Sophie was special. Still, it was hardly likely he would find someone this evening with Wolf at his side. Wolf exuded the air of a man about to get married, repelling advances from females. Siegfried smiled ruefully. A few short months ago that had been him. Now look at him!

The night was cool, the traffic still busy. Siegfried walked the short distance to his local pub, unaware of the phone ringing in his empty flat. Wolf's flat, in a less desirable area, was not far away, so the pub was a handy halfway house. Siegfried arrived first, pushing his way into the crowded, smoke-filled bar. It was what they liked about the place, anonymous and discreet, yet full of atmosphere and life. He elbowed his way into a place at the bar, ordered two beers, keeping his eye on the door for Wolf's arrival. Two men came in, wearing denim jeans and leather jackets, their long, unkempt hair greasy. Siegfried eyed them curiously, wondering what manner of work they did looking like that. No self-respecting employer would have them on his books!

"Have you been waiting long?" Wolf had crept in while Siegfried's attention was diverted by the hairy pair.

"No, only a minute. Here's your beer. *Prost!*"

They raised their glasses in salute and took a mouthful. "Thanks for coming, Wolf. That empty flat's beginning to get to me. I can't wait for Sophie to come home."

"I know how you feel. It's the same for me. I keep thinking of having Bina with me, but she won't come until we're married. Mind you ..." He had been about to reveal all to Siegfried about Sabina's sudden capitulation in the forest at Medebach, but decided on discretion. Siegfried may have been a reformed character as far as his family was concerned, but there were limits to Wolf's trust in him.

Siegfried picked up on his old friend's hesitation and made his own conclusion. Wolf's smug grin had been too revealing.

"You lucky sod! I never thought she would. It just goes to show what a little gentle persuasion can achieve." He continued his teasing. "So she won't be wearing white for the wedding."

Wolf was an old hand at sparring with Siegfried. "Wasn't Sophie in white?" Remembering his last telephone conversation with Sabina he added: "Which reminds me. We were discussing what the men should wear. Sabina suggested we wear our loden. Make it as much a German event as possible for my benefit."

"What? In England?" Siegfried asked in astonishment. "Things must have changed a bit since I was there. I seem to remember my father hated displaying his nationality."

"That was a long time ago. I guess things have mellowed a bit since then. Anyway, I like the idea, so that sorts that one out. Do you think Sophie will be able to come and meet all your father's family?"

"We don't know yet. It depends how –"

A noisy exchange in a corner of the room drew their attention. Three young men were arguing over a card game, while a fourth had jumped up in anger, accidentally spilling Dubonnet down the front of a woman's fawn-coloured jacket. The dispute soon spread to the woman's companions, with tempers fraying dangerously. Other customers were beginning to move away nervously, and Siegfried noticed the hairy pair among them.

"I'd have thought they'd want to be in the thick of things," he remarked to Wolf, pointing them out.

"Too nervous about losing their wigs!" Wolf laughed.

"Wigs? Are you joking?"

"No. I saw them come in, and one adjusted his to make sure it was straight before they walked through the door. They must be going to some hippie convention and didn't want to feel left out!"

Siegfried's eyes narrowed with suspicion. The pair now had their backs to the bar where Siegfried and Wolf were sitting, but a large wall mirror enabled Siegfried to see their faces. They were not looking at the developing row, but into the mirror towards the bar where he was sitting. Their hurriedly averted gaze gave them away.

"I don't like the look of them," he told Wolf. "Finish your drink. I want to see what happens when we leave. We'll go up the road to the T-junction, see if they follow."

"What if they do? What if they're undercover police keeping an eye on us? We can't jump them!"

"What if they're not?" Siegfried countered. "They could equally well be a hit-squad. I think we assume the worst. If they are police, we can give our reasons for jumping them."

"Hang on a minute, Siegfried!" Wolf objected, but Siegfried was already on his way to the door, eager for the chase. Reluctantly Wolf followed.

*

Sabina's duck was proving troublesome. She had accidentally gouged out too much around the neck on one side. If she made the other side to match, the neck would be too thin.

"You could always turn it into a swan or a goose," Dieter suggested, seeing her spirits sinking.

Sabina held the roughly hewn block up to eye level and scrutinised it carefully. She could lower the level of the back, lengthening the neck, and achieve the proportions of a swimming goose. "Good idea, Opa. I'll have a try."

Dieter left her to her labours in the living room and wandered out to the kitchen where Stefan and Anna were sitting over mugs of hot chocolate. Their youngest son, Lothar, a strapping seventeen-year-old who was normally out with one of the local girls at this time of the evening, sat head in hands at the table bemoaning being dumped by his latest beloved.

"Want one, Papa?" Anna asked, getting to her feet. "We were just trying to console Lothar."

"Who was it this time?" Dieter asked his grandson gruffly.

Lothar looked up, his eyes clear, but his mouth decidedly down-turned. "Martina Fischer. She's going off to train as a nurse and doesn't want the distraction of a boyfriend."

"Good for her!" Dieter declared with a nod at Anna for some hot chocolate. "Sounds like she's got some sense, that one. She should make a good nurse."

"Perhaps I should go off and study something," Lothar muttered. "Though there's not much point until I've got my national service out of the way."

"You wouldn't rather do community service instead?" his mother asked.

Lothar shook his head. "No, it's longer. I want to get it all over and done with."

"You never know, you might learn a useful trade in the army. Just look at Wolf and his electronics," Stefan commented.

"I know." Lothar seemed revived enough by the conversation to take a sip of his chocolate. "Are we really all going to go to England for Bina and Wolf's wedding?"

"Yes. Onkel Karl wrote to say we can all be found beds of one sort or another. Robert Murdoch's parents have suggested you younger ones can all sleep in a tent on their lawn."

Lothar's eyes were shining with anticipation now. "I can't wait! Richard and Paul have told me so much about the place. Can we visit the livestock market in Hereford?"

"I don't know what's so great about a load of cattle and sheep all crammed in together," his father laughed, "but I'm sure if that's your heart's desire it can be managed!"

"I want to see the cathedral," Dieter declared. "Karl tells me there's a very old map of the world in there."

Sabina walked in on the party. "Are you talking about Hereford? I came to see what all the noise was about!"

Her nose wrinkled at the delicious smell. Anna had boiled enough milk for Sabina too and promptly handed her a cup full of steaming chocolate.

"Yes," Anna told her. "We're all looking forward to your wedding."

"Mummy's almost more excited about it than I am," Sabina said. "She's written a long list of questions and suggestions about the reception, who to invite, where I'm getting the dress from, bridesmaids, the cake. You name it, she's asked about it! She suggested we ought to be there to hear the last banns read, but I'm not sure Wolf will be able to get so much time off work, what with the honeymoon as well."

"Have you decided where you're going?" Lothar asked.

"Somewhere in England, but that's all I'm saying!" Sabina declared smugly.

Out in the hall the telephone rang. Stefan went out to answer it, returning a few moments later. "It's Wolf for you, Bina."

"Thanks," Sabina said and went out to the hall.

*

Outside the pub Siegfried and Wolf turned right and began walking briskly up the road. It was a side street with comparatively little traffic, but the streetlights were bright enough to spot anyone following them. As they crossed a minor road they turned to check for traffic behind.

"They're following!" Siegfried hissed.

Wolf swore under his breath. "Shit! What do we do now?"

"At the T-junction you turn right, I'll turn left. See which one they follow. We then each go down the next side street, back into this one and meet up. If they turn up too we'll know for sure they're following us. Then we confront them."

"What if they're armed?"

"We'll manage," Siegfried said confidently. The adrenalin was starting to flow and he felt the old familiar buzz of excitement in his veins. They had reached the main road, where, making a show of bidding each other goodnight, he peeled left and Wolf right. Increasing pace he headed for the next side turning. On the corner he paused, looked at the reflection in a shop window and saw both men heading his way. So it wasn't Wolf they were after. He strode out, turned left again and caught sight of Wolf hurrying silently towards him. Before their tails had turned the last corner, Wolf slipped into a dark alley and waited. Siegfried had slowed his pace right down so the men would come upon him suddenly.

Hearing their footsteps close behind now and judging them to be by Wolf's alley, Siegfried turned on his heel. In his hand was the penknife Gustav had given him as a small boy, and which he always kept with him. The blade was sharp and open. Before the hairy pair realised what was happening, Wolf ducked out from the alley behind them and forced the nearest man against the brick wall of the house. Before his partner could react, Siegfried had grabbed his left arm, pinioned it behind him and held the blade to his throat. He could smell beer on the man's breath as he pressed him hard against the wall.

"What do you want?" he demanded, scraping the penknife blade gently against the man's throat. With a deft flick of the penknife, Siegfried caught a lock of long, curly hair and whipped the wig off the man's head. Underneath he was close-cropped.

Without all the hair the man was older than he looked. He was breathing hard but remained silent, casting anxious glances towards his companion. Wolf had the second tail's face pressed into the brickwork so he could not move.

"I asked you a question," Siegfried repeated, allowing the tip of the blade to press into the man's throat. A trickle of blood ran down his captive's neck onto his shirt collar.

"We – we were to follow you," he gasped.

"I can see that!" Siegfried snorted contemptuously. "Who sent you?"

The man licked his lips nervously. "I can't tell you."

"Can't or won't?" Siegfried pressed the blade a fraction deeper, his knee pushing behind his victim's left leg, crushing his kneecap against the wall.

The man yelped in pain. "C-can't."

Siegfried maintained the pressure a few moments longer as he came to a decision. Then with a satisfied grunt he eased back slightly. "I used to be in charge of your outfit. I know how it works. But it's got too amateurish. Tell your new boss to get his act together. And I don't expect to see you two again. Understand?" To emphasise his point he leaned hard against the man, grinding his face into the brickwork.

There was an infinitesimal nod. Siegfried stood back, withdrew the knife and let go of the man's arm. Wolf did likewise and the pair hurtled off into the darkness, one of them limping noticeably.

"Pathetic!" Siegfried spat after them.

Wolf, however, was far more shaken by the incident. "Why are they following you?"

"I don't know. In their shoes I would have done us in without any warning. They're obviously not sure of themselves." He noticed that now the action was over, Wolf was trembling slightly. "Let's go back to my place. Have something to steady our nerves. You can stay the night if you like."

"My nerves, not yours. Thanks. I think I will." They set off back towards the more upmarket quarter where Siegfried's apartment block was situated. Nobody seemed to have witnessed the event, fortunately, and they had the street to themselves.

Wolf looked across at his friend. "You enjoyed that, didn't you? Quite like old times."

Siegfried grinned back. "To be honest, yes. I did enjoy it. But that's what I was brought up to do. Old habits die hard, so they say. It almost makes me want to take up the reins again and sort them out."

Wolf stopped dead. "Sort them out? As in organising them? You're joking!"

Siegfried stopped too and gave a sigh of resignation. "Yes. I'm joking. I'm supposed to have turned over a new leaf, aren't I?"

Wolf made no comment but the look of reproach he gave Siegfried showed he took a dim view of such jesting. They continued walking in silence, their ears straining for sounds of following footsteps, but they reached Siegfried's flat without further incident. As they entered the flat, however, Siegfried instantly went on the alert, cocking his head for sounds of an intruder.

"What is it?" Wolf silently mouthed.

Siegfried ignored him and went cautiously from room to room, followed by Wolf, looking behind doors and curtains. Satisfied there was nobody in the flat except themselves, Siegfried explained his reason for alarm, taking Wolf back to the hall.

"The rug by the door's flicked up at the corner. Somebody's been in here while I was out."

"You're sure about that?"

"Positive. I remember looking back before I shut the door to check I'd switched the light off in the kitchen. The rug was fine then."

"Has anything been taken?"

Siegfried was bending down to pick up the rug. It was of natural-coloured cream and brown wool from Norway, lightweight and easily rucked up. "Not that I noticed," he replied. He shook the rug out, laid it back down then headed for his writing bureau in a corner of the living room. "They were probably looking for something – papers, letters or whatever. Let's see."

He stood in front of the bureau and scrutinised it. There were no obvious signs of disturbance. Opening the flap he studied the inside before noticing the bundle of letters from his mother propped on one side. Something about the angle they leaned at struck him as wrong. Picking them up he flicked through, checking the postmarks. At the mid-point he double-checked the sequence then declared: "There's one missing!"

"Are you sure?"

He nodded. "My mother writes regularly on Saturday afternoons without fail. One of her February letters is definitely missing."

Wolf sat on the arm of a chair behind him. "But why would they want one of your mother's letters?"

Siegfried shrugged. "As a way of finding out where my loyalties really lie, perhaps? They're possibly in some doubt – don't want to kill me unless they're absolutely sure I'm not just deceiving the police and all my family. They must reckon my mother's the one most likely to know the truth."

"What about Sophie? She knows your views on Nazism now, doesn't she? Couldn't they ask her?"

Siegfried grimaced. "She's convinced herself and her parents I'm still one of them, but that doesn't guarantee they'll believe her."

"Bina's still not sure about you, you know."

Siegfried shrugged, unconcerned. "The bigger the smokescreen the better. I don't really care what people think. I know the truth. Everyone else can think what they like. All I'm doing is protecting myself and my family. You ought to try doing the same, Wolf, for Sabina's sake."

Wolf looked askance at him. "It's too late now. I've been totally open about my change of heart. But you ... You're covering up."

"I know what I'm doing, Wolf. I know how their minds work."

"So do I, but –"

Siegfried raised his hands, demanding silence. "Let's get that drink I promised." As he made for the drinks' cabinet across the room, he turned suddenly with an afterthought. "Try thinking about my influence rubbing off on you. If they doubt I'm a turncoat, they could be made to doubt you too."

Wolf flipped himself over the side of the armchair where he had been perching and made himself comfortable until he began to think about what Siegfried had just said. It seemed a good idea, but he could lose Bina's trust if she thought he was wavering.

"Do you mind if I use your telephone?" he suddenly asked. "I want to warn Bina to be vigilant, after what happened tonight."

"Sure. Go ahead."

Wolf got up out of the chair and went out to the hall. Dialling the number of Haus Fichtenblick, he heard Stefan's voice answer as the connection was made. A few moments later Sabina's voice came on the line.

"Hi, Liebling. How's things?"

Now he had made the call he was having second thoughts. She would only be frightened if he told her what had happened. "I just wanted to tell you, I love you."

Down the line Sabina heard a clock begin to chime ten. She recognised its deep, melancholy tone as one in Siegfried's apartment. "That wasn't really why you called, was it? Has something happened?"

"Happened? No? Why should it have?"

"Because you're phoning from Siegfried's," she explained patiently.

Wolf acknowledged defeat. She was too perceptive to be lied to. Briefly he told her the events of the evening.

"And you're all right?" she demanded when he had finished regaling how the men were sent packing.

"Fine. A bit shaken. Siegfried lapped it up though."

"Well he would, wouldn't he." She thought a moment. "And he wasn't frightened at all?"

"Didn't seem to be. Why?"

"Are you sure it wasn't all a set up? You know, to convince you he's reformed when he hasn't?"

"Bina, really!"

"I'm sorry. I just can't shake my suspicions of him. It's just the sort of convoluted, scheming thing he'd do."

Wolf was tempted to let her believe her theory. At least it might ease her fears for their own safety. He let the matter rest. "Well, I'll leave you to whatever it was you were doing."

"We were in the kitchen drinking hot chocolate."

"Lovely. I'll let you get back to it, Liebchen. Sleep well." He blew a kiss down the line, feeling calmer himself for talking to her. Her theory had a strange ring of truth to it, after what Siegfried had said about Sophie.

*

Karl replaced the receiver, cutting off the ringing tone. He was disappointed not to have got hold of Siegfried, but should have expected him to be out somewhere at this time of the evening. Strangely enough he now felt relieved Siegfried was not in. Richard had not believed his mother capable of having an affair, and nobody else would either. Everyone would say it was a Kellett practical joke and tell him not to be so stupid as to believe it. But they had not seen Kellett's face when he made the accusation.

The only way he would get at the truth was to ask Katherine outright. If he did it as sensitively as he could, with no recriminations, then surely it would turn out all right. It would have to. He could not carry on as normal much longer with this dark suspicion lurking. Again and again he and Katherine had told each other they must have no secrets from each other. Now it was her turn to confess.

He returned to the study and made an effort to deal with the paperwork, but his mind rehearsed his approach to her, trying out different questions and likely scenarios from the optimistic to the pessimistic. Would she shrug it off and say it was nothing? Would she burst into tears and make a scene, saying it was all his fault anyway? For once he had no idea how she would react.

Time passed slowly. She was not due back until ten thirty. Karl abandoned the paperwork and went outside to seek company in the work shed. It was a cool night with a stiff breeze hurling clouds past the moon. Despite the cold he paused outside the door. Richard and Paul were deep in discussion.

"I hope Dad doesn't do anything stupid," he heard Paul's voice, squeaky with adolescence.

"Like what? Kill Robert? Don't be daft, Paul," came Richard's retort.

"I didn't mean he'd kill anybody. At least, I don't think he would. Would he?" he added doubtfully.

There was a long pause. Karl could imagine Richard weighing up the likelihood of their father turning killer again. "It depends on whether he loses his temper, but somehow I can't see him doing anything like that. I think we ought to warn Mum, though. Tell her what's troubling Dad. Then she can plan how best to deal with him to avoid ... problems."

"Well you'll have to tell her," Paul whimpered, suddenly sounding like a frightened child rather than the strapping lad of fifteen that he was.

Karl could not bear to listen to any more. He crept back to the house to the warm kitchen. He had to pre-empt the boys and deal with this tonight when Katherine returned from rehearsal. Searching in the dresser he found a bottle of schnapps then put it back untouched. The smell of alcohol on his breath might antagonise her. She disapproved strongly of solitary drinking. He wanted her friendly and sympathetic. He just hoped the rehearsal was going well.

The boys wandered in at eight, Paul to commence his homework, Richard to watch 'The High Chaparral' on television. They made no comment at seeing their father sitting doing nothing in the kitchen, although Richard gave him a shrewd look. Taking the hint Karl got up from the rocking chair and joined him in the living room. He seldom watched television, but needed something to occupy his mind until Katherine got home. Monday proved a good night on BBC2 and the time passed quickly. As ten-thirty approached Richard yawned and took himself off to bed. Karl stayed up. Katherine always took some time to wind down after a rehearsal and would be wide awake. At last he heard the car keys clunk down on the hall table then she stepped into the living room.

"Are you still up?"

"Katherine, I need to talk to you."

The full use of her name, the fact he was watching television, and the incident earlier that day with Andrew Kellett warned her something serious was coming.

"Just let me get my coat off. Do you want a cup of tea?" An air of normality usually helped in these situations.

"Might as well." Karl switched off the television and followed her out to the kitchen. He watched her fill the kettle and put it on the range. "How was rehearsal?"

"Quite good. It's starting to take shape at last."

Karl was relieved. He perched against the range and watched the steam as it began to emerge from the spout of the kettle, knowing he too needed to let off steam. But how to start?

"What did you want to talk about?" Katherine asked casually while ferreting around in a cupboard for two mugs. She sensed he needed help. "Was it something to do with Andrew Kellett?"

"Yes. Something he said today." He took a deep breath. "I don't want to make a big thing of this, Schatz, and I'm not casting blame or anything, but I just need to know some answers."

"Oh?" she said slowly. "What about?"

"He said today that I was not the only man who had 'had' you. He wouldn't explain, but was very smug. I need to know what he meant, Schatz."

He hoped he had sounded unprovocative enough. He watched her reaction carefully. She slowly put down the mugs on the table, remarking only: "That's quite an accusation."

She went about the business of making tea, leaving Karl in an agony of suspense, but he was not going to rush her. She would say something when she was ready. He could see she was deliberating exactly what. Eventually she poured the tea and sat down at the table. He joined her at the table, facing her over the steaming mugs.

"Well?" he prompted.

"Well," she repeated. "I don't know what Andrew was trying to achieve. If he's accusing me of sleeping with someone else since we've been married, then he's lying."

She was hedging, he could tell. "He wasn't lying." He reached across the table and picked up her hand in his. She seemed astonished by the move but did not withdraw her hand, obviously comforted by his non-confrontational approach.

She reconsidered her tactics. "Look, Karl. I think I know what he was getting at, and I'll explain it just because I can see you won't drop the subject until you know. But I can promise you it will achieve nothing. In fact this is a pointless exercise –"

"Pointless?" he snapped, abruptly withdrawing his hand from hers. "I would hardly call –"

"Karl, just shut up and listen, all right? This is difficult enough for me without you interrupting." She calmly took a sip of tea and was pleased to see her action had a soothing effect on Karl. This was not going to be easy for him, so she had to do it right. She looked into his eyes. "Promise me that whatever I tell you there will be no recriminations, no repercussions, nothing. What happened, happened and can't be altered."

"That's not so easy. I don't know what you're going to tell me," he protested, but more reasonably.

"I know, but I won't say anything until I have your promise. No recriminations."

He shrugged. If she wanted forgiving, he would readily forgive her. He had to. It would be hypocritical of him not to, after what she had done for him. "No recriminations, I promise."

"Good." She leaned back in her chair. "I know we always promised not to hide anything from each other. Well, I'm afraid I didn't keep that promise. It was for your own good. Telling you would have only caused too many problems. I don't want to tell you even now, but you're insisting and so I shall. What happened was before we were married, so I can hardly see the relevance now. Do you still want to hear?"

Karl nodded, as she knew he would.

"Right. Here goes then. Andrew was talking about himself. He's 'had' me, as he so eloquently put it."

Karl was stunned. It blew apart all his theories about Robert. He felt immediate relief that Robert was in the clear, but puzzlement too. "I thought you said you and he never got that far when you were engaged."

"We didn't. It happened during your breakdown when I was coping with the farm on my own. Andrew tried to win back my affections. He partly succeeded for a while, but when he twigged that you and I had slept together he was very angry. I think he hoped that if he possessed me like that, I would be irretrievably his."

"And you let him?"

Katherine looked away. This was the hardest part. "No. He raped me."

She had expected a violent and vitriolic outburst against Kellett, but instead he was strangely quiet.

Eventually he said: "And you've told nobody this?"

"Only Gertie. She said I should tell the police, but I didn't think it was worth the trouble. How could I have proved it was rape? We'd been going out together, and Andrew would have claimed it was a grudge accusation."

"I can understand that."

"So?" she prompted.

"So what?"

"No recriminations?"

With great reluctance he nodded, but then negated his promise by growling. "Just don't let that bastard get within a mile of me."

It was as much, if not more than she could have hoped for. Curiously enough it was a relief to have told him at last, even though he was strangely lacking in sympathy for her plight all those years ago. It was almost as though he didn't want to share the experience with her by talking about it.

Upstairs Richard hung over the banisters, straining to catch every word from the kitchen. How could Dad leave it like that? he fumed. It had not been Mum's fault, of course. He had been stupid to think it might have been. Kellett had raped Mum, and Dad wasn't going to do anything about it?

Satisfied, however, that his mother needed no protection from his father's wrath, he disappeared into his room, the anger of youth raging in him. God help Kellett if he ever showed his face here.

SIX

Gustav held Ilse's letter to her son. It had been delivered to him in Berlin, together with a report on the bungled surveillance and Siegfried's remarks about doing a better job himself. The more Gustav heard about him, the more he wanted to meet Siegfried again. But he could not risk that unless he was absolutely certain of his loyalties. The report suggested Siegfried still considered himself part of the network, if no longer an active member. He turned to the letter, settled back in his chair and read it carefully.

Montevideo, 17.2.68

My darling Siegfried,
I'm roasting here, sipping a cold beer, trying to keep cool and thinking of you in the ice and snow of February. I've been following the reports of the Winter Olympics, wishing I was there myself. Perhaps one day they'll hold them in South America, but I doubt it. Paul says there's no reason why I shouldn't make a trip back to Germany to see you all, but until this new project of his really gets under way, we'll be relying on you for funds. Hopefully another two or three months should see us on our feet. He has plenty of contacts here and in Paraguay, and now that Stroessner's been safely re-elected there, we should be able to get on with things. I'm necessarily being vague with the details, for obvious reasons!
I do hope poor Sophie's feeling a bit better. Fortunately I didn't suffer too much with morning sickness, but enough to know how miserable it can be. She doesn't have much to take her mind off it, does she? I've begun knitting little cardigans – difficult to think about in this heat! – and am so excited at the prospect of having a grandchild. Almost all the other ladies I meet up with at the Club here are grandmothers already, and have been giving me lots of advice on the subject! I don't know what advice to give you about being a father. You've certainly had three very different role models to work from. I trust you won't be remotely like your first stepfather, but a cross between your second and your real father

might be good. Goodness, I must sound like some Hollywood starlet with all these men!
I hardly dare ask for news of your father, but you will let me know what the result of the trial is, won't you? Knowing, as you do, the way I feel about him, you'll appreciate my concern for his welfare. It does seem so unfair after all he's been through in his life to spend the rest of it in prison. I suspect Paul secretly feels the same, but won't admit to it. He's very bitter about what's happened, although I keep telling him Wolf's the one to blame, not you. I think in time he might relent. I show him your letters, which at least he reads, so he isn't totally disenchanted with you! If you could only get together I'm sure everything would be all right. The fact that he never got to speak to you before he left Germany is much of the problem, I think. Well, it's time to join the other grandmothers at the tennis court. What a sight we are! By the time you get this, the trial should be under way. I'll be thinking of you all. Please give my love, as ever, to dearest Sophie.
    All my love,
    Mutter.

It was with a pang of jealousy that Gustav put down the letter. He had lost all his immediate family during the war – mother, father and three elder sisters. The naval dockyards of Kiel had not been a good place to live near. The apartment had suffered a direct hit, a broken gas main had finished it off. Their remains now lay in a communal grave, but he had never been back to Kiel to see it. Perhaps one day ...

Shrugging off his morbid thoughts he read through the letter again. There was nothing concrete that suggested Siegfried was a traitor. He merely seemed to have made his peace with Karl, and if Paul Zopf was prepared to believe Siegfried was simply avoiding trouble with the police then he could too. In the meantime observation would continue, more discreetly than before, he hoped. Siegfried's continuing association with Wolf was a dilemma, however. Did it mean Siegfried was going soft, putting friendship before duty, or did it mean both were traitors, or both were still loyal to Nazism?

Gustav had always had a soft spot for the boy, had followed his achievements in the party with pride. Siegfried's skill at arranging accidents for undesirables was legendary. He was far too useful a member of the party to lose. Gustav felt his earlier decision not to see him personally was wrong. In two weeks the play's run would be over and he could leave Berlin and pay Siegfried a visit to find out exactly what was going on.

*

Three weeks after Wolf's late night phone call, Sabina still had difficulty concentrating on her work. She was constantly anxious about him, despite her theories about Siegfried's part in events, with the result that her appetite took a nose dive. She tried to act normally around the house, but Anna had noticed her hollowing cheeks and untouched meals. After scraping yet another plate clear of leftovers, Anna pressed Sabina to confide her worries.

Sabina told her of the telephone conversation. "If I was with him, at least I would know he was all right," she continued, wiping the evening meal dishes her aunt had washed up. "I don't care if it put me in danger too, but this not knowing all the time is just ..."

Anna rested her frothy hands on the edge of the sink. "If you think it would help, why don't you move in with him? Your health is beginning to suffer as it is, and we don't want you falling ill before your wedding, do we?"

Sabina looked at her aunt in astonishment. "You mean live with him before we're married? What on earth will everyone say?"

"Not a lot, I shouldn't think. We all know what's going on."

Did Tante Anna mean everyone knew what she and Wolf got up to in the woods during his weekend visits, or was she referring to the danger Wolf was in? Sabina did not like to ask. She energetically dried a pan and hung it on the rack, her back turned to hide her burning cheeks.

"I think I'll ring Wolf and see what he says," she said, draping the tea towel over the rail on the stove to dry. "It looks like Onkel Rudi will be back to doing the accounts himself sooner than he thought."

"He won't mind. As long as you're happier."

Sabina went out to the hall telephone and dialled Wolf's number. It rang for longer than usual before he answered and Sabina found her heart pounding with fear.

"Hi, it's me," she said hardly able to disguise her relief.

"Hi, Bina. You just caught me. I was just on my way out when I heard the phone ringing. Everything all right?"

"Yes, fine. Brilliant, in fact! You know how much I worry about you since that evening? Well, guess what?" Too eager to wait for a reply she hurried on. "Tante Anna just suggested I come to live with you now and not wait for the wedding! What do you think of that?"

"My God! What brought that on?" Realising how that might sound, he added: "Your Aunt, I mean. What made her say that?"

"She's noticed I'm looking a bit peaky and not eating very well because I'm worried about you all the time. She didn't want me falling ill before the wedding."

"Is that true? Are you really not eating?"

Sabina smiled with the warm feeling his concerned voice gave her. "Well, I suppose so. I just don't feel hungry. I'm sure I would feel better if I was living with you. Take just now," she charged on, as though he needed convincing, "when you didn't answer the phone. If I'd been a few seconds later in ringing and missed you, I'd have been frantic with worry all evening, not knowing if you were all right. Whereas if I lived there, I'd have been going out with you – I expect," she added tactfully, not wanting him to feel she had to tag along everywhere he went.

"I was just going out for a meal actually, with Siegfried. Of course you'd have come too!" He paused a moment to think things through. "Tell you what, I'll come down as usual this weekend and then you can come back with me. That'll give you time to get all your things packed, and me time to get the flat tidy!"

"You'll need more than three days!" she rebuked him with a laugh. "I suppose I'd better let Mummy and Daddy know. Though I don't see how they can have any objections, as I have my suspicions they got up to mischief before they were married."

She gave an earthy chuckle, and Wolf was glad she sounded so light-hearted again. "You're probably right," he agreed, his mind meandering through pleasant liaisons in Medebach Forest.

Sabina, however, had moved on to more mundane bodily requirements. "Well, I'd better let you go and eat, or else I'll be hearing your stomach rumble. Take care, won't you?"

"I will, don't worry. You too. And try to eat something yourself!"

"I'll try. *Tschüs!*"

"*Tschüs!*" Wolf put down the receiver, smiled at it wistfully, then went out to meet Siegfried.

"Sorry I took so long," he apologised, hurriedly getting into Siegfried's Mercedes. "Bina called just as I was leaving." He glanced up and down the street on the lookout for potential assailants as Siegfried drove off at speed, hurtling through a set of traffic lights as they were changing to red. "She's going to come to live with me from next weekend."

"Oh? Isn't that risky?"

"Who knows? But she's got to come once we're married."

"True." Siegfried was concentrating on his driving and the grey VW Beetle that had reappeared in the rear view mirror. "Shit! There they are again! I though I'd lost them at the traffic lights."

The traffic was building up as they neared the Westfalenhalle and the ice stadium. Nipping in front of a coach-load of ice hockey supporters, he made a sudden exit towards the new university buildings. Checking his mirror again, he smiled. "That got rid of them. They've got to learn, I don't like being followed."

"I wish we knew what their game was," Wolf remarked, looking back again, but seeing no sign of the grey Beetle. "But at least as long as they're simply following us, we're not in any real danger." He also wished he knew what Siegfried's game was: whether he was secretly directing this whole farce or whether it was for real. Settling back in his seat he asked: "Where are we headed?"

"Nowhere grand. I thought we'd try the new Balkan Restaurant near the university. I fancy a *Zigeunerschnitzel.*"

"And a drop of beer?"

"Naturally!"

Their mood stayed light throughout their meal. Wolf tried out the house goulash, Siegfried ordered his schnitzel and both had several beers. Nobody seemed to be observing them, and no one followed them on the journey home.

It was past ten o'clock when Siegfried dropped Wolf off at the door of his apartment block and headed back to his own. He parked his Mercedes in the underground car park, sharing the lift up to his floor with another resident. The familiar smell of her perfume filled the enclosed space, awakening pleasant memories.

An attractive widow in her forties, Frau Eberhardt had once called upon Siegfried's services late one evening when a bathroom tap had stuck full on. Her gratitude had included a drink of schnapps and the offer to share her bed for the night. Since Siegfried had learned most of his sexual techniques from his mother's large circle of friends, he was quite at home with older women. He had left in the morning confident his services would be called upon in the future – but then he had met Sophie. Beate Eberhardt had respected his engagement, but now she eyed Siegfried up again, the need for brevity making her bold.

"Your wife's been in hospital a long time, hasn't she? You must let me cook you a meal one evening, Siegfried."

They had already arrived at their floor. He stood back to let her leave the lift first.

"That would be most entertaining," he replied, welcoming the prospect of her company.

"How about tomorrow? At eight?" she breathed, her full lips curving upwards in anticipation of the delights to come.

Siegfried took her hand and kissed the back of it. "Tomorrow," he agreed. With a gentle squeeze, he let go of her hand and headed towards his door.

Entering the living room he switched on the light to find a man sitting on the sofa.

"At last we meet again, Siegfried!" the man greeted him, rising to his feet.

The curly brown hair was greyer, the face fuller and now Siegfried looked down into the brown eyes rather than up, but the soft, soothing voice took him back eighteen years. "Gustav?" His pounding heart began to settle back into its natural rhythm, although he knew he should be extremely wary of this supreme actor.

"Yes, it's your old friend Gustav. Very clever of you to remember me after so many years." He held out his hand and Siegfried shook it warmly.

"I could hardly forget you, could I?" he said. "You made such a big impression on me, helping me survive those years in England. I modelled myself on you, you know?"

"Until you met Paul Zopf?"

Siegfried smiled in unashamed acknowledgement of the truth. "Well, I have to admit, Paul became my hero after you, but I never forgot you or what you taught me." He reached into his jacket pocket and pulled out his trusty penknife. "Remember this? You gave it to me the day you left the farm. It's got me into a lot of trouble over the years, but it's also got me out of it."

"Like three weeks ago?" Gustav asked ruefully.

Siegfried nodded, suddenly apprehensive. "They weren't under your orders, were they? I'm afraid I made some derogatory remarks about –"

Gustav waved aside the criticism. "Certainly not. But that's why I'm here. The organisation's a shambles at the moment. I've come from Berlin to sort it out – with your help."

Siegfried's heart lurched again but outwardly he maintained his calm. "It's a shambles because we don't dare stick our heads out at the moment." He needed time to gather his wits, to relax more. "Can I get you a drink? Beer, schnapps, coffee?"

"Peppermint tea, if you have it."

"Yes, I think so. Won't you sit down? I'll be back in a moment."

Siegfried hurried out to the kitchen, grateful he still had some peppermint tea left over from his entertaining days before Sophie. He boiled the kettle and set a tray with cups, then found a lemon to slice for his own black tea. When he returned to the living room with the drinks he found Gustav standing by the bookcase, examining his wedding photographs.

"Lovely girl, Sophie. Such a shame about her legs."

"She told me you'd been to see her." Siegfried put the tray on the coffee table then joined Gustav by the bookcase.

Ignoring Siegfried's comment, Gustav carefully set the silver-framed photograph of Sophie and Siegfried back on the shelf next to the family group photo, which he picked up next. He studied the figures, pointing to the woman in the blue suit and hat. "Your mother? You're very like her, aren't you?"

Siegfried had to smile. "You're one of the very few people who says that. Mostly they say I'm just like my father."

As Gustav looked up, his dog-like brown eyes seemed to penetrate Siegfried's soul, but he held the stare until Gustav's eyes returned to the photograph.

"Yes, your eyes are his, from what I remember, but the cheekbones and facial structure are definitely your mother's. Your hair could be from either one of them." Once again Gustav's eyes fixed on Siegfried's as he commented: "They look rather like each other, don't they?"

"My parents?" He shrugged. "Perhaps they do."

"And Sophie resembles your mother, doesn't she? Same fair hair, fine features – very attractive really."

There was something in his tone of voice Siegfried found disconcerting. It was deliberate too; Gustav could have hidden his feelings, but he wanted Siegfried to feel threatened. Or was Gustav actually intimating he found him attractive too?

"What are you getting at?" he asked coldly.

Gustav put down the photo with a dramatic flourish. "My dear boy! Nothing at all! Now where's that tea?"

Their eyes held for long enough for them both to take each other's measure. Neither was taking trust for granted.

They sat on opposite sides of the coffee table, Gustav relaxed in his armchair, Siegfried sitting forward to pass the tea and reach his own. For a few minutes Gustav chattered lightly about his time in Berlin, his meeting there with Sophie and how he had told her of Siegfried's reputation for ruthlessness.

"I was very proud of you, very proud. As though you were my own son. The ingenuity of some of your ... annihilations was astonishing. Your father's trial was nothing compared with what yours would be if the details ever got out."

Another threat, but Siegfried had to make sure.

"There's no evidence."

The corners of Gustav's mouth twitched into a smug smile. "Perhaps there is."

Siegfried banged his teacup down in alarm onto its saucer, spilling half the contents. "Where?"

"In a safe place, I assure you," Gustav soothed.

"Paul told me there would be no record –"

"Paul didn't know everything."

Siegfried was finding Gustav's calm voice intensely irritating. "I don't believe you!"

Gustav only chuckled at the outburst. "That's up to you." He took a final sip of his tea, put down the empty cup and saucer on the table and leaned back in his chair again, a figure totally at ease. He formed his fingers into a steeple in front of him and smiled warmly. "But I'm sure you'd like to know why I'm here."

"Too right I would! And how you got in."

The smile left Gustav's face. Dismissing Siegfried's second question out of hand he replied: "There are certain people, Siegfried, myself included, who want only to believe well of you. The events of the last few months have caused us to have grave doubts about you and your friendship with Wolfgang Garisch. His betrayal of us is acknowledged, but your complicity in it is less cut and dry. So I have been asked to set you a test to prove your loyalty to us." He paused, eyeing his protégé keenly.

"What is this test?" Siegfried snapped.

Gustav smiled again. "We want you to kill your father." He waited for a reaction from Siegfried, but there was none. That was a good sign. "It's something you've always wanted to do, but held back on, I suspect, out of respect for your stepfather's friendship with him. Since Josef Garisch's unfortunate demise, you have had everyone's blessing to fulfil your dreams."

"I tried to kill him that day – with this knife!" Siegfried informed him, brandishing the closed penknife.

Heedless of the weapon in Siegfried's hand, Gustav calmly replied: "I'm aware of that. I'm also aware that it's not been easy or ... prudent to get to him since then. We've been patient, you've been patient, but now we want to see some results." He looked coldly at Siegfried. "When is Sophie's baby due?"

It was a direct threat, unspoken but transparently clear to Siegfried that if he did not knuckle under and kill his father, then the baby's and possibly Sophie's lives were at risk.

"August," he said evenly, as though the threat was unnecessary.

Once again Gustav smiled. "Still plenty of time to make preparations. I know how thoroughly you like to plan things."

Siegfried's brain was already racing, going over the implications of Gustav's threat. "And what about Wolf?" he demanded. "Is he on the list too?"

Gustav shrugged. "That depends on whether you can convince me he shouldn't be on the list. It's up to you. But let's just say I have every confidence in you." He raised his eyebrows enquiringly at Siegfried.

Siegfried nodded.

*

Sabina's request had hardly surprised Katherine. In fact she was surprised it had been a request and not just a *fait accompli*. But then Sabina had grown up to be as sensitive of her father's moods as she was herself. Sabina adored her father and hated crossing him, very much like herself and her own father, Katherine thought fondly. She gave the tea a quick stir in the pot then poured it out into four mugs and began locating her men-folk. She knew Richard and Paul were out in the work shed, so went there first.

Over the years the tool shed had been enlarged to a full-blown workshop where Karl had constructed the furniture for their guest accommodation, as well as their new double bed. Now their two sons had set up residence there of an evening, producing rustic garden furniture. She was surprised how well they worked together, with relatively few squabbles that she was aware of.

"Haven't you any homework, Paul?" she asked, placing the tea tray on the windowsill where the mugs would not get full of sawdust.

"Only a bit. I can do it later. We want to get this table finished before the light goes."

"All right, but don't forget," Katherine sighed, and left them to it. The boys had their father's practical mind, which she could seldom argue with. Clutching the remaining two mugs of tea she went to find Karl. She found him as she had expected, leaning on the field gate overlooking Hay Bluff, watching the deep orange glow of the sinking sun, Molly the sheepdog at his side. Since his release from prison it had been his favourite haunt after doing the evening rounds of the farm. It was his thinking time and she seldom interrupted, but tonight she needed to talk. Molly whined at her approach and Karl turned to see why.

"Beautiful sunset," he commented, taking one of the mugs from her. The sun's rays were highlighting the auburn of Katherine's hair. He put out his left hand and stroked it.

Katherine smiled. His mood seemed beatific, which bode well for Sabina's request. She stood by him looking out at the familiar view, reluctant to disturb the peace and quiet of the moment. She waited another minute then took the plunge. "Bina just phoned."

"Oh? Is she all right?"

"Yes, fine. She just wanted our approval for something."

"Did you give it?"

"More or less, but I said I would discuss it with you as well."

Karl grinned at her. "So what is it I have to approve? More guests for the wedding? Wolf's mother, even?"

Katherine sipped her tea then rested her mug on the top of the five-barred gate. The ewes beyond looked at her curiously down their long Roman noses then carried on grazing as peacefully as they could while being butted on the udder by their lambs. Katherine leaned cosily against Karl's side then casually said: "She wants to move in with Wolf this weekend." She wondered whether to expand on her daughter's reasoning and decided she might as well. "She's very worried about his safety, and feels she would worry less if she was there with him."

"Sounds reasonable," Karl said simply.

"So there's no problem?"

"No. Why should there be?"

"Good. I thought you would see it like that."

There was a long pause disturbed only by the loud bleating of lambs seeking their mothers.

"Schatz?"

Katherine looked up at Karl. "Yes?"

"I love you."

*

It had been another long day. There was a glimmer of hope for Zopf Construction with a request to tender for a school annexe arriving on Siegfried's desk that morning. It was a start, and even if their tender was not successful, at least they were back on the list. He had found it difficult to concentrate on the tender, however, with Gustav's terrible ultimatum hanging over him. At least Gustav was not expecting a rapid outcome. Siegfried had been given as long as he needed – within reason.

There was so much else to think about, that was the trouble! Dropping his briefcase on the hall floor as he entered his flat, Siegfried loosened his tie and went to get a bottle of beer from the kitchen. Drinking straight from the bottle he washed the glasses and pile of crockery left from several days' breakfasts then headed for the bedroom, bottle in hand. The bed was still unmade, dirty underwear kicked in a corner. He looked at it, sighed and left it, remembering he had promised to ring Sophie at seven.

She was ready and waiting by the phone. After a single ring he heard her voice.

"Hello?"

"Schatz, it's me. How are you?" He perched on the edge of the telephone table, knowing a detailed account of her latest physiotherapy session would follow.

"They got me on my feet today! Isn't that wonderful?" She sounded elated, and he was pleased for her. "Only for a few seconds at a time – my left leg's still painful – but I've got a load more strengthening exercises to do now."

He sat and listened to her detailed account, occasionally taking a swig from the bottle, until she finally changed the subject.

"Any news of the house?"

He put the empty bottle down on the telephone table. "Yes. It should be ours by the end of May. The current owners can move out then. Isn't that great?"

"So we'll be in well before the baby's born. That's a relief! I must phone my parents and let them know. They'll be thrilled. My mother will be round like a shot, once we're in, to help put up curtains and things."

Siegfried gave an amused grunt. "You should see the state of the flat. I'm seriously thinking of getting a cleaning woman. I don't know why I haven't already. Finances I suppose, but things are beginning to look up a bit."

"Really? You must have been working hard, Schatz. I can hear by your voice you're tired."

"I am rather. I'll probably try to get an early night tonight."

"I'd better not keep you then. I don't suppose you've eaten yet, have you?"

"No."

They said their goodbyes then Siegfried went to the kitchen to fetch another beer. He had just prised the top off when the phone rang.

Beate Eberhardt's sultry voice greeted him. "Siegfried, I was just ringing to say don't dress up this evening. It's quite casual!"

Clothing optional, you mean, Siegfried smiled to himself. "Understood. I'll see you at eight." His voice had not betrayed the fact he had totally forgotten about the evening's arrangements. Gustav's visit had wiped it from his mind, but after the stresses of the day, a night with Beate Eberhardt was just what he needed.

*

When Wolf arrived at Haus Fichtenblick, Sabina was waiting for him on the road outside the house. He had barely got out of the car before she was in his arms.

"It's been so long!" she gasped as their lips parted from their kiss. "I thought the week would never end."

"Well I'm here now," he laughed. "Did you speak to your parents? What did they say?"

"I spoke to Mummy. I thought she'd understand my fears for you better, after all she's been through with Daddy. She seemed OK about it."

"But you don't know what your father thinks."

Sabina grinned. "He'll be OK too, once Mummy's done her bit to convince him. Besides, they could only forbid the wedding, and what would be the point in that?"

She led him round to the back of the house where her grandfather was sitting enjoying the late April sunshine over a glass of beer. Dieter stood up to greet Wolf, shook his hand then reached for another beer bottle.

"So what have you been up to at work since I last saw you," Dieter asked, deftly pouring beer into a glass and handing it to Wolf.

Wolf sat down on the wooden bench next to Sabina and took a swig. "Still testing out colour televisions. What's so astonishing is how much whiter white is than on the monochrome. Instead of being like dull slush, it now sparkles like fresh snow."

"Well, I suppose we'll get one, one of these days. It would be nice to see what colour the moon is, when they get around to landing on it," Dieter chuckled.

"True. I guess I'll be glued to my set too, if and when they finally touch down next year."

Dieter looked dreamily up at the sky to where, in a few hours, the moon would rise. "So much has advanced in so short a time. When I was a boy Jules Verne's stories seemed fantastic enough, but now it's actually going to happen."

"Thanks to German rocket scientists," Wolf said provocatively.

Dieter sportingly took up the gauntlet. He enjoyed these verbal fencing sessions with Wolf. "True. We can't deny the part our country played in developing rockets, but you mustn't forget all the other developments needed – tracking and communication systems, computer controls. Who knows where it will all end?"

Sabina squeezed Wolf's hand proudly. "Hopefully making people like Wolf rich. All this new technology's bound to come in use here on earth, and Wolf's in the right business!"

"Well as long as he shares his wealth with the rest of us, there's no harm in that," Dieter joked. "I'll not be making a fortune with the sawmill, that's for sure." He caught sight of Rudi and Stefan appearing round the corner of the barn. "Come on boys, beer's waiting!" he called out to them with a flourish of his glass.

Rudi and Stefan ambled across the cobbles towards them. They both greeted Wolf with a handshake before sitting on the high-backed bench in the last of the evening sunshine.

"You've made good time, Wolf," Stefan commented. "Traffic not so busy?"

"I left work early to avoid it. I knew Bina would be anxious to see me!"

Sabina gave him a peck on the cheek. "True, but right at this very moment my conscience is pricking me about Tante Anna all alone in the kitchen, so I'll leave you men to your beers. *Tschüs*, Onkel Rudi. See you on Sunday."

She wandered in through the back door. Sure enough Anna was hovering over a steaming pan of chicken noodle soup. A large rye loaf sat on the table awaiting slicing so Sabina set to work.

"We'll miss you, you know," her aunt told her without turning round from the stove. "Papa especially. Once you're gone, I'll been the only female around here. He likes having the attention of women, does Papa!"

Sabina smiled affectionately. "I've noticed. He loves to flatter us, doesn't he?"

"Can't help himself. That's why we all love him so much." Satisfied the soup was simmering gently Anna joined Sabina at the table, setting out cutlery. "He's really looking forward to your wedding. I've never seen him so excited about anything before, not even mine or Monika's weddings. I think it's such a contrast from all the doom and gloom we've had recently that he's over the moon about it."

"What colour moon?" Sabina asked herself.

"Pardon?"

"Oh, nothing. We were just talking about colour televisions and things. Opa said he'd like to get one to see what colour the moon is when they land on it."

"Ah. I'm sure Wolf could oblige."

"What would be nice," Sabina went on, "would be some film of our wedding. Onkel Rudi must bring his cine camera along. It would be lovely to have everyone on film! Photographs are usually so stilted."

"I'm sure he's thought of it. It'll already be on Papa's list of things to take, you'll see!"

"Well, tell him not to bring his woodcarving tools as Daddy has plenty!" She paused, her thoughts heading homewards. "Apparently Richard and Paul have started producing rustic garden furniture as their sideline – bird-tables mostly, but they've had a few orders for tables and benches too. The Murdochs were their first customers and they've spread the word among their friends!"

"I'm so pleased for Karl that he's got such a lovely and talented family," Anna declared, moving to the back door to call the men in for their meal. "He deserves it. You can sometimes still see his painful memories of the war deep inside him, can't you? We all have them, of course, but your father's must be so much worse." She bit her lip and grew sombre. "I never knew all the details of his time at Dachau until the trial. That man, Goslar, deserved to be –" She broke off, having momentarily forgotten she was talking about the man who had pretended to be Wolf's father.

"'Shot' is the word you want, Anna," Wolf said, entering the kitchen ahead of Stefan and Dieter. He stopped and wrinkled his nose. "Mmm, that soup smells good."

"Well sit yourselves down then," Anna told them, beginning to ladle soup into warm bowls. "We're not waiting for Lothar. He's out on a mission – to do with girls, I suspect."

Sabina sat next to Wolf and found she had an appetite at last. Raising her spoon to her lips she shovelled the noodle soup down until her bowl stood empty.

"That's what I like to see!" Anna declared, beaming at her niece.

Just as everyone was preparing to leave the table, Lothar appeared at the door, his face flushed.

"Good. There's some left," he said, eyeing the pan on the stove.

"Of course!" his mother remarked. She filled a bowl for him and put it down in front of him. "So what's her name?"

Lothar had crammed his mouth with bread so they could barely understand his muffled reply. "Sonja."

"Who would believe there could be so many girls in Medebach?" his father jested. "You're beginning to live up to your name, young man!"

"Isn't that Friedrichsmeier's youngest girl?" Dieter commented. "From Medelon? Have you tried all the Medebach girls, Lothar?" he asked, joining in the gentle ribbing.

Lothar blushed and got on with his soup, secretly enjoying the banter and the reputation he seemed to be acquiring. He caught Wolf's friendly wink and grinned back. Those two had gone further than he had, despite all the talk about his name. He had seen them disappearing up into the forest. No doubt they'd be up there again tomorrow. Good luck to them. They deserved some fun after everything they'd been through.

SEVEN

"So you admit Gustav's visit wasn't just a social call," Siegfried challenged Sophie. "He was asking questions about me?"

Sophie was sitting in a wheelchair by her bed. She wished Siegfried would sit down as she had to crane her neck to look up at him while he paced about the room. And why hadn't he asked her all this when he phoned the other day? "Yes," she admitted. "He wanted to know if you had ... changed at all. If I had any doubts about you."

"And do you?" he demanded.

"No!" she retorted, horrified at his suspicion. "I remember you telling me you'd changed your point of view. But that was so the firm wouldn't lose business. You had to appear 'Persil white'. I think that was the phrase you used."

So Gustav's doubts about him had not made her waver. She still believed he was a committed Nazi, unavoidably having to shun the limelight. Until Gustav's visit to his flat, Siegfried had been sure in his own mind where his new path lay, but now it was all thrown into turmoil again. He was trapped in the middle, playing a dangerous game, but Sophie at least was proving predictable. Darling Sophie. He smiled and sat down on the visitor's chair next to her wheelchair. Taking her hand in his, he caressed it with his thumb.

"Yes. Persil white." He beamed at her, promptly changing the subject onto safer ground. "Like you in your wedding dress. Beautiful." His other hand moved to her gently swelling belly, savouring its growing dimensions. "I can't wait to have you home again, Schatz. I miss you so much. If only you didn't need all this physiotherapy you could be home already."

"I know. I miss you too. Don't you think I'd far rather be home than stuck in here? At least I'm beginning to make progress." She wriggled her toes and lifted both badly scarred, wasted legs up and down for his approval.

"Bravo! Keep it up. You've got a pram to push in a few months' time."

"I've got to push it out first!" Sophie laughed, patting her belly.

"Do you think you'll be out of here by the middle of June?"

"Why then?"

"Wolf and Bina's wedding, remember? I've got to go, since I'm best man. But it's in England."

"This is where the pretence comes in, isn't it, Siegfried?" She thought about it for a moment. "I really don't think I can face all that travelling."

"That's all right. I quite understand, Schatz. I rather thought you wouldn't be keen. As long as you don't mind me going."

"No, of course not. I know how important it is to get back in with your family. I think I'd feel a bit out of place, anyway."

He nodded. "You're probably right. Safer for the baby too. We'll visit next year perhaps, when things are easier."

How he wished he could confide in her, tell her of his Faustian dilemma, but as he struggled with his conscience he suddenly felt a slight fluttering in the mound beneath his fingertips. "Was that...?"

She grinned. "Yes. Amazing, isn't it?"

She was unprepared for the ferocity of the hug he gave her, for the powerful emotion surging through his arms, and for the dampness of his tears on her shoulder.

"A bit overwhelming too," she added, stroking his silky, blond hair.

Pulling himself together he raised his head off her shoulder and sniffed. "Sorry. I don't know what got into me." She was gazing deep into his eyes, her obvious love for him threatening to choke him, and he had to fight to hold back the tears. He wiped his eyes with the back of his hand, then reached for his handkerchief to blow his nose. "I wouldn't want anything to happen to you, Schatz," he said by way of explanation.

"It won't, I promise," she reassured him. "Besides, what could possibly happen to me in here?"

There was no way he could tell her.

*

Of the two, Katherine preferred the lime green dress to the gold and green flowers, but thought it might look a bit young for her. "What do you think?" she asked, holding it up against her.

Her sister, Sarah, pursed her lips, giving the matter deep thought. "No. The other one," she said eventually. "It's more you."

"Perhaps I don't want to be 'me'," Katherine pointed out, holding up Sarah's choice and studying her reflection in the shop mirror. "Perhaps I want to go for a more daring look, for once."

"Trust me!" Sarah laughed. "You won't feel comfortable in the lime. You'll be too self-conscious and it'll spoil the day."

"Perhaps we ought to go back to that one I liked in Harrods, though it was rather on the expensive side."

"No. You've got to remember it's a rural wedding in Herefordshire, not some posh, city do. You'd feel out of place in that one."

Katherine sighed and looked at herself once again in the mirror. "I'll try them both on, but I'll probably bow to your superior wisdom. Besides, I don't think my feet can stand traipsing the streets much longer. It's exhausting work, shopping!"

"You're telling me!"

While Katherine disappeared into yet another changing room, Sarah looked at her watch. It was four fifteen already and they were expected back at their cousin Evelyn's in Colliers Wood for tea at six. They needed to get a move on.

After what seemed an eternity, Katherine stepped out of the changing room, wearing the green and gold dress. She gave a twirl. "How does it look?"

"Perfect. The shoulders don't pull, the waist's just right, and the length is spot on. Are you going for that one?"

Katherine hesitated then made up her mind. "Yes. It's this or nothing now. I can't manage another shopping trip to London before the wedding." She turned back towards the curtained doorway. "Won't be long."

Sarah began gathering up the bags of purchases they had already made: shirts, ties and underwear for Karl, Richard and Paul, exotic lingerie for Katherine – which had been rather a surprise until she thought about Karl's long absence – and a new work suit for herself. She would have to buy her own wedding outfit some other time. When Katherine had finally paid for the dress after waiting an age in the queue, they set off at a brisk pace for Oxford Circus underground station to catch the Bakerloo line to Charing Cross, changing to the Northern Line for Colliers Wood. The Saturday afternoon shoppers crammed the platforms and trains to bursting point, forcing the two sisters to clutch their bags tightly to themselves against the crush.

When they finally reached Evelyn and Bill Bagnold's semi-detached house they were gasping for a cup of tea. Piling all their bags into the spare room they would be sharing that night, they returned downstairs to find sandwiches and cakes all ready in the dining room, with the table set for six.

"Shirley's bringing a friend from the hospital round," Evelyn explained on seeing Katherine's inquiring glance. "She and Judy are going out to the cinema later, but she wanted to pop in and see you. They'll be here any second. I just saw the bus go by."

Shirley was Evelyn and Bill's daughter, a ward sister at St Thomas' Hospital, Lambeth, and seemingly married to her career. Katherine knew her well from the numerous holidays the Bagnolds had enjoyed in the guest accommodation at Lane Head Farm. Bill Bagnold's initial reluctance at the idea had very quickly been overcome by his enthusiasm for fishing in the River Wye, and the family had made it a regular jaunt.

Katherine followed Evelyn into the front room to look up the road for signs of Shirley and her friend, Judy. Seeking news of Shirley's brother, she asked: "How's Trevor enjoying his job with BP?"

"Not too bad, he says. He's supposed to be going off to Iran shortly, which will be rather exciting, considering he's never been abroad before in his life. Not even a day-trip to Calais." She craned her neck forward. "Ah. Here they are!"

Katherine looked through the bow window. She was surprised to see Judy was a coloured girl, until she remembered that many of the nurses in the London hospitals these days were of Caribbean origin. In Hereford she hardly ever saw a black face. She waited with Sarah and Bill in the front room while the newcomers took off their coats and chatted to Evelyn before entering the front room at last. Shirley greeted them all with a kiss each on the cheek, then introduced Sarah and Katherine to her friend.

"Judy, these are my mother's cousins, Miss Carter and Mrs Driesler."

Judy had been shaking Sarah's hand, but at the sound of Katherine's name she froze, then remembered her manners and quickly shook Katherine's hand, clearly excited about something as her teeth flashed in a huge grin. "*Driesler* did you say? My word, fancy comin' across dat name again so soon! It can't be very common over here."

Katherine smiled politely back, her interest roused. "No, it's not. My husband's German."

"Well dat explains it. Siegfried was German."

"Siegfried? Siegfried *Driesler*?" Katherine asked in astonishment.

Judy was aware she was causing a stir, and began to milk it for all she was worth.

"Yes. Nice man. Such a shame 'bout his poor wife's accident."

"Nice?" Shirley exclaimed in surprise. "I thought he was supposed to be awful!"

Now it was Judy's turn to be surprised. "Oh? Why's dat?"

"Hang on a minute," Sarah interrupted. "Let me get this straight. You've met Siegfried, here, in London?"

"No-o-o!" Judy laughed at Sarah's confusion. "On St. Lucia in the Caribbean – where I come from. I was home visitin' and he was dere on his honeymoon."

"That's Siegfried, all right," Katherine murmured.

"Why don't we all go on through to the dining room where tea's ready?" Evelyn urged with a glance at her husband, sensing trouble. "Do you want to wash your hands first, Shirley, Judy?"

The topic would not be buried however, and once seated around the table, Judy quickly returned to it, wanting to defend the reputation of someone she had found charming in his distress. She took a fish-paste and cucumber sandwich then began to interrogate Shirley.

"So who is he? A relation? And why did you say he was awful?"

"He's a neo-Nazi!" Shirley blurted out, eager to reveal the skeleton in the Driesler cupboard. "He's also Katherine's stepson."

Judy put down her sandwich and stared at Shirley in horror. "No. I don't believe it! He was so nice. Are you sure?"

"It was in the papers last summer, when Karl – that's Katherine's husband – was on trial –"

"Shall I explain, Shirley?" Katherine hastily interrupted, fearing an over-dramatic version of events.

"Go ahead. You know the facts better than I do."

Judy was clearly agog to hear what this was all about, while Bill Bagnold resignedly got on with his tea, used to the trials and tribulations of Katherine's German family.

"First let me say," Katherine began, "that Siegfried *was* a neo-Nazi. He was brought up by his mother and stepfather to believe in all that, and never questioned it until he met you, Judy. Let me also say that I'm only repeating what Siegfried told Karl – my husband, and Siegfried's father," she explained carefully. "Apparently Sophie's accident finally brought home to him what family love and the love of his fellow man – black, white or whatever – was all about. The help and support you and your people gave him in his time of crisis jolted him into realising what, until then, Nazism had hidden from him – that we are all brothers and sisters on this earth." She paused, debating whether to reveal her own thoughts, and decided she ought to.

"As I said, that is what Siegfried told Karl. I've not seen him since his change of heart, but Sabina, my daughter, has. She tells me she can't be absolutely certain he's no longer a Nazi. It's just her gut feeling, which I must admit I share, that when it comes to Siegfried, you never believe a word he says. Changing his colours was very convenient for him at that point in time. But on the other hand, Karl is convinced Siegfried is telling the truth, but he won't explain why he's so sure. He just says that he and Siegfried have common ground and understand each other. Now, what you make of that is up to you."

Everyone's eyes turned to Judy. "What I saw was real. He loved his wife and he was grateful for our help, but ..." She looked up at everyone, confusion written on her face. "Perhaps I saw what I wanted to see. A white man, a German even, humbly indebted to black people. Dat is what I saw. What it meant, I don't know any more. I'd have to meet him again, knowin' what I do now."

"But that would prejudice you against him, wouldn't it?" Bill asked, amused by the turn of the conversation. "You'll be reading things into his words that possibly aren't there. Your initial, unbiased assessment could have been the right one."

"Whose side are you on, Bill?" Evelyn asked, astonished at her normally disinterested husband's provocative stance. "Not Siegfried's, surely?"

"Well, he's not here to defend himself and you lot seem intent on condemning him as a liar and con artist."

"You've never met him, Bill," Katherine said quietly.

"No, but I've met Karl, and I remember having similar thoughts about him, until I got to know him well. Sorry, Katherine, but it's true. You hear the word 'German' and immediately have misconceptions."

"Yes, but it's the word 'Nazi' we're talking about here, Dad," Shirley reminded him.

Sarah had heard every argument there was to hear on the subject over the years, and knew how tedious it was for Katherine. "Well anyway, we'll all get the chance to meet him at Bina's wedding." She looked at Judy. "Except you, of course, Judy. You ought to come too and give us your verdict on him. I suspect he'll give a very good performance at a family wedding."

"You know, I *would* like to meet him again. I still t'ink I'm right, but you've got me worried now."

"Come by all means!" Katherine told her warmly. "It'll give us the chance to thank you properly for the help you gave Siegfried."

"Oh I don't need no t'anks," Judy beamed, "but I sure would love to come to the weddin'. I jus' love weddin's! When is it?"

"The twenty-second of June," Katherine told her. "With haymaking and sheep-shearing to contend with as well. You'd have thought she'd have known better than to choose a date like that, but she wanted a mid-summer wedding."

"Love is blind, so they say" Evelyn commented, then threw her stone into the pool. "But what about Sabina's fiancé? Wasn't he a Nazi too? He's a close friend of Siegfried's, isn't he?"

Katherine and Sarah exchanged glances then both burst into giggles.

"Our family! Honestly! We do pick them, don't we?" Sarah laughed.

Smothering her laughter, Katherine gave a quick explanation of Wolf's history.

"So when he found out his father wasn't his father after all, and that he'd been lied to all his life, he turned them all in to the police and gave them the evidence they needed to convict even his own mother," she concluded. "After that, we trust Wolf completely."

"Does Wolf trust Siegfried?" Bill asked perspicaciously, through a mouthful of jam sponge.

Katherine replied, allowing a hint of doubt in her voice. "Enough to ask him to be best man."

"I can't wait to come to this wedding!" Shirley declared. "It's going to be a hoot, watching everyone watching each other!"

"I hadn't looked at it like that, I must say," Katherine said, her spirits sinking. "I don't want anything going wrong to spoil Bina's day."

"It'll be lovely, you'll see," Sarah reassured her. "Nothing can go wrong with your German lot organizing things down to the minutest detail." She knew that would bring the smile back to her sister's face, and she was right.

"I'll hold you to that!" Katherine laughed.

*

Karl tightened his grip on the rope and let the branch swing gently down to the daisy-covered lawn where he stood in the front garden of one of the Penchurch cottages. The elderly couple who occupied the cottage had been advised by the Post Office to have their ancient and unproductive apple tree cut down, as it was interfering with the telephone lines. Karl had brought along a young apple tree as a replacement, and hopefully the Jennings would get more fruit off it than they had off the gnarled old one. The Jennings would have to make sure the new tree was kept neatly pruned to prevent the same problem occurring in years to come.

Karl untied the rope from the branch so Richard could haul it back up into the tree to prevent the next trimming from crashing down into Mr Jennings' tulip bed. Richard was the tree monkey these days, Karl preferring to keep his feet on the ground when he could. That's what sons were for, after all, to save their ageing fathers from the more strenuous work. As Richard began sawing at the next bough, Karl dragged the first branch across the lawn to a small area of hard-standing by the cottage where he had set up the electrical circular saw to cut the branches into logs for the Jennings' winter fire. A chain saw was going to have to be the next purchase, he decided, although Katherine would need some persuading of the safety of such potentially lethal tools being used up trees.

He was about to switch on the circular saw when he heard a car draw up and park on the valley road next to the Land Rover. He recognised its purring engine and immediately felt the hairs on the back of his neck bristle. The sound of sawing from the tree stopped as Richard also became aware of the arrival of Andrew Kellett's dark blue Jaguar. The question was, was it Andrew or his wife, Audrey, driving?

"Oh, no!" Richard groaned. Hurriedly he began scrambling down the tree to join his father.

"Driesler!" Kellett hailed Karl heartily, getting out of his car. "I saw your vehicle there as I was passing and thought I'd stop and ask if you could do a tree job for me. It's the old cedar, you know. Need to prune a lower branch that's cracked badly and is in danger of falling off."

"Can't one of your estate workers tackle it?" Karl replied brusquely.

Kellett only grinned at the rebuff. "Are you turning down work?"

"For you, yes."

Kellett stood hands on hips on the pavement and guffawed with laughter at his adversary's self-restraint. "She told you then?"

Karl purposefully crossed the front lawn so he would not have to shout. "She told me you raped her," he hissed, aware of Richard's rapid approach behind him. He glanced back over his shoulder and saw his son's angry face. "Stay out of this, Richard!"

His son had other ideas. "You can't let him get away with it, Dad!" Richard yelled. "I know what he did to Mum."

Without any warning he launched himself at Kellett, threw back his arm and punched him hard in the face. As Kellett reeled against the Jaguar, Richard dived towards him again, fists raised.

"For Christ's sake, Richard! Don't be stupid!" Karl shouted, leaping after him. He tried to grab his son's arm but Richard twisted aside, colliding with Kellett in the process and winding him. Kellett, however, still had wits enough to stick out a leg and try to trip Richard before his next punch landed. As Richard teetered, Karl got a good grip of his arm and hauled him off, leaving Kellett gasping like a landed fish.

Held fast by his father, Richard made no further move except to glare ferociously at the man who had once raped his mother.

"Don't think you can get away with it, *Mister* Kellett," he taunted. "The whole county will get to hear what you did."

"That's enough, Richard!" Karl snapped. "Leave this to me."

Alarmed by the shouting the Jennings appeared at their front door to be confronted with the sight of the local squire wiping a trickle of blood from his nose. Dora Jennings tried to hold back her husband, but Reg insisted on going out to investigate the rumpus.

"Did you see that?" Kellett demanded of him, holding his handkerchief up to his nose. The Jennings were tenants of the Froxley Grange estate and he expected their support. "That lout punched me."

Support was not forthcoming, however. "I'm sorry, Captain Kellett, I only heard the shouting," Reg said, then to make his point he added: "Mr Driesler and his son were very kindly taking the old tree down I'd reported to you some months back. I couldn't wait any longer for you to see to it, as Mrs Jennings has not been so well of late and I didn't want problems with the telephone lines if she needed the doctor."

Kellett glared at the old man. "We're not talking about your blasted tree. I've just been attacked and all you can do is complain. Go and call the police! I want them here immediately!"

"Mr Kellett," Karl said coolly. "A word of advice. If the police get involved we'll have to say why my son punched you."

"Katherine won't press charges," he scoffed as Reg reluctantly shuffled back into the house. "She didn't then so why should she now? Besides, I didn't rape her. She was perfectly agreeable," he said with a leer. "As agreeable as I'm sure you found Audrey when you bedded her." The look of shock on Richard's face made him grin, but then he winced in pain, which inflamed him further. "You didn't know your father's had half the women in the county, did you?" he taunted the boy. The flow of blood seemed to have dried up and he removed the handkerchief from his nose. Satisfied he had stirred things up enough, he turned his attention back to the case at hand. "Anyway, I'm certainly pressing charges against you." He turned to Karl. "Like father, like son, eh, Driesler? We all know you've just done time for breaking your bastard son's nose. I'm going to make bloody sure this one doesn't get away with the same thing!"

"Dad!" Richard protested. "I'm going to punch him again if he doesn't shut up."

"I'd join you, but that wouldn't help matters," Karl said evenly, refusing to be riled by Kellett's deliberate provocation. "Let's just get on with the job until the police get here. Mrs Jennings wants her winter firewood."

Richard could not bear to let Kellett get away with it but had to follow his father's advice. Giving Kellett his blackest scowl he turned and made his way back to the apple tree, more shaken than he cared to admit. He had never been in trouble with the police, and whereas Kellett was a man of influence, as far as the police were concerned the Drieslers were notorious troublemakers in the area. Siegfried had left a legacy of violence and mistrust, while his father had, by all accounts, given the police plenty of problems when he was still a POW here. Not to mention the women! Was what Kellett said really true? Had his father really been the local Don Juan? He knew only too well that many females found the Driesler men a handsome bunch. He himself was never refused a dance at the local hops. Had Dad really –

"No, I didn't have half the women in the county," Karl said, reading his son's expression absolutely correctly.

"I never thought you had, Dad," Richard spluttered in embarrassment.

"Rubbish. It was written on your face just then. Audrey, yes, but that was before your mother and I got together. She –"

"It's alright, Dad," Richard interrupted, still deeply embarrassed, his ears burning bright crimson. "I don't need to hear all the gory details." He meekly faced his father. "I've got other things to worry about, haven't I?"

Karl laid a hand on his son's shoulder. "It'll be alright. You've no previous convictions, you'll get good character references from everyone. Nobody will have a word to say against you except for Kellett. You'll probably get off with a fine or something."

"But Kellett knows all the magistrates –"

"Then they'll know what an unpleasant, self-important creature he is. Don't worry, Richard. You'll be OK. Boys get into fights all the time." He paused. "No, it's your Mum I'm worried about. I don't want her having to get involved in this."

Richard looked bleak. "We'll have to tell her when she gets back from London. Kellett's going to milk this for all it's worth. Even I had some doubts when he said Mum agreed to ..."

Karl was silent. He had had doubts too, but was not going to admit it.

Suspecting he had been too honest, Richard hastily began his climb back up the tree to where he had left the saw, leaving his father to wander slowly back to the circular saw, deep in thought.

Leaning against his car as he waited for the police to arrive, Kellett watched the pair carefully, satisfied he had done a good day's work.

*

Katherine was horrified when she heard what had been going on during her absence. They had let her get in the house, hang up her new purchases and dispense the items she had bought for Karl and the boys. It was only as they sat over a cup of tea that Karl told her about Kellett and their time spent with the police. It was even worse when she discovered Richard had heard about the rape.

"Oh, it's all so sordid!" she moaned. "But thank you for trying to protect my honour, Richard, even if Andrew would have nothing of it. He seems intent on making out I've falsely accused him of rape. We'll just have to do the best we can to make people think otherwise. Gertie knows the truth –"

"The truth as you told it to her," Karl had to interject. "She doesn't know for certain. Only you know whether he raped you or not. Kellett seems to think you were willing."

Katherine frowned. "Well I wasn't," she snapped, "or don't you believe me? I suppose," she went on more calmly, out of long habit to avoid arguments, "that I didn't put up much of a fight, but I was frightened of him. I rather froze and let him get on with it rather than risk ... I mean it's not as if I was a vir-" Too late she remembered Richard's presence. "I'm sorry, darling. You don't want to hear all this." She looked anxiously at Karl. "Does Paul know?"

"I think Richard's filled him in on most of the details. Isn't that right, Richard?"

Richard blushed. "Yes."

"Including about me and Audrey?" Karl asked in an attempt to lighten the general mood.

Richard lowered his eyes and muttered with a concealed grin: "Yes."

"Oh, he didn't bring that up against you, did he?" Katherine exploded. "The swine!" Then she laughed. "You lot can't stay out of trouble for one minute, can you!" She grew more thoughtful. "This is the last thing we need, what with Bina's wedding approaching. We've got to do something to stop Andrew pressing this charge against Richard."

"Yes, but what?" Karl asked.

All three looked blankly at one other.

*

News of the brawl and Richard's predicament soon got out. At Hereford market the following Wednesday there were two distinct camps: those who supported the Drieslers and those in league with Kellett. Richard found himself discreetly patted on the back by some and cold-shouldered by others. Kellett himself chose to avoid the market that week, whether out of discretion or cowardice nobody knew.

While Karl and Richard were out buying Welsh hill lambs for fattening up on their richer Herefordshire pastures, Katherine took the opportunity to telephone Audrey Kellett. Audrey had originally been one of Sarah's friends, but since her sister left home they had got to know each other quite well, despite Andrew's disapproval.

Katherine got straight to the point. "This whole stupid business has got to stop, Audrey."

"I agree. Andrew's being his usual pig-headed self. He's like a little boy with a new toy over this and won't let it go."

"The thing is, Audrey," Katherine said rather more delicately, "I don't know if he's told you the full story."

"About why Richard hit him, you mean? Because you claim he raped you."

"I'm not claiming anything. It's true, he did rape me. But he's the one who first brought up the subject, boasting to Karl."

"Why would he do that? Even Andrew's not so daft as to deliberately get on the wrong side of Karl. He's too much of a coward."

Katherine had to smile at Audrey's lack of loyalty to her spouse. "I think it was a casual boast that went further than he anticipated when I had to explain what he had meant to Karl."

"Oh, I see. So you're saying Andrew really did rape you?"

"Yes, but that's not the issue now. That's ancient history. It's Richard I'm concerned about. I don't want him having a police record."

"Unlike his father," Audrey pointed out.

"Yes, unlike Karl," Katherine had to agree. "So I'm asking you to persuade him to drop the charges. The people who'll get hurt from this are Richard and Andrew. And besides, what will your two think when they hear what their father's accused of? Mud sticks, Audrey. Most people in these parts are going to believe my story rather than Andrew's, even if the magistrates and police don't."

Audrey was silent. Katherine could only hear the buzzing and crackling of the line. "I'll try, on one condition," came her eventual reply. "If you want this badly enough, you'll grant me a favour in return."

"What's that?" Katherine asked cautiously.

"You know how I've always felt about him. I want another night with Karl."

Katherine slammed down the receiver.

Five minutes later the telephone rang. Katherine had returned to the kitchen to do some ironing. She was still fuming about Audrey's outrageous request when she picked up the receiver again.

"Hello," she said brusquely.

"Katherine, I'm sorry, don't put the phone down on me. It was a joke, that's all."

"Some joke, Audrey," she snapped.

"Yes, well, I suppose it was in rather poor taste, but you know me. I like my men – always have and always will probably."

Katherine needed Audrey's help so was prepared to be magnanimous, accepting her apology even though she did not believe a word of it. Negotiations had been resumed, and that was the important thing. "I can just picture you at ninety," she replied more lightheartedly, "spoon-fed by an adoring Adonis."

"Well it won't be Andrew spoon-feeding me, that's for sure. He'll stick me in a nursing home at the first sign of senility." She paused to draw breath. "As to the other matter, I'll try but I can't promise anything. I might just make matters worse. You know what Andrew's like. When he gets the bull by the horns, he won't let go."

"I know, but do your best, please, Audrey. Let me know how you get on."

"I will."

Katherine returned to her ironing with Audrey's words buzzing round her head. If Audrey could not persuade him, then she must try herself.

EIGHT

Ilse returned from the travel agent's exhausted after her fact-finding mission, which had been negotiated in a mixture of basic Spanish and English. She really should have taken up Paul's offer to get one of his friends to help her. Still, it was all done now and she had the flight information at her fingertips for when the time came. She would only need to change planes in Buenos Aires and London, but it would be an awfully long haul. Well worth it, though, to see everyone again, especially Siegfried – even Karl, with any luck.

Paul had been so good about her little misdemeanour with Karl, apart from forcing her to tell Katherine about it. That had been a truly awful experience, mostly because she knew that it had nothing to do with being cuckolded, but was Paul's way of punishing Karl for killing Josef Garisch. Fortunately for Karl, Katherine seemed to be a forgiving sort of person, much as Paul had forgiven her.

She had so much to be grateful to Paul for. He had saved her from a ruinous marriage and given her back her looks, her health, her happiness. She loved him deeply, but her love could not compare with what she had felt for Karl in those fairy-tale days during the war.

She poured herself an orange juice and went to sit out on the balcony in the late morning sunshine. Her life here was pleasant but empty. She had no family to consider, no garden to occupy her, shopping was difficult unless she went with one of her Spanish-speaking tennis friends. Her social life was picking up, with invitations to coffee mornings and dinner parties, even a weekend on a yacht, which she was looking forward to immensely as it would remind her of her happy childhood in Hamburg. Nevertheless she yearned for her old life entertaining friends back in Iserlohn, for summers and winters spent in their lodge in the Bavarian Forest, skiing, riding, swimming. Life here seemed aimless. She could only daydream while Paul worked hard to build a new life for them.

Construction was his forte, and with the contacts given them by their Nazi friends he had soon found a niche in an expanding firm. They were both learning Spanish, although she did not get nearly as much practice at it as Paul. It was her own fault for not getting out more, but she preferred to stick with her fellow German expatriots at the tennis club. Give her a few more years and she guessed she would be reasonably fluent, but her heart really was not in it. She wanted desperately to be back in Germany.

She spent the rest of the morning pottering about the apartment, reading a novel, filing her nails, attempting a crossword puzzle. At midday she got changed and went out to meet Paul for lunch. He knew she was bored and tried his best to meet her for lunch when he could, along with anyone else he had recently met.

Today when the taxi dropped her off at their favourite steak house she could see he was already at their table along with a young man. Both men stood to greet her as she entered the restaurant and Ilse eyed Paul's companion with curiosity. He was much younger than Paul's usual lunch partners and more casually dressed, in an open-necked white shirt and beige slacks. He was more handsome too.

"Ilse, this is Ricardo de Benito, a student at the university."

Ilse offered her hand. "*¿Qué tal?, mucho gusto.*" It was nearly the limit of her Spanish and she hoped he would not gabble too quickly back at her.

The student shook her hand and replied in perfect German. "Pleased to meet you, Frau Zopf."

Paul resumed his seat. "Ricardo is studying German," he explained, "and wants someone to practice conversation with. Isn't that right, Ricardo?"

Ricardo flashed a gleaming white grin at Ilse. "Yes indeed. My father and Herr Zopf are business acquaintances. Herr Zopf said he was looking for a Spanish tutor for his charming wife, and my father offered my services."

"For a small fee, of course," Paul added.

"Really it is not necessary as I will benefit too from speaking German."

Ilse was taken aback. She had not expected Paul to find her a tutor who was male or who was quite so ... good-looking in a rather too Latin kind of way. She quickly got a grip of herself and said: "Of course you must be paid for your services. It sounds to me like you don't need much practice at German."

"You are very kind, Frau Zopf."

The waiter brought cold beers all round then went to fetch their food. After they had toasted and taken a sip of beer Paul said to Ilse: "I know how much free time you have, so Ricardo has agreed to come for an hour or so each day to the apartment. He'll soon get you fluent in Spanish, aren't I right, Ricardo?"

"Indeed, Herr Zopf. I'm sure Frau Zopf and I will have plenty to talk about."

Ilse felt hugely uplifted by the thought of some purpose to her days at last and Ricardo seemed a very pleasant young man. She raised her glass of beer in another toast. "To fluent Spanish!"

Their steaks arrived, Paul's discreetly cut up for him in the kitchen so he could eat with his single hand. As they began to eat Ilse remembered her morning's work.

"I've looked at flights for my trip to Germany when the time comes," she informed Paul, then remembered Ricardo would now need to know her plans. "I hope to be away for a couple of weeks later this summer," she explained, quite forgetting about the southern hemisphere's opposite seasons, "to see my first grandchild."

"You don't look old enough to have a grandchild," he gallantly replied.

Ilse smiled. Ricardo was just too perfect. It was almost as though Paul had hired him chiefly to keep her mind off Karl, seeing even a distant Karl as a far greater danger than a close but unthreatening Ricardo. She looked across at Paul and his beneficent expression seemed to confirm he was giving her a gift. If that were the case then she and Ricardo could have a lot of fun together, but Paul would be fooling himself if he thought she would so easily forget her feelings for Karl.

*

Audrey Kellett caught up with Katherine in the churchyard after several days spent fruitlessly begging Andrew to consider all the ramifications of pressing charges against Richard Driesler.

"It's no-go, I'm afraid," she said hurriedly in passing. "Sorry. I did my best."

Katherine nodded her thanks and watched Audrey thread her way through the Sunday morning worshippers to re-join Andrew, who was striding on ahead. Her heart sank as she realised she must now try herself to change Andrew's mind. She did not have long as Richard was to appear before the magistrate in Hereford on Tuesday. That only left tomorrow. What on earth could she achieve in one day?

Beside her Gertie Murdoch asked, "What was that all about, dear?"

"Oh, it's this stupid business between Richard and Andrew Kellett. Audrey was trying to get Andrew to drop the charges, but he's refused."

"It would take a miracle, I think."

"A miracle indeed," Katherine muttered, her decision made.

After she had accompanied Gertie and Donald to the Walnut Tree for their pre-Sunday lunch drink with other members of the congregation, she returned home. Seeing Karl and the boys sorting timber near the woodshed she went straight to the telephone and called Froxley Grange. To Katherine's surprise Audrey answered. She had been expecting a maid but times were obviously changing at the Grange.

"Ah, Audrey. It's Katherine here. Look, I've been thinking. Would it help if I came round personally and had a word with Andrew, do you think?"

"I doubt it, but if you want to try, by all means do."

"When would be a good time? It would have to be before Tuesday."

"Um, not this afternoon or evening, we've got guests. Tomorrow morning perhaps. He's usually around on Mondays. I'll tell him to expect you around ten, shall I?"

"Fine. If it's not convenient for him, give me a ring."

"Of course. I won't be here, I'm afraid. I've got an appointment at the dentist's. But it's not me you're wanting to see, is it?"

"No. Tomorrow at ten then. Good luck with the dentist."

"Oh, it's only a small filling, I hope. Shouldn't stop me doing some shopping afterwards."

Or anything else, Katherine could not help thinking as she put down the receiver. Knowing Audrey, there was probably a lover or two stashed away in Hereford somewhere. As for herself, she did not want Karl or Richard to know she was going begging to Andrew. She would have to find some excuse to go out on her bicycle tomorrow morning. Perhaps some shopping of her own at the village stores.

That night she could not sleep for mentally rehearsing what she would say to Andrew. Beside her Karl was sound asleep, dream-free. She wondered how Richard was, whether he was worrying about the events of Tuesday. Clenching her fists with determination she knew she must succeed with Andrew at any cost. No child of hers was going to have a police record.

The following morning, with immediate chores accomplished and the chickens fed, she put on a headscarf, wheeled out her bicycle from the barn and pumped up the tyres. Karl knew she was going out for the morning but, to her great relief, had not asked where.

It was a good twenty-minute ride to Froxley Grange up the valley road, but the spring weather was fine, the birds twittering in the hedges, frantically finding food for their offspring. Katherine found the ride a pleasant one despite her anxiety. A car tooted its horn at her as it passed and she waved as she recognised the new vicar. At least he was one of the least likely people Karl would come across, so her secret visit should be safe.

At five to ten she began the ride up the long sweep of drive, through parkland grazed by prize Herefordshire beef cattle, to the Georgian edifice that was Froxley Grange. She left her bicycle by the main steps up to the front door, removed her headscarf, and at ten o'clock precisely pulled the handle of the doorbell.

This time there was a maid on duty. Katherine was shown in to Andrew's dingy study, which did not seem to have been touched since Victorian times. Ancient tomes and lithographs lined the dark green walls obscured by a haze of cigarette smoke. At the source of the smoke she could see Andrew seated at an enormous desk dealing with paperwork. He stood up to greet her, extinguishing his cigarette as he did so.

"Welcome, Katherine. To what do I owe the pleasure, or can I guess?" He suddenly remembered his manners and signalled to the departing maid to wait. "But first things first. A coffee perhaps?"

Katherine felt she needed a little time to settle down with Andrew. "Yes please." She sat down on the high-backed chair by his desk, surprised not to have been received in a more comfortable parlour. It must be his way of saying he was a busy man and she must be brief. "I'm sorry to be taking up your time, Andrew," she began somewhat hesitantly.

"Audrey said you needed to see me before tomorrow. I should have been going out to see one of the tenants this morning but I changed my plans just to fit you in. You see, I can be reasonable."

Katherine did not like his tone of voice. It was not as friendly as she had hoped. Her job might be a whole lot harder than she had reckoned on. "I'm very grateful. Relations between our families have not been good over the years, have they, Andrew?" she said with a soft smile of reconciliation.

"The operative word there is families, Katherine," he replied less brusquely. "It's not you who's the problem, is it now?" Her smile had suddenly suggested an agreeable solution to the current conflict and he grinned at the delicious idea.

Unaware of his intent Katherine grinned back, relieved he seemed in lighter mood. "It's silly, isn't it, how we avoid each other. In such a small community it makes life quite difficult at times, and I do miss coming to the Hunt Ball."

"There's no reason why you shouldn't come to the next one, Katherine, that is if you can persuade your husband to attend. He's not totally lacking in social graces, is he?"

"You know as well as I do, Andrew, that he's perfectly able to keep up with you and your friends. I think even you were secretly impressed by his performance at that dinner you invited us to during our last attempt at reconciliation."

He nodded. "I did my best to goad him into an argument, but he had a lot of help from the ladies, especially Audrey, at deflecting my attacks. He's a popular man with the fair sex, as I'm sure you've noticed!"

The coffee arrived and conversation halted while the maid poured then retreated. Andrew watched the door close then said:

"Now, tell me. What's it like being married to a jailbird? Has he picked up any nasty habits while he was inside?"

Katherine helped herself to cream and sugar, ignoring Andrew's attempt at frivolity. She was not going to let him goad her into an argument. In fact the time had probably come to take the bull by the horns herself. "I didn't come to talk about Karl," she said stirring her coffee vigorously. "I came to reason with you about this stupid court case tomorrow. I know Richard punched you, and I'm really very sorry about that, but he was angry when he heard what you had done to me."

"And what did I do to you?" he demanded, his eyes boring into hers. "Tell me, Katherine, because I seem to remember events rather differently from how you described them."

She sipped her coffee, choosing her words carefully. "You did rape me, Andrew. I may not have screamed or kicked but I did not want you to do what you did. You forced yourself on me and I knew there was nothing I could do or say to make you stop, so I gave in. But it was without my consent."

Andrew smiled and leaned back in his leather chair. "Now that's interesting, because as I remember it I made love to a rather frigid young woman who had no idea of what making love was really about. Your experiences with that Kraut of yours had obviously left you in some doubt as to the pleasurable nature of the whole thing and I hoped I may have changed your opinion as a result of my services."

At first Katherine thought he was joking, but as his words sank in she realised it was just the typically egocentric view of things Andrew would have. She could hardly believe her ears when he went on: "Are you still frigid, or have you perhaps learnt more since then? I doubt it somehow. They're not famous for it, are they, the Krauts? Now if he were a Frog or an Eytie, that would be another matter."

He had stood up as he spoke, now he stepped around to her side of the desk. He moved her coffee cup aside and sat on the edge of the desk his hand reaching towards her hair, fondling it. Unseen by Katherine he inserted a finger into a tight curl. "Would you like to find out more, Katherine?" he asked gently.

Katherine suddenly realised Andrew's intentions. Horrified, she moved his hand away from her hair and tried to stall him with conversation. "I never said anything all these years because I honestly didn't want your reputation tarnished, Andrew. If you like I can deny saying you raped me, but it would be far, far simpler if you just dropped the charges against Richard."

"I will, if I get some compensation for my trouble, Katherine." He grinned. "Your son punched me. I have a right to seek redress. Your dress!" He laughed at his own joke then went to the door and turned the key.

"Andrew, this is ridiculous!" she snapped as he moved across to the window and pulled down the blind.

"No it's not, Katherine. You want something, I want something. Our little secret and just harmless fun. You do this for me and I promise to get straight on the telephone and withdraw charges against your son, then we're quits. What do you think now? Isn't that a bargain?"

Katherine felt trapped, revolted by the idea of letting Andrew have her, but unable to think of any other way of getting Richard off the hook. "How do I know you'll keep your word?"

Andrew gave a smile of victory. "I'm a gentlemen. But how do you know you won't want to come back for more?" he teased, standing close now and laying his fingers on her thin cotton dress, feeling her breast underneath.

Katherine stood helpless as he slowly unbuttoned the front of her dress. I'm doing this for Richard, she told herself, closing her eyes and allowing Andrew to gather her into his eager embrace. He could not get his hands on her quickly enough, it seemed. Dragging her dress half down over her arms, leaving them pinioned by the fabric, he groped for the fastening of her bra, releasing it with a satisfied sigh. Katherine tried to shut her mind to what was happening, then tried to imagine it was Karl making love to her, but it was impossible. She felt herself pushed backwards by the sheer force of his ardour until the small of her back crashed against the desk edge. His hands were all over her now, pummelling, possessing, pinching even, reclaiming the territory that had been lost to him twenty-two years ago. Katherine forced herself not to protest at his rough treatment, encouraging him to be more gentle by trying to reach for his hands, but the dress encumbered her. By now his hands were tugging at her knickers.

They dropped to the floor and she was tilted backwards to lie across the edge of the desk. Keep calm, she told herself. It will soon be over at this rate.

She was right. The coffee was not even cool by the time Katherine buttoned up the front of her dress again and tidied her hair. No wonder Audrey looks elsewhere for pleasure, she thought, if that's the best he can do. Satisfied she was presentable again she turned to him in a business-like manner.

"So, it's time for you to keep your part of the bargain." She pulled the telephone extension closer to him and handed him the receiver.

Taking it from her he replaced it on its cradle, enjoying the moment of teasing her before picking it up again with a self-satisfied grin.

*

Cycling home Katherine could not believe what had happened. Still, it was done now. Andrew had officially dropped all charges against Richard and hopefully the entire affair would soon be forgotten.

Affair. That was the wrong word. It was not an affair in the sense of Karl's fling with Ilse. This had been an act of self-sacrifice she did not ever want to repeat. The sooner she got home, had a wash and a change of clothes and got rid of all trace of Andrew, the better. She would need to wash her hair too, unless she could blame the smell of cigarettes on someone else, but how was she to explain away the bruises on her back?

As she began the steep climb up the lane to the farm she caught sight of the Land Rover making its way up the lane ahead of her. Blast it! That would mean no chance of getting in without being seen. She stopped pedalling and paused for breath by the gateway to the paddock. From here she could see across to the farm buildings. In the gap between the sheep sheds and the converted feed store she could see the Land Rover now parked and being loaded up with something. If she waited a little longer they might return down the lane.

Sure enough, two minutes later she saw Karl get back in the driving seat and pull away from the yard. She immediately began pedalling again and met him on the next bend. He stopped and let her by so she did not lose momentum, gave a wave then drove on. Katherine was not sure whether it was the effort of riding uphill or anxiety that was making her heart pound so loudly. As soon as she had put away the bicycle she rushed inside and straight upstairs.

This is awful, she thought as she brushed her teeth and put her clothing in the washing basket. How am I ever going to look him in the face?

The question plagued her the rest of the morning as she continued tidying up the house. The moment could not be put off when she heard the Land Rover draw up outside as Karl and Richard returned for lunch.

"You've got changed!" Karl remarked as he entered the kitchen clutching a sack of potatoes, which he dumped in the larder. "Present from Bob Groves," he explained.

Katherine ignored his first comment. "That's kind of him. By the way, where's Richard? I've got some important news for him."

"Just sorting out the back of the Land Rover. He'll be here in a minute, I expect."

Katherine filled a jug with cold water and put it on the table with the lunch things. Sure enough Richard appeared a moment later. With a broad grin on her face she told him: "Tomorrow's off. Andrew's withdrawn all charges!"

"What! How on earth ... When did you find that out?" Richard spluttered.

"I had a word with Andrew," Katherine beamed, keeping her eyes off Karl. "I managed to persuade him how stupid this all was."

"Well done, Mum," Richard cried, giving her a bear hug. "Thank you!"

"Is that where you went?" Karl asked, equally pleased.

"Yes. I didn't want to tell you where I was going and get your hopes up unnecessarily, but as it turned out ..."

"Whoopeee!" Richard yelled, giving her another big hug.

As soon as his son had made way, Karl put his arm round her and kissed her proudly. "What a miracle-worker you are. I don't know how you did it."

"Neither do I," she replied, not ever intending to tell him, "but at least now it's all over we can concentrate on Bina's wedding."

*

Ilse watched the ceiling fan rotating over Ricardo's head. He was a good lover and she did her best to please him too, but her heart just wasn't in it. It was fun, a means of passing the days, but their lovemaking lacked that essential spark of passion she felt with Karl. She had tried closing her eyes and imagining it was him, but Ricardo would insist on continuing their Spanish lessons as he performed and it totally shattered the illusion. She could not complain however, as she felt herself responding at last to his embrace. Paul's complicity in the arrangement meant she could relax and enjoy it for what it was: innocent fun.

Her fingers dug into his back, urging him on, and she was glad he at least seemed to find their meetings wholly satisfying. Of course he had other girlfriends. She could not expect a young man to devote himself solely to an almost grandmother. Nevertheless he was tactful enough not to mention what he did of an evening. Daylight was their time together, and Paul still had her for himself at night. He was right when he saw Ricardo as no threat, merely a means of keeping his wife occupied both mentally and physically.

"Your mind is elsewhere," Ricardo said when he lay beside her again.

"Is it? No, really, I was just remembering your Spanish words of love. Should I try them out on Paul, do you think?"

"He'll know where they come from!"

"Of course, but he knows anyway."

"What, about us?" Ricardo asked in horror.

"Yes. I thought you knew that was part of the deal."

"You Germans amaze me with your cold-blooded schemes. No self-respecting Latino would pay another man to -"

"Are you sure? You wouldn't know unless you asked, would you?"

Ricardo relaxed again and smiled. "True. It might be going on all over Montevideo right now, for all I know." He kissed the hollow of her throat. "You are a very beautiful woman, Ilse, and your husband is right to try to keep you happy." He stroked the spot he had just kissed. "But you are not happy, are you? I try my best for you, but I can tell you wish I were someone else. Who is that man, Ilse?"

Ilse groaned and closed her eyes. "Don't ask me questions like that," she said quietly, rolling over and reaching for her wrap.

Ricardo watched her walk away to the bathroom, knowing he had bad news to report to Paul.

*

Katherine stroked the soft silk camisole she had bought in London but not yet worn. She must put Andrew behind her and concentrate on the purpose for which she had bought them. She wanted to show Karl she was as desirable as Ilse. Not that she was in any doubt. Since his unexpected release and the first few awkward hours in London, there had been no problems with their love life. She just felt the need to show him she wanted him still. Even more so, after her experience with Andrew. How could Audrey bear him? Perhaps she couldn't. Perhaps that was why Andrew had been so desperate yesterday. Would he want to come back for more?

A chill ran down her body at the sudden fear. His parting words had been 'See you again, Katherine.' Innocuous enough, she thought as she laid her clean laundry over the silk underwear. It was too soon to wear it for Karl, the memory of Andrew too fresh in her mind. It would spoil things for her. She left it carefully hidden under her everyday knickers.

A quick glance at her watch told her she had time for some paperwork before the men wanted their tea. She went down to the compact study and sat at the desk her father had installed when her parents had extended the small farmhouse in the early years of their marriage. Her mother was suburban born and expected the comforts of suburbia even in rural Herefordshire. Along with the study and an extra bedroom, a proper bathroom had been built, electricity and telephone installed with money her mother had brought with her. It was her mother who had gentrified the farm, her mother who had encouraged Katherine and Sarah to ride, and it was her mother who had most encouraged her friendship with the heir to Froxley Grange. She had often wondered whether her mother would have approved of Karl as a son-in-law. Her father certainly had, as Karl had been his worker and companion of choice. She suspected her mother would have come around to the idea eventually, but always with regrets her daughter had rejected a far higher status in the county.

Katherine smiled fondly at the memory of her parents and got on with the paperwork. Karl mostly left the more tedious business to her, although he did prepare his own bills and liked to keep track of everything and know how the finances stood. He was reasonably up to date with his billing, but there were a couple of invoices under the Medebach stone paperweight that had not yet been entered into the ledger.

As she reached across to the nearby bookshelf for the ledger the telephone rang in the hall. So much for getting some work done, Katherine thought as she went out to answer it.

"Hello, Lane Head Farm," she said brightly, anticipating a possible bed and breakfast booking.

"Katherine," a familiar male voice replied. "I'm glad you're in. I wanted to thank you for our little meeting yesterday. I did enjoy it."

Katherine's heart sank. This was the last thing she wanted. "Andrew," she responded politely. "How nice of you to phone. How was Audrey's visit to the dentist? She wasn't in too much pain when she got in, was she?"

"Never mind Audrey, you little minx. I wanted to know when we could get together again, for a bit longer this time. When are that husband and son of yours next out for the day?"

Katherine gripped the receiver hard. "That wasn't the deal, Andrew."

"Wasn't it?" he asked in feigned surprise. "You made a down-payment on a loan, but there is a lot yet to be repaid."

"That's not what we agreed at all, Andrew, and you know it. You've had your payment and that's all you're getting!" Katherine slammed down the receiver, her hands shaking in anger. She marched back to the study and shut the door. Standing behind the chair she grasped the back of it, wringing it like she wished she could wring Andrew's neck.

"Oh God, what have I got myself into?" she raged.

By the time Paul came home and clattered up the stairs to get changed out of school uniform, Katherine had calmed down. She hoped Andrew had got the message and would not trouble her again, but if he did she could not call on Karl for protection, or Richard. That would be far too dangerous. This was where having someone like Siegfried would come in useful.

Her sudden train of thought horrified her as she realised how easy it was to step onto the slippery slope.

NINE

The keys to the new house sat comfortably in Siegfried's pocket as he drove to the hospital to fetch Sophie and bring her home at last. There were no curtains at the windows or rugs on the parquet floors and most of the boxes remained unpacked, but that was something he and Sophie could do together in the evenings and she could do with her mother during the days. To brighten it up he had asked a local florist to deliver a mass of potted plants and flowers, which now stood on strategic windowsills and on the balcony outside their bedroom. All the house needed now was Sophie herself to put her mark on it, and, in due course, the baby to fill it with life.

The big-band music on the car radio made way for the news, which concentrated on Robert Kennedy's assassination and the subsequent arrest of an Arab. Siegfried switched it off. The topic was too close to home for comfort. It was now early June and he had heard nothing from Gustav since their meeting in his flat in April. But he did not want such thoughts to spoil the day. Today was the first day he and Sophie would live together at home as man and wife. It was a day for celebration, not despair, a day for opening a bottle of champagne and toasting his beautiful bride's arrival in the house.

As he turned off the road and headed for the wrought iron gates of the private clinic, the sun burst from behind a towering cumulus cloud, spotlighting the white façade of the building like a scene from an El Greco painting. He felt a surge of renewed optimism. Everything would be all right. He had always found a way in the past and he could do so again.

He parked the car close to the entrance doors and hurried inside, nodding familiarly to the hefty woman at the reception desk who knew him well by now. He took the lift to the second floor and was soon knocking on Sophie's door.

"Come in!" she called excitedly.

She was standing by her wheelchair, dressed in a loose-fitting summer frock, hair up in its familiar coil, showing the elegance of her neck and the softness of her skin. Siegfried could not reach her quickly enough, carefully hugging her to him, his lips kissing her neck, working their way over her cheek and onto her eager mouth.

"At last! I thought today would never come!" he said, leaning back slightly to inspect the object of his desire. "You're looking gorgeous." Releasing her shoulders, he reached into his jacket pocket and brought out a long blue jewel box. "A welcome home present for you."

"Schatz! You shouldn't have! I thought we had to be careful about –"

"I wanted something you could always remember this day by. The day you came home as my bride."

"You sentimental old thing," she laughed, sitting down on the bed to open the box. Inside lay a silver and flower-enamelled locket, which opened to reveal a miniature photo of each of them, one on either side. She realised its monetary value was not great, but she treasured the thought behind it. "It's beautiful!" she gasped, closing it up again, then getting awkwardly to her feet. "Here, help me put it on."

He took it from her, unclasped it and draped it carefully over her shoulders, unable to resist the urge to kiss again the fine, downy hairs on the nape of her neck. He noticed the goose pimples rise on her skin at the touch of his lips.

"My beautiful Sophie," he murmured in her ear, his hands cradling the huge belly in front of her.

She turned round and stroked his face, her fingers running gently over the slight bump of his broken nose. "Let's get going, shall we? I can't wait to get home." She sat down in the wheelchair, ready for him to push her out. "But first we must say goodbye to everyone. They're all in the day-room."

Siegfried could have done without the further delay, but Sophie had been at the clinic so long, she knew all the staff and many patients well. There were hugs and kisses, promises to write, then at last they were in the lift and on their way out. The receptionist bade them farewell and wished Sophie well with the baby, then they were finally on their way, her wheelchair stowed safely in the boot.

The road up to Soest was busy with lorries and families headed for picnics by the Möhne Dam, but they made good progress, arriving in their new village just outside Soest at midday. The house was quite recently built in a cul de sac of similar, chalet-style houses. Siegfried parked in the short drive then helped Sophie out of the car. Sophie was determined to walk into the house with the aid of her walking sticks, but having unlocked the front door, Siegfried had other ideas. Sweeping her up into his arms, her sticks dangling over his shoulder, he carried her across the threshold.

"Welcome home, Schatz," he gasped, easing her down onto the hall floor. "My goodness, that baby's heavy!"

"Now you know what I have to put up with," she laughed. She looked eagerly around her, smelling the scented air and running her fingers over the carved wooden banisters. "It's as beautiful as I expected it to be." She hobbled into the living room to be greeted by a sunburst of cut and potted flowers in a bare but bright room. Rugs stood rolled up against the walls, furniture stacked likewise, awaiting her directions and guidance for their layout.

She turned in rapture to Siegfried. "Thank you for leaving it all for me. I'll have such fun deciding where to put everything." The smile left her face. "You can't imagine how boring it's been in hospital all those months."

He held her close to him, as close as her belly allowed. "I know, Schatz. I know. But you're home now. We can start a new life together." He grabbed her hand and led her slowly out towards the kitchen. Opening the fridge door he pulled out a bottle of champagne with a flourish, then produced two glasses from a boxed set of twelve standing on a marbled worktop. "One of our wedding presents I needed to open," he explained. "The rest are stacked in the cellar. I'll bring them up a few at a time for you to open."

"For us to open," she corrected as the cork exploded from the bottle.

He poured the champagne into the long-stemmed glasses, handing her one. "*Prost!*"

"*Prost!*"

He allowed her a sip then took her glass from her so she could inspect the cupboards and cooker and the separate laundry area, then opened the door leading out to the garden. "Not much except lawn and a few shrubs, but ideal for the baby when he's older." He helped her outside, finding her leaning heavily on his arm. "Are you getting tired, Schatz? Let's sit on the wall here and drink our champagne and enjoy the view. Look! There's a squirrel coming down that tree."

He pointed over the wire netting fence into the adjacent woodland where a red squirrel was scampering down a pine trunk. It sat in a pool of sunshine on the ground, its tufted ears and tail glowing a deep reddish gold.

"There's another one," she observed. "It must be its mate. We're their new neighbours and they've come to welcome us! Hans and Lotte I'll call them."

The name Lotti had other connotations for Siegfried, other than the famous underwater filmmakers, Hans and Lotte Hass. Lotti had been a live-in servant in his parents' home, who had introduced him into the joys of adulthood at the age of sixteen. Strangely enough, her hair had a touch of reddish gold in it too, he mused.

They sat happily sipping their champagne, watching the squirrel pair suddenly chase each other back up into the trees, running along the branches like over-wound clockwork tightrope walkers, chattering as they went.

Sophie gave out a long sigh and rested her head on Siegfried's shoulder. "It's all so perfect."

"You haven't seen our bedroom yet."

She looked up and saw the twinkle in his eye. "I can't wait!"

*

Karl and Richard surveyed the long sweep of Steps Meadow. Before them the long grass rustled and billowed in the gentle summer breeze.

"What do you reckon, then?" Karl looked across towards the sharp outline of Hay Bluff on the horizon and sniffed the air. Perfect weather for haymaking. "Is it ready to cut, do you think?"

Richard knew he was being tested, but answered confidently. "You bet! Besides, we'll run out of time if we leave it any longer.

Once Bina and Wolf get here for the last reading of the banns, nothing's going to get done."

"That's what I think," Karl agreed. "Come on then. Let's get cracking! Just count yourself lucky you don't have to cut this lot by hand."

"You say that every year, Dad!"

They both laughed and headed back to hitch the tractor to the mowing machine, Molly close at their heels. Karl had other tasks to see to and soon left Richard to his own devices, taking Molly with him.

It was hot and dusty work driving the tractor, but Richard loved the satisfaction of seeing the swathes of grass left by the mower in ever-increasing rows. By the time he cut the last swathe in the meadow, Paul was returning home from school. Richard left the tractor by the gateway to the next meadow, and headed for the house for his tea break. Paul would want to take over driving the tractor as soon as he had changed out of school uniform and eaten a plateful of sandwiches. Richard entered the welcome shade of the kitchen, where he downed a pint of water in one go, then wiped his mouth with the back of his hand, leaving a smeared streak of dust across his lips.

Katherine finished cutting a fresh round of cheese sandwiches and refilled the plate on the table. There was no sign as yet of Karl.

"Where did Dad get to?" she asked Richard, wondering whether to make another batch just yet.

"The tree nursery. Those rabbits have been in again and he had to fix the fencing. Shall I give him a shout?"

"No. He'll be in when he's ready. How's the hay?"

"Steps Meadow's cut. I've left the Mead for Paul when he's ready."

"Just be grateful you don't have to cut it by hand."

"Honestly, Mum! You and Dad are just the same!"

"I hope not!" Katherine laughed. "There's no way I'm giving a speech at Bina's wedding. Dad can have that honour. Which reminds me," she added. "Have you tried on your best shoes recently? I don't want you finding they're way too small on the morning of the wedding."

"Not yet, but I will. Have you heard yet whether the Thorntons are coming?"

"Yes. Olive wrote to say they've finally moved into their bungalow, and that now John's wheelchair's been delivered they can get out and about. It'll be lovely to see them up here again. Church services were never the same when he retired." She gave him a wistful smile. "I suppose I'm old-fashioned like most people round here, and this new young man isn't proving very popular."

"Bina likes him. So do I."

"You're young too. You're on the same wavelength. But you should have seen the raised eyebrows amongst the older generation at his choice of clothing for the St Valentine's dance! Pink shirt, purple tie and maroon hipsters indeed!"

"Very trendy," Richard laughed. "But he was only trying to inject some life into the proceedings."

Just then Paul appeared at the kitchen door dressed in T-shirt and shorts, his arms and legs already deeply tanned. Richard and Sabina, who had their mother's freckles and auburn hair, burnt rather easily, but fair-haired Paul stripped off at every opportunity.

"Are you talking about me?" he asked.

"No. The Reverend Williams," Richard told him.

Paul laughed. "Oh yes! Bit different from the old fuddy-duddy Reverend Thornton, eh?"

"Paul, show some respect, please" his mother chided him. "They're coming up for the wedding and are great friends of ours. He was very kind when Dad first came to the village, and was one of the reasons why Dad was accepted here so well."

"Sorry," Paul muttered and scuttled out, side-stepping his father who was on his way in.

"Hasn't he got an exam tomorrow?" Karl asked Katherine, sucking blood off a cut on his finger.

"No. Last one today. That's why he's in such a hurry to get outside. Here, let me find you a plaster before you drip all over the floor."

She rummaged in a bottom drawer of the tallboy, through the saved paper bags and string, until she found the box of plasters. "Nearly empty," she told herself. "Must get some more."

While attending to Karl's finger she told him of the Thorntons' letter. "Bina will be pleased they can come. Christened, confirmed then married by him. Luckily Reverend Williams is quite happy to share the service." She threw the backing strips into the waste bin and began washing the dirty glasses and plates as Karl sat down at the table to have his snack.

"How much still needs organising?" he asked, taking a large bite out of a sandwich.

Katherine spoke over her shoulder from the sink. "I wanted to wait until Bina gets here before Vera ices the cake. Gertie's arranging the flowers, and all hosts know what guests they're having and when. Bina's sorting her dress out, I've an army of helpers for the food and drink. That leaves you and the boys to renovate the dog-cart –"

"That's in hand," he told her.

"– and clean the horse's tack and harness."

"I've written that down for Thursday. Plus the service sheets must be collected from the printers and checked. We can do that this Wednesday when we go in to market. Is that all?"

"I think so, unless you can think of anything I've missed. How's your speech going?"

"In my head and working on it. The rabbit fencing proved very fruitful until I caught my finger on a sharp end."

"Photographer!" Katherine suddenly blurted. "Write that down on the list, Schatz, before I forget again. I need to confirm the time with him."

"Right." Karl reached behind him for the notepad on the dresser where a long list of items had already been crossed off. He skimmed through it. "My suit to the dry cleaners. Mustn't forget." He perused the list again. "Oh, and there's the dripping tap in the guest bathroom. Must get Werner to come up and sort that out."

"Can't you do it?"

"I'll let him. Makes him feel involved. He's really excited about the whole thing. Can't wait to meet my family and have a good long chat in German." He checked a detail on the list. "Thursday the twentieth, German crowd arrives about eight p.m. I just hope they all manage to keep together in convoy. At least they can put one English speaker in each car, although quite how much English

Siegfried remembers, I don't know. He was telling me he found communicating harder than he expected in St Lucia."

Katherine dried her hands and sat down at the table beside Richard, who had eaten his sandwiches and was silently waiting for Karl to finish his. "Are you absolutely sure about Siegfried?" she asked tentatively. "I know I've asked you before, but ..."

Karl smiled indulgently at her. "I know. It's hard for you to accept, but I'm convinced he meant what he said to me. He's not going to do anything to upset the wedding, I assure you, Schatz." He could see she remained unconvinced, Richard too, but there was nothing else he could say or do that might change her mind.

Katherine nodded in acquiescence. "It's such a shame Sophie isn't coming too. But I wouldn't want to either in her condition. Never mind, at least the Röbel clan can all make it. That brings our German guests up to sixteen, you realise, now that Monika's Jens is able to come after all."

"It'll be strange seeing Heinrich and the girls again," Richard ventured. "It's been three years since we last saw them at Siegfried's twenty-first. I wonder if Margit's still as bossy as ever, and Edeltraud's ears still stick out? How Ilse ever produced three such ugly ducklings, I don't know!"

There was an awkward silence from his parents at the mention of Ilse's name, until Katherine said: "It must be very difficult now for them, with their parents away in Uruguay. I expect they're glad to have Siegfried's family around. Makes them feel less cut off."

Richard was unaware of his parents' discomfort as he prattled on: "I'm surprised Bina didn't invite Ilse along to the wedding too. I know Paul wouldn't be able to enter the country, but I'm sure Ilse would have jumped at the chance to see Siegfried and the others again."

"I expect she'll come over when the baby's born," Karl said, his eyes deliberately avoiding Katherine's.

"Oh yes, of course," Richard agreed. "I'd forgotten about that."

Karl pushed his empty plate away and stood up. "Right! Back to work. If Paul's taken over the tractor, then you can come and help me with that broken bit of fence by the sheep dip."

Katherine watched them set off. Ilse remained a thorn in the flesh, pricking away every so often, refusing to budge. And there was another pain that would not go away. Each Sunday at church Andrew had given her the eye, winking lewdly at her, but fortunately it had amounted to no more than that. He was blatantly teasing her, but she suspected it was his lack of courage that was keeping him away. Whatever else his shortcomings, Andrew was sensible enough not to incur the wrath of Karl.

*

His desk covered in architects' plans, Siegfried groped to find the switch to answer the intercom. His secretary's voice told him there was a Herr Halstrup on the line wanting a word.

Siegfried's heart jolted but his voice kept steady. "Put him through, Frau Schiersmann." There was a click as the connection was made. "Hello, Gustav," Siegfried said jovially. "What can I do for you?"

Gustav's reply crackled down the line. "Meet me for lunch today. There are things we need to discuss."

Siegfried felt his heart sink. "I think that's OK with me. Twelve o'clock suit you?"

"Fine. I'll be outside your office. See you then."

The line went dead. Siegfried flicked the switch and got his secretary back. "I'll be leaving the office at twelve for a lunch meeting. I'm not sure what time I'll be back in, but it'll be before Huber comes at three."

"Very well, Herr Driesler."

Siegfried tried to turn his attention back to the plans on his desk but found it impossible. He knew exactly what Gustav was going to ask him, namely how far he had progressed with his plans to kill his father. He glanced up at the wall clock and saw he had an hour to prepare his answer.

*

It had taken Christian Bracht a few weeks to track down Gustav. All he had to go on was the actual city until he had a lucky break courtesy of a mutual friend in the theatre world, who eventually supplied him with Gustav's address in Dortmund. Following Gustav's movements was tricky in the unfamiliar territory and he had repeatedly lost him at first, but now he was finding his bearings and had managed to keep track of Gustav's car as far as a modern office on the outskirts of the city. The bold sign on the wall proclaimed it to be the headquarters of Zopf Construction.

"What on earth does he want there?" Christian asked himself, lighting a cigarette and blowing the smoke out of the car's window. It was a hot day. He reached for the bottle of warm lemonade on the passenger seat and took a long swig as Gustav sat waiting in his car. A nearby church bell was mournfully striking twelve as a tall, slim figure in a light grey suit left the office and glanced around before heading for Gustav's car. Christian saw Gustav beckon the blond young man inside, and began to seethe with jealousy. So Gustav had a new lover! A handsome bastard at that!

In a moment the car had set off. Flinging his stub out of the window, Christian followed discreetly behind Gustav's ancient black Mercedes. After only a short distance it pulled into the car park of a small restaurant. Christian drove past the restaurant before turning up the next side street. He parked and hurried back to observe Gustav and his friend entering the restaurant. Now Christian was in a quandary; whether to enter the restaurant himself and risk being seen by Gustav, or whether to simply wait outside and resume his surveillance in due course. Christian was aware he was becoming obsessed with following Gustav, wanting still to be a part of his life, even if only at a distance. Ultimately he knew he was being driven by the burning hope that Gustav would notice his devotion and come back to him. But for now he just wanted to observe and assess his new rival. Taking advantage of a group of businessmen entering the restaurant to shield him from Gustav's view, Christian loitered in the foyer with them until the headwaiter directed them to a large table in the middle of the restaurant. Christian spotted Gustav and his companion seated at a corner table, studying the menu. To his relief, Gustav had his back to the room, so Christian decided to take the risk and ask the waiter for a table near the bar, not too close to his quarry.

Looking at the prices on the menu Christian blanched. He would just have to order the cheapest item and leave before the others, but at least he would have about half an hour to observe them. The waiter accepted his order of spaghetti carbonara and a beer without comment, then left him alone to watch Gustav and friend.

The blond young man patently knew Gustav well. This was certainly not a first meeting, the conversation too serious for introductory chit-chat. His face betrayed little emotion, indeed seemed almost too much under control, as Christian could not guess at the nature of their conversation. A brief frown, a snatched smile were the few clues available. There was certainly no overt friendliness, nor animosity. Yet Christian sensed from Gustav's relaxed posture that he was content with what he was hearing.

Perhaps the young man already had a lover and was having trouble getting rid of him, but had promised to sort it out as quickly as possible. Or maybe he was not sure he was homosexual even. Or perhaps this was simply a business transaction. Christian began to feel frustrated. By the time his spaghetti arrived he was no nearer deciding on the facts. Winding the long threads carefully round his fork he was just leaning forwards to shovel it into his mouth, when a movement caught his eye. Surely Gustav had his hand on the young man's! It was only for a moment, but it confirmed a close bond between the pair. An agreement had been made, the conversation lightened up. The young man smiled more, laughing even at something Gustav said and seemed to be enjoying the meal at last. Which was more than could be said for Christian. His fears seemed confirmed. This was Gustav's new lover. He guessed they had not yet slept together – there had been too much wariness on the young man's part initially – but Christian felt certain they would. He would have to keep watching Gustav. Fired up with jealousy, he felt a masochistic desire to know the truth.

The waiter whisked away Christian's empty plate. "Can I get you anything else, sir?"

"No. Just the bill, please." Christian wanted to be out of there before Gustav stood up and turned round.

"Certainly, sir."

Leaving the restaurant, Christian returned to his car and drove it round to the restaurant's car park. There he waited for half an hour until Gustav and his tall companion left the restaurant. He followed them back to the office where they had met and saw Gustav give an affectionate pat on the shoulder as the young man left the car.

Suddenly the spaghetti in his stomach felt like lead. Christian's anger boiled up inside him. He must find out who that man was! And he knew where to make a start – the employees of Zopf Construction.

TEN

Sabina carefully lifted her wedding dress in its plastic cover from the rear seat of Wolf's car. It seemed to have travelled without mishap. The hardest part now was to get it inside her parents' house without any mud or manure leaping up from the yard onto it.

Her mother rushed to her assistance. "Here, let me take one end."

Between them they carried it safely up to Sabina's old room and hung it on the back of the door.

"Can I take a peek?" Katherine begged, her hands hovering over the cover's edge.

Sabina grinned. "Go on then, Mum. I know you've been dying to see it. You wouldn't believe the trouble I've had keeping Wolf from sneaking a look!"

Katherine raised the grey plastic cover up over the dress and stood back. "Oh, it's beautiful! Not too fussy, just as you said. And I love these sleeves," she declared, lifting up one of them, feeling the satin-smooth material slide under her fingertips. "They look almost mediaeval. Very Lady of Shallott!"

"I'm glad you like it. It's a bit different from the yards of frills and petticoats on all the dresses in the shops, and I didn't fancy a mini-dress either. I was lucky Frau Friedrichsmeier could make exactly what I wanted. And of course it fits perfectly."

"You'd never have found anything like that in Hereford, nor even in London, I shouldn't think. I can't wait to see you in it!"

"It's going to be fun, isn't it," Sabina declared, giving her mother a hug. "At least, I hope so," she added, her smile slipping away.

Katherine guessed the reason for her daughter's doubts. "You're worried about Siegfried?"

Sabina nodded. "I can't help it. He just gives me the creeps. He's so slick. It's different for Wolf, who's been friends with him for years. But I can't get used to the idea of him being so friendly."

"I know, Treasure. I'm having the same problem, but Daddy insists we've nothing to worry about." Katherine pulled the cover back over the wedding dress. "Right! Let's get the rest of your stuff up here. I expect Wolf's safely installed in the old feed store by now. I hope he doesn't mind shifting down to Gertie and Donald's on Thursday when everyone else gets here, but we rather wanted Opa to stay here with us."

"No, that's fine. He can keep an eye on Siegfried and enjoy his stag night better down there." Sabina grinned at her mother. "Had we better warn them at the Walnut Tree?"

"Done. Daddy's sorted it with Alf. He's said he'll keep the saloon bar free for them. He's even getting in some extra help behind the bar, anticipating a lot of drinking going on!"

They went downstairs to find Karl and Wolf in the hall with Sabina's luggage. Stepping between her cases and the old grandfather clock Sabina hissed in Wolf's ear: "Don't peek at the dress!"

"I won't," he promised for what seemed like the tenth time since leaving their flat in Dortmund. Once the way was clear he picked up a case and followed Karl up the stairs. He had already cracked his head on a low beam in the hall, but he noticed how Karl automatically ducked to avoid them, and guessed he would soon learn to do the same or suffer the consequences. The floorboards creaked, the half-timbered walls bulged in places, but the farmhouse oozed character and a warm welcome. It was a happy home, unlike his mother's house, which had always seemed dark and forbidding, overshadowed by the stern portrait of his grandfather in the parlour.

"This way," Karl told him at the top of the stairs.

Wolf followed him into Sabina's bedroom where they deposited her two tightly packed suitcases. The room was small and cosy, overlooking the yard and converted feed store just beyond, where he would be sleeping for the first few days. He was used to sleeping with Sabina now, but custom dictated otherwise until the following Saturday. He sensed Karl knew what he was thinking and abruptly turned away from the window.

"I felt like you must now, the first time I came in here," Karl told him, trying to set him at ease. "Except I had a bad dose of flu at the time. But it was still rather strange being in Katherine's bedroom." He saw Wolf's puzzled looked. "She moved into her sister's room and let me sleep in her bed rather than out in the feed store. It was rather draughty in those days, with no toilet facilities, except down those old stone steps and across the yard. Not a trip I could have made, feeling as I did!"

Karl had been accepted into Lane Head Farm, and now, a generation on, Wolf was too. He grinned at his prospective father-in-law. "Thanks, Karl. You've been great about letting Bina come to Germany and ... everything. Some parents would have been awkward about letting their only daughter go off like that, but you and Katherine have –"

"Bina's a sensible girl," Karl hastily interrupted, embarrassed by Wolf's flow of gratitude. "We trust her not to do anything silly, and our trust is rewarded. Usually."

Wolf caught Karl's drift. He was unsure whether to broach such a delicate subject, but decided, after a moment's hesitation, that it all ought to come out into the open. "Reefers, you mean?"

"I was thinking on those lines, yes," Karl admitted. "But I know Siegfried put you up to giving them to her, and it was before you fell in love with her, so it's all in the past."

"Thanks, but I don't see how you can be so tolerant about it."

Karl put a fatherly hand on Wolf's shoulder. "We've all made mistakes. I know you'll look after her now. I also know that might not be so easy." There was a moment's deathly silence before Karl added quietly: "If you think you'll be safer here with us, you're very welcome to stay here."

"Thank you," Wolf replied steadily, "but our lives are in Germany. I've a feeling I could go far in my work and I don't want to let that opening pass me by."

"Understood," Karl said, stepping aside to lean on the windowsill and look out down to the yard below where Katherine and Sabina were removing the last oddments from the car. He lowered his voice lest they heard him through the open window. "You'd probably not be any safer here, anyway."

"No, probably not. They'll be after you too." It was not a subject Wolf wanted to dwell upon. Turning abruptly he made for the door, remembering just in time to duck under the frame.

*

Sophie's parents had given her a room downstairs in their new home for the eight days of Siegfried's trip to England. Delighted to have their daughter to stay they reassured Siegfried she would be well looked after.

"You've got our phone number with you, haven't you?" Peter Wendt asked through the open car window as Siegfried prepared to pull away.

"Yes. And you've got my father's in England?"

"Yes. She'll be all right," Peter Wendt promised, seeing his son-in-law's anxious face."

"I know. It's just one hell of a time to be going abroad. It would be just typical if anything happened while I was away."

"It won't. She's got weeks to go yet."

Sophie leaned in through the window to give him another last kiss. "Don't worry, Schatz. I'll be fine. You just enjoy yourself for once, and make sure you give my love to all your family, both Karl's and Ilse's."

It was all very well, Siegfried thought as he headed west from Soest towards the town of Iserlohn, but Sophie was blissfully unaware of the threat that was Gustav. Siegfried was the piper, with Gustav calling the tune, and still Siegfried could see no way round it. The devil and the deep blue sea were on either side of him and neither would go away.

He noticed his speed creeping up along with his agitation and made a conscious effort to slow down to one hundred kilometres an hour. As he tucked his Mercedes in behind a cruising Alpha Romeo he noticed the car behind him likewise nip in and slow down. It was hardly surprising really. A small car like that would be pushing it travelling so fast. When the same green Beetle followed him off towards Iserlohn, Siegfried began to have his suspicions. Was Gustav still having him tailed? If so, why? Gustav knew full well he was off to England today, along with his four Röbel half-siblings. Were they going to be followed the whole way? It would make far more sense to send someone directly to Herefordshire if Gustav wanted to keep an eye on him, as Gustav certainly knew his father's address.

Sure enough, the little green car was stationed a discreet distance back when Siegfried pulled up in front of the apartment block near the centre of Iserlohn where Margit, Heinrich, Edeltraud and Roslinde Röbel were now living. Siegfried watched the green car chug noisily by and disappear round the next corner. The driver seemed to be a young man in his twenties, clean-shaven with mid-brown hair and a white shirt. Siegfried shrugged and decided to ignore him. If he saw him again in Hereford, then he would ask him what his business was.

Roslinde had been looking out for him and welcomed him into the flat the four shared. It was the first time he had actually been inside, since relations between himself and his half-siblings had been somewhat strained since their mother's departure to Uruguay. He was surprised even now that they had wanted to attend Wolf's wedding, since he was the cause of all the family's disruption, but it seemed the friendship between them and Sabina ran deeper than their parents' politics, especially when Sabina asked Margit to be a bridesmaid.

"You're prompt!" Roslinde declared, offering her cheek for a ritual kiss. Siegfried had never been particularly close to his Röbel half-siblings or, for that matter, to his Driesler ones either. He had been caught in the middle, the eldest, born out of wedlock, attached first to one family, then to the other, then back to the first again, never feeling comfortable with any of them. He knew they only tolerated him as a family member, and were accepting his offer of a lift simply as their chance to visit England on the cheap.

"I don't like to keep my customers waiting," he joked, in an effort to be friendly. "Are you all packed and ready?"

The others had joined Roslinde in the hallway, and exchanged greetings. Margit, the eldest at twenty-one, took charge as usual. "We're all ready. We've got some food to eat on the way, and you'll need a decent break from driving before we reach the Hook of Holland. Are you sure you don't want any of us to drive for a bit?"

Siegfried winced at the thought of any of them driving his precious car. "We'll see. You might not be so keen to offer once we get over to England and have to drive on the left!"

"All the more reason to get used to your car while still on the right," Heinrich pointed out. "Though I don't mind driving in England. We've got quite a journey once we get over there."

"I'm going to be navigator," Edeltraud declared, "as I'm good at map-reading."

"No you're not!" Heinrich protested. "Remember the time you took us up the wrong autobahn on the way back from Bonn last month."

"That was hardly my fault! There are so many roads round there and the lorry hid the signpost just as we were passing it, and I didn't know which lane we should have been in."

Margit intervened. "My God, you're still as bad as when you were kids! Stop bickering and let's get the cases into the car!"

As they began carrying bags down to the car, Siegfried sighed. Margit heard him and raised her eyebrows in query. "Worried about Sophie?"

"No, as it happens. I was wondering how I was going to survive this journey with you lot."

She smiled. "Marriage has certainly mellowed you. I had been wondering the same thing about you, but you seem more tolerant these days."

His laugh sounded like a grunt, but he acknowledged the truth of her words. "Relationships are important. I've learned that recently."

Margit paused on the bottom step of the apartment's staircase and turned to him. "Good," she said quietly, making sure the others were out of earshot. "I always felt you were on the outside of everything. Now you're one of us!"

"Are you sure about that, Margit?"

"What do you mean?"

Siegfried gazed into the distance then shrugged enigmatically and carried on towards the car. Margit watched him a moment before following in his wake. Her friendly overtures had been rebuffed. It seemed Siegfried was not prepared to bend beyond his limits.

What had distracted Siegfried, however, was the figure in a white shirt looking into the Italian ice-cream shop window, apparently choosing what flavour to buy. Studying him from under the raised boot, Siegfried could see it was the same young man who had been driving the green Beetle. There was no doubting he was following Siegfried and not very skilfully either. Gustav had seemed happy to let Siegfried get on with the job without interference, so why the tail? Puzzled, Siegfried wedged the last of the cases in the Mercedes' boot, locked it and retreated back into the apartment block while the Röbel females collected their handbags and took a last look around for items forgotten.

"Passports, money, wedding present?" Siegfried prompted.

"All set," Margit declared. "England, here we come!"

"Yes. Here we come," Siegfried breathed, dreading the task ahead of him.

*

Christian drew his eyes away from the pistachio and raspberry ripple tubs in the window and watched the Mercedes drive off jammed to the gunwales with its full cargo of bodies and cases. He felt there was no point in following further. Siegfried Driesler and his friends were obviously going on a long journey for some time. At least he assumed they were friends. They could have been relatives, he supposed. The four dark-haired ones seemed to be the same family, so it seemed more likely his quarry was related rather than just a friend of one of them.

Having stood looking at the ice cream for so long he decided he might as well enjoy one. He could just about afford it. The weeks spent shadowing first Gustav and then more recently Siegfried Driesler as well, had taken a severe toll on Christian's finances. Standing on the hot pavement again, licking the dripping ice cream from its double-cupped cone, Christian decided to check out the names on the apartment doorbells. There were half a dozen names, none of which was Driesler. He felt compelled to find out. Crunching the last of the cone, he licked his fingers clean then rang the bell labelled Dietz, since it was the closest he could find to Driesler. As he heard footsteps labouring down the stairs he wondered what on earth he was doing. He was obsessed about Gustav's apparent new lover, trying to glean every last little detail about him. He already knew Driesler was head of Zopf Construction, despite his relative youth, and was married to a heavily pregnant cripple, a beautiful one if women were your taste, but a cripple nevertheless. If Christian had not seen Gustav's pat on Driesler's shoulder as he left his car that first meeting, he would have rejected the idea of Driesler as a rival. But Christian knew Gustav too well not to recognise the signs of a close friendship.

The door was opened by a wizened and white-haired old lady who was wearing thick-lensed glasses and walked with the aid of a stick.

"I'm so sorry to trouble you," Christian began, wishing he had selected a different bell to try, "but I'm looking for a friend of mine, a young woman of twenty with dark brown shoulder-length hair."

"One of the Röbels?" she suggested, eager to be of help.

"Yes, that's right," Christian nodded, giving his most disarming smile.

"I'm afraid you've just missed them. They've gone away on holiday."

"Oh, that's a shame. I was hoping to see her before she left," Christian lied glibly. "I'm so sorry to have troubled you." He decided to offer no explanation as to why he had rung the old lady's bell. With any luck she would not question it. In fact she seemed pleased to have someone to talk to.

"They're away for a week," the old lady added helpfully. "Did you want to leave a message or anything? Young Roslinde comes in every day to read my letters for me, my eye-sight not being what it was, so I can pass any message on to her when they get back."

"No, it's quite all right, thank you. I'll wait till she returns." He paused and half-turned as if about to go away then added as an apparent after-thought. "Who was it they left with, do you know? The tall, blond man with the Mercedes," he prompted.

The old lady smiled. "You must mean their half-brother. Roslinde told me they were going over to his father's farm in England for a wedding."

"Yes, that's right. That must be him." Realising he had given away the fact he had seen them go, Christian decided not to risk any more conversation. "You've been very helpful. Thank you so much, Frau Dietz."

"You're welcome ... I'm afraid I didn't catch your name."

A name he had recently heard on the news sprang to mind. "Brandt. You take care now, Frau Dietz. Goodbye."

Back in his car, Christian pondered his situation. With Driesler away for a week he had a clear run at Gustav. It was time to head back to Dortmund. As he drove, he mulled over what he had discovered during his period of observation. Gustav seemed to have generated a remarkable number of friends and contacts in the short time he had been living there, spending much of his time socialising in bars and restaurants. His associates were invariably male, sometimes smart businessmen, on other occasions very shady-looking characters. And almost always Gustav seemed to dominate the proceedings. Christian never dared go near enough to overhear a conversation, but he was fast gaining the impression that Gustav was at the centre of some kind of organisation, probably illegal, but whose members came from all walks of life. Siegfried Driesler was possibly one of them, although Gustav had been alone both times he met him. Driesler had certainly not yet been to Gustav's rooms, nor had anyone else spent the night there. Celibacy was not normal for Gustav unless he was fixated on and hunting down a new lover. Well, Driesler was away, so perhaps Gustav would play.

*

Edeltraud's navigation skills proved equal to the job. Only half an hour after their estimated time of arrival of eight p.m., Siegfried drove up the narrow, hedge-bound lane he dimly remembered from his early schooldays. It was still broad daylight, with the sun streaming over the distant escarpment of Hay Bluff, as he negotiated the last bend and was faced at last by the farmhouse he had once run away from as an eight-year-old, in a bid to reach Germany and his mother. It was weird being back, especially as the old fears and hatred of those years were still fresh in his memory. He drove slowly, making use of the gravel turning area at the end of the lane, then, almost reluctantly, applied the handbrake.

"We're here," he declared rather superfluously, as the others were already streaming out of the car to meet the familiar figures gathering by the seldom-used front door of the house.

Siegfried found his own reservations reflected by Katherine who, despite trying hard, was not succeeding in sounding pleased to see him.

"Welcome back, Siegfried," she said in German, placing her hands on his upper arms and stretching up to give a brief peck on his cheek. "Did you have a good trip?"

"Very good, thank you." The awkwardness between them proved overwhelming, and Katherine quickly turned to the Röbels.

It was left to Karl to make a fuss of his eldest son with a hug and a gentle thumping of his back.

"It's good to have you here at last! We're so glad you could come, especially with having to leave Sophie behind at such a crucial time for her. Is she well?"

Siegfried managed to relax more, although he still felt ill at ease. "Yes. Blooming, as they say, and walking much better now, though she still needs her wheelchair at times. She should get on a lot better once the baby's born."

"That's marvellous."

"She sends her love, by the way."

His words sounded surprisingly genuine. Karl told himself to stop being so suspicious of his son, though whether Sophie truly accepted him now was another matter. The little he had seen of her made him doubt she would be easily swayed, whatever Siegfried said. He saw Wolf and Sabina had begun shepherding everyone around the outside of the house and followed them into the garden where a rustic table, benches and numerous seats were stationed near the old pear tree. He checked that Richard and Paul were assuming their duties as waiters, handing round glasses of home-brewed cider to the thirsty travellers. Picking up two glasses from Paul's tray he offered one to Siegfried.

"Did you meet up with Opa and the others on the boat?" Karl asked him.

"Yes. We managed to stick together from Harwich as far as er ... Gloucester." He had trouble pronouncing the name, and Siegfried remembered with some embarrassment that Gloucester was where the police had found him during his youthful escape bid. Rejecting the memories he carried on: "But they all stopped for petrol. We decided to come on ahead to save four carloads arriving all at once."

"Good idea. So they shouldn't be far behind you."

"No. Rudi said he'd be able to recognise the way up from the village all right."

"That sounds like them now!" Richard called out, hurrying along the flagstone path to the front gate.

Everyone except the Röbels followed suit, crowding into the lane as three more cars with German registration plates squeezed into the small parking area, over-spilling back down the lane. Bodies piled stiffly out of cars, backs were slapped and cheeks were kissed. Proudly Karl led his father to the garden, where Dieter stood a few moments and gazed around at the English farm his son had taken over and made his own. He could only see a small part of it, but what he could see impressed him with its order and air of prosperity.

"Very nice," he declared, finding a brimming glass in his hand and Paul hovering at his side.

"We'll show you round everything tomorrow, Opa. I'm taking the day off school especially because you're here."

"Really? We're honoured!"

Karl saw that everyone by now had a glass of cider or juice, so raised his in a toast. "Finally you've made it. Welcome one and all! *Zum Wohl!*"

Twenty-one other glasses raised and twenty-one voices repeated the toast. "*Zum Wohl!*" Sabina put her arm round Wolf's waist and squeezed. The wedding celebrations had begun and it was all going to be perfect. She looked around her large family and four friends. Tomorrow and Saturday the English family members would be gathering. The enormity of the whole thing suddenly hit her and she felt tears of happiness pricking her eyes. Tomorrow would be her last full day of being single.

Out of the corner of her eye she noticed Siegfried standing slightly apart from everyone else. Overcome with bonhomie she dragged Wolf over to him to include him in the party.

"Come on, best man! Cheer up!" she berated him.

"Sorry, it's been a long drive. Also I ..." He grinned sheepishly. "You'll think me daft."

"No we won't. I promise. Go on."

"I remember spending a lot of time as a boy in a secret hideaway. I was wondering where exactly it was. I don't seem to be able to place it."

"What was it like?"

"Some kind of a bush you could easily get inside. With fluffy seeds!" he added in triumph as memory won over time.

"Sounds like the old-man's-beard," Sabina said. "We used to camp in there too. Are you desperate to see it now?" Siegfried hesitated, but Sabina could see he wanted to wallow in nostalgia, although from what she had understood of his life at the time, there had been precious little he would have enjoyed. "Come on then, I'll show you. Are you coming, Wolf?"

Wolf sensed Siegfried wanted to be alone in his reminiscing. "No. I'll chat to Margit and Co. They look a bit lost."

Sabina led Siegfried away from the crowded garden, out of the garden gate and up a grassy track towards the woods which crowned the hill. Once on the right path, Siegfried let memory guide him and they soon stood by the ancient clump of traveller's-joy clinging to the trees and shrubs at the woodland's edge. He stood staring at it, breath seemingly held in rapt concentration, oblivious to Sabina's presence, although she could strongly sense his desire to be alone.

"I'll leave you to it," she said. He made no response or sign he had even heard her, so she turned on her heel and walked back down the track. The western sun still shone fully on the woodland but the wood's interior seemed strangely gloomy and ominous. She had walked this way a thousand times before, both in daylight and darkness, never feeling as she did now. Something rustled nearby and a male blackbird shot out of a bush in front of her, sounding its loud, rhythmic warning and sending her heart pounding. She tried to shrug off her fear, but was glad when she could once again hear the friendly buzz of voices emanating from the garden. Trotting up the garden path, she made her way back to Wolf's side and slipped her arm through his.

He glanced at her and saw her strange mood. "All right?"

"The ghosts must be out this evening," she said with a laugh, determined to make light of it. "Perhaps Alex Kellett's come back to haunt me!"

"Alex?" Margit asked. "Your friend who died of a heroin overdose?"

"Yes. We used to meet quite often up by the woods. I suddenly got the creeps as I was walking back down here."

"Wolf said you were showing Siegfried where his old hideout was. Is he still up there? Perhaps Alex will pop up out of nowhere and give him a real fright!" she giggled.

Wolf felt uncomfortable. At Siegfried's request, he had supplied Sabina with reefers. She, in her sixteen-year-old innocence, had given one to Alex, who had then procured more from friends at his boarding school. Although Sabina had assured him that Alex's death two years later from a heroin overdose had been inevitable, given his general state of misery, Wolf still felt he had contributed to Alex's death.

"I don't believe in ghosts, but you've certainly managed to put the wind up me!" he told Sabina. "You won't catch me up there!"

Margit was game for some fun. "But what about Siegfried? He's all alone up there."

Heinrich snorted in derision. "The devil looks after his own. He's all right."

Sabina noticed her mother approaching their circle and stepped back to allow her entry. Unaware of the group's concerns Katherine said breezily: "We thought it's about time we went down to Donald and Gertie's and got you all settled in before it gets dark. Our guests are an hour ahead anyway and Opa's quite tired after the long journey so he'll be wanting to bed down here soon."

"OK," Sabina replied and translated quickly for the others' benefit.

"Who's going to go and fetch Siegfried?" Margit asked, her eyes wide in mock terror.

"We can all go," Sabina declared. "It'll give you the chance to stretch your legs a bit more before getting back into the car." Noticing Lothar on the sidelines of the Medebach group, and Rudi's two offspring, Andrea and Martin, starting a squabble over whose turn it was on the old rope swing, Sabina called out to them: "Come on! This way!"

Like the Pied Piper of Hamelin she led them all up to the woods.

*

The old-man's-beard had grown in places and died back in others, but small bodies forcing themselves through its thick stems over many years had kept the inside clear. Finding a gap in the leafy fronds, Siegfried crouched down and pushed his way into the soft green interior. It was, of course, far more cramped than when he had been little, but as he sat down on the dried leaves inside, time receded. Breathing deeply, he opened his mind to the past so he could become again that small boy, so full of hatred and bitterness, who had come up here to read his mother's letters and hide from the father he despised. He had once found a knobbly twig there in the shape of a man, and had cut off its head with Gustav's penknife. He still remembered, as if it had been yesterday, the immense satisfaction that small gesture of defiance had given him.

Now he must concentrate on the terrible task in hand. What Gustav demanded of him could only be achieved by shutting his mind to recent events and summoning up all his old memories. He closed his eyes and allowed the smell of the foliage to permeate his nostrils, mentally transporting himself through all his old resentments. But thoughts of his current dilemma crept in, blocking his journey into the past. To keep Sophie safe he had to sacrifice his father. There was no way out, no escape that he could see. There could be no question of not co-operating with Gustav. The safety of Sophie and the baby depended on it.

Clutching his head in anguish, Siegfried cursed his predicament. 'You can't play with fire without getting burnt' went the old saw, and he had been playing with it for as long as he could remember. At the age of five in Dortmund he had burnt down Herr Cornelius' shed. He had started off bad and gone to worse, to the point where he could cold-bloodedly kill anyone he was ordered to. Now he had been ordered by Gustav to kill his father as a test of his loyalty. Nine months ago he would have relished the prospect. Now things were very different. His former feelings towards his father were still fresh enough in his mind to be accessible. Deeply ingrained animosity had left its mark, but he knew he did not want to kill him now. Although more time was needed to complete the healing process in their relationship, not enough time had yet passed for them to have grown truly close to each other. But his love for Sophie, even for the unborn baby, was undeniable. They were the most important members of his family now, and he must protect them any way he could.

Screwing his eyes up tightly, he made another effort to conjure up images from the past. There was his father lying on the ground, his leg broken after falling from the ladder Siegfried had sabotaged, berating him for not hearing the cries for help. Next came the time his father had punched him on the jaw. But Siegfried could not help his adult mind from making excuses for his father's behaviour. He had sorely provoked his father and the punch had been deserved. Clenching his fists hard under his chin, he tried again. This time he remembered the moment his father rejected him finally, the moment he told him he could go back to his mother in Germany, even if it meant being beaten by his stepfather. The young Siegfried had won the war, and, although initially he had felt the pain of rejection, later he had felt only utter contempt and scorn for his father. That had felt good. That was what he must now hang on to if he was going to succeed.

Loud voices disrupted his concentration. People were calling his name. He had obviously been there longer than he thought. Getting to his knees he crawled out from his old hideaway, stood up and rapidly brushed off the dry leaves and old seeds clinging to him. Down the track a short way was a posse of familiar faces, and upon seeing him, they waved him towards them.

Feeling slightly foolish at being caught out in what they would imagine to be a severe case of nostalgia, he forestalled any comments.

"Is it time to go already?" He had reached the large group of assorted cousins and half-siblings. With a sudden jolt he realised he was the unifying link between them all. Only he was related to everyone else by blood. Nevertheless they would all, even the Röbels, be devastated by what he intended to do. He felt his recent resolve begin to waver. Clenching his fists at his side he mercilessly shoved aside such weakness. He had to think of Sophie!

The others did not notice his distraction, being too concerned with frightening away the ghost of Alex Kellett. Sweeping Siegfried up into their midst, they trooped noisily back down the hill to the awaiting family elders.

Glad to see his son back in the thick of things, Karl nodded him over and asked with a smile: "Been exploring old haunts, Siegfried?"

Siegfried looked his father boldly in the eye and without hesitation replied: "Yes, and reviving old memories too."

"Really?" Karl asked dubiously. "Pleasant ones, I hope."

"Y-e-e-s." His own uncertainty made Siegfried inwardly swear and strengthen his resolve to show nothing of his turmoil to the world outside.

Karl put his hand on his son's shoulder. "I expect this is difficult for you, coming here. It's all right, I understand. Take your time to settle in."

Siegfried felt the urge to look at the grass under his feet, but managed to avoid the temptation. "It's all right. I've no problem. I'm fine."

Karl gave Siegfried's shoulder a squeeze. "Good. Oh, and any time you want to phone Sophie, just go ahead. You must be worried about her."

Siegfried's reply could not have been more heartfelt. "I am, *Vater*. You don't know how much I am."

ELEVEN

"Message from Wildfowl," Sophie read from the letter delivered to her parents' house that morning. "You are asked to be waiting this afternoon, Saturday, at two p.m. near the duck house by the village pond."

So they had finally contacted her, and exactly when Siegfried was away. They had even known she would be staying with her parents. She had to laugh at the association of Wildfowl with duck houses. Was it designed to put her at ease? If so, they had succeeded. She knew better than to expect any more details. Whoever was meeting her would find her if, and only if, they thought the coast was clear. The village pond was accessible by wheelchair, so there would be no problem going there alone. At a pinch she could have walked there, but did not want to over-exert herself. Her parents had to be ultra-careful about being seen again with neo-Nazis, so there was no way they could or should accompany her.

At five to two her mother helped her manoeuvre her wheelchair out of the front door then she set off up the road to the pond. As village ponds went it was quite manicured, having a paved path all around with several benches to sit upon and throw bread to the incumbent ducks. A willow draped its fronds into the water near the duck house, dominated at present by a large grey and white Muscovy duck. Sophie stopped by the bench nearest the duck house and looked around. A mother with a pram and a toddler running beside it were circling the pond, while an old man in hat and coat despite the warm day occupied a nearby bench. Sophie looked at her watch. It was just after two, but no doubt whoever was meeting her was assessing the situation. She had brought some bread with her as cover, so opened up the bag on her lap and began breaking small lumps off and throwing it to the ducks, who rushed over in a flurry of wings and excited quacks.

Presently she realised the old gentleman was shuffling slowly her way. Puffing and wheezing he sat down again on the bench beside her.

"Hello, Sophie," Gustav's gentle voice came from underneath the hat.

Careful not to react, Sophie apparently spontaneously offered him some bread to throw to the ducks. Gustav made a show of polite surprise and acceptance, sliding nearer to reach more easily from the bag.

"Another hour local time and they'll all be at the church, " he said softly. "I don't suppose young Sabina would welcome any 'interruptions' on her wedding day, would she?"

Sophie looked askance at him. "Sorry?" Gustav's brown eyes were boring into hers, seeking information and finding it.

"You don't know what I mean, do you?" he asked in surprise. He had assumed Siegfried would have discussed his intentions with her, if not the details, bearing in mind how like-minded they were.

"No. Should I?"

"I thought you might."

"Is that what you came for? To find out if I knew something ... whatever?"

"Partly." Gustav threw another handful of bread to the gaggle of impatient ducks at his feet. So, Sophie knew nothing. Siegfried was either keeping his cards very close to his chest or had no intention of carrying out his orders. A pity for Sophie. She was a bright girl. He would be sorry to lose her.

Throwing a last handful to the ducks he decided there was no point in hanging around longer than necessary. He had all the information he was likely to glean from her. Keeping his eyes on the ducks he asked: "You'll tell Siegfried I was here, of course?"

Again she was not sure what he meant. "Do you want me to?"

"Yes." Gustav felt Siegfried must be convinced of the threat to Sophie and her unborn child. He needed Siegfried back in the fold, under duress if necessary. It would be easier to order Sophie's execution than Siegfried's, but hopefully it would never come to that. Siegfried *would* obey orders. He *must*!

Sophie grew impatient. "Oh come on, Gustav! This is all so melodramatic. I know we have to be careful, but really! Or are you simply practising a new role for a spy film, or something? I must say, your disguise fooled me."

"This is no joke, Sophie. Watch yourself!" With that warning, he slowly stood up and shuffled off towards the village's main street, scattering aggrieved ducks as he went.

Watching him walk away, Sophie felt a chill pervading her body. Gustav was double-checking on Siegfried, that she could deduce. But what about?

From his hiding place in a nearby shrubbery, Christian Bracht was equally perplexed.

*

Gustav shuffled into his car and drove off, carefully keeping to the speed limit within the village, then speeding off and discarding his disguise once on the road back to Dortmund. Always alert for possible surveillance, he noticed once again the green VW desperately trying to keep up with him. Easing his foot off the accelerator, Gustav allowed his Mercedes to slow to a more comfortable speed for his former lover.

Christian's dedication was commendable, even if his performance was not. He was becoming a nuisance and needed seeing to.

At the first opportunity Gustav stopped at a café for a cup of coffee. He took his time, watching through the window to see if Christian left his car, which was now parked a discreet distance from his own. There was no sign of life. Draining his cup he left the café and walked briskly across to Christian's car. Standing by the locked passenger door he waited for a startled Christian to lift the catch and allow him in. He sat down and came straight to the point.

"What's your game? Why are you following me?"

Resting his hands on the steering wheel in front of him Christian made an effort to appear nonchalant. "Can't live without you, I suppose," he said eventually. "I want to be with you, be a part of your life, even if only at a distance."

"I don't like it," Gustav snapped. "You're history. I don't want to see you following me again. Is that clear?"

Hearing it again so brutally proved too much for Christian's tenuous self-control. "Please, Gustav! I miss you, I love you! Can't you understand that? How can you just shut me out so completely after all we had together?" Tears were welling in Christian's eyes. Angrily he wiped them away with his hand.

With a despondent sigh Gustav realised this was a bigger problem than he had thought. The young man was besotted with him.

"Look," he said more gently. "I'm sorry you feel more strongly than I do, but that's life. I want a break from being involved with anyone and –"

"What about that Siegfried Driesler! Aren't you involved with him?" Christian blurted out.

Stunned and appalled by the extent of Christian's knowledge, Gustav had to take stock of the situation.

Mistaking Gustav's pause for guilt, Christian barged on: "I've seen you meeting him, and the way you touched him on the shoulder. I know the look you gave him. You've got him lined up as your next lover, haven't you!"

"Now wait a minute, Christian. You're –"

"How can you do this to me, Gustav?" Christain pleaded, reaching for Gustav's hand.

Snatching away his hand Gustav barked: "That's enough!" He opened the car door and turned to get out. "It's none of your business," he said over his shoulder. "Leave me alone or you'll be sorry! Go back to Berlin and find yourself a job and someone else. I don't want to see you ever again. Clear?"

Without waiting for Christian's answer he stood up and marched over to his car, fuming with rage at Christian's intrusive adherence. When he drove off he noticed Christian did not follow, and his rage gradually began to subside. He did not want to have to resort to more desperate measures. Despite what he had said, he was still fond of the young man.

*

All eyes were on Sabina as she appeared at the doorway of St Michael and All Angels, Penchurch. Swathed in the simple white 'Lady of Shallott' dress, she clung onto her father's arm. He smiled encouragingly and began to lead her up the aisle to the strains of the 'Bridal Chorus' from *Lohengrin*. Behind them, wearing dresses of pale lilac satin, came the two bridesmaids, Margit and Sabina's best school chum, Amanda. The small church was packed, and Karl was pleased that Richard and Paul had managed to divert a large proportion across to the groom's side to join Wolf, Siegfried and the remaining Röbel three, with Werner and Vera amongst them. Robert Murdoch and his family also swelled the ranks on the right hand side of the church, no doubt remembering the similar problem at Karl and Katherine's wedding, when the vast majority of the guests were the bride's.

Ahead of them at the altar steps stood Wolf and Siegfried, reasonably alert after the party of the night before, when Wolf had revealed his nervousness about speaking English in front of so many people. He looked confident enough now, Karl thought. He led Sabina past a host of smiling faces, before coming to a halt next to Wolf and Siegfried. Wolf took his place beside Sabina, and the organ fell silent as the ceremony began.

After giving her away, Karl left his daughter's side to stand beside Katherine in the front pew. Holding her hand he watched with pride as vows were given, rings exchanged and his only daughter took another man's name; a name that had caused him so much grief and pain. Beside him he felt Katherine wipe away a tear and he turned to her but she looked serenely up at him, just as she had twenty-one years ago and only a few paces away from where they now stood. He felt an overwhelming need to reaffirm how much he loved her, to renew the vow he had so shamefully broken. As Wolf spoke the words out loud, so Karl mouthed them to Katherine.

"I do."

He saw she understood, and when it was Sabina's turn to respond, Katherine too mouthed the same words as her daughter. He hoped it was a final healing of the wound. The trauma of the past year could finally be laid to rest.

The wedding service passed without mishap and the afternoon sun shone brightly as the happy couple left the dusky-red stone church and posed for photographs in the churchyard. Locals thronged outside to view the spectacle of so many Germans gathered in their village, while the local Press took advantage of the event to glean an interesting story and photographs of the groom's and best man's unusual outfits.

There were many in the village who remembered the best man as a troublesome eight-year-old who had proved too much of a handful for his father and stepmother and had been packed off back to Germany. Siegfried was aware of the curious stares and whisperings of the crowd and felt old hostilities rising to the surface. Of all the visitors he knew he was least welcome, and had trouble refraining from glaring back at the likes of Mrs Winters. Twice he had wounded her son, John, at school, the second time with Gustav's penknife. He only recognised her now by the large wart on the side of her nose, as she had been dubbed 'Witch Winters' by the other schoolchildren. Memories such as these, buried for nearly twenty years, were surfacing freely, but he needed more to fire up the old resentments and make his task easier.

Standing still beside Wolf for yet another photograph, a solitary black face over by the lych gate suddenly caught Siegfried's eye. He was instantly reminded of his Caribbean honeymoon, of Sophie's accident, and of his need to get this job done for Sophie and the baby's sakes.

"Thank goodness that's over!" Wolf muttered to him, as the photographer turned his attention to the bride and bridesmaids. "I'm getting bloody hot in all this lot."

They moved over into the shade of the yew hedge where many guests stood awaiting the call for the group photograph. While exchanging a few comments on the service with Heinrich, Siegfried became aware of a figure beside him and turned to see who it was. Towering over her, all he could see at first was a floppy-brimmed straw hat trimmed with large silk roses. As its owner looked up at him her black face was revealed.

"Judy!" he gasped. Struck dumb by surprise and a sudden lack of English he could only blink in astonishment.

Judy gave one of her deep, throaty laughs at his shock. "Surprise! I asked Mrs Driesler, Katherine, not to tell you I was comin'. I wanted to see de look on your face when you saw me, and it was wort' it!" She giggled heartily again. "Yep, it sure was wort' it!"

Siegfried found his voice at last. "Why ... how are you here?"

Heinrich appeared nonplussed, as much by Siegfried conversing with a coloured woman, especially one who seemed so friendly towards him, as by the change into English. Stepping aside, narrowly avoiding Katherine's father's headstone, he left them to it.

"It's a long story, as dey say," Judy chortled. "Mrs Driesler's cousin's daughter is a friend of mine at St Thomas' Hospital in London. We met by chance when Mrs Driesler was in town buyin' her weddin' outfit. Her name straightaway connected her to you, and she was kind enough to invite me here so I could meet you again." She paused for breath before continuing, "How is your wife now?"

It was all nearly too much for Siegfried to follow, but he felt he had the gist and answered happily, "She's much better now. She can walk a little bit. But ... do you know ... she will soon have a baby?"

"No-o-o-o!" Judy grabbed his arm in her excitement. "Really? You must be t'rilled." She gave him a sly nudge. "Our Caribbean sunshine did some good, eh?"

Siegfried could not help grinning back at Judy's forthright, friendly manner. "Yes. It was good."

"Is your wife here?"

"No. The journey was too much."

"Of course." Overflowing with glee, she grabbed his arm again. "You will let me know when it's born, won't you, Mr Driesler? I can't wait to write and tell my folks at home. My ma'll be crochetin' a shawl for the baby the moment she hears."

Siegfried's English was beginning to let him down. 'Shawl' sounded like '*Schal*', and in connection with babies it was probably what she meant. "Thank you."

Judy was already burrowing in her handbag and pulled out a pencil and old envelope. "Here, let me have your address so she can send it on to you."

Siegfried wrote it down carefully, then realised he would need hers to inform of the baby's arrival. He did not have his usual address book on him so had to get Judy to raid her bag again for another scrap of paper. By this time the group photograph was being called and everyone made their way across the grass to gather around the bride and groom.

Judy found her way back to Shirley's side, and whispered: "I don't believe a word bad about Siegfried. He's just as I remember him."

"I haven't met him properly yet," Shirley whispered back. "I'll reserve judgement until I have." She set her mouth in a smile and looked towards the camera.

The photographs finally over, Wolf and Sabina processed towards the lych gate under a shower of confetti, to where the gleaming horse and cart stood waiting to take them to the Murdochs' large, Victorian house on the hillside behind Penchurch. The guests followed at their own speed, in their own manner, arriving at Yew Tree Lodge in dribs and drabs. In the hall they were greeted by the bride and groom, and by the bride's parents. Richard and Paul had already stationed themselves at the drinks' table in the living room, handing out glasses of sherry or lemonade.

Sabina felt ecstatic as she kissed one cheek after another. The day was going perfectly, and the weather had not let them down. It meant the guests could wander in and out of the house and around the large gardens, and nobody would feel cramped. The gentle breeze served only to cool, and would not create a problem with tablecloths and napkins. They had decided to risk eating outside, after hearing the weather forecast, and the three ladies hired from the village for the day were busy laying out the food on trestle tables in the shade. At her side Wolf did his best to greet everyone politely and work out who they all were, although she noticed Siegfried keeping out of the limelight. She turned her attention back to the next guest in line.

"Shirley! How lovely to see you. Thank you so much for coming."

"Congratulations, Mrs Garisch. May I kiss the groom?"

"Be my guest!" Sabina laughed, then smiled warmly at Shirley's nurse friend. "You must be Judy, Siegfried's saviour. My mother was telling me how you met in London. What a coincidence! Have you spoken to Siegfried yet?"

"Yes, briefly. I hope to have a longer chat later. But I must congratulate you, Mrs Garisch, on your special day and on your lovely husband. Isn't he charmin'!"

Sabina knew Judy was looking beyond Wolf's warm green eyes, brown hair and even white teeth to his innermost qualities. "I think so." She turned to her new husband and explained in German: "This is Judy, who was such a help to Siegfried in St Lucia."

Wolf instantly sprang to attention, took Judy's hand and kissed the back of it. "I am honoured to meet you," he said in English.

Judy giggled loudly at all the fuss being made of her. "Anyone else would do the same."

"Not anyone," Wolf contradicted her. "You were ... important to Siegfried. I thank you."

Judy felt she had held up everyone else for long enough. With a smile and a kiss for the bride and groom, she moved on down the reception line. She received a warm smile and a friendly handshake from Katherine Driesler, then came face to face for the first time with Siegfried's father. She gave him a long look as they shook hands.

She saw the same eyes as Siegfried's, but with more depth of feeling and without the reserve she now realised was present in the younger Driesler's eyes. When before she had felt happy to believe Siegfried's sincerity, suddenly she could see what true honesty in those eyes would look like, and it was not the same.

"Welcome, Miss Bridges," Karl greeted her warmly.

"Judy, please." She hung onto his hand a while longer, not wanting to be moved along. "What a lovely family you have, Mr Driesler. You must be very proud of them all."

"I am, Judy. But I must thank you for what you did for Sophie at the accident. I might not be looking forward to my first grandchild's arrival without you."

"Oh, dat was nuttin'. Just doin' what I'm trained to do."

"We're all grateful, Judy." The firm clasp of his hands about hers reinforced his words.

I believe this man, Judy thought to herself. But what is more, I'm not so sure now about Siegfried. Something in him has changed since I first met him on St Lucia, and it's not for the better. She remembered the look the young German standing with Siegfried in the churchyard had given her. But she was aware of Siegfried's past now, of his former neo-Nazism. That other young man probably thought Siegfried still held similar beliefs – or held them himself.

Judy grinned and moved on to do a spot of stirring.

Karl watched her go. So that was the person who had helped Siegfried turn away from Nazism and made him appreciate his own family. They had a lot to be thankful to Judy Bridges for! He had felt his own soul being examined as she had looked into his eyes. He just hoped he had passed the test.

He looked back towards the doorway. A few more guests were still to be received, Olive and John Thornton amongst them. John's wheelchair had delayed them, getting it in and out of their car, but now they were here and the celebrations could start. Katherine, looking every inch the bride's mother in her green and gold outfit, finally passed on the last guest to him and then he was free to mingle.

"Here, Dad," Paul said, handing him a glass of sherry. "You look as though you could do with this!"

"A bucket of water would be more like it!" Karl retorted, running a finger round his collar and feeling extremely overdressed on such a hot day.

Katherine came to his rescue with a glass of lemonade. "Come on outside where there's some breeze. Most people seem to be out in the garden now."

Karl followed her and the bridal couple through the Murdochs' living room and down the two stone steps into the old conservatory. Hurrying through its oppressive heat they stepped out into the fresher air of the garden. Werner and Donald had spent many hours weeding, trimming and tidying ready for the big day and the garden was looking magnificent in a riot of summer blooms. He noticed his father standing with Werner and Donald, examining the extensive herb garden. The other members of his family all seemed at ease, chatting with each other or making the effort to communicate in English with Katherine's relatives. Completing his sweep of the garden, Karl spotted Siegfried sitting alone on the low wall enclosing the rose garden. Something about his apparent isolation made Karl join him, brushing a few crumbs of soil from the top of the wall before he sat down.

"All right?" Karl asked.

"Yes, fine," Siegfried replied a shade too quickly.

"You just looked a bit lonely. Missing Sophie?"

"I suppose that must be it. Also ... I don't feel ... accepted here."

"They'll get used to you. Go and chat to a few of them. By the time you've made your speech they'll love you. It's a good one and shows you as very much a part of the family."

Siegfried smiled. "Yes, thanks to your little 'alterations'! It's just as well you've translated it for me. I'd never have managed it on my own."

"Nor Wolf, either! At least it means we all have to keep our speeches short, even if we do have to say them twice over." Karl decided Siegfried was man enough to look after himself and rose to leave. "Speaking of which, I was going to go over mine in my head before we eat. Excuse me, won't you?"

Siegfried watched his father wander off down the path to the large, enclosed vegetable garden, then breathed a huge sigh of relief. What an ordeal that was! He took out his handkerchief and wiped the sweat off his brow. He could feel himself being sucked into the family vortex, despite battling against the current. It was imperative he stayed outside. His family was in Soest, he reminded himself focusing on the golden rain of the nearby laburnum tree.

Laburnum and yew. One of the things he had remembered on his visits to the house as a boy was Dr Murdoch's repeated warnings about their potentially lethal nature. They had fascinated the young Siegfried, although he had never tried them out. Poisoning had not seemed dramatic enough at that time, although since then he had used many different methods of annihilation. That had been his strength: his ability to suit the manner of death to the circumstances.

A shadow fell across him and he looked up. It was Judy.

"A penny for them," she offered.

"*Wie bitte*? Sorry. I mean ... I don't understand."

"What were you thinking?" she explained, sitting down carefully, so as not to spill her sherry. "You seemed miles away."

"I was in Soest." It was a convenient excuse. Everybody believed him.

"Love is a funny t'ing, isn't it?"

He looked at her, awaiting explanation, which she was quick to give.

"You're sittin' dere, mindin' your own business, and whoom! It grabs you and won't let go. Changes your whole life, it does, and you can't do nuttin' about it."

"That is not true. It is always possible to ... think for yourself."

"No-o-o-o," she replied adamantly. "In my experience, love wins every time."

"Your ...experience is different than mine."

"Maybe you just haven't seen the end yet." She patted his knee in a motherly fashion. "Come on. I came to fetch you. Everyone's startin' to line up for food. You don't want to miss out, do you?"

He cursed that hand on his knee. What was it about Judy that breathed confusion into him?

"No. I am hungry." He stood up, offering his hand to help her up off the wall. "I hope there is much to eat."

Somehow her hand transferred itself to his arm, and he found himself escorting her to the trestle tables groaning with cooked meats and salads. Most of the guests had already started to tuck in as they joined the end of the queue. Seating was informal around more trestle tables and chairs borrowed from the village hall. His plate piled high with food, Siegfried felt himself towed in Judy's wake towards a table where only English people sat. Casting his eye around in desperation, Siegfried could see no spare places at tables occupied by Germans. Sensing his intent and refusing to allow him to break away, Judy shepherded him into a place between the Rev. John Thornton in his wheelchair and Gertie Murdoch. He did not see the unobtrusive nod of thanks Gertie gave Judy as she settled down next to Robert and Alice Murdoch.

"How's your head after last night, Siegfried?" Robert asked him jovially. "I hear the party got quite riotous after we 'oldies' left!"

"No problem," Siegfried declared. "I can drink. I learned it in the army." He could remember the Murdochs well, all of them, from his time there as a boy. They had always been kind to him, despite his aggression, but he felt uncomfortable with them now. It was as though they were well practised at dealing with potential troublemakers, and were engaged in that activity right now. John Thornton's priestly, slightly censorious air was also vaguely familiar. Siegfried felt himself bristling under their combined gaze, sure they would interrogate him about his new life. He wanted to impress them, needed them to like him, but his other more pressing need was to distance himself from them and everything to do with his father. To do that he had to take control.

"You were always keen to join the army," Donald Murdoch said lightly. "Did it live up to your expectations?"

Siegfried was surprised how well he was coping with English. He must have picked up more than he had realised as a boy. "No. I wanted to fight, but of course for we Germans it is not allowed." He grinned disarmingly at them all. "But now I will soon be a father I do not wish to fight. War is something for young men without families, yes?"

"No," Judy protested. "Nobody should fight a war."

"Naturally. But sometimes a war is ... a war just comes, and men must fight. Some men are ready to fight, but I no longer wish so."

"I'm glad to hear that," Donald applauded as John Thornton too gave a nod of approval.

"I remember with our generation in the Great War, don't you recall, Donald?" the Rev. Thornton began, his fingers forming an elegant spire in front of his chin. "We were all so anxious to go off and fight for our country. We none of us knew what we were letting ourselves in for until we were confronted by the stench of rotting flesh"

"John, we are eating," Olive Thornton swiftly interrupted. "I don't think we want to hear about –"

"Sorry, dear. It's just that when I get back with Donald here ..." His voice trailed off under his wife's glare.

Alice Murdoch, Robert's mousy-looking but vivacious wife, stepped in and steered the conversation onto safer ground by asking Judy about weddings in St Lucia. Siegfried was able to withdraw his attention, apparently concentrating on spearing a recalcitrant piece of tomato with his fork, but inwardly trying to deal with the turmoil within. It was all Judy's fault. If she weren't here it would have been so much easier. During the two days so far he had almost succeeded in working himself into the right frame of mind to deal with his father. He still had not worked out a method that was sure-fire, but he had begun to feel more confident in his task. And then Judy had turned up with her big brown eyes and infectious giggle, and sent him into turmoil.

He looked up from his plate to see her happily conversing with Alice, Gertie and Olive, instant friends with them all. Robert, Donald and John Thornton were likewise engaged in discussion, leaving himself on the sidelines as an observer and outsider. The sense of exclusion he had previously sought and cultivated now only provoked a deep loneliness and desire to be included. Seeing Judy he should have thought of Sophie and thus the need to kill his father. But it was not working like that. True, he thought of Sophie, but then his reconciliation with his father flamed into his memory. Judy was the spark for that ignition. She exuded warmth, compassion, love and rectitude. He must distance himself from her.

Feigning thirst he slipped away from the table and helped himself to a long drink from the assortment of bottles laid out near the food. He stood there a moment, drinking deeply from his glass and observed the festivities. Sabina and Wolf at the table in the shade of the yew tree looked radiantly happy and too engrossed in each other to eat much. Katherine was fussing over Opa, making sure he had enough to drink, while his father was ... watching him.

Their eyes locked across the intervening tables of guests. Guilt shot through Siegfried so unexpectedly it caused him to look away. Cursing his lack of control he looked back at his father, who was walking over to him.

"You should be sitting with us, Siegfried!" Karl called out. "The best man should be with the groom, giving him moral support before he has to make his speech."

Siegfried forced himself to grin. "What about me? I have to speak too."

"And me, so come and join us."

Siegfried's hand crept into the pocket of his loden jacket where he had hidden some laburnum flowers and a single early pod of seeds. Now was not the time. He still had three days left. He withdrew his hand and strolled across to the bridal table. Wolf beckoned him to the empty chair beside him.

"Where've you been? I need you here!"

"Judy kidnapped me," he explained ruefully. "Besides, there wasn't a seat free when I came to eat."

Sabina laughed at his pathetic excuse. "I don't believe it of you! The Great Siegfried kidnapped by a woman?"

Siegfried sat down with his empty glass still in his hand. Katherine was quick to notice and moved over from Dieter's side, bringing a bottle of German white wine with her.

"This is one you brought, isn't it, Siegfried? It's rather good. You'll have to bring some more of this next time you come." She filled his glass. "Have some Dutch courage." She saw he had not understood and sought the word for 'courage' in German. "*Mut*," she explained.

If she only knew, Siegfried thought. If she only knew.

TWELVE

Through tears of rage Christian watched Gustav driving off from the café. His impulse to follow was thwarted by the tempest within himself. Embracing the steering wheel, Christian sobbed for a full five minutes as all his emotions spilled out and ran down his nose. He felt no better when he stopped crying. His throat hurt, his eyes were puffy and his nose was still running tears but he could not sit there all day. Giving his nose a final blow he started the car's engine and set off towards Dortmund, but after a few kilometres he realised something was pulling him back towards Soest. He had unfinished business there.

At the next junction he turned off and drove back in the opposite direction, his mind racing with the traffic. Gustav didn't want him anymore because he had a new quarry – Driesler. So what was the solution? Get rid of Driesler, or else put him out of the running somehow. And how to do that?

He pulled up twenty minutes later outside the chalet-style house he knew was the Drieslers'. The cul-de-sac, *An der Waldecke*, was deserted. No net curtains twitched or dogs barked, but, cautious as ever, Christian drove off again and parked in the village's main square. His Berlin registration plates were too obvious to be seen so near the house. He walked back to *An der Waldecke*, up to the Drieslers' front door and rang the bell. Expecting and getting no reply he hurriedly ducked round the side entrance and into the back garden. A pair of squirrels chittered at him from the woodland over the fence but he ignored them, peering instead through the kitchen window. Everything was tidily put away. He could see the rest of the house through glass doors leading to the dining room and hall. He stepped back and peered upwards, locating the bathroom by its frosted glass window and the main bedroom by its small balcony. A barred window at ground level indicated the cellar.

Housebreaking was not something Christian had tried before, and it did not seem an easy task as all the doors and windows looked well secured. Seeking inspiration he looked through the garden-shed window. The usual array of tools and garden furniture met his eye, along with the motor mower and petrol can.

He was unprepared for the idea that forced itself into his mind at the sight of the petrol can. A part of him recoiled at the horror of it, but another part embraced the solution it offered. Eyes riveted on the can, he saw his rival disposed of simply and with minimal risk to himself. But the idea terrified him. Not a violent person, Christian had never intentionally harmed anyone. Now he was contemplating maiming or murdering a man and his disabled, pregnant wife. Yet she had a connection with Gustav too, one that Christian could not fathom out. Gustav's disguised and covert approach to Frau Driesler perplexed him no end.

A sudden flash of gold through the nearby trees finally drew his gaze from the shed. The squirrels were racing along the branches like tongues of flame in a forest fire. Christian watched them a moment before their haste made him realise he had spent long enough there. He must be careful in case anyone had seen him approaching the house.

Leaving nonchalantly by the side entrance he was careful to stroll up the quiet road and back towards the market place. Since it was not the first Saturday in the month, the shops had already shut for the afternoon. Only the occasional window-shopper and a few children riding bicycles disturbed the scene. Keeping his face to the shop windows, Christian reached his car and sank down onto the seat, feeling as guilty as if he had already done the deed. Could he possibly do such a monstrous thing, and get away with it?

Slowly he drove out of the square and set off back towards Dortmund. Gustav filled his thoughts, memories of nights of passion, meals shared, conversations enjoyed. Gustav was so strong, so clever, always knew the right way to do a thing. Without Gustav Christian felt helpless. Life had no meaning without him to share it with. If Gustav was ever going to look at him again, then Driesler had to go. There was no avoiding it.

By the time he had parked outside his tiny rented flat in Dortmund, Christian knew he had no choice in the matter. Another thing he had no choice in at the moment was earning a living. His funds were all used up and the only way to get more quickly was to find a client willing to pay for his body. Food would have to wait until later.

*

The round of applause that greeted the end of his speech surprised Siegfried in its warmth and sincerity. Gertie Murdoch was beaming at him, Robert looked pleased and Judy gave him a broad wink. The English speakers had had to wait to hear their version, but it had obviously been worth waiting for.

"Well done," Wolf murmured in his ear. "They've taken you into their hearts at last."

"Seems like it." Siegfried glanced at his father, who was also beaming at him. He smiled back, hiding his despair that no matter how hard he tried, he could not hate him again. Everyone else could relax now the speeches were over, but Siegfried felt unbearably tense. He had to get away from the overwhelming sense of family unity that surrounded him. As the wedding guests began to mingle again Siegfried felt able to sneak away by himself. Wandering down the flagstone path towards the far end of the Murdochs' extensive garden he came to a small orchard, the branches beginning to set with immature apples. Amongst the trees a garden seat faced out across the valley, its back to the rest of the garden. Siegfried sighed and slumped down onto it, his face grim. He looked at his watch. It was half past six, and the sun was still hot. Honey bees buzzed about the clover in the grass. He wished his life could be as simple as theirs. They had their queen and hive to serve with no other demands made on them. Decision-making was a chore unknown to them, whereas human beings developed the ability to override instinct. He must choose between his wife and child on the one hand, and his father on the other. All his instincts went with his wife, but his mind kept telling him there was no answer.

It was hopeless. Gustav believed his killer instincts remained intact. But the months of dealing with Sophie's accident, the problems with the business and his father's trial, impending fatherhood and the need to buy a house had all served to deflect his thoughts from his former purpose in life. He had changed more than he realised. It was not simply a question of finding his father. He had found an alternative way of life: a life that no longer held a place for Nazi doctrine. Yet he was unable to escape its demands. He was trapped, his task inescapable. He had no choice but to comply.

"Do you mind if I join you?"

There was no mistaking that voice. He looked up and saw his ever-alert guardian angel, Judy, her head haloed by the sun.

"You look as if you need to talk to somebody," she added when he did not reply.

He could not look into the brightness any longer, his gaze dropping to the grass at his feet. Saying nothing, Judy sat down on the bench beside him, waiting patiently for him to speak.

The bees buzzed hypnotically in his ears, the sun beat down on his lowered head. Suddenly the rest of the world did not exist. He was alone in the Garden of Eden, with Judy simply a part of his inner self, a manifestation of his conscience, invisible to others. Her mere presence was enough to give him his answer.

"Why do you do this to me, Judy? I came here to kill my father and now I can not." His hand reached into his jacket pocket, bringing out the laburnum flowers and seeds. He scattered them on the grass, then ground them into the mud with his heel. "There! See? I can't even think of a way to do it. But if I do not, my wife and baby may die. What can I do?" He stared out across the valley, too ashamed to look at her.

Judy somehow contained her shock. She should have expected something like this from a man with such a past as his. She tried to think what to say to him. Whatever she said could make the difference between life and death ... for somebody.

"I don't know. But one t'ing's for sure. You won't be killin' anybody."

"You believe that?"

"Yes," she said emphatically.

"I've killed before."

His stark admission horrified her, but again she controlled her revulsion, knowing he needed her help. "But you never felt guilty before, and now you do."

He thought about that. "No. I don't feel guilty, because then I felt what I did was right."

"Dat's your excuse? Den you're still a Nazi!" She allowed her voice full censure.

He hung his head. "I don't know what I am, Judy." He looked around at the surrounding hills. "Here I am a different person. I thought I would hate it here and could find again the hate in me to kill my father, but everyone is so ..."

"Forgiving?"

Siegfried shrugged, uncertain of what he wanted to say.

Judy too needed clarification. "But why must you kill your father?"

The right words came slowly for Siegfried. "To see if I will obey them still. They are not sure if I am still a Nazi. They ask me to do this as ..."

"As a test of your loyalty still to them?"

"Yes."

"But why your father?"

"Because he killed someone important to them."

"The court said he didn't."

Siegfried shook his head. "No. The court said they could not find him guilty. That is different."

Judy swallowed hard. Suddenly the world was not so cut and dry. She was in the company of killers, and the dreadful thing was she liked both of them – very much. "So what can you do? If you don't kill your father, the Nazis will kill your wife?"

"I'm not sure, as she is ..." He had been going to say 'a loyal supporter', but decided against it.

Judy mistakenly thought he did not know the English word. "Pregnant?" she suggested. "Who else knows about this? Your wife?"

"No. No one else."

"What about your friend, Wolf? Can't you talk to him about it?"

"This is my problem, not Wolf's."

"But he knows these people too, doesn't he? He might have an idea ..." Her voice trailed off as she saw the hopelessness in his eyes. She reached for his hand. "You've shared your problem with me, but I can offer no help except to advise tellin' the police, and I know you won't. Now you *must* share this with your friend."

"No!"

"But you can't kill your father now, because you've told me."

Siegfried looked at her, and for a brief, awful moment she saw the killer in his eyes.

*

Karl had not been able to eat. Too hot, too excited and too busy before the speeches, now he could relax and dip in to the leftovers on the buffet tables. Alice and Gertie were busy slicing up the wedding cake after Sabina and Wolf's ceremonial cutting of it, Katherine was helping Sabina change into her going away outfit up in one of the Murdochs' bedrooms, and Wolf was laughing about something with Margit and Heinrich. Richard, Paul, Lothar, Edeltraud and Roslinde all lounged on the grass together, but of Siegfried there was no sign. Nearly seventy guests were at the reception, but one was conspicuous by his absence.

"Looking for someone?" Robert asked him, likewise finding the need to empty a plate or two of salmon fragments, tomato slices and cucumber.

"Yes. Siegfried."

"I saw him wandering off down the garden towards the orchard."

"Oh?" Karl glanced behind him but verdant shrubs obscured any view of the orchard. "I don't really like the thought of him being alone. Despite what he said in his speech, he still doesn't feel a part of the family, understandably enough."

"He sounded sincere"

Karl raised his eyebrows. "You know what Siegfried's like. Still brilliant at deception, even though he's changed sides."

Seeing the salmon all gone, Robert turned his attention to the beef. "He certainly convinced a few doubters today, I think." He picked up a slice, wrapped it around a gherkin and popped it in his mouth, chewing a few moments before adding: "How much of his speech did you actually write?"

"Not a lot," Karl grinned at his friend's suspicious mind. "Just a few words here and there. I know the British better than he does, and knew what you would like to hear – and what not. Actually it was more what I cut out that was important."

"Like what?"

"Oh, a few references to the dim and distant past, that sort of thing. Subjects best avoided."

Robert saw his opening. "Speaking of which, I haven't really had the chance to ask you how you are. Any problems after your stint inside?"

Karl scowled. "None I haven't dealt with. But this is hardly the time or place to –"

"Alright, alright," Robert interrupted, dismayed to have hit a raw nerve so quickly. "You can tell me later. In the meantime, tell me more about Siegfried. You said he seems to have a lot on his mind." Robert stared over Karl's shoulder. "Talk of the devil, there he is. He looks a bit serious, doesn't he?"

Karl turned and saw Siegfried, accompanied by Judy, walking slowly back towards the wedding party. "Something's going on, and I'm not sure what," he murmured.

Before they had the chance to find out, Sabina emerged from the house in a pastel-blue suit and made a beeline for her father. "We're all changed and ready for the off, but I just wanted a moment to thank you for everything and for your lovely speech. Wolf and I were both very touched." She hugged him then kissed his cheek.

"My pleasure!" he beamed. "I've only one daughter and you've made me very proud." He looked around the garden. "Now, you'd better find that husband of yours and get on your way. Where is he?"

"Heading towards Siegfried," Robert informed them.

They all looked towards the path from the orchard where Judy and Siegfried strolled, deep in conversation, while Wolf approached unobserved.

"I'll go and grab him," Sabina said, setting off towards them.

Siegfried saw Wolf approaching, and behind him Sabina. He abruptly ended his conversation with Judy, who melted away into the shadows. "All ready?" he called to Sabina, seeing her change of clothing.

"Yes. I've come for Wolf," she explained, "but we were wondering what you and Judy were up to."

"Up to? Nothing!" he replied innocently. "We were just talking about family matters and babies." He looked for an escape. "Now I'm thirsty and need a drink."

Sabina sensed a lie but gave up interfering. Instead she turned to Wolf and said: "We'd better say a few goodbyes. Come along."

They wandered off together, wrapped in each other's company, while Siegfried headed for the drinks' table alone. Katherine, who had just emerged from the house, saw him there and noticed he had a strangely faraway look about him. She made her way over to him, feeling more sympathy towards him than she had ever felt before. She had never liked Karl's eldest son, despite the striking similarity in appearance between father and son. Now there was the same air of vulnerability about him she had always found so appealing in Karl, and she found herself wanting to help him.

"Thinking of Sophie?" she asked.

His grey eyes looked down into hers, but his thoughts were hidden from her. She was just deciding that the stubborn little boy of yesteryear had not gone when he nodded almost imperceptibly and her heart warmed to him again.

"I tell you what, Siegfried," she suggested. "Why don't you ask the Murdochs if you can put in a call to Germany. They won't mind and then you can set your mind at rest and enjoy the rest of the day."

He nodded again. "I will do that, as soon as Wolf and Sabina are away."

Katherine smiled. "Good. Send her our love, won't you?" She sensed movement behind her and turned to find Karl.

"Bina and Wolf are ready to go, Schatz. It's time to wave them off."

"Right."

The three of them joined the throng in the drive, where Wolf's car stood bedecked with flowers and toilet paper. The obligatory tin cans were tied to the rear bumper, along with a painted card saying 'Just Married'. Siegfried shook Wolf's hand, kissed Sabina, threw confetti, waved them off, then turned to Dr Murdoch.

"May I use your telephone to call my wife? Katherine said you would not mind."

"Go ahead, laddie," the kindly Scotsman told him. "Katherine's already told me you're worried about her." He pointed in through the open front door. "The phone's in the hall there."

Siegfried leaped the steps to the door and was momentarily blinded by the darkness within until his eyes accommodated to it.

His call was swiftly connected and he was soon speaking to Sophie's father.

"She's out in the garden. I'll call her in," Peter Wendt told him. "Hold on."

Siegfried waited patiently until Sophie's slightly breathless voice came down the line.

"Liebling! How are you? How was the wedding?"

She sounded strained, Siegfried thought. "Great, but ours was better. Wolf and Bina have just left for their honeymoon. But how are you, Schatz? You sound a bit ... odd." Her silence crackled down the line. "Schatz? Are you there?"

"Yes, I'm here. But you're right. Something odd did happen today. I had a ... visitor."

Her hesitation warned him to be discreet on the open telephone line. "Oh? Anyone I know?"

"Yes, you know him very well, from long ago."

Gustav! Siegfried's heart skipped a beat. "What did he want?" he asked, trying to keep his voice steady.

"He asked me some strange, vague questions. I hadn't a clue what he was talking about, but he was content to leave it at that. He seemed to suggest I should tell you he called."

"I see." Siegfried began to tremble with simultaneous fear and anger.

"Is everything all right?" Sophie's voice was trembling too now. "He didn't seem nearly as friendly as usual. In fact he quite frightened me."

Siegfried desperately thought of something to calm her. "It's nothing. He and I have a little bet on about something, but it would ruin it if I told you what it was. Just play along with him and reassure him all's well if he calls again. Oh, and Sophie ..." He knew he might frighten her again but he had to warn her. "Don't go out alone from now on – what with the baby and everything. I don't want you falling over or anything like that. Make sure your parents are with you."

She sounded irritated. "You're getting as bad as they are. Don't worry so much."

"How's the baby? Still kicking?" Having eased the conversation off dangerous ground he listened to her account of her latest purchases for the baby and the state of her back and indigestion problems. He could have listened for longer but was conscious of people gathering in the Murdochs' hall. Some of the wedding guests were preparing to leave. "I'll have to go now, Schatz. It's getting a bit noisy here. I'll phone again tomorrow. Take good care of yourself. I love you." He blew a kiss down the receiver before replacing it in its cradle. He had forgotten to pass on Katherine's message. Never mind. There was always tomorrow.

Robert Murdoch brushed past on his way to the kitchen with an empty jug. "Did you get through all right?"

"Yes, thank you."

"Is Sophie well?"

"Yes, very well."

"Good."

As Robert disappeared down the corridor to the back of the house, Siegfried felt in his pocket. Gustav's penknife was there as usual, and a fragment of laburnum flower, reminders of his commitment to protect Sophie. But now Judy knew. How stupid to have confided in her! What damned foolishness had made him do that? He leaned against the doorframe to the living room, head resting on his left hand. Why was he messing this up? He had done this sort of thing so many times before, but now, when it mattered most, he was just making things harder for himself. Until today he felt he could do it. Until he met Judy again. Perhaps once she left he would forget his qualms. Throughout history sons had murdered their fathers. It was nothing new. It happened all the time. He could do it to protect his wife and child. He had to!

"We're off now, Siegfried," Judy called from the front door.

Startled Siegfried stood upright and turned towards her. Shirley, Evelyn and Bill Bagnold were with her on the steps, Bill's car keys dangling impatiently from his fingers. Siegfried strode over to them, shaking each of the Bagnold's hands before coming to Judy.

"You have a wonderful family here, Siegfried," Judy told him purposefully. "You're lucky to have dem. Enjoy the rest of your stay over here, and remember to let us know when the baby arrives."

My God! Did she know he still had doubts? Siegfried thought. He shook her hand. "Thank you, Judy. It was very good to see you again."

She laughed. "Come on, don't be so formal!" She stood on tiptoe and kissed his cheek, giving herself the chance to whisper in his ear: "Don't disappoint me. You'll find a way round dis, I know you will."

He made no reply, promising nothing. Judy stepped away from him, gave him a last smile of encouragement then joined the Bagnolds as they headed for their car. It was a long way back to South London and they were amongst the first guests to depart. As the car disappeared down the hill of Cutbush Lane, Siegfried felt a curious sense of loss at Judy's departure.

Rejoining the festivities he found most guests prepared to stay much longer, and of course, those Germans staying at Yew Tree Lodge, such as himself, were there to the bitter end. The youngsters present, English and German, were gathering on the croquet lawn, mingling sociably together. Werner and Vera Gimpel had taken it upon themselves to integrate the Medebach elders into the general company, while Katherine and his father sat quietly alone together, gathering their strength and their emotions after seeing off Sabina and Wolf. Dance music played gently from the open windows of the house, but as yet nobody was making a move as a local band was busy tuning up ready to provide the real thing. A gathering at the Murdochs' house was never complete without country dancing.

"It's a shame Wolf and Bina are missing the dancing," his father's voice suddenly interrupted his solitude. Katherine was there by his side too. He had not noticed them coming over to him, so lost in thought was he.

"They should have chosen a hotel closer than Shrewsbury. Sophie and I danced until late in the evening at our reception."

"I think they were glad to have some time to themselves. It's been a busy two days since you lot arrived," Karl said. "And we've plenty more sightseeing to fit in before you go on Thursday. Opa's thoroughly enjoying himself, don't you think?"

Siegfried looked across at his grandfather who was laughing jovially along with Werner, Donald Murdoch and an elderly gent he did not recognise. "Yes, he is."

"Are you enjoying yourself, Siegfried?"

"Why do you ask?"

"You seem to be alone nearly every time I see you."

Siegfried looked down at Katherine and then across to his father again. It was not nosiness, he decided, just concern. "I had a long talk with Judy," he told them lightly. "And now I'm going to join in the dancing. I see the band is ready to play."

Katherine put her hand in his. "Then you and I can have the first dance, Siegfried. Let's get those youngsters on their feet!" She led him over to the croquet lawn, beckoning other guests to join them as they passed. Soon the lawn was covered in couples dancing an energetic polka or gyrating on the spot, according to age and inclination. Karl held his hand out to Gertie, who at first declined, but after a little coaxing was persuaded to glide very gently with him around the lawn.

As darkness began to fall and Werner lit the coloured lanterns dotted about the garden, Siegfried paused with his current dancing partner, Margit, by the laburnum tree. They watched Heinrich cavorting with Amanda on the lawn, while Lothar was equally lively with another of Sabina's old school friends.

"I do miss having family gatherings," Margit said wistfully, lifting the hem of her long bridesmaid's dress to allow some air to circulate round her hot legs. "Promise me, Siegfried, when the baby's born, you'll hold a proper christening and invite as many family members as you can. Especially Mutti."

"You think Paul will really let her come?"

"I don't see how he could stop her."

"He could."

"But he won't. Despite his philandering, he loves her too much to upset her, and there's nothing going to stop her seeing her first grandchild."

"You're forgetting something. You said all the family should be there. That includes my father." Siegfried raised his hand and fingered a frond of laburnum flowers. "Do you think that's such a good idea?"

"Oh, gosh! I hadn't thought. That would be tricky, especially if Katherine came too. But you can't *not* invite one or other of them."

Siegfried plucked the frond from the tree. "Perhaps he won't come."

"Of course he will! You try stopping him!" She noticed the laburnum in his hand. "That stuff's poisonous, you know?"

Siegfried felt himself blanche, but it was too dark for Margit to notice. "Want a drink? I'm thirsty." He dropped the laburnum. It was too obvious now. Both Margit and Judy had seen him with it. He would have to find some other way: a way that not even the suspicious Judy would connect with him – and a humane way.

Shit! He couldn't even think about it now. As he poured them both a glass of cider, he knew time was ticking by and he still had no real plan how to carry out Gustav's order.

*

Sophie returned to her sun-bed in the garden and began to mull over the day's strange events. First there had been Gustav's visit, now Siegfried's phone call and warning to be careful. Sophie recalled Gustav saying as much too, although his actual words were 'Watch yourself'. What had he meant exactly?

Lisl Wendt noticed her daughter's troubled expression as she came out with a tray of cold drinks. She handed Sophie a glass of iced orange juice. "Are you all right, Liebling?"

"I don't know. Gustav is obviously checking up on Siegfried, and Siegfried is worried about me. I'm supposed to report to Gustav if I'm suspicious at all of Siegfried and he seemed to threaten me today, hinting I might come to harm if I don't. Siegfried seems aware of a threat to me too, but tried to fob me off with some cock and bull story about he and Gustav having a bet on. For once I could tell he was lying. He sounded frightened for a moment, although he quickly changed the subject."

"I think we'd better talk about this." Lisl called her husband over from his task of edge-trimming the flowerbeds. "Peter, sit down and have a drink and listen to what Sophie has to say."

Peter Wendt sipped his beer while Sophie recapped her fears about Siegfried. "That's the trouble with Siegfried," he said when she had finished. "You can never be sure what he's doing. It could all be perfectly innocent, or you could turn it right around and say Siegfried's worried that Gustav is up to no good where you are concerned, Liebling. After all, we all know what Gustav's like with the ladies as well as the men. I've rather felt he's always had his eye on you and was glad when you and Siegfried got together."

"No, Papa. It's not like that. This is definitely something between Gustav and Siegfried. My role is merely as a spy for Gustav. I'm to tell him if I have doubts about Siegfried's loyalty, and I think I ..." She hesitated. Could she do it? Could she betray her husband to her parents? Her strong sense of duty prevailed. "I think I'm starting to doubt him again, but I just can't be sure. Everything he says about pretending to have changed his ways makes such sense. Of course he and Wolf have had to try to repair the damage after Josef Garisch made such a hash of things and got himself killed, but sometimes Siegfried seems a bit remote now."

"You think Wolf is just play-acting too?" her father asked carefully. "His mother certainly doesn't. She won't even speak to him, but others amongst us are not so sure."

"I thought there must be some doubt in high places, as he's still alive. Traitors are traditionally hanged, aren't they?"

"Times have changed. We have to be more careful. Wolf will only get his comeuppance once we're convinced of his guilt."

"Convinced? So you're not."

Her father put his finger to his lips. "As you well know, it was Karl who killed Garisch and blew his cover. Wolf only provided the evidence, securing his, and probably Siegfried's, freedom in the process. Let's just say, I've been told his case is on hold. The waters are too muddy still."

Sophie had to smile at Siegfried and Wolf's guile. Siegfried's continued association with Wolf was acting like a protective shield. As long as Siegfried was not under suspicion, then Wolf had a stay of execution. Her smile faded rapidly as she realised she held both of their fates in her hands. Denounce Siegfried and Wolf went too. Gustav was asking an awful lot of her.

THIRTEEN

Richard wanted a quiet word with Siegfried before everyone disappeared off sightseeing round Hereford. He had not had the chance before the wedding, but now things had quietened down a bit, and he reckoned he had got to know Siegfried well enough to make his approach. Never in his wildest dreams had he thought the day would come when he would ask Siegfried for advice, considering how much he had hated Siegfried after their father's arrest, but his anger at Mr Kellett was proving overwhelming.

As he sat in the back of the Land Rover with Paul on the way down to the Murdochs', Richard wondered how best to make his approach. Siegfried had never been an easy person to talk to, holding himself aloof from his half-siblings, although he had been trying hard these past few days to be more friendly. It had helped having all the Drieslers gathered together. If Siegfried had visited on his own it might have been much more awkward for them all. But with so many people milling around, no one would notice if he and Siegfried disappeared into a quiet corner.

By the time they pulled into the Murdochs' semi-circular drive it was already full of cars, the other family members having assembled from their respective billets about the village. Richard realised he would not have much time before they were all ready for the trip into Hereford. His father had hardly applied the handbrake before Richard jumped out and headed for the house. The ornate glass-panelled front door stood wide open. On the front steps his young cousins, Andrea and Martin, sat in the warm sunshine playing with a collection of snails gathered from the garden. Avoiding stepping on the molluscs, Richard headed into the dark recesses of Yew Tree Lodge, seeking out Siegfried. He found him perched on a windowsill in the huge kitchen, mug of coffee in hand, as Gertie and Donald Murdoch nobly struggled to communicate with their guests in a mixture of pigeon English and mime.

"Good morning, Richard!" Gertie beamed at him. "Are your parents with you?"

"They're just coming in." He turned and saw them with his grandfather negotiating the dark passage to the kitchen. "Here they are."

As Gertie waved them in, Richard sidled up to Siegfried. Time was of the essence and he wasted none in small talk. "Can we go outside, Siegfried?" he asked quietly.

Siegfried looked at him in surprise, but drained his mug, put it down in the sink and nodded towards the side door of the house. When they were a safe distance from the house Siegfried stopped and asked: "Well? What is it?"

Richard had to look up into Siegfried's blank grey eyes, which expertly shielded his thoughts from the outside world. Age and height gave Siegfried dominance, and Richard suddenly felt nervous about what he wanted to ask. Completely forgetting his carefully chosen opening he gabbled: "How would you set about paying someone back for something terrible he once did?"

Siegfried's eyes narrowed in alarm. Did Richard suspect him already? Had Judy said anything? Looking past Richard to the house he checked to make sure nobody had followed them out, then scrutinised Richard. "Why do you ask me?"

"You and Heinrich were always plotting against each other, and I'd got the impression you still did that sort of thing ... but for real," Richard mumbled, not wanting to offend his half-brother.

"What sort of thing?" Siegfried snapped.

This was not going well, Richard thought. For some reason he had got Siegfried's hackles up straight away. I mustn't sound accusatory, Richard told himself. "Dealing with nuisances," he explained, as though he meant something as mundane as shovelling away snow. He hurried on: "There's someone I need to deal with, but I'd like some advice on how to do it and not get caught."

"You think I'm an expert at that?" Siegfried asked as casually as he could.

"Well, yes, I mean, I think so." Richard felt he was getting nowhere and needed to hurry things along. "Perhaps if I tell you who it is and why, it'll help."

Siegfried understood at last. Richard did not suspect him at all. He really was asking for help. "Go on then. Who is it?"

Richard sighed. He was over the first hurdle. "Do you remember the Kelletts at Froxley Grange? The big house up the valley."

"Er, vaguely."

"Mr Kellett was engaged to Mum before she met Dad. When he found out she was in love with Dad he ..." He realised he did not know the German word for 'rape' and had to find a way round it. "He did something to her she didn't want."

"He raped her?" Siegfried guessed from Richard's blushing face.

Now Richard had heard the word its meaning sounded right. "Yes. Admittedly this was years ago, but he's got away with it all this time. When I found out I punched him and nearly got into awful trouble with the police and everything, but Mum managed to sort it all out. I still want to see him punished, but of course I'd be under suspicion."

"Does Father know?" Siegfried found himself being drawn into the drama.

"Yes, of course."

"And he's done nothing?"

"He daren't with his record."

Siegfried allowed himself a smile. "No. I can see that." He grew serious again as he thought over the information. Richard was taking it upon himself to be the avenging angel when the true wronged parties were content to let the dust settle. Richard would be heading down a dangerous path if he embarked on revenge. "My advice is to forget about it."

"What?" Richard gasped at Siegfried's totally unexpected response. "I thought you at least would understand –"

"Maybe I do. And maybe I understand more than you do. Leave it be. It's not worth the risk to you, or to Father and Katherine."

"But that's why I'm asking you for help. You could think of a way to pay him back."

"Yes, but not one you would want to, or should, carry out." Siegfried knew he had to drive his point home. He looked hard into Richard's eyes. "Stay out of this. It's not your problem, nor is it mine. I don't want to get involved and you shouldn't either.

You're right, I do have experience of such things, and I know you live to regret it." He laid a friendly hand of warning on Richard's shoulder. "You'll only be harming yourself if you do anything. You get entangled in the web of deceit and can never escape. Believe me!"

Richard was amazed not only by Siegfried's advice, but also by the real pain in his voice.

"You're caught in the web, aren't you?" he said, but Siegfried was already walking back to the house, leaving Richard to wonder exactly what Siegfried was caught up in.

Hearing his name called he ambled back to the kitchen where everybody finally seemed ready to set off. Richard was acting as guide for the livestock market party, which consisted of Lothar, Uwe, Heinrich and Siegfried, so made his way to Siegfried's car, wedging himself onto the back seat alongside Lothar. Siegfried proved to be an aggressive driver, and Richard flinched on a couple of occasions as Siegfried forced his way through the thickening traffic near the market.

"We ought to park soon," Richard suggested, wanting to avoid the numerous cattle trucks and sheep trailers cluttering the area. "There's a place, just ahead on the left."

The din of lowing cattle, bleating sheep, squealing pigs and clanking gates greeted them. Through the cacophony the auctioneer's voice could be heard as the small party threaded its way round the hurdles and pens of the stockyard, the reek of dung and livestock omnipresent. Richard pointed out different breeds, exchanged greetings with local farmers and introduced his relatives. They stood for a while watching a pen of wether lambs being sold, then looked on as a recalcitrant young Hereford bull tried to batter its way out of a pen. Eventually its florid-faced young handler got it going in the right direction towards the sale ring.

"Shall we watch it being sold?" Richard suggested when he sensed his companions had seen enough outside.

There was a general nod of consent and Richard led them into the already crowded ring area. A couple of tweed-clad farmers recognised Richard and made room for him and his four companions. As they stood leaning against a rail, watching the muscular bull paraded round, behaving perfectly demurely at last, Richard spotted another familiar face at the rail, bidding for the bull. He nudged Siegfried and pointed out the stocky figure to him.

"That's Kellett over there. Dark brown jacket and hat, just raised his hand to bid. See him?"

Siegfried followed Richard's gesture towards the man in the trilby who had just bid for the bull. So this was the man Richard wanted revenge upon. He was a formidable opponent, by the look of him: a man of status and influence, not easily trifled with, who wore a trilby where everyone else wore flat caps. No wonder Richard wanted help. Automatically Siegfried began assessing Kellett's solid physique and probable lifestyle until he suddenly realised what he was doing. He was supposed to have left all that behind him.

"Forget it, Richard. I won't help you." He had to speak directly into Richard's ear to compete with the din.

At that moment Kellett looked up and saw a face that made him do a double-take. Anger, then puzzlement followed by comprehension crossed his face as he worked out who was standing with young Richard Driesler.

"Shit. He's seen us," Richard swore. "And he doesn't look best pleased."

"I think it's me he's looking at," Siegfried said, feeling himself being sucked into the dispute against his will.

"What's the problem?" Uwe asked, seeing his cousins' anxious faces.

"Someone best avoided," Richard replied. "Doesn't like Germans," he added by way of explanation.

"Oh. I see. Should we go?"

"Perhaps it would be best. It's a bit public here. We don't want any trouble."

"And he would make trouble?" Heinrich asked. "But we outnumber him, surely."

"He has a lot of allies here. Anyway, that's not the point. I daren't get into trouble again with him."

Heinrich seemed disappointed. He was game for a fight with an Englishman, but Uwe and Siegfried saw the sense of a tactical retreat. Lothar was totally oblivious to everything but the market around him and was surprised when his jacket was tugged by Richard to show they were heading back to the stockyards.

A file of jostling bullocks being loaded into a truck held them up. When they finally got round the obstacle they found Andrew Kellett blocking their way.

"So you're Siegfried," he boomed, ignoring Richard and the others. "Come back to make more trouble, have you?"

Siegfried found his fists clenching. He shifted his feet uneasily. He must keep control of his temper!

Seeing Siegfried's scowl, Richard reluctantly decided he had better intervene. "My relatives have come over here for Bina's wedding, Mr Kellett," he said perfectly politely. "Now we're sightseeing. I see you just bought a bull. A good price was it?"

Kellett grinned as he realised he had the upper hand in this game. Young Richard Driesler was clearly frightened of a confrontation. "Not bad. Perhaps we should put you lot in the ring and see how much we could get for a bunch of feeble Germans. Not much, I reckon!"

A crowd was beginning to gather round, sensing trouble. Lothar and Uwe stood back, unsure of what was brewing, but Heinrich kept close to Siegfried, keen to be in the thick of things. Richard, however, was determined not to let the situation get out of control.

"That may be your opinion, Mr Kellett, but others here might think differently." There was a low murmur of assent as friends of the Drieslers showed their support. "Now, if you would kindly step aside and let us be on our way, please?"

Kellett realised young Richard Driesler was not going to be provoked and turned instead to the other Driesler, the one who was the image of his father. "You're the Nazi one, aren't you?" he demanded, jabbing his finger in Siegfried's chest. "I read about you in the newspaper. You were a friend of that Nazi your father killed." He spoke to the men around him, intent on drumming up support. "We don't want his sort here, do we?" This time there were murmurs of agreement from Kellett's friends amongst the crowd as well as from those who had until then been neutral.

"What's going on?" Uwe hissed in Richard's ear.

"Big trouble," Richard said, trying not to show his nervousness. He could see the crowd beginning to side with Kellett, even those who were friends of the Drieslers. Siegfried had no friends here.

Siegfried decided it was time to take control. He stepped a pace forward, his chest brushing against Kellett's, and stared aggressively down at him. "I am not a Nazi," he said loudly so all could hear. "You are more Nazi than I."

There was a gasp of shock from the onlookers at his effrontery. Kellett had taken an involuntary step backwards as he began to realise the might of his opponent. There was something in those cold grey eyes that he had not even seen when Karl Driesler had attacked him all those years ago. He was starting to wish he had left well alone.

Siegfried pressed home his verbal attack. "You think you can do what you like because you are important here, Mr Kellett. But you are wrong." Now he jabbed a finger in Kellett's chest. "For me you are not important, you are just a man who lost his girlfriend to my father and cannot forget it. You lost, Mr Kellett. Understand that!"

To everybody's astonishment, especially Siegfried's, Kellett suddenly laughed in his face. "I lost? Don't you be so sure!" With that final gesture of triumph he hastily stepped back into the crowd which silently parted to let him pass. Once he was gone a babble of noise erupted and a few onlookers offered words of support and congratulations to Richard for handling the situation so calmly. Nobody spoke to or went near Siegfried.

As the eldest of the party Uwe decided it was time he took charge. "Come on. Let's go before anything else happens. I think we've outstayed our welcome here."

The others agreed, although Heinrich gave a rueful backward glance, hoping someone would yet decide to start a real fight. It was not to be. Karl was too familiar and respected a figure at the market for anyone to want to make trouble for his family. Besides, there was business to attend to. The crowd rapidly began to disperse, and Richard led his little band off to find alternative entertainment. They browsed amongst the market stalls for a while then walked within the city wall into Widemarsh Street and up into High Town. Richard showed them the black and white 'Old House' in the centre of the shopping street then they stopped for a cup of coffee and doughnuts near the cathedral.

Siegfried found he remembered some of the city sights although his memories of the place were very hazy. He guessed he had not often been brought here. The city had a pleasant, friendly atmosphere, which had quickly managed to dispel his earlier anger. He saw himself bringing Sophie and their baby here one day, showing them the sights: the dusky red cathedral and the River Wye's clear waters swirling under the six arches of the old stone bridge.

As he leaned over the parapet of the Wye Bridge, he saw a mallard duck paddling to keep stationary against the current. That's me, he thought. If I stop, I'll get swept along where I don't want to go. I've got to keep trying to find a way out of this.

He looked beneath the bright sunshine sparkling on the surface to where green weeds waved darkly below. They reminded him of the prank he had played in the lake in Bavaria when he was sixteen, persuading Paul Driesler to hide so his parents thought he had drowned. Life had been so simple then. He had known exactly where he was going. Now he was in a maze with no way out that he could find. It would be so easy to follow the route he had taken before the trial. Kill his father and be done with it. He knew he could still kill. Kellett had shown him that. But how could he cut himself from all this? If he killed his father he would never return here. His newly found conscience would never let him.

"Siegfried? Are you coming?" Uwe called back.

Siegfried gripped the warm stone of the parapet, reluctant to let it go. The past was here, the future could be too. He so wanted it to be.

*

Kellett's last words had troubled Richard all day long. 'I lost? Don't you be so sure!' What had he meant? Should he mention it to his father? Or mother?

As Siegfried drove the five of them home late that afternoon, Richard made up his mind to speak to his father. No doubt someone would mention the events of the day when they next went to market and Dad ought to have some warning, he thought.

It proved easier said than done. It was the last evening they would all be together and they were meeting up in the Walnut Tree's beer garden along with Penchurch's host families. As more and more people gathered to enjoy the balmy summer's evening, the pub's few pieces of garden furniture had to be supplemented with chairs and stools from the bar. Werner and Vera arrived last with Monika and husband, Jens, in tow, as Richard despaired of ever finding his father alone. It would have to wait until tomorrow.

Heinrich had other ideas, however.

He told Margit and Margit told Karl that somebody called Mr Kellett had been mouthing off at Siegfried at the livestock market.

Katherine's ears pricked up too at the mention of Kellett's name and she moved closer to Karl to hear what it was all about as Karl beckoned Siegfried over to quiz him.

"What's all this about Mr Kellett?" Karl asked with some apprehension.

Siegfried put his beer glass down on the table and perched on an upturned ornamental barrel. "He wanted to pick a fight with me because you stole his girlfriend," Siegfried laughed. "I told him to forget it."

"Yes, but he seemed to win the argument," Heinrich, who had come over with Siegfried, pointed out. "He said he hadn't lost. I understood that part at least!"

Katherine's heart leapt into her throat. Andrew was bragging about it. She should have known he would not keep quiet.

"Lost what?" Karl asked, sensing more was meant than just losing the argument.

"The girlfriend," Heinrich cheerfully supplied before suddenly putting two and two together. He had not followed the argument properly as it occurred, but now he grasped that Katherine was the former girlfriend in question, confirmed by her frozen expression. He shut his mouth and wished he were elsewhere.

Siegfried too saw the danger signs in Katherine's face and wondered how to defuse the situation. "Kellett was in a corner. He didn't want to lose face in front of all those men. He had to say something. It worked for him too. No harm done and no fight, much to Heinrich's dismay!"

They all laughed and Siegfried breathed a sigh of relief. He saw Katherine's too. He also saw the curious glance his father gave her and his mind immediately began to race feverishly. Was something going on between Katherine and Kellett? Was this a situation he could turn to his advantage? Could he possibly kill his father so suspicion would fall on Kellett? Alternatively, could he make it look like his father killed Kellett? That way his father might again face the prospect of being jailed for life, but at least he would not have to die. Would that be enough for Gustav? Regretfully Siegfried doubted it. Gustav wanted Karl dead. Kellett could be the decoy murderer.

Why had he not found all this out sooner? He could do little once he was back in Germany.

He picked up his beer glass and wandered back to join Uwe, Jens and Lothar, his emotions a curious mix of elation and depression. He had found a solution at last, but could not, nor did he even want to, carry it out. The longer he stayed here the harder it was to even contemplate such a thing. It would be so easy to kill Kellett. So easy. Perhaps that was the way out of this dilemma? Again Gustav's face came to mind and again Siegfried realised Gustav would not be palmed off with half-measures.

"I expect you're looking forward to seeing Sophie again," Monika said, breaking into his thoughts.

"What? Oh, yes." He smiled distractedly at his cousin.

"It's been lovely here, hasn't it?" she went on. "Everyone's made us so welcome. It would be nice to come back some time soon – not so many of us at once though!" she laughed. "Onkel Karl was certainly lucky to end up here."

"Yes, it's a bit better than a shallow grave on the Russian Front, isn't it?" Siegfried joked. Uwe frowned and he realised his awful blunder. "Forgive me, Uwe. I forgot about your father. I suppose I've always thought of you as Onkel Stefan's son."

"That's alright," Uwe said, exchanging his frown for a smile. "I never knew my real father and Stefan's been a great Dad to me. I couldn't have asked for a better one." He turned the subject away from his own tragedy. "I'm really pleased you've finally accepted Onkel Karl. It's wonderful seeing you both together at last."

Siegfried nodded but said nothing, letting the conversation drift to other matters as he sat watching the swallows swooping after insects in the sultry evening sky.

Why do they all have to make it so hard for me? he wondered gloomily. If Sophie had been here with me I would have had no problems. She would have spurred me on to have done something by now. Yet here I am, the trip almost over and next to nothing achieved. My heart's simply not in it, but I can't leave it like this.

He looked across to where his father sat with Katherine and Opa. All three were silent, Opa because he was nearly asleep, while his father and Katherine looked tense, as though there was a whole lot they wanted to talk about but could not here. Siegfried found himself curious as to what was going on. For years he had made it his business to snoop, and the habit was hard to break. Perhaps a little eavesdropping was called for later tonight?

*

Karl bid his father goodnight then went outside to his thinking spot at the gate overlooking Hay Bluff. The boys were settling down in their room, while Katherine was sorting out the breakfast things ready for an early start tomorrow. She had been horribly quiet since hearing about Kellett's boast that he had not lost. He knew she was a hopeless liar and could not hide her thoughts. She was extremely tense, and he hoped she might follow him out so they could talk in private. He had not asked her to, leaving it up to her. He had no right to make demands, not after what he had done. He just hoped she would come.

The night sky was palest green in the north-west, the stars struggling to appear. Up in the woods a vixen screamed, making him jump and he thought he heard a rustling by the sheep sheds nearby. A hedgehog probably, he thought. He realised he was thinking in German again, what with all his family being over. It had taken him a while to switch back to thinking in English after his release from prison, but time made no difference to his dreams. The ones he remembered were always in German.

He heard a soft footfall on the stony ground and he turned round.

"I thought you'd be here," Katherine said quietly, coming to his side but keeping a slight distance. "I sensed you wanted to talk."

"Yes. It's something to do with Kellett, isn't it, Schatz?" He tried not to sound harsh or accusatory, but felt he had failed.

Katherine gritted her teeth, steeling herself to deliver the news that would surely hurt him. "I did it for Richard," she said quietly. "It was nothing like you and ... Siegfried's mother." She still could not bring herself to say the woman's name, but her long-simmering anger now gave her the armour she needed to explain her actions. "It was nothing except a bribe for his co-operation."

Karl felt the ground knocked out from under his feet. He gripped the top of the gate hard. "What are you saying?" he breathed, unable to look at her. "That you slept with him?"

Katherine shuddered at the explicit image his question cast in her mind, and knew it was what he imagined had happened. She must swiftly disillusion him of that. But if she told him the whole truth, that Andrew had virtually forced himself on her, she would be courting disaster as Karl would feel duty-bound to take action. She must cast blame on herself, she decided, as much as on Andrew and hope for the best. "I went to his house one morning when I knew Audrey was out. I made him promise he would drop the case against Richard if I granted him a favour."

"A favour!" he exploded, turning to confront her. "Is that what you call it?"

She had to be cruel to be kind. "Karl, you of all people can not make an issue of this. Unlike you and Ilse," she spat out the name now, "this was a job I had to do to protect my son. You mustn't read anything into it. I've volunteered the information because I saw you were worried and wanted to put your mind at rest. I can assure you, you have nothing to worry about."

"Except Kellett is now bragging to the whole world he has you back!"

There was a deep, dividing silence between them, then Katherine spoke forcefully again. "If you have a problem with this, Karl, it's a problem of your own making. I'm not going to apologise for what I did. I didn't enjoy it for one second and would hate for it to happen again."

"But don't you see? Now he has you. He can demand your ... favours any time he likes. You can never accuse him of rape again, and he can make up all sorts of lies about Richard or me knowing you'll be there to stop him telling anyone." He gripped her shoulders in angry frustration. "We'll never hear the end of this, you realise?"

Katherine quailed under his grip. He was right of course. Andrew would not leave her alone now. She had procured a temporary reprieve only. "I could tell Audrey what's happened, what Andrew did. She would sort him out."

"At a price," Karl snarled. "Me!"

"What do you mean?"

"You know her! I'd have to pay for her co-operation with my services."

If he only knew how right he was, Katherine thought, catching her breath. "This is ridiculous, Karl. We're letting our imaginations get out of control. There must be another way out of this. If Andrew thinks he can pressure me into doing anything, he's got another think coming!" She felt Karl's fingers increase their grip. The violence locked within him still had the power to frighten her once in a while, but she knew she had nothing to fear from him. It was others who were at risk. That was what she had striven so hard to avoid throughout their married life.

"If he does try anything again, I'll kill him."

"No you won't, Karl. You wouldn't be so stupid."

She had used the calm, soothing voice that usually had the knack of reaching him, even when he was at his most irate. She waited for his response, then felt it in the release of his grip on her shoulders.

"How can I face him now and do nothing?" he said eventually, fingering a lock of her hair. "I've done a lot of stupid things in my time, Schatz." He gave a hint of a smile. "I can do plenty more, I'm afraid."

"Then I'll just have to continue keeping a jolly good eye on you, won't I?" she replied, her hand applying gentle pressure to the back of his neck, bringing his mouth closer to hers. She would prove to him she was still his.

He kissed her, with the scent of hay in his nostrils and the glint of moonlight on her upturned face. As their lips parted he murmured: "I love you, Katherine. More than ever."

The peace of the evening contrasted starkly with the recent feverishly busy days. They were alone, in the darkness, and he wanted her. He drew her body towards his and she responded, but as his hands dropped to caress her she shrank back.

"Not here!" she whispered. "Someone might see."

"Who?" he smiled, but gave in to her caution and opened the gate, leading her through to the shelter of the hedge on the other side where they had only sheep for company.

Siegfried watched them disappear, envious of what they were up to. It made his own need for Sophie all the greater. What he envied more, however, was their total openness with each other, the way they could discuss everything with no pretence or subterfuge. When he was with Sophie, Siegfried was still a Nazi. With the rest of his family he was a former Nazi. It was proving impossible to maintain the two roles he was playing. Something would have to give.

He decided to leave them in peace and began to wander slowly down the lane to the valley road where he had left his car. He knew he should not really be driving after drinking so much at the pub, but the night was beginning to refresh him, even though it left him feeling maudlin and alone under the emergent stars.

FOURTEEN

Siegfried's dilemma kept him preoccupied during the long drive home. At the Dutch/German border Heinrich and Roslinde were arguing again and Siegfried tried to shut his ears to their squabbling. He knew he must decide before he got home to Sophie. Once there all his objectivity would disappear. He also needed something positive to report to Gustav.

At the next service station Siegfried suggested putting Heinrich behind the wheel to silence the dispute. Back on the road again Siegfried rested his head on the passenger seat and closed his eyes. Every argument he had held with himself during his stay in England ran through his head; every conversation with his family played itself back to him, and through it all he could hear Judy's voice telling him he could not kill anybody. He smiled ruefully to himself. As they drove through the smoke and dirt of the Ruhr conurbation his spirits sank as he decided he had only one option, and it needed Gustav's co-operation.

Arriving outside the Röbels' flat in Iserlohn, Siegfried half-expected to see the strange young man who had been following him before the trip to England. There had been no sign of him in England, fortunately, and Siegfried had put him out of his mind, but now he was reminded of him and wondered where or when he would next turn up. He felt certain, somehow, that he would.

"Are you coming in for a drink, Siegfried?" Margit asked once their luggage was safely inside the flat.

"No, thank you. I want to get on to see Sophie. She'll be waiting at home."

"Alone?"

"No. Her parents were driving her back and staying until I arrive."

As they stood on the threshold to the flat there was a shuffling of feet and old Frau Dietz appeared.

"Good afternoon, Margit. I do hope you had a good holiday?"

Margit smiled apologetically to Siegfried and gave the old lady her full attention. "Very nice, thank you, Frau Dietz."

"I won't keep you when I know you've just got in, but I did want to mention the young man who was looking for you, just after you had left. I told him you were away for a week. He didn't leave a message. But his name was Brandt," she added as an afterthought. "I wrote it down so I wouldn't forget."

"That's very kind of you, Frau Dietz. Thank you for your trouble."

"My pleasure. Now I'd better let you get on with your unpacking." She turned and shuffled back towards her front door.

Margit looked puzzled. "Well, I've no idea what that could have been about. No doubt I'll find out in due course."

"No doubt," replied Siegfried gravely. So the young man knew when to expect them back and would be on the lookout. Well, two could play at that game, he thought, itching to be away. He called through the open door. "I'll leave you all to it. Goodbye, you three."

"Goodbye, Siegfried, and thanks for the ride," Edeltraud called back, echoed by Heinrich and Roslinde.

"Yes, thanks, Siegfried," Margit added in turn. "It was good fun. We must see you and Sophie more often, once the baby's born. And don't forget about that christening party you promised!"

"We won't." He stooped and kissed her cheek. "Take care."

He kept an eye open for the young man's green Beetle all the way back to Soest, but saw nothing suspicious. As he pulled into *An der Waldecke* he saw the Wendts' white Mercedes parked on the road outside, leaving the drive clear for his own car. Sophie was watching out for him and opened the front door as soon as he pulled up. Her rolling, faltering gait towards him tugged at his heartstrings and he engulfed her in a bear hug, curved awkwardly over her belly.

As their lips parted and he stood back a bit from her, Sophie broke her news. "I was waiting till you got home before telling you. Mama and Papa don't know this yet either." She paused for dramatic effect, making sure they were all paying attention. "I had an ante-natal last week and they reckon I'm expecting twins!"

"Twins?" Siegfried gasped.

"Liebling!" Lisl cried.

Peter Wendt was speechless.

Siegfried rested his hands on her belly as if he would be able to feel the two babies inside, but apart from unidentifiable bumps there was no way of knowing. "Are you pleased? It's going to mean so much more work for you, Schatz."

"Yes, I think I'm pleased. I'm just about getting used to the idea now. I was going to tell you over the phone, but I decided I wanted to see your expression when I told you. I'm glad I did. We all know what a good liar you are, but I can see you're pleased."

Siegfried wondered exactly what she meant by her remark, whether it was meant with suspicion or pride. But now was not the time to dwell on it. "Of course I'm pleased. Two for the price of one, so to speak!"

They all laughed, and Sophie's parents kissed their daughter proudly, telling her how thrilled they were. Appreciating her need to be alone with Siegfried on his homecoming they did not linger, however, staying only long enough to enjoy a glass of beer before making their departure.

As soon as Siegfried and Sophie had finished waving her parents off up the road they returned inside the house, shut the front door and kissed each other hungrily. Their passion soon took them up to the bedroom. Hurriedly stepping out of his clothes, Siegfried then helped Sophie with hers. Her girth made her awkward and he felt again the tenderness towards her that had so surprised him the first time it struck early on in their relationship, which had told him she was the one.

He stood now in front of her, his hands caressing her swollen breasts. "I've missed you, Schatz. I've missed you so much." He kissed her before she could reply, savouring the taste of her mouth, the softness of her cheeks and silky blonde hair. He knew his own urgency must be tamed so as not to be too rough with her. She always read his moods so well, and this time was no exception. Silently she lay down upon their bed, smiling sweetly up at him. Lying down beside her he stroked her belly, feeling the rolling movement under his fingers as the babies stirred. His fingers moved lower, but she was ahead of him. Her fingers found him and guided him towards her. He was always fearful at first he would somehow hurt the baby, but reason swiftly departed and he thrust hard into her as their bodies overwhelmed them both.

"I missed you too," she grinned, as he regained his breath.

"I noticed!" He lay down beside her, tracing a circle around her left nipple with his forefinger. There was so much he needed to tell her, so much he had to explain, but she would not understand or want to hear, and so he kept silent.

"Do you want the shower first?" she asked after a few minutes of him lying strangely quiet beside her.

"Yes. I'll get it warmed up for you. Gone are the days when we could both fit in there!"

As he soaped himself in the shower, he was reminded of their honeymoon and how simple life had been then. But he could not return to those times. He had tried and failed. His life had irrevocably changed since Sophie's accident had brought home what life and relationships were really about. With that had come a deeper understanding of the world at large. He had matured. Did that mean his stepfather, Paul Zopf, and Peter and Lisl Wendt had never matured? They still believed wholeheartedly in Nazism. Why was he different? But it was not they who had done the dirty work. That privilege had always been his own or someone else's. He had to live now with his violent past thanks to Judy's comments in the Murdochs' garden. At the time she asked him he had not given it any thought. Since then the seeds of guilt she had planted in his soul had slowly germinated and over the long drive home he had understood what she had meant. It had never been right to kill all those people who had been a threat to security, even though he had believed it was right at the time. From now on his whole life would be spent in shameful regret and anticipation of his crimes coming to light. The evidence was there. Gustav had told him so.

"Are you still in there?" Sophie's voice called through the rush of water from the shower. "Hurry up, Liebling!"

"Nearly finished." He stood under the gush of hot water, washing the soap away, then opened the shower door. Sophie handed him a towel before taking his place.

By the time she joined him in the kitchen, wrapped like him in a white dressing gown, he had prepared egg mayonnaise sandwiches and tea for them both. It was still quite light outside so they sat on their little terrace, thankful their garden was secluded.

"The grass needs cutting," Siegfried said through a mouthful of rye bread. "I must get some more petrol. Can you remind me?"

"I'll try." Sophie shuffled uncomfortably on the garden chair. "My back's beginning to ache again."

"I'll give it a rub when we go to bed," he offered.

There was no sign of their friends the squirrels, so they watched a neighbour's cat stalking a vole in the woodland undergrowth. The cat had infinite patience, far longer than their own attention span.

"I'm going in. This chair's killing me," Sophie declared eventually, picking up the tray of empty crockery. "Can you lock up?"

It was not yet ten o'clock, but Sophie seemed tired and he had had a long journey. He shut all the downstairs windows, locked the doors, switched off the lights and followed Sophie upstairs.

*

The nearby street lamp showed the Mercedes was parked in the drive. So Driesler was back! Dressed all in black and wearing gloves, Christian stood poised at the top of the cul-de-sac, looking down towards the house where his quarry lived. He could not believe he was actually here, about to set fire to Driesler's house. The enormity of the crime hit him, and he knew he must be careful to give Driesler and his pregnant wife a chance to escape. All he wanted was for the house to burn down and for Driesler to be too preoccupied with sorting out the mess to have time for Gustav. The fire must start with an explosion sufficient to waken them. He looked at his watch. It was nearly two in the morning. A black and white cat skittered across his path, diving into the shrubs of the neighbours' garden. Everywhere else was as silent as the grave. No lights shone from any houses. Summoning all his courage he continued down the pavement.

He had debated with himself whether to bring his own petrol or use Driesler's, deciding eventually that there was too much risk in carrying such an item down the road. With pounding heart he stepped onto the drive. He looked up anxiously. The sky was clear with sufficient moon- and starlight for him to see by as he approached the side of the house. The hinges of the garden gate were well oiled, he remembered, and did not squeak as he opened it. Once safely through he paused, listened intently for a moment, then crept down the concrete path alongside the house to the back garden. In front of him stood the garden shed. His previous visit had shown him the window was not very secure. Sure enough, with a bit of effort and a piece of wire he managed to lift the window catch and open the window wide. Awkwardly he climbed through the narrow aperture into the shed, then reorientated himself. He put his hand straight on the can, despite the darkness within the shed, but as he lifted it he groaned in dismay. It was empty!

Cursing himself for not bringing his own petrol, Christian began to climb out of the window then froze as an upstairs light came on in the Drieslers' house. A few moments later the kitchen light came on. Christian flung himself to the ground and slunk behind the shed. He sat there trembling with fright and cursing himself again for embarking on such a stupid project. He had let his jealousy get the better of him until reason had flown out of the window. Fate was telling him through the empty petrol can that this was the wrong thing to do.

He peered cautiously round the edge of the shed. Lights were on all over the house, but no curtains were twitching aside or blinds being raised. Had they heard something? What was going on? Whatever it was he dared not make another move. Presently the upstairs lights were switched off and he thought he heard the sound of the front door closing. A few moments later a car door clunked shut followed a few seconds later by a second, then the Mercedes' engine coughed into life.

Two doors. Driesler and his wife? At this time of night it probably meant one thing. Her labour had started. Christian relaxed, leaned back against the side of the shed and sighed with relief. Nature had solved the problem for him. Driesler would be far too preoccupied from now on to have time for Gustav, who had surely picked a losing horse in Driesler. Christian felt renewed confidence he could win the race himself.

*

Siegfried stood proudly over the two tiny forms asleep in their cots, one wrapped in a pink blanket, the other in a blue, their pink and wrinkled faces clean and sweet-smelling now after the trauma of birth. The name cards on the cots proclaimed their identities to the world: Friedrich Driesler and Freia Driesler. He put his finger next to Friedrich's tiny hand and stroked it. The baby gave a lurch then curled his fingers around his father's hand. Siegfried put his other hand on Freia's tightly clenched fist. She too responded to her father's touch but with a kick and a whimper, before settling again into a deep sleep.

"Congratulations, Herr Driesler," the nurse beside him said. "You must be very proud."

Siegfried blinked hard and avoided looking at her, keeping his eyes downcast to the cots below. "Yes, I am. Very proud." Gently he pulled his finger away from his son's grasp. "Will they sleep long?"

The nurse smiled. "An hour or two, I expect. Then they'll let us know they're hungry. You go back and see your wife before she has a sleep too. She's pretty exhausted."

Siegfried was exhausted too after the very long night and morning. The twins had finally been born shortly after eleven. He was told Sophie had been very brave throughout, but was beginning to flag by the time Freia joined her brother in the world. Leaving the nursery he found his way to the room Sophie had been moved to from the delivery suite. Popping his head round the door he saw she was expecting him, even though her eyes were half-closed.

"Have you seen them?" she murmured.

"Yes," he replied, walking into the room. "They're perfect. Well done, Schatz." He stooped to kiss her forehead. He could see how exhausted she was now the excitement was all over and the adrenalin had subsided. He would come back later with the biggest bunch of flowers she had ever seen. "You have a good rest now. You're going to need it!"

"Have you told my parents yet?"

"No, I wanted to see you and the twins first." She smiled vaguely, her eyes already closing. "You sleep now, Schatz. I'll go and phone your folks, and then get some rest myself. See you later. Sleep well." After kissing her lightly on the lips he crept out of the room, then found a nearby telephone.

Lisl Wendt was naturally thrilled at his news. "And they're all well?" she kept asking, as if he was keeping something back from her.

"They're fine, all beautiful and all well," he reassured her yet again. "Sophie's looking forward to seeing you later and showing off your grandchildren to you."

"My grandchildren!" Lisl sighed as if still unable to believe the news.

Siegfried felt like that himself. He could hardly believe he was now the father of twins, with all the responsibilities that entailed. The thought brought him abruptly back to reality. He replaced the receiver, his hand lingering on it, deep in thought. Suddenly he felt very tired and alone. If only time would stop here and now and he could hold on to that feeling of elation, but time would march inexorably on with all its terrible consequences, thanks to Gustav. The blank hospital walls stared back at him. Unless he did something about it he faced a lifetime in jail as a murderer, with his wife and children dead. Gustav's secret visit to Sophie had left Siegfried in no doubt as to his intentions. He must focus his thoughts on the present and begin preparations. Whatever he did from now on must be above suspicion. Sophie and the children's futures depended on that.

He had to act normally, and normally he should have been back at work today, so his next call was to his office. He imparted his news to his secretary, Frau Schiersmann, who was thrilled for them both and promised to send flowers from the firm immediately. As he was about to put down the receiver Siegfried thought of something else.

"Oh, Frau Schiersmann. Could you arrange a meeting for me with Herr Huwald as soon as possible?"

"Certainly, Herr Driesler. But don't you worry about things here, sir. You go home and get some sleep."

His next tasks were to telephone England, then Medebach and send a telegram to his mother in Uruguay, but he decided to do that from home. His eyes almost closed as he drove there, but he would not sleep until he had made the calls.

*

Katherine had to wait until Karl and Richard returned from a tree surgery job away up the valley before giving them the news. It was evening by the time they returned, tired and hungry. She stood at the back door and watched them empty the Land Rover of tools and ropes, waited for all to be safely put away, before calling out to Karl as he was shutting the tool shed door: "Good evening, Opa!"

Karl spun around. "Opa?" he queried, then saw her beaming face. "It's arrived already?"

"Not it. They! Sophie's had twins. Friedrich at five past eleven and Freia at eleven fifteen. Both a bit on the small side of course, since they're rather early, but otherwise healthy and well."

Richard wanted to be in on the celebrations too. "Hey! That means I'm an uncle!"

His mother laughed. "Uncle Richard and Uncle Paul! Honestly, it makes you too sound positively aged."

"What about me?" Karl laughed, giving her a hug. "I'm an Opa. That's positively ancient."

Katherine led them inside the kitchen where the smell of sausages hung in the air. "And I suppose I'm an Oma of sorts, although they've got two already. Except I don't suppose they'll see much of ..." Even now she still could not say Ilse's name.

"So when did Sophie's labour start?" Karl asked quickly, taking off his work boots and leaving them by the back door as Richard shot back out to the boys' garden furniture workshop to share his new status with Paul.

"At about two a.m. Nine hours in labour. That's pretty good for a first time."

Karl looked at his watch. "Seven o'clock here, eight there. He'll probably be at the hospital visiting her, but I'll try ringing."

"Dinner's ready in about ten minutes."

"Right. Oh, we must have some wine to celebrate. Can you find a bottle?"

"Already done!"

As he listened to the phone ringing in Siegfried's empty house, Karl wished for once that he lived in Germany. To have grandchildren and hardly ever see them would be unbearable. There would be the photographs and progress reports, of course, but they could never make up for the cuddles and play that was a grandparent's right. It would be even worse for poor Ilse. It would really bring home to her how cut off she was from her family.

Frustrated in his attempt he replaced the receiver and went up to the bathroom for a wash and brush up before dinner. He supposed Bina and Wolf would wait a bit before having children, but they too would be in Germany. For the moment though, they needed to be told the news.

"Do we have the number of the hotel Bina and Wolf are staying at?" he asked Katherine upon his return to the kitchen.

"It's all right. I've already let them know."

"Ah. How are they? Enjoying themselves?" he asked with a twinkle in his eye.

"They seem to be. They've done lots of walking, found some nice pubs." She put a dish of mashed potato on the table then called the boys in from the workshop. Before they arrived she had one more thing to say. "Karl, if there's any visiting being done, we're both going."

She did not want him in Germany alone. Ilse's name had cropped up. Karl had no time to react as Richard and Paul burst into the room, hungry for dinner. He wished she had not said that, not then and not like that. His elation was shattered. He hardly heard Paul's question. "Pardon?"

"What sort of a name is Freia?" Paul repeated, shovelling sausage and cabbage into his mouth.

"Freia?" Karl paused to think where he had heard it before. "A character in one of Wagner's operas, I think. One of the goddesses in the Ring probably, knowing Sophie."

"Blonde and beautiful?" Paul asked.

Karl shrugged. "Bina would know." There was a snigger from Paul. "What's that supposed to mean, Paul?"

Paul blushed. "Nothing. Just ..." He looked guiltily at both his parents, then decided to share his lascivious thoughts. "I was just thinking she'll be the one producing babies next."

Karl smiled. "I was thinking that earlier too. But I was thinking it because, like Friedrich and Freia, Bina's children will live in Germany too." He gazed across at Katherine and saw she understood his plight, only with Bina's children it would affect Katherine more directly.

"We'll all have to move to Germany then," Paul suggested.

"Not likely!" Richard retorted. "What about the farm? We couldn't leave here!"

"You maybe not," Paul replied. "But I'd quite happily go and work in Opa's sawmill."

"Nobody's moving anywhere," Katherine butted in, worried by the turn the conversation was taking. "There's a perfectly good ferry service across the North Sea. It's not as if we're ..." She broke off, sought a distraction and began pouring more wine for them all. 'Across the Atlantic Ocean' was what she had been thinking. Ilse again, damn her! She could see Karl had followed her train of thought and she smiled at him reassuringly. This business between them was still present. It was her own fault, she knew, ever anxious, ever suspicious now of Karl's loyalties, despite his protestations of remorse and shame. Ilse's name seemed like the Sword of Damocles hanging over her.

As if in response to her mood, the conversation settled down into routine farming matters again of sheep to be dipped, vet's bills to pay and numbers of guests booked in for bed and breakfasts.

Paul had sensed his mother's discomfort at all this talk about grandchildren in Germany. Of all her family, Paul thought, only Richard would object to a mass removal over there. As the years went by, his father seemed to miss his own family more and more, jumping at any excuse for a trip over. There had been no real need for him to take Sabina there last summer when she had gone to live with Ilse and Paul Zopf, but he had insisted, with all the resultant drama that followed. No wonder his mother was so wary about Germany now.

"Did you sort out that fence near the river, Paul?" his father asked, interrupting his ruminations.

"Yes, I found where the sheep had forced a hole. It's all patched up. Which reminds me. Mr Duggan was passing by across the river and he asked if you would phone him about that ram you were interested in."

"Right-o." Karl looked up at the kitchen clock. "I'll do that now, then try Siegfried again. See if he's in yet."

As her family dispersed from the meal table Katherine felt a cold hand clutching at her heart. The baby – babies, she corrected herself, had been born. There would be a christening. Ilse might be there.

*

The telegram arrived as Ilse was about to set off for the tennis club. She immediately phoned Paul at his office, sent a telegram of congratulations in return, then went to bask in the glory of new grandmotherhood amongst all her friends. Returning later to the apartment, she made herself a coffee then sat on the balcony overlooking the vast River Plate estuary. Down in the docks ships were loading, while one was just heading out into mid-channel en route, no doubt, for Europe or America. Wistfully she imagined herself sailing one day to Hamburg, her birthplace, though scarcely recognisable to her these days. From there she could catch a train to Dortmund. Siegfried would meet her at the station and take her to see Sophie, Friedrich and Freia.

The names rolled delightfully off her tongue as she repeated them several times. She could not wait to hold the twins in her arms, rock them to sleep and enjoy them as she had never been able to enjoy her own children when they were small. She longed to spoil the twins, give them everything they wanted, as even a sweet had been a rarity for her offspring at first. Poverty and the aftermath of the war had denied her any pleasure in motherhood. Now she was to be denied the pleasures of grandmotherhood as well, through loyalty to her exiled husband.

When he came in from work, Paul found her still sitting there with dried tears on her eyes. He carried a bunch of flowers, which he presented to her with a kiss on her blonde hair.

"For the new grandmother," he said tenderly, guessing the reason for her distress.

"Oh, Paul, thank you!" she cried and burst into tears again.

"What say you we go out to celebrate tonight? We'll paint the town red, drown your sorrows and look forward to your trip over to see them."

Ilse swiftly reached for a handkerchief from her bag and dabbed at her eyes. "You're so generous, Paul. Thank you."

"Rubbish! I just wish I could go with you." He leaned on the balcony rail, sniffed the breeze then turned back to his wife. "Time for a drink, then we'll go out to that new steak house near the cathedral. An acquaintance of mine owns it now."

Ilse had to smile. Paul always mixed business with pleasure. It was why he was so successful. No doubt they would end up as a threesome with this acquaintance, but she was used to that. Their news would warrant free drinks and that would be Paul set up for the night. She stood up. "I'll go and get changed while you pour me a martini."

Paul moved over to her and took her chin, tilting her face up to his. He kissed her gently. "You can visit them whenever you like, you know."

"Thank you." She hastily disappeared to her room, before her thoughts betrayed her. Trips to Europe would leave Paul free to philander. But then, wasn't she used to that too? She doubted whether she would have been quite so ready to pursue Karl again if Paul had not been so liberal with his affections. But then again, Karl was Karl. She suspected she would have wanted him whatever her circumstances. Sorting through her jewellery box for a brooch to pin on her black satin dress, she came across the wooden hair clasp he had carved for her during the war. Its interlocking wild roses spoke of a love that had once been true – still was as far as she was concerned. She had experienced his continued love for her last August, but unlike Paul, Karl was not comfortable loving anyone other than his wife. If Ilse went over to the christenings it would mean frustratingly close contact with Karl once again. It was the price she would have to pay for seeing her grandchildren.

She replaced the clasp in the box, closing the lid on its memories. One day it would be Freia's. She had promised as much to Siegfried when she had tried to purge herself of Karl's memory by giving her only memento of him as a gift for Sophie. Siegfried had refused to take it, saying she should keep it still. He had been right.

Paul came and stood at the bedroom doorway, admiring his wife's still sleek figure. He knew she worked hard to keep it that way – for him or for Karl? It didn't really matter which. "Ready?" He handed her a glass of martini and lemonade.

"Just about. I've forgotten to put on my earrings." She raised her glass. "To Friedrich and Freia!" She took a sip then rummaged again in the jewellery box, finding the pendulous drops of local silver Paul had recently bought for her. She deftly clasped them on each ear lobe, then turned to Paul. "Ready."

"Beautiful as ever, my Ilse," he breathed. "And a grandmother twice over too."

"Don't rub it in!" she laughed, kissing his fleshy cheeks. If she had kept her figure, Paul had not. Wealth and age had brought him a wider girth and thinning hair, but no diminution of his undoubted love for her. Loved by two men. Wasn't she lucky!

FIFTEEN

Settling down in a chair by the window overlooking the street, Gustav glanced through the day's post. On top lay a bank statement proclaiming the dire state of his account, then came a letter from some charity connected with children in Africa. He tossed the latter unopened into the waste bin. How had they got hold of *his* name? Then there was a handwritten envelope, postmarked Soest. He ripped it open to reveal a birth announcement card for Friedrich and Freia Driesler with a note from Siegfried.

29.6.68

Dear Gustav,
As you can see, it's turned out to be twins and they're five weeks early! Thankfully all is well with them and Sophie, and they should be coming home next Wednesday.
I had meant to get in touch earlier about our little project, which I am still busy with and have not forgotten about, although recent events have of course meant a temporary lull in preparations.
We must get together soon as I want to discuss certain details with you. Excuse my brevity as Sophie and I have many of these to send off. I'll be in touch.
        Siegfried.

Gustav smiled with relief. It was about time he heard something from his young protégé. He had hoped there would have been more progress by now, an outcome even, but he was content to let Siegfried choose the right moment. The family wedding was obviously not it. Perhaps the next opportunity would be the twins' christenings, when Karl would no doubt be over in Germany on Siegfried's home territory.

He folded the paper and stuck it back in the envelope with the announcement card, making a mental note to send Sophie some flowers and a gift for the babies. What did people give these days?

It was so long since he had had the occasion to welcome a new life into the world. Gazing out of the window for inspiration, his thoughts were instantly sent reeling in another direction. Christian Bracht's car was parked outside.

"Damn him! What does he want now?"

As he spoke, his doorbell rang. Gustav debated whether to answer it. Were there any incriminating documents or letters lying around? Only Siegfried's note and that was innocuous to all but the initiated. The doorbell rang again. Christian obviously knew he was in and would pester until he was admitted. Reluctantly Gustav operated the remote opening, allowing Christian access to the inner hall of the apartment block. Christian was up the stairs a few moments later and Gustav had his door ready open.

"Come in," he said, not wanting loud discussions for all the neighbours to hear.

Christian eagerly stepped over the threshold. "Thanks, Gustav. I thought you might not want to see me after last time, but –"

"I don't. But since you're here and I've nothing better to do, you might as well stay for a drink. I'm not a demon, you know. I'd still like us to be friends, but I want to make it quite clear to you, Christian, that just at the moment I've no time for a lover."

Except Siegfried Driesler, Christian thought. Ignoring Gustav's last comment he moved on into the strangely tidy flat. It was stark and uninviting, unlived in even, with nothing of Gustav's personality or life in evidence except some recent post on the occasional table by his side. "I'm sorry if I'm interrupting anything."

"I was just looking at my post. It can wait. Can I get you a drink? Beer, coffee?"

Christian had not been thirsty until he glimpsed the post-mark on the uppermost envelope. He chose the drink that would grant him most time alone. "Coffee, please."

As Gustav disappeared out to his kitchen, Christian reached for the envelope. It took no more than a minute to read the card and the note, then replace the envelope exactly as it had been lying. So Driesler was still interested in Gustav despite his new family, and wanted a liaison soon! Christian felt his face burning with rage and the stranglehold of his uncontrollable jealousy twisted even tighter.

With a massive effort of self-control he composed himself and sauntered out to join Gustav in his kitchen.

Gustav had his head in the fridge searching for milk. Hearing Christian's entry he withdrew it and stood upright. "Sorry, I seem to be out of milk. Do you mind it black?"

"No. Black's fine." Christian gave a wry smile. "You never were much good at housekeeping, were you? You still need me to do all that for you." He looked Gustav boldly in the eye, challenging him to deny it.

Gustav accepted the challenge. "I don't need you. But you need me, don't you? You can't live without me, can you?" He poured water over the instant coffee and carried the two mugs through into the living area, Christian following as meekly as a lamb. Gustav ensured they sat on opposite sides of the coffee table. "What exactly do you want, Christian?" he asked once they were settled in their chairs. "Are you hoping to move in with me again?"

"In a word, yes."

It was certainly tempting, Gustav thought, but too dangerous in the present circumstances. Christian was a possessive, nosey individual who would very likely jump to the wrong conclusions about his clandestine activities. But then again, with Christian suspicious and stalking about the neighbourhood, there was no knowing what he might discover. Besides, he could do with someone to share the rent. And Christian was an inventive lover – a remarkably inventive lover, he remembered, feeling the first stirrings of excitement.

Christian could see Gustav mulling over the idea and his hopes began to rise. He kept his mouth shut, however, knowing Gustav hated to be cajoled into a decision. He sipped his coffee and waited, heart thudding, for a decision, but when it came his heart lurched with disappointment.

"Sorry, Christian. I've decided I like my independence too much for you to move in. I'd love you to stay the odd night, but not permanently." Hopefully the offer was sufficient to keep Christian from stalking him further.

Christian bit his tongue. It was better then nothing and still left him with a foot in the door. "How about tonight?" he ventured.

"How about now?" Gustav countered.

*

Siegfried let Sophie lie in. Her breasts were drained from feeding the twins at five o'clock and she now lay in exhausted sleep beside him. Last night he had wanted to make love to her, but it was too soon and she had no inclination. He would have to wait. Today he had other matters to attend to. There was the meeting with his financial advisor, Herr Huwald, to secure the twins' interests, then he had a mountain of paperwork to attend to, a site call to make, then he ought to speak with Gustav. He had yet to thank him for Sophie's flowers and the teddy bears he had sent for each of the twins. It was strange how teddies and Gustav seemed to be associated. He remembered Sabina calling a teddy after him. Incongruous really.

He showered and shaved without waking Sophie, dressed for work then crept downstairs to make up a tray of breakfast for her to eat when she woke – orange juice, a glass of milk, bread rolls, cheese and cold meats and a pot of her favourite honey. She always seemed famished these mornings after her long night. He drew a kiss on a scrap of paper, tucked it beneath the plate and went back upstairs to leave the tray by the bed for her. He looked down on her sleeping form, her fine silver-blonde hair splayed across the pillow like a dandelion clock. So beautiful. She meant the world to him, and there was nothing he would not do to protect her. Nothing. Before leaving he popped his head round the nursery door. The room was already filling with toys sent by relatives and friends for the new arrivals, who were both sleeping, their tiny heads displaying the merest shimmer of silvery hair. Freia snuffled and twitched, Friedrich sucked at a dream nipple. He felt an unfamiliar urge to cuddle them, something he could never have imagined himself capable of before their births, but he resisted the temptation, not wanting to wake them. Their future lay in his hands. He must make sure he did things right.

The day promised to be a scorcher. The bright sun filled the car as he drove in to Dortmund. The Monday morning traffic was its usual impatient self, made worse by the fine weather. Summer holidays beckoned or had recently been enjoyed and work was the last thing on people's minds. A minor accident caused a long tailback, so that by the time Siegfried arrived at his office he already felt stressed. Frau Schiersmann adroitly sensed his mood and swiftly brought him coffee before outlining the day's schedule.

"Your meeting with Herr Huwald is at nine," she told him, "then you are expected at eleven-thirty at the state planning office, going on to the shopping development after lunch. Herr Flinterhoff of FWP Electronics wants you to call him this morning about the new factory."

There was so much to be done. Clear thinking was vital, yet his thoughts kept wandering back to Sophie and the twins. Was his decision the right one? Could he do it? Was this really the only way to keep them safe?

"Herr Driesler?"

"Sorry?"

"Your call to Herr Flinterhoff. Do you want me to find the tender documents?"

"Oh, yes. Thank you."

Alone in his office again Siegfried tackled the post Frau Schiersmann had set out for him. By the time he had scribbled notes for further action by his staff it was nearly nine. Huwald, prompt as ever, was shown in on the dot. Siegfried wasted no time.

"The reason I requested this meeting, Herr Huwald, is that I have new responsibilities since becoming a father. I want my children's futures to be secure, as any parent would. Now, tell me what I should do to achieve this."

Huwald grinned broadly, sensing lucrative commission, but pretended his smile was for Siegfried. "First, let me offer my congratulations on your double good fortune, Herr Driesler. I hope Frau Driesler is recovering well from her confinement?"

"Yes. Tired, of course, but her mother is a great help during the day."

"It's wonderful to have family around at such times. Now, let's see what we can do!" He reached for his briefcase, pulled out a notebook and began to jot down a financial strategy for the Driesler family. After an hour and a half of detailed questions and answers, phone calls to brokers and promises to send on the relevant paperwork as soon as possible, Huwald had gone.

Siegfried watched him leave then sat back in his chair with a sigh of relief. He only had an hour before he was expected at the planning office. He had not touched the pile of paperwork at his side, but on an impulse he picked up the telephone and dialled Gustav's number. It rang several times before a sleepy voice answered.

"Yes?"

"Gustav, you lazy old man. Are you still in bed?"

"Siegfried? Is that you?"

"Yes. Look, I was wanting a brief word about things on my way to the planning office, but if you're not up then –"

"I'll be up," Gustav snapped, now thoroughly alert. "I'll expect you in ... what ... fifteen minutes?"

Siegfried sensed a problem. "Are you alone?"

There was a dry laugh. "Soon will be. Don't worry!"

*

Christian sat in his car and watched Siegfried Driesler pull up by Gustav's apartment block. Having been hustled ignominiously from Gustav's bed and sent on his way without breakfast, Christian had felt sure whom to expect, and he was proved right. His knuckles turned white on the steering wheel. "Important visitor, my arse," he hissed through clenched teeth. "New lover, more like. And you couldn't even wait for your bed to get cold, you two-timing bastard!" He shifted angrily in his seat, watching and waiting, his mind unavoidably conjuring up the activities going on in Gustav's apartment. It proved to be a quick session. A quarter of an hour later Driesler left the apartment block, unruffled and debonair in his city suit, and drove off.

As he sat there fuming, the street door opened again and Gustav himself stepped onto the pavement. He spotted Christian's car and came over. It was another hot day and Christian had his windows open. Gustav ducked down and rested his elbows on the doorframe.

"Spying on me still, Christian? I thought I made it clear I wanted a life of my own now."

"I didn't expect you to make your preference for your new lover so obvious by chucking me out like that!"

"New lover? Come off it, Christian, that was business! You don't think I'd be so heartless as to treat you like that, do you?"

"Business? With those looks? Don't take me for a fool, Gustav. I know your tastes and he fits the bill perfectly. Why business at your apartment? What sort of business?"

"Nothing to do with you," Gustav replied curtly, annoyed now and regretting his reunion with Christian.

Christian felt a strong urge to drive off in a huff, but then Gustav would have won. Taking a deep breath he managed to say: "If that's how you feel, fine. I'd just appreciate a bit more respect."

His meekness caught Gustav by surprise. Christian was really trying hard to be co-operative. Gustav decided to be tolerant. "Yes, you're right. I shouldn't have thrown you out in such a hurry. But you can see my point of view, can't you? Herr Driesler only had a few minutes spare and I couldn't have my lover around, could I? It would hardly have looked business-like!"

Christian still did not believe Gustav – what business could he have in the construction industry? – but he kept up the verbal fencing. "No, I suppose not." He reached for the ignition key and turned it on. "I'd better get some shopping in, since you don't seem to have time." He gave Gustav a beatific smile. "Any money?"

Gustav smiled in gracious defeat, reached into his pocket for his wallet, and handed over a ten mark note. "Milk, proper coffee, eggs, bread. You know the sort of stuff I need."

"Can I join you for breakfast?"

"If you prepare it!" Gustav agreed. Despite the privacy problems he caused, it was good having Christian's company and household skills again. But he was definitely not moving in.

*

Lisl Wendt handed her fed, bathed, powdered and now sleeping granddaughter over to her daughter. She surveyed the twins' bedroom. Friedrich was already asleep in his cot and everything was tidied away for the night. "Right, Liebchen," she said quietly to Sophie. "I'll be off home. Papa wants us to go out tonight so I must be back promptly. Are you expecting Siegfried at the normal time?"

Sophie shrugged. "I don't know what the normal time is any more. He has so much work at the office." She kissed her tiny daughter's forehead. "Vati seems very stressed at the moment, doesn't he, Liebchen?" she confided to Freia, then looked anxiously back at her mother. "He hides it well, but I think he's working too hard, what with the business nearly going under and all."

"I thought things were on the up at last."

"They are, but only because he's worked so hard to get the customers back. And his trip to the wedding in England didn't help. What we really need is a holiday together, after our honeymoon was such a disaster. But that's impossible right now," she added, giving the sleeping Freia a wistful look.

"The time will come soon enough. Babies have a habit of growing up, but I know that's no consolation when you're up all hours with them. Are you sure you can't afford an au pair even? Surely there must be something tucked by to help you out?"

"You're forgetting it's Siegfried who's stressed, Mama, not me!" Sophie laughed, laying Freia in her cot.

"Well then, come round for dinner tomorrow and bring the twins with you. Siegfried will have to be home on time then."

"Thanks, Mama. That would be nice."

At the front door Lisl Wendt kissed her daughter on the cheek. "Till tomorrow then. I won't be round till after lunch. What about a gentle stroll around the village? Do you think you can manage that?"

"You bet! I know you're desperate to push the pram."

Lisl laughed. "A grandmother's simple pleasures." She sobered as her thoughts turned elsewhere. "Poor Ilse, denied that pleasure. She was so looking forward to having grandchildren."

"She'll come for the christening."

Lisl nodded. "Of course she will. But so will Siegfried's father."

Sophie smirked. "I know. That should be fun to watch! I just hope Katherine won't want to come too, but I have a feeling she won't let Karl out of her sight now. She'll be all gracious forgiveness on the surface and seething anger underneath. Ghastly!" Sophie shuddered at the thought. "I suppose we do have to have them christened, do we?"

"Of course. Appearances are everything. You have made yourselves acquainted at your parish church, haven't you?"

"Not yet, but we will this weekend. But stop worrying about that now, Mama, or you'll never get away. Papa will be waiting."

Sophie sat for an hour after preparing supper before Siegfried arrived home. He looked like she felt, washed out and exhausted, and disappeared straight upstairs to get changed out of his suit. She wished she felt like giving him some bodily comfort, but the doctor had advised against it for a few weeks yet. Besides, one of the twins would be bound to wake up just as ...

"Schnapps?" he asked, popping his head round the kitchen door, bottle in hand.

"Go on then, just a small one. I shouldn't really, but maybe it will make the twins sleep longer."

He appeared a moment later with a full glass for himself and handed her a smaller one. "Prost!" He took a large swig, then perched on the edge of the kitchen table. "I was thinking today, Schatz, we must get this christening organised. Best done while it's still reasonable weather, since my father will have to travel a long way."

"Doesn't it depend on the farming calendar? Apple-picking or whatever?"

"That's a point. I'm not sure what comes first. Sheep-tupping maybe. I have a feeling late summer is a quiet time for them, before the apple harvest."

Sophie took a sip of schnapps. "We must be psychic. Mama and I were talking about the christening before you came home."

"That just goes to show, we need to get on with it. Let's set a date and fix the church. Mid-September, do you reckon? Is that long enough to organise everything?"

Sophie shrugged. "Probably. Your mother will need to get her flights booked. Where will she stay? With us?"

"Definitely. She'll want to see as much of the twins as possible."

"And your father?"

"What about him?" Siegfried snapped.

Sophie eyed him curiously. "Nothing. I just wondered if he would be staying at Medebach or nearer us."

"Oh." He drained his glass. "Medebach of course. That's where the christening will be."

Sophie blanched. "I thought it would be here. Your church at Medebach is Catholic."

Siegfried realised his mistake. Sophie was Protestant while he floated freely, not a believer of either church. "Sorry. There's so much to think about. Protestant it is. Local church will do." He stifled a yawn. "God, I'm tired. Let's eat."

Despite his exhaustion sleep evaded him that night. His meeting with Gustav was fresh in his mind, then there were the plans for the christening, business commitments to deal with and, above all else, the minutiae of his plan to sift through. There must be no problems, no hitches and no clues left behind. It must be foolproof and untraceable. Was it possible?

Friedrich woke shortly after twelve, followed by Freia. Siegfried finally fell asleep at three but was woken again at four. Sophie dealt with both twins since she could sleep in, but Siegfried could not get back to sleep. At five he got up, showered and shaved, and was in work by six-forty.

Frau Schiersmann found him asleep at his desk when she arrived at eight. She shook him gently. "Herr Driesler! Herr Driesler!" she repeated more loudly. She saw his eyes crank open. "You need to read this report before you attend the meeting with FWP Electronics at nine."

Siegfried raised his head from his desk and rubbed his bleary eyes. He felt dreadful. He needed his assistant. "Is Herr Nagel in?"

"Yes, but he's due out at the shopping complex this morning."

"Blast!" He reached for the coffee she had brought in.

"A bad night was it, sir? With the twins?"

"Yes." He made it plain he did not feel up to idle chatter and Frau Schiersmann quickly left him in peace.

He tried to clear his brain but it felt like it was stuffed with cotton wool. He picked up the report but could not focus his eyes on it. "Shit!" he swore, downed his coffee and poured himself another. They would need to promote someone as extra assistance. He jotted down the name 'Eduard Schüngel', then fixed his eyes on the report once more.

*

Sabina dumped her handbag on the bed then peeled off her damp blouse after a particularly tedious and sweaty day back at her work in a travel agent's. Despite the heat outside, Wolf's flat in

Dortmund seemed cheerless and bleak after the glories of the Shropshire and Herefordshire countryside. Seeing her parents looking so happy together again had made Sabina's wedding perfect. For a while she had been able to forget about the constant threat of danger, but her fears had resumed upon their homecoming.

She went into their tiny bathroom and ran a bath of tepid water as she continued stripping off clothing. As she stepped into the soothing water she heard the front door of the flat open and close as Wolf arrived home.

"I'm in the bath!" she called out on hearing him drop his keys on the dresser. The bathroom door opened and Wolf entered, grinning broadly at the sight of her naked body. Sabina decided on a bit of fun and at first played hard to get. "Hi, Liebling. I thought we might visit Siegfried and Sophie soon," she said, ignoring his obvious arousal. "We can meet the twins then get out into the countryside for some fresh air."

"Good idea. But don't go getting broody seeing those babies. I want some fun first." He leaned over the edge of the bath to kiss her. "Can I join you in there?"

"With pleasure." She grabbed his tie and pulled his face down towards hers, planting a big wet kiss on his mouth. Still kissing him she untied his tie and unbuttoned his shirt.

"Hey! You're making my shirt all wet," he protested, laughing at her sudden attack.

"So what? It's going in the wash anyway, isn't it?" Deftly she threw it in the laundry basket, then proceeded to unzip his trousers, hauling them down along with his underpants, before making room for him in the bath.

"How come I always get the tap end?" he asked, avoiding the taps by kneeling in front of her. There was a glugging noise as water rushed down the overflow outlet.

"Because you're a gentleman and wouldn't have it any other way," she giggled as he reached for the soap, worked up a lather on his hands then began soaping her breasts.

By the time they had finished it seemed like there was more water on the bathroom floor than in the bath. Sabina hugged a towel around her and hurried to the kitchen for a mop before water started to seep through the floor into the downstairs flat. With a towel about his waist, Wolf was moving the laundry basket out of a puddle.

"Shall we eat out tonight?" he asked, wanting to save her the effort of preparing anything after a hard day's work.

"I'm really not hungry. It's too hot. A beer or two would be nice, watching the world go by, and a snack, nothing more." She squeezed out the mop into the basin. "A rollmop or hamburger from a stall."

"A rollmop it is."

As they were getting dressed to go out into the hot evening, Sabina remembered her plans for the weekend. "I'd better give Sophie a ring before we go, and see if we can call in for a short visit on Sunday. We won't stay long as I'm sure she's got enough to do without having to entertain us."

"Fine."

"What about your mother?"

"What about my mother?"

"Don't you think we ought to make some effort to see her?"

Wolf smiled. "Ever the bridge-builder, aren't you?" He hesitated. "She won't want to see us. She made that quite clear before our wedding." He saw her determined expression. "But I suppose we still ought to make the effort to keep in touch, just in case she changes her mind."

"Good. I'll phone Sophie, then you can phone your mother." She sat down by the phone and dialled Sophie's number.

Sophie was delighted at the chance to show off her babies and talk about christening details. Sabina was taken aback, however, when, out of the blue, Sophie said: "You and Wolf must be godparents, of course. You will, won't you?"

Wolf saw Sabina's surprised expression and mouthed: "What's up?"

"Let me just check with Wolf," Sabina said into the phone, then put her hand over the mouthpiece. "They want us to be godparents. Do you mind?"

Wolf too was taken aback. "Goodness. What does it involve?"

"Oh, this and that, but do you want to be one?"

He shrugged. "I suppose it's an honour. OK, say yes."

Sabina took her hand off the mouthpiece. "We'd be honoured, Sophie. Thank you. We'll see you on Sunday to talk about it then, OK? *Tschüs.*"

Wolf's phone call to his mother, however, was far from friendly. "She hardly spoke to me," he told Sabina a short time later as they walked towards the city centre. "She said she was busy this weekend and couldn't see us, although it was perfectly clear she didn't want to see us, and had said goodbye and put the phone down before I knew what was happening."

Sabina gave his hand a squeeze. "Don't let her win. Keep on in there and act as though nothing was wrong. She'll come around eventually. You'll see."

"You really think so?"

"Yes, I do. The day will come when she realises she needs you. She'll be grateful then that you kept in touch."

"I suppose so."

"Perhaps grandchildren will make a difference."

Wolf stopped dead in his tracks. "I thought we agreed –"

"Not yet, you idiot!" Sabina laughed, punching him gently on the arm, then hugging him close to her side.

"Phew! You got me worried there. The thought of babies leaves me cold."

Sabina remembered with a shudder her own fears after they had first made love in the forest at Medebach. No, she too was not ready for a family yet. Perhaps when she was twenty-five or so. Wolf needed to get his business established; they would need a larger flat, a house even. Babies were too much of a responsibility when you're young and want to enjoy life, given the chance, she thought with a nervous glance around her.

They stood patiently with the crowd of pedestrians waiting for the traffic lights to change. Any one of them could put a knife in Wolf's back, or knock him into the path of a bus at any moment. She lived in constant fear for his life, just like her mother lived in constant fear for her father's mental state. She remembered seeing Robert Murdoch alone with her father at her wedding, no doubt satisfying himself that he was coping with the after effects of the trial and prison.

The lights changed and the crowd surged across the road. She studied the faces in the crowd, wondering if there was an assassin lurking behind the expressionless masks; an assassin like Siegfried.

*

"Excuse me, please."

Katherine looked up from pulling out dandelions, chickweed and groundsel from between the rows of cabbages. A man in a green felt hat adorned with a badger's-hair brush was peering over the hedge by the lane. She guessed he was in his late forties and thought he looked rather pale and unfit, considering the rucksack on his back. A German hiker moreover, his hat and heavy accent had immediately told her. She stood up and brushed the soil off her knees. She was wearing shorts and was immediately conscious of the man's eyes on her bare legs.

"Can I help you?" she called, keeping her distance. His accent had frightened her after all the recent talk of neo-Nazi retribution.

"Yes, I look for Karl Driesler. I read in the newspaper he live here in England so I take a holiday to find him." The man smiled warmly, but Katherine's heart froze. Seeing her hesitation, the man continued pleasantly: "They tell me in the village where you live."

There was no denying it then, Katherine thought, wondering what on earth she should do. Karl and the boys were out making a delivery of some garden furniture in Hereford and would not be back for an hour or so.

"I see you have worry," the man hurried on. "Let me explain myself. I am an old friend of Karl. We were in the army together, in Norway and Russia. Then he is make officer. I am not. I hear he is shot, then I hear no more until I read his name and see his photograph last year in the newspaper in Germany. Then I read he is free and goes home to England. I say to myself, I must find him and talk about the old times. We were good friends."

Despite herself, Katherine believed him. She approached the hedge and, reaching over it, offered her hand. "I am his wife, Katherine."

The man shook it warmly and introduced himself. "Ernst Winter."

The name meant nothing to her, but Karl never spoke about his life in the war. It was taboo territory. It might be interesting to hear what Ernst Winter had to say.

"Karl is out at the moment," she said slowly and clearly, having assessed the German's level of English. "Would you like to sit in the garden and wait for him? He should only be about an hour."

Ernst beamed with delight. "Thank you. Most kind."

Katherine showed him the front gate then suppressed a grin as she saw the lower half of him. There was absolutely no hiding the fact he was German in his half-length hiking trousers, long red socks and walking boots. His distinctive hat was the icing on the cake. He was the epitome of an innocent hiker. It could almost be a disguise. She felt another sudden panic. Any fanatical Nazi could have read about Karl's past and taken it upon himself to exact revenge. But it was too late now to go back. She must just remain vigilant and try to warn Karl of the man's presence before they met.

She led him to the garden seat in the shade under the pear tree where he took off his hat and rucksack and laid them beside the seat with a sigh of relief.

"In the old days we skied all day with three times that weight," he boasted.

Skied. At first the accurate word reassured her until she realised anyone reading Karl was in the First Mountain Division could safely assume they skied in winter. Maybe she was just being too suspicious. "Can I get you a drink?" she asked, mindful of her duty to a guest. "Coffee, beer, cider, lemonade? It's English beer," she added to remind him it would be warm, not icy cold.

He understood her reasoning. "I will try your cider. I hear it is a speciality of this area."

"Yes. We make our own here on the farm." She left him alone while she hurried indoors to fetch a bottle of cider and some lemonade for herself. She returned to the garden to find him studying the roses.

"Very beautiful flowers," he told her, his blue eyes twinkling at her as if to say it was not only the flowers that were beautiful. Another flatterer, she thought. Just like Gustav. The thought jolted her back to reality.

She poured the drinks then they sat on the garden seat, a polite distance apart.

"So, tell me about your time with Karl," Katherine prompted, keen to hear more details from the man who claimed to be Karl's friend.

"*Prost!*" Ernst said quickly, so he could take a sip of cider.

Katherine had forgotten the German formality with drinks. "*Prost!*" she replied.

"You speak German?"

"A little. Not very well." He seemed to be diverting the conversation, she thought anxiously.

"Like my English," Ernst laughed. "But Karl, he must speak good English now, yes? Like I speak Russian very good."

"Oh really?" Katherine asked. "Why's that?"

"I was prisoner there, a very long time. It was a very hard life. To live I must be clever. So I learn Russian. I am only here now because I make friend with guards." He sipped at his cider again. "Karl was very lucky. To be shot and sent away from the front," he clarified seeing her puzzled expression. "We stayed and some of us ..." He lifted his hands in resignation at his fate. "Our comrades went on to Yugoslavia, I hear later, but we were prisoners already. The newspaper said Karl was in Yugoslavia, where he met the man he later shot – Garisch?"

"Yes, Garisch or Goslar, whichever name you care to choose." Ernst seemed to be in his stride now and she prompted him to carry on talking, hoping to hear more about her husband's past from the man she was beginning to accept had been a friend. "So when did you meet Karl?"

"Our first days in the army. We went to Norway together, drank together and told our secrets to each other. He spoke always of his girlfriend at home, very beautiful. He told me he wanted to marry her, Ilse I think her name was, but of course ..." He broke off in embarrassment, realising who he was talking to. "I am sorry, Frau Driesler. You do not want to hear about former girlfriends."

"It's all right," she said quietly. "I know Ilse."

"Really?" He looked puzzled, then worked it out. "But of course. It was in the newspaper. His son, Siegfried, is Ilse's. You see? There is much about him I know only from the newspaper. Tell me about you and Karl. That I do not know."

The hour sped by as they exchanged information. Katherine heard of the thrills and excitement of Norway followed by the cruel hardship of Russia. At least the Mountain Divisions had been equipped for the cold, but still she could not imagine the full horror of fighting a war in winter out there. She thought she could almost hear the grinding roar of tanks, then realised it was the Land Rover driving up the lane to the farm.

"They're back!" she told her guest.

Ernst jumped to his feet in eager anticipation of meeting his long lost comrade and followed Katherine to the yard where the Land Rover was just pulling in, allowing her no time to warn Karl of Ernst's presence. Molly was barking a welcome as Richard and Paul got out of the vehicle first. They did not notice their mother standing by the garden gate and headed straight for their workshop. Karl was more sedate, but his attention too was fixed on emptying the back of the Land Rover of purchases made in Hereford.

Katherine called over to him above Molly's barking. "Karl! You have a visitor." She opened the garden gate and led Ernst Winter out to the yard.

Karl dumped a roll of wire netting at his feet and looked up. He did not recognise the man in hiking garb standing at Katherine's side, but there was no mistaking his nationality. His heart lurched.

The man strode forward, hand outstretched in greeting, and called out in German: "Karl, you rascal! Don't you know your old comrade, Ernst Winter?"

"Winter? Ernst Winter?" The voice sounded familiar. Karl peered closer at the man. It was strange how easily he had recognised Goslar from all those years ago, while an old friend was almost a stranger. "My God! It is you under all those wrinkles."

Katherine breathed a huge sigh of relief. The man was who he said he was, and what was more Karl was pleased to see him. She had feared Karl would shun reminders of history, but the comradeship the two men had once shared did not seem to have faded with time. She watched as the pair embraced, slapping each other's back then staring at each other as if unable to believe the changes they saw in each other's faces. They seemed rooted to the spot until Katherine decided to intervene.

"We were sitting in the garden, Karl, having a drink and Ernst was telling me about your time in Norway. I believe it when he called you a rascal, some of the things you two got up to!"

Ernst grinned wickedly. "I couldn't tell your wife the half of it."

"We were young men, away from home. It was normal," Karl laughed. "But you speak English, Ernst! You understood my wife just then."

"Between us we managed with her German and my English." His smile faded. "I told her my Russian is much better."

Those few words told Karl all he needed to know. Ernst had been a prisoner of the Russians. "You poor sod," he muttered. Sweeping away the grim past he abruptly turned to Katherine. "Can you fetch the schnapps I keep for special guests, Schatz? Today there'll be no more work done, I fancy"

Ernst laughed. "I knew you would speak good English. You were always good at everything!"

Katherine smiled to herself at the veracity of that last remark as she went inside to fetch the bottle and glasses. She decided she ought to throw some food together as well to soak up the alcohol. Karl rarely drank to excess, but today might be one of those days. Rummaging in the kitchen cupboards she found some potato crisps, stuck a lump of cheddar cheese on a plate along with some biscuits, threw some knives and butter on the tray too and hurried outside with her offerings.

Karl and Ernst were well ensconced in reminiscing already as she placed the tray on the garden table, alongside the one holding the drinks from earlier. She wondered whether to go, but Karl beckoned her to join them.

"Sit down, Schatz and make us keep our language clean before the boys hear us swearing like the old soldiers we are."

"You swear, Karl?" she asked in disbelief. Apart from the odd expletive, his language was usually mild. Then she thought she understood. Karl was suspicious of his old friend turning up out of the blue, and wanted reinforcements in case of trouble. She moved a chair closer to the table and sat down as Karl poured her a glass of cider.

"So, did you ever get married, Ernst?" he asked, resuming the conversation.

"Briefly, in 1957. But it didn't work out. I had been a prisoner too long. I just couldn't seem to adjust to a normal life. We went our separate ways, and I've been a bit of a nomad ever since, working here, there and everywhere. I was in India for a year, working on the railway. That's where I learned my English."

"India!" Katherine exclaimed, managing to keep up with the spoken German. "How fascinating!"

Ernst shrugged. "Yes, if you like poverty. I was pretty much of a tramp myself, carrying everything I owned in one bag. I had to be free, free to move on, free of walls that held me in. India gave me that and somehow, eventually, I managed to turn the corner and settle down a bit after that. Got myself a job back in Germany with the Bundesbahn in the end. Cheap rail-travel. That's how I got here all the way from Berlin!"

Yet another soul shattered by war, Katherine thought sadly.

"Do you ever use your Russian in Berlin?" Karl asked.

"No, except to shout abuse at the border guards," Ernst quickly replied.

Karl topped up their glasses, and Katherine promptly held out the bowl of crisps. At the rate they were going she would need to send Richard out to the village store for some more.

"I was in Berlin in early '43," Karl said. "Officer-training and convalescence after being wounded. The city was still intact then, of course. I would hate to go back now and see how much was destroyed or lost to the Russians."

"The two halves are certainly very different," Ernst informed him.

"But which half is better?" Karl demanded suddenly.

Ernst lowered the glass, which had been half way up to his mouth. "What are you driving at, Karl?" he asked slowly.

Karl scratched his head as he worked out how to phrase what he wanted to say. "We all have ways of surviving, Ernst. As you read in the reports on my trial, I survived a prison camp by joining the SS, against my better judgement. I think you may have survived by becoming a communist and working for the Russians."

Ernst slapped his thigh and guffawed with laughter. "Goal!" he roared. "How did you guess?"

"Just a hunch. Did you stay in Russia, marry a Russian girl then work your way down towards India from there?" Ernst's broad grin gave him the confirmation he needed to continue. "No doubt they gave you papers that got you into the West when you returned."

"You've been watching too many James Bond films, Karl, but you're right. So now you know my secret. I'm a spy. But I'm very small fry. In fact the only reason I can admit this to you is because I don't do anything at all for the Soviets. I used them as a means to an end. I have no real loyalty to them. My loyalty is to Germany – always was and always will be." Ernst's speech was beginning to slur. "You'd understand that, I'm sure, living here in England like you do." He thumped the table as he suddenly demanded: "Are you English or German?"

Karl smiled. He could see where Ernst was heading. "British passport, but I suppose that underneath I'm still German."

"There, you see? Even when we were loyal Nazis, you and I, we were Germans first and foremost. Politics mean nothing and politicians are all liars, cheats, thieves and murderers! I'm not surprised you killed that trickster who called himself Garisch. I'd go and shoot the whole bloody lot of them if I could. They ruined our lives, Karl, ruined them."

To Katherine's horror she saw tears streaming down Ernst's face. Karl motioned her to stay seated. He would handle this.

"So you hate the Nazis now, Ernst?"

"Only because they let us down. Those were such good times in Norway, Karl, weren't they? We truly believed we were the Master Race and could do what we wanted. Then the Russians showed us otherwise. Man, how they showed us. I've never felt the same about myself ever since. I can't live with the disgrace of it all, Karl. I can't seem to accept the world as it is now. I'm just a sad old soldier who wants to return to the glory days." He sniffed hard then smiled again. "Imagine my excitement when I saw your son interviewed on television immediately after you shot Garisch. The likeness is so striking I thought at first it was you, until he started speaking about his father and I remembered twenty-odd years had passed since I last saw you. Then I followed every word spoken or written about your trial, heard all about what happened to you, and how the Nazis treated you. I thought, surely Karl would know how I feel. I was tempted to write to you in prison but never quite plucked up the courage. Then, when I heard about your release, I thought, right, this is my chance to find you again, an old comrade, somebody I can pour out my woes to."

"I'm honoured you felt I could help you, Ernst. But why didn't you go to any of the reunions? Surely there are others who survived?"

"No doubt there are, but they would look on me as a traitor for siding with the Soviets. There were a few released from Soviet prisoner of war camps in the end. Not many, but a few. But you are a traitor to the Nazis too, aren't you, Karl? You killed one of them – I know – they couldn't prove you intended to, but you would have. I know you too well. A natural killer you were. I could see the same in your son."

Karl was uncomfortably aware of Richard and Paul hovering close by, hearing every word, and of Katherine's pinched expression, but he had to let Ernst say his piece, just as he had once needed to pour out his soul to Robert Murdoch so many years ago. He saw the boys sit down on garden chairs nearby, watchful of this German stranger but curious to hear what he was saying.

"And then your son changed sides," Ernst went on, unable to quell his outpourings. "And I thought how happy you looked together and I just pictured myself with you, and I cried every time I thought how good life was in the army, and how alone I am now and ..." Ernst gulped back the sobs which overwhelmed him now. In an effort to regain his composure he drained his schnapps, held out his glass and Karl dutifully poured him another, which he downed in one.

As his eyes began to glaze over, Katherine got up and put her hand on Karl's shoulder. "Shall I ring Werner and ask him to come up this evening," she whispered in his ear. "It sounds like Ernst wants a soldiers' reunion party and to feel good about himself again."

"You recognise the signs do you, Schatz?" Karl asked with a wry smile.

"Indeed I do. Now it's your turn to rescue the lost soul, and I don't mind if you have to sing your old soldiers' songs in the process. Help him out, Karl. He needs it."

Ernst's head had sunk onto the table by now and Karl had to smile. "He never could hold his drink. You go and phone Werner, and I'll get the boys to help me carry him to the feed store. We haven't got any guests booked in for tonight, have we?"

"No. There's a couple arriving this weekend, but we're all right until then."

Karl stood up and nodded to Richard. "You help me with him and Paul can carry his rucksack up."

Paul let his father and Richard struggle across the garden with their barely conscious burden, then picked up the stranger's pack and hat. His father was really too trusting, Paul thought. Wolf and Sabina were terrified of being attacked and now here were his parents offering hospitality to someone who could have been sent by Siegfried, for all they knew. He bent down and unbuckled the strap on the rucksack and peered inside. Maps, phrasebook, passport, spare socks and underwear, flask and, rolled up in a shirt, a revolver.

He waited in the yard outside the old feed store until his father and Richard came out from putting their guest to bed. "Dad, look," he said, beckoning him to inspect the contents of the rucksack.

Karl frowned. "You shouldn't be looking in other people's –"

"Just look, Dad," Paul interrupted. "It's important."

Karl took his son's word for it and crouched down to look in the rucksack. He found what Paul had found. "Did you touch it?" he asked, carefully avoiding doing so himself.

"No. I felt it through the shirt and guessed what it was before I unwrapped it. What do we do now, Dad? Shall I call the police?"

Karl rocked back on his heels, hands clasped round his knees, deep in thought, then he reached forward again and removed the passport to look at it. All the details tallied with what Ernst had told them. It had been issued in Berlin in 1963 and gave his details as a railway worker, born in Brunswick in 1920, which Karl knew to be true. The Russians had not given him a new identity then, merely furnished him with the means of quietly returning to his homeland, presumably to act as a 'sleeper' until he was needed by them.

"I thought Siegfried or someone might have sent him to ..."

"Or someone, Paul It wouldn't be Siegfried. But you could be right. It's impossible to know where his loyalties lie. He could be a communist, or an ardent Nazi still. Perhaps he carries a gun to remind himself of the good old days or as self-protection. There could be any number of reasons."

"But we can't take any chances, Dad," Richard intervened. "We can't just leave it with him."

"I don't want to get him into trouble." Karl stood up and looked towards the old feed store as if to check that his old comrade still lay sleeping. "My instincts tell me to believe him," he explained, "and I'd betray his trust if I turned this over to the police. I know what your mother would say," he hurried on, seeing both his sons about to protest. "She'd be scared witless if she knew he had this, but there's no way I'm touching it. We'll hide his rucksack somewhere safe, and I'll confront him about it when he wakes up. I'd like to give him the chance to explain why he has it."

Richard and Paul looked at each other. They could each see the other disagreed with their father's decision but knew it would be pointless to argue.

Karl buckled up the rucksack and carried it over to the boys' workshop where he buried it behind the pile of wood in the corner. "I suggest you stay around here to keep an eye on it," he told them. "I'm sure you've plenty of work to do in here."

As he came back out Katherine found him. "I've rung Werner and he's coming up at seven. He seemed quite excited at the prospect!"

"I just hope Ernst has managed to sleep it off before then. He's got five hours, so he should be all right."

After a late lunch Katherine returned to her weeding but found herself brooding over something Ernst had said about Karl. When he joined her later in the garden for a tea break she asked out of the blue: "Were you really a natural killer, Karl?"

Karl laughed off her question. "Don't take any notice of that. I was a born show-off. Whatever I did, I wanted to do well. Naturally gifted, shall we say, and I was used to killing animals. That is what he meant."

"But you did kill Goslar, didn't you?"

"Katherine! We've been through all this –"

"I know, I'm sorry. It's just that your friend seemed so sure you could do it, it just made me think again whether you had really meant to ..." Her voice tailed off and she shrugged awkwardly. "Your life has been so different from mine. I can't always understand you, but I want to. You know I wouldn't blame you if you had meant to kill him."

"I know. But it's like I've always said. My memory of the event is very hazy. It's like the moment I saw him I stepped out of the present and time stood still. The next thing I was aware of was being taken away in the ambulance. I was in shock and bleeding a lot from the dog bite and my thoughts were ... elsewhere."

"I see. I'll just have to live with that, then. Not that it matters really, does it?"

"Of course it matters," he contradicted, knowing she had deliberately provoked him to. "Would it help you if I admitted I did intend to kill him, then you wouldn't harbour any doubts about me."

"No, that's not what I'm after. I just want the truth, and if the truth is you don't know, then you don't know."

Karl reflected on her words, 'I just want the truth'. She was right. She should not be kept in the dark. "You want to hear some more truth?" he asked. "Ernst has a gun."

"What!" Katherine gasped.

"I wasn't going to tell you, as I didn't want you frightened, but the boys thought I was wrong, and I probably was. Don't worry," he soothed seeing her about to jump up to find the boys. "It's safely hidden and he doesn't know we know. Paul found it, suspicious lad that he is. Ernst is right. We see too many 'James Bond' and 'Man from U.N.C.L.E.' films. But in this case it paid off."

"So what do you intend doing about it? He could be here to kill you! Shouldn't we call the police?"

"Back then I would have trusted him with my life. I trust him still."

"But people change. Look at you! You're nothing like you used to be, and I should know. When you had amnesia you were young and arrogant, the Karl that Ernst knew. A few weeks later you were a reformed character again, once your memory came back. Don't tell me that after all he's been through at the hands of the Russians, he's not changed too, and maybe for the worse."

"You believed him."

"Yes, until I heard he was carrying a gun. Normal people don't carry guns about with them, Karl."

"He's not normal. He's a Soviet spy."

"Stop acting the fool, Karl! This is serious. He could be here to kill you."

"Then why is he lying out cold in our guest room? You don't trust my instincts with Siegfried and you don't seem to trust me on this one either."

"I just want you to see sense. You can't afford any repercussions from this. If anything happened with that gun, anything at all, and you with your record –"

"I was cleared!"

"Not proven. It's different and you damn well know it!"

She had sworn. Karl knew how upset she was. "Look, Schatz," he soothed, "just as soon as he wakes up I'll ask him about it."

"No you won't. You'll tell the police now. I'm not going to wait and have you shot in front of my eyes. You've had too many lucky escapes in your life."

She was on her feet already but he grabbed her arm. "Sit down, Katherine!" he bellowed.

She had rarely seen him this angry except with Siegfried, who had more than once ended up getting hurt. Suddenly she noticed Richard and Paul lurking anxiously in the yard, aware of the row. Their presence made her calm herself somewhat and remember her rule number one, which was to avoid upsetting Karl. Out of long habit she sat down so as not to provoke him further. She always had to let him feel he had won. He could not abide being forced to do anything against his will. She usually managed to get her own way in the end by stealth.

As she sat Karl immediately softened his grip on her arm. "Thank you. Just let me explain. You don't appreciate how strong the bond of comradeship is. We trained together, lived together and were prepared to die together."

"But that was years ago!"

"Even so, I can't go behind his back to the police. I must speak to him first."

Her frustration with him evident, Katherine let out a long sigh. "Right, well you'd better go and ask him now, because I'm not waiting for him to wake up and start prowling around searching for his gun before we know what he's up to."

"Fair enough," Karl agreed. "We'll all go. Safety in numbers, but I also want you to see how much you'll upset him by your distrust." He stood up and noticed Richard and Paul for the first time. "Did they hear all that?"

"I think so."

"Right, so I don't need to explain what's happening. Come on then."

They all marched over to the guest accommodation in the old feed store. Karl knocked twice then put his head round the door. Stepping inside he beckoned them all in.

"See, sleeping like a baby."

Ernst grunted, licked his lips and rolled over. Karl sat down on the bed next to him and gently shook his shoulder. He got the reaction he expected. Despite his drink-sodden state, Ernst sat up remarkably alert, ready to defend himself.

"It's all right, Ernst, nothing to worry about," Karl told him. "We just want to know why you're carrying a gun in your rucksack."

Ernst smiled slowly and flopped back onto one elbow. "Ah! You found it." He stretched unconcernedly and yawned widely, displaying numerous gaps in his teeth. "I'd better explain. It's to shoot myself with if the Soviets ever call on my services." He smiled weakly to hide his fear. "I'm not going to betray my country for them, ever. They may never call on me, but if they do then ..." Now he managed a braver smile at the four faces round his bed. "I've got into the habit of carrying it with me everywhere I go. Don't worry, Karl. I haven't been sent by Garisch's comrades to avenge his death, if that's what you're thinking." He paused, still smiling but this time with amusement. "I can see by your faces that is what you were thinking."

"It was a possibility we had to consider, Ernst," Karl explained. "You obviously appreciate our concerns since my trial."

Ernst swung his feet round over the side of the bed and shook his head to clear it of sleep. "Only too well, I'm afraid, Karl. But I can assure you, I'm not your assassin."

"That's good enough for me, Ernst," Karl replied. He looked round at his wife and sons and saw scepticism written large on their faces, but that was only to be expected. They did not know Ernst.

"So, where is my rucksack?" Ernst asked looking round his room for it.

"Karl, please don't ..." Katherine begged.

Ernst saw her fear. "If it will reassure you, Frau Driesler, then keep the gun hidden from me while I am here. But I would still like my rucksack. I seem to have woken with a headache and I need some aspirin."

There was a gentle chuckle all round and Ernst knew he had convinced them.

SIXTEEN

Ilse's bulging suitcases finally appeared on the carousel. She strained forwards through the waiting passengers to grab the first one. Settling it carefully on the baggage trolley she paused to regain her breath before forcing her way back to the carousel for her second case. She had had to pay excess baggage, but it would be worth it to see everyone admiring the gifts she had brought with her.

The journey had been exhausting. With stopovers and time differences she was now hopelessly muddled as to time of day, whether she should be eating breakfast or dinner. Only her adrenalin was keeping her going; any moment now she would be seeing her beloved Siegfried again, and in a couple of hours her grandchildren! When she had first introduced Sophie to Siegfried she had hardly dared hope it would come to this, but her matchmaking had been perfect, with Friedrich and Freia the results.

Clutching her handbag tightly, she steered the trolley through customs to the arrivals' hall. To her relief and immense joy she saw Siegfried standing at the front of the crowd waiting there.

"At last!" he greeted her, giving her a rapturous hug. "You're here!"

"What a journey!" Ilse cried, wiping an emotional tear from her cheek. She stood back and held her son at arm's length to get a good look at him. She was distressed at what she saw. He looked more exhausted than she felt, but she made no comment, simply giving him another long hug. Finally she broke away. "Let's get going. I can't wait to see those grandchildren of mine."

"Come on then. We should just beat the evening rush hour."

"Evening, is it? It should be morning, except I don't think I've slept yet. Never mind. There'll be time for that later."

Siegfried pushed the trolley out of the terminal building and they were soon in the Mercedes headed east down the autobahn towards Dortmund. He let his mother relax and absorb her surroundings, sensing she was too tired for much conversation. By the time they were approaching Soest, however, she found her voice again.

"Paul sent his love, and wishes he could have come too."

"He's definitely forgiven me, then?"

"There was nothing to forgive. You only did what you had to under the circumstances. You made a good job of it by all accounts. Things are starting to get going again after our slight setback. I hear Gustav Halstrup has taken over the Dortmund area now."

"That's right. I've met him several times recently. He even sent the twins a gift when they were born. Teddy bears!"

Ilse smiled. Paul would be very pleased to hear that bit of news. It confirmed Siegfried was well and truly accepted back in the neo-Nazi fold. She probed further. "And how was your father? You didn't really tell me much in your letters about Bina's wedding. It must have been very strange for you going back there again and being so ... friendly to everyone," she teased.

"Yes, it was. Most of them were still a bit suspicious of me, but they began to come around. My middle name ought to be Janus, I had to be so two-faced! You'll see at the christening how well it works."

"Your father's still coming, I take it?"

"Yes, and Katherine too," Siegfried warned his mother.

She smiled at his concern. "I'm glad you appreciate what I feel for him still." She gave a girlish giggle. "Do you think Katherine will speak to me?"

"I doubt it, but I can't see her publicly shunning you. She's not one for creating scenes – especially at occasions like that. She'll be very cool but polite."

"Yes. I think you're probably right. Typically English. I don't think I'd be so polite if the tables were reversed. Ah well, let's just make sure we all enjoy the occasion. It'll be good to see everyone again."

Siegfried heard the wistfulness in his mother's voice. He took his eyes off the road for a moment and saw her surreptitious wipe of a tear. He put a hand on her arm. "We miss you too."

He was surprised by her reaction. She gave a choking sob and tears gushed down her powdered cheeks. Hurriedly she delved in her handbag for a handkerchief and delicately wiped her eyes, although her mascara had already smudged. At the next lay-by Siegfried pulled in to give her time to repair her make-up before they arrived home.

As she put away her lipstick and compact, Siegfried asked: "All right now?"

"Yes, thank you, Liebling. It must have been because I'm tired. I promise I won't do that again."

"It's all right, Mutter. You do whatever you want."

How tired he looks, Ilse thought with a mother's critical eye. She decided to say something before they got home and were enveloped by the rest of the family. "You've changed a lot since I last saw you, Siegfried. Despite Sophie's accident, you were full of the joys of forthcoming fatherhood. Now you seem ... troubled."

Lying was second nature to Siegfried, but he had seldom kept anything from his mother before. He scratched the side of his nose and smiled reassuringly at her. "Troubled? No, I'm fine, really – just tired and trying to sort out the business still. We're promoting Eduard Schüngel to help ease my load, though I don't suppose it'll make much difference for a while, until he finds his feet. Paul taught me well, but I don't have time to teach Eduard, I'm afraid."

Ilse nodded, apparently accepting his words, but inside she knew when her son was lying. Everything was not all right, and for Siegfried to lie to her it must be serious indeed. Perhaps there was trouble between him and Sophie? Her long stay in hospital must have led Siegfried into temptation of a night. He had always been one to sow his wild oats, but unlike herself, Sophie would not turn a blind eye to such misdemeanours if she ever found out. She would have to keep a watchful eye open during her visit, Ilse decided. She put her handbag back down by her feet. "Shall we press on? I'm quite recovered now."

Siegfried started the engine and steered back onto the road for the short distance to Soest. Ilse suddenly remembered all the questions she had wanted to ask about the twins, Sophie's health, about Margit and the rest of her children. She kept Siegfried busy until they pulled up in his driveway and saw Sophie watching out of the window for them. Ilse waved excitedly, grabbed her handbag and hurried out of the car and up to the front door just as Sophie got it open.

"Ilse!"

"Sophie!"

Siegfried stood with the luggage, waiting patiently for the hugs and kisses to subside then he too kissed Sophie, aware of his mother's watchful eye. He gave Sophie an extra-long hug, for his mother's benefit and saw she was satisfied.

"You're looking well, Sophie. And walking without sticks now?" Ilse commented.

"Most of the time, as long as I don't overdo things."

Ilse's impatience became apparent. "So where are they then – my little grandchildren?"

"Come on in and I'll show them to you," Sophie beamed. "They're both awake and waiting to see their Oma." She led Ilse through to the living room where Ilse enjoyed the delights of grandmotherhood for the first time. She crooned and fussed over them, held each in her arms, comparing them to their parents, until Freia had had enough and started to cry. Siegfried took his mother's bags up to her room, leaving the two women to tend to the babies' needs. He found himself wondering whether Katherine would be so effusive in her adoration of her step-grandchildren. Hardly likely, he supposed, but you never knew with Katherine. As for his father, he had no idea how he would respond. There was so much about him he didn't know.

*

The journey to Germany was becoming almost routine to Katherine, after all her visits while Karl was in prison and for his mother's funeral. On each of those occasions the wretched Ilse had been uppermost in her mind, and now she was going to have to meet her again and be civil to her. She gazed out of the aircraft window at the fields and woodland looming closer as they prepared to land. She knew Karl was excited about seeing his grandchildren, and had scarcely mentioned Ilse, but for Katherine she was the bogeyman destined to blight the celebrations. Katherine felt it must be obvious to Karl that she was only accompanying him to the christening to fend off Ilse, but he had said nothing about the subject, probably finding it too tricky to tackle. It was his usual method of dealing with emotional problems – trying to forget about them. He had once succeeded only too well, with his bout of amnesia after the traumas of the Second World War, but Katherine could not simply forget about Ilse and how she had brazenly boasted about sleeping with Karl.

The aircraft banked, heading ever downwards then she heard the undercarriage lock into position. Rudi would be waiting at the airport to drive them to Medebach, where she would be welcomed into the bosom of the Driesler tribe. Then it would be another day before the christening at Soest and the meeting with her foe.

There was a lurch and a rumble as the plane landed. The terminal buildings sped by then it was time to step out onto German soil, or rather tarmac, again. She had never forgotten the feeling she had on her first visit to Germany back in 1950 when travel restrictions had been lifted. Everything had seemed so strange then. It was her first trip abroad; her first meeting with Karl's family; the first time she had seen him on home territory, relaxed and familiar with people and customs as he seldom was in England, where he was always conscious of his nationality. It was the first time she had truly appreciated what he had given up to allow her to stay on the farm in Herefordshire, and the first time she had felt uneasy as a member of the conquering allies. Karl's family had welcomed her with open arms, but in Medebach she had never been able to rid herself of the feeling that the locals considered Ilse to have prior claim as Karl's wife.

"Ready?" Karl asked as the seat-belt sign went out.

Katherine smiled. "To face the fray, you mean? You must have been reading my thoughts!"

"You were looking a bit grim. Enjoy the break. Richard and Paul will be fine. Just relax. Don't forget we'll be seeing Bina and Wolf again tomorrow." He stood up and reached for the overhead locker, passing Katherine her flight bag.

Katherine tried hard to lighten her mood as they passed through the arrivals' procedures and met up with Rudi. It was good to see him again. Even though Bina's wedding was not very long ago, there was still news to catch up on. She let Karl sit in the front of the car with his brother, while she watched the country pass by, so different now from that decimated land she had first seen. No wonder Zopf Construction had made such huge profits. Paul Zopf must have considered himself in serious trouble to have fled from so much wealth.

She listened to Karl and Rudi chatting away. When Karl spoke German in England he used *Hochdeutsch*, which she was better able to understand than the dialect he used with family and friends in Medebach. Nevertheless she managed to catch some of what they were saying and smiled to hear how pleased their father was at being a great-grandfather. Dear Dieter. It would soon be the first anniversary of Gisela's death, but now he had two great-grandchildren to help distract him through that unpleasant time. Counting the months she realised that in years to come, cynics might cast aspersions on the twins' births, coming rather short of nine months after their parents' wedding. She found herself wondering when Sabina and Wolf might produce a grandchild for herself, but had to admit that Sabina showed no desire for motherhood yet. Strange, as she herself had always wanted Karl's child, even before they were married. Fortunately it had not resulted in that, thanks to Robert Murdoch's help in acquiring contraceptives. She smiled at the memory of just how useful Robert had been.

Karl's voice speaking in English broke through her contemplation. "You look happier!"

She laughed. "Well, I won't tell you exactly what I was thinking, but you were a part of it."

"I'm glad I made you smile at last. You're worried about meeting Ilse, aren't you?"

Just hearing him say her name still hurt, but there was no way it could be avoided. "Yes, but don't worry. I don't intend making a scene."

"I know, Schatz. Enough said."

Karl turned back to face the front and spoke to Rudi, while Katherine sank back into her seat, realising how awkward it was going to be for him too. And what about Ilse? How was she looking forward to meeting Karl and herself again?

As they turned off the autobahn and headed into the hills of the Sauerland towards Winterberg, passing ever more picturesque villages full of half-timbered houses, Katherine suspected Ilse's feelings would be very different from her own.

*

Siegfried watched the clock ticking away as Sophie and his mother fussed over the twins in their white christening robes, making sure both were clean and tidy before the first family members arrived. Peter and Lisl Wendt were staying out of the way, going directly to the church; the Röbel offspring had visited their mother the previous day so were also making their way direct to the church. The Driesler contingent, on the other hand, was coming to the house first to see the objects of all the attention before the event.

Wolf and Sabina were first to arrive, Sabina sporting the pastel-blue suit she had worn as her going away outfit. Wolf wore his loden suit, as did Siegfried. Sabina placed the two presents she had brought with her on the hall table, kissed Sophie and Siegfried, then faced Ilse. This is not going to be easy, Sabina thought. Their last encounter had been at Siegfried's wedding, when Sabina had stood outside the reception hotel and shouted insults at Ilse for trying to steal her father.

Fortunately Ilse took the initiative, taking hold of both Sabina's hands in hers. "Hello, Bina. You look well. Wolf too." She let go of Sabina and presented a cheek to Wolf for him to kiss. "My congratulations on your marriage. How's life treating you?"

Sabina found herself responding automatically to the question. "Great, thank you." It really wasn't so difficult after all to be polite to Ilse. "How's life for you and Paul?"

"Oh-h-h ... different. I miss everyone here, of course, especially now my grandchildren have arrived. Aren't they gorgeous? You've seen them already, Sophie told me."

"Yes, a few weeks ago, though. No doubt they've changed tremendously. We brought a camera this time."

"And so have I," Ilse cheerfully informed them.

The thought flashed across Sabina's mind that possibly Ilse wanted pictures of her father as much as of the twins, but she shoved the idea to the back of her mind. If Ilse needed such memories when stuck in exile in Uruguay, what the heck did it matter?

Sophie moved them all through to the living room, but just as they were all settled, more cars drew up outside. Sabina was back on her feet in an instant, ready to greet her family and also to observe her mother's meeting with Ilse. Nothing had ever been said by her parents about Ilse, but Richard had overheard Siegfried bragging that his father had gone back to Ilse. Sabina had managed to persuade Richard it was all lies, but she strongly suspected there was truth in what he said, hence her outburst at Ilse at Siegfried's wedding. Perhaps she would find out now. She spotted Ilse hanging back, furtively looking through the window as the numerous family members filed up the front path.

Uwe was first to the door, she noticed. None of the Driesler side of the family had been invited to Siegfried and Sophie's wedding, which was hardly surprising, given the circumstances at the time, but it had hurt Uwe in particular. As a seven-year-old he had taken his younger cousin, Siegfried, under his wing and helped him settle in with his new family at Medebach. They had remained close through childhood, so Siegfried's treachery had come as a real blow. But since the trial and her wedding, contact with Siegfried had been re-established and Sabina guessed Uwe wanted to be the first to set foot in Siegfried's home. Onkel Rudi and Tante Adele were close behind with Andrea and Martin; Tante Anna and Onkel Stefan, Lothar and Monika with husband Jens were next, while Sabina's parents brought up the rear with Opa. If they were deliberately hanging back it was not obvious, but Sabina was careful not to get embroiled with the incoming crowd so she would have a good view of her parents' meeting with Ilse.

Sophie and Siegfried, each holding a twin, stood at the door to greet their guests, so Karl and Katherine's arrival into the living room was somewhat delayed as they were shown the babies. When they finally appeared in the now crowded room, Ilse was hidden behind the mass of bodies and almost invisible. It was a tactical withdrawal but it tended to confirm that Ilse was anxious about meeting Sabina's parents.

Then Sabina saw what she was looking for. Her father, far taller than her mother, had spotted Ilse skulking by the window. Their eyes met; Ilse looked wistful, her father looked awkwardly away, then thought better of it, giving her a nod of recognition, nothing more. Very cool, Sabina thought. She watched her mother closely now, but Katherine was as yet unaware of Ilse's presence and made her way straight over towards her daughter and Wolf.

"Hello, Mummy," Sabina greeted her, positioning herself so that her back was towards Ilse. "Did you have a good trip out here?"

"Yes. No problems whatsoever. Richard and Paul send their love, of course, as does the whole of Penchurch. Gertie told me to tell you ..." Her voice faded away as she suddenly saw Ilse over Sabina's shoulder. Sabina saw the narrowing of the eyes, the hardening of the mouth, which betrayed her mother's wrath, but Katherine made a good recovery and carried on. "... that your wedding photo has pride of place on her piano beside Robert and Alice's."

Katherine moved sideways so she did not have to look at Ilse and began chatting to Wolf. Karl joined them and kissed his daughter. He too positioned himself so Ilse was out of sight. A definite snub, Sabina noted. It was true then. As far as her parents were concerned Ilse was *persona non grata*.

Sophie had noticed the situation and was not having her mother-in-law ignored, whatever the reason. She weaved her way over to Ilse, gave her Freia to hold, and brought her into the middle of the room for Dieter, Anna and Adele to talk to. Ilse was now only a few feet away from Karl and it was impossible for him to ignore her any longer, given the company she was in. He turned aside to open up the circle to include his family and Ilse. Katherine looked steadily at the floor, but then Ilse made her move.

"Hello, Karl. Do you want to hold our granddaughter?"

It was her deliberate stress on the word 'our' that angered Katherine and Sabina. They both bit their tongues and watched Karl's reaction. Dutifully he stepped forward, but Ilse was holding Freia close to her chest. Karl had no option but to put his hands between the baby and Ilse's breasts to safely pick her up. Ilse looked smug, Karl looked momentarily peeved, but he settled the gurgling Freia in the crook of his arm and returned to his place in the circle. Sabina caught her mother's eye and in her look, Katherine knew her daughter was aware of the situation.

Karl looked down into his granddaughter's blue eyes, the genealogical product of one of the liaisons with Ilse in the forest around Medebach back in the Easter of 1943. First had come Siegfried, the son he hardly knew. Now there were Freia and Friedrich. He determined they would see plenty of their grandfather, whatever it took. He touched Freia's peach-soft cheek and she turned her head to try to suck on his finger, just like Sabina, Richard and Paul used to.

He became aware of both Katherine and Ilse watching him. There was no doubt Ilse was totally smitten with her grandchildren. For Katherine bonding with them would be harder, but he needed her to feel close to them. He caught Katherine's eye and was not comforted by what he saw. Ilse's proximity to Freia was not working well for her. Karl put himself between Ilse and Katherine and gave his wife his full attention.

"What do you think of her then? Another Beauty, eh?" Beauty had been Katherine's parents' pet name for her.

"Definitely," Katherine smiled, determined not to spoil things for Karl. She held out her hands. "May I hold her?"

"With pleasure!" Karl deposited the tiny baby into his wife's arms then stood back as Adele and Monika gathered round to ogle. Siegfried joined them, still holding Friedrich, apparently loath to let him be passed to anyone else. Both twins were now gently nodding off, much to Sophie's satisfaction.

"I hope we've timed this right," she said to Sabina. "With any luck they should last through the service." She looked over at the ornately carved wall clock. "Speaking of which we ought really to be setting off soon." She touched Siegfried's arm gently, careful not to disturb the sleeping Friedrich. "Time?"

Siegfried nodded. For the first time he passed Friedrich to another person – to Karl. It seemed a symbolic gesture to Karl, done with a certain gravity and sense of occasion. Siegfried was handing him the bloodline. "Look after him for me," he said quietly, holding his father's gaze for several seconds before turning to face the assembled family.

Clapping his hands he called: "Can I have your attention, please!" The voices gradually subsided and he continued. "We'll be setting off for the church soon, so if anyone needs to make themselves comfortable first, now's your chance. There's plenty of room to park at the church, but could you please leave space nearest the door for our car."

There was a general flurry of activity as people disappeared upstairs, looked for handbags, and assembled into car-loads. Karl was still holding Friedrich but Ilse took the baby off him as the room began to empty.

"Come to Oma," Ilse crooned. "Opa can have you back later."

Beside him Katherine seethed in silence.

*

Christian's foot was sticking out from under the bedcover. He was fast asleep still after a busy night of passion. Satisfied he would not wake for a long time yet, Gustav crept out of the bedroom, picked up his car keys and eased open the apartment's front door. It gave a click as he shut it, but should not have been enough to waken Christian, whose visits to Gustav's flat were now regular, sometimes lasting more than just one night. Gustav had always managed to turf him out at some point, but he was fast becoming part of the fixtures and fittings again. Today of all days he had hoped for some time to himself, but Christian had sensed Gustav's distraction last night and turned on the sex appeal full blast. There was no escaping it – Gustav was hooked on him. But today was the big day and he had to get to Soest to witness the event.

Siegfried's instructions the previous week had been clear. The christenings were at eleven, the guests returning to Sophie's parents' house afterwards for refreshments. The Drieslers would then be driving back to Medebach. Gustav was to wait in a lay-by near the Wendts' home where Siegfried would pick him up. When pressed for details, Siegfried had only given an inscrutable: "You'll see." It was typical of the lad to keep his cards close to his chest, Gustav thought fondly. During the subsequent week his curiosity had steadily mounted, not just as to what Siegfried had planned, but also what Katherine and Karl were like now. Especially Karl. The newspaper photos had shown him to have worn surprisingly well and now Gustav had a deep desire to see him in the flesh. He had never forgotten the overwhelming attraction he had felt on first seeing Karl, nor the frustration of knowing he could never show that attraction. Instead he had showered affection on his son, an affection that had bloomed over the years into desire. With Karl he had been absolutely certain he would make no headway, but now with Siegfried ... He was a different kettle of fish altogether!

Gustav smiled smugly as he got into his car and pulled away from the kerb, his mood buoyed up by physical satisfaction and anticipation of a job approaching its conclusion. He wanted to be a part of the action, but dared not show his face. No suspicion must fall his way. Nevertheless his curiosity was overwhelming. He would observe the christening from a safe distance using one of his disguises.

*

Christian let Gustav get well ahead. It had been a mad panic after being woken by the front door closing to get some clothes on, find his car keys and race out of the apartment. He saw Gustav's car had gone from its customary parking place and had to make a guess as to the direction he had taken. Any traffic policeman nearby would have collared him immediately, but by great good fortune he spotted Gustav's car ahead of him within a couple of minutes. Once they were on the main road headed east he knew exactly where Gustav was making for – Soest. It was a Sunday, early. Could Gustav have been invited to the babies' christenings? If so, why hadn't he mentioned anything about it? And what did Gustav expect him to think when he woke up and found Gustav gone? Admittedly, Gustav had made it clear he would come and go without explanation, but surely he could mention a simple christening?

Driesler had been round again recently. Christian had seen his car parked near the apartment. He had stood at the corner and watched for a good hour until the tall, blond man emerged, handsome as ever, and drove off. Gustav was so convincing when he swore there was nothing going on between himself and Driesler, but then the man was a supreme actor. Unless Gustav gave Christian a key of his own, he could never catch them in the act. Christian could almost believe him, wanted to believe him. But if he knew for certain that Gustav was lying then God help him!

Christian's knuckles showed white on the steering wheel as he kept a safe distance behind Gustav. When Gustav took the expected turning he dropped right back out of sight. Arriving in the village, Christian tested his theory by parking well away from the village church and walking back to it, keeping his eyes peeled for Gustav. Villagers were already making their way to the Sunday service, and cars were drawing in to the car park. He noticed several registration plates were not local, but were from the Hochsauerland area just to the south. Driesler's family perhaps? Definitely! The tall, blond man getting out of one of the cars had to be his father. Or was it his uncle? Certainly family as now there were two men who fitted that description, surrounded by wives, children and a grandfather. As yet there was no sign of Siegfried Driesler, or of Gustav.

The church must have been nearly full before the car he recognised as Driesler's Mercedes drew up near the door, disgorging wife, two babies in white shawls and a grandmother, aided by the blond beast himself. Christian grinned smugly. So he was right. It was the christening. So where was Gustav? Already in the church, perhaps? Did Driesler's wife know her husband's lover was one of the guests?

Christian hung about outside the church. A bald man, who made up for his lack of scalp hair by a profusion of facial hair, sat on a bench nearby, watching the world go by and nodding off gently in the late summer sunshine. Christian too began to feel sleepy, gently warmed by the brickwork of the wall he was leaning against. His stomach suddenly rumbled loudly, reminding him he had not eaten breakfast. The village baker's shop was open, selling traditional Sunday cream cakes, and he nipped inside to find something not too expensive to eat. When he returned to his post, clutching a bag of crusty rolls, he noticed the bald man had gone, then spotted him walking up the road. The man's walk strongly reminded him of Gustav, and he looked harder at the man. He was of the same medium height and build, and yes, that was one of Gustav's jackets he was wearing. Gustav had been disguised as an old man when he visited Driesler's wife before the babies were born. This time he wore a different disguise. Was it to deceive her or someone else? Christian took a large bite out of a roll, confused and bewildered by Gustav's growing web of deceit. What was going on?

The bag of rolls lasted until the end of the service. Christian now felt very thirsty after standing for an hour in the hot sun, but he dared not disappear again as he could not assume the christening party would be going back to Driesler's house. There was still no sign of Gustav, so Christian returned to his car and cruised slowly towards the church where the congregation was beginning to leave. He watched the twins being loaded into the Mercedes, then followed the convoy of family cars as they drove away.

*

It could have been Sabina's wedding all over again, Katherine mused. Guests gathered in their best clothes in a large, sunny garden, with occasional bursts of laughter breaking the gentle babble of voices. Except these voices spoke solely in German, Ilse's cheerful tones prominent amongst them. For Karl's sake Katherine remained tight-lipped. She longed to let rip at the over-confident Ilse, who was playing her role as doting grandmother for all it was worth and dragging Karl into her conversations at every opportunity. Between them Ilse, Sophie and her parents had managed to exclude Katherine from every part of the ceremony, as though she had no right to be there. Even Sabina had noticed her mother's ostracism, and was doing her best to rally Karl's family around her. But Ilse took a lot of beating.

It did not help matters that Katherine's spoken German was mediocre; she could not take a prominent part in any conversation. Even so, Katherine felt that Ilse was striving to dominate and was easily winning. Her displeasure must have showed on her face as she felt Sabina's hand on her arm.

"Don't let her get to you, Mummy. She'll have won if you do. Ignore her and enjoy yourself."

Katherine nodded, deciding to give up the unequal fight and simply try to make light of the whole thing. The event must be a pleasant memory in years to come, not a saga of jealous rivalry. The trouble was, that was easier said than done. She took another sip from her glass of champagne, exchanged a few words of German with Anna and Dieter then stepped back into the shadows of the Wendts' well-tended garden. She paused for a while by an ornamental stoneware urn planted with lavender, and began to feel soothed by its powerful but balmy scent. Another sip of champagne continued the calming process as she watched the proceedings around her.

The twins were fast asleep in their pram, shaded by a small silver birch. Sophie sat nearby chatting to a formidable elderly lady who had been introduced to Katherine as Sophie's Great Aunt Hilde. Ilse was laughing loudly with her three daughters, Margit, Edeltraud and Roslinde, while her son, Heinrich, was joking with Wolf and Lothar. Even Karl looked happy, animatedly chatting to Rudi and Stefan. The one exception to this happy scene, she suddenly noticed, was Siegfried. He was just like he had been at Sabina's wedding. Rather than lording it over everybody, as she would have expected, he seemed very restrained, nervous even. He was taking numerous gulps from his glass, and must have refilled it several times from the bottle on the drinks' table behind him. He kept looking round the assembled gathering, especially in Karl's direction, smiling artificially brightly when he caught his father's eye.

Why should Siegfried of all people look troubled? Was she the only person who had noticed? Certainly everyone else was engrossed in conversation. Even Bina had been quickly sucked back into the family circle. She looked back at Siegfried and, as if by telepathy, he looked at her, noticing her solitude. Topping up his glass and bringing the bottle with him, he ambled across the lawn to join her.

"Feeling left out, Katherine?"

He had spoken in German, but she replied in English. It was easier for them both that way. "A little, I must confess. How about you?"

He seemed surprised at her question. "Me, the father of the heroes of the day? You must be joking!"

He was looking at a bee buzzing at the lavender and she felt certain he was lying. He seemed to remember the bottle in his hand and waved it towards her glass, pouring a trifle unsteadily as she held it up for him. Was he drunk? Surely not Siegfried!

"I see you're keeping well away from my mother," he continued. "Very wise." He paused before adding rather stiffly: "Thank you." His gaze reverted to the buzzing bee as if the next thing he was going to say would be difficult for him, but when it came he looked directly at her. "I wanted to say sorry for what happened. You might never have known if it weren't for Sophie and me. I wanted to make trouble. Now I'm glad everything's all right." He saw the flicker of her eyes. "It is, isn't it?"

Katherine was touched by his unexpected, but welcome, concern. She smiled warmly at her stepson. "Yes. Although it is difficult for me, seeing your mother here, but I didn't want to spoil things for everyone. It's in the past. Almost forgotten."

Siegfried smiled wryly at her choice of words. "Almost but never entirely?" She nodded as he went on: "It's impossible to forget the past, isn't it?"

She nearly made light of his remark with a reference to Karl's bout of amnesia, but sensed how serious he was. "It has a habit of coming back to haunt us, yes," she agreed.

He gave a noncommittal grunt, drained his glass and walked away without another word.

Katherine sighed. She would never understand Siegfried. Never. She watched him join Sophie and her parents then decided she ought to be more sociable too and went to stand by Karl.

*

Sat in his car outside, Christian could see little of the events in the garden. The house stood somewhat distanced from the village so all the cars parked there belonged to guests, but there was no sign of Gustav. Was he still incognito and lurking somewhere? Had Gustav spotted his car and gone off in a huff at being followed? Christian decided the only thing to do was to sit it out in the hope that Gustav either appeared or something interesting happened. There was certainly nothing else to do in this godforsaken place.

The afternoon dragged on and Christian became hungrier and thirstier by the minute. The morning's rolls were a distant memory, and, to make matters worse, he kept catching wafts of roast pork from the garden. His stomach growled loudly, a rush of saliva helping to lubricate his parched mouth. It was no good. He would have to find something to eat and drink.

A short way down the road he came to a farm displaying a sign for fresh eggs and vegetables. A few negotiations swiftly resulted in a bottle of water, a leg of cold chicken, several tomatoes, a cucumber and some slices of bread, together with a large bag of plums. He drank half the water then pulled out onto the quiet country road again, heading for a shady lay-by up ahead. It was only when he pulled in that he noticed Gustav's car partially hidden in a gateway to a field, with Gustav apparently asleep inside until the sound of the car disturbed him and he looked up. Recognition was instantaneous. Gustav shot out of the car and strode angrily over to Christian to confront him. Christian noticed he was no longer in disguise.

"What the hell are you playing at, Christian? I told you, I won't have you meddling in my life!"

Christian slowly got out of his car and tried to sound placatory. "What else was I to do when you left me all alone with no explanation? It was a game to see if I could find you." He gave a disarming smile. "It looks like I won!"

"Very clever, but I don't believe a word. It's your stupid jealousy again, isn't it? You can't get it into your thick skull that I can have business dealings with people that don't concern you. Now get going and leave me in peace!"

Christian did not like the mood he saw developing in Gustav, but could not leave it like that. "Business? What business can you possibly have here and now. There's a christening party going on, and you're skulking around, waiting for something by the look of things. A meeting with him, perhaps? Here, in your car in this nice secluded lay-by?"

"It's not at all what you think, Christian. There are other things in life –"

"Not where he's concerned there aren't! I can see you're besotted with him. He's got everything, hasn't he? Looks, money –"

"And a wife and children, for God's sake!"

"That means nothing where you're concerned. You probably lust after his wife as well. In fact," Christian went on, carried away by his imagination, "I bet you're planning on a threesome as soon as he'll let you!"

Gustav swallowed hard. Christian knew his sexual pleasures only too well. The thought had certainly crossed his mind, but he was not going to admit that to Christian. Besides, Siegfried would never share Sophie with him, not unless he had no choice but to agree. He stepped a pace towards his young lover, jabbing a finger into his chest as he spoke. "The trouble with you, Christian, is that you impose your dirty mind on the morals of others. This has nothing to do with sex or with you. Now clear off, take your filthy mind with you and don't come back to my flat. Ever!"

Christian shoved Gustav's finger aside, positioning himself aggressively close to Gustav's face. "You bastard! You're lying and you well know it. Well that's it! I don't want to live with a creep like you, Gustav. I've had it with your arrogance and selfish egotism. It's the end, all right!" He spat at Gustav's feet, short of hitting him outright, span on his heel and leapt into his car, driving off in a spray of gravel.

A few hundred metres up the road he stopped and waited.

SEVENTEEN

Ilse could not imagine a crueller form of torture than holding Karl's grandson in her arms yet unable to embrace Karl himself. In her memory she had replayed that night with him a year ago over and over again, until she felt they had made love hundreds of times, and not just the once. She craved his presence, the sound of his voice, the smell of him, the touch of his hands on her breasts, his lips on the back of her neck. It was not just his physical self she craved either. It was his caring nature, his concern for her, his love. She knew he loved her still, albeit in a very controlled fashion. Paul loved her too, of course, but having experienced the full force of Karl's love so many years ago, she knew what he was capable of, and Paul had never come close.

Gently she stroked Friedrich's soft blond hair. He wriggled in her arms, stretching out his legs, reaching out for her hand. If only Karl would reach out for her. How much longer could she maintain this pretence at decorum? He knew she was covertly watching his every move; their eyes had met several times, but he was always the first to look away. It's only because I can't have him that I want him so much, she kept telling herself.

She sneaked another glance in Karl's direction. He was helping himself to a plateful of pork and parsley potatoes, having managed to detach himself from his faithful shadow, Katherine. No, she shouldn't be unfair. Katherine hadn't spent all day stuck to his side. She and Bina were chatting with Wolf over by the pram where Freia still slept soundly. Ilse took a step forward, hesitated then decided she must speak to him.

As Karl left the buffet table to find a seat Ilse moved in on him. "Karl, can I have a quiet word?" She saw how his eyes immediately cast about for Katherine, how anxious he was about being seen talking alone with her. "It's about Siegfried."

"Oh?" His curiosity aroused, Karl found a pair of garden chairs and made sure they were both steady before indicating to Ilse she should sit down.

Ilse settled Friedrich so he was looking over her shoulder at his mother nearby. His father, the subject of her concerns, was well out of earshot over by the french windows, changing the film in his camera under the cover of some heavy velvet curtains. Ilse guessed she would not have long alone with Karl before someone joined them, so got straight to the point.

"Maybe I'm just being hypersensitive, and I know I haven't seen him for a long time, but he strikes me as being very worried about something. Had you noticed?"

Karl put his plate down on a nearby table. "No, but then I don't know him as well as you do. Has Sophie said anything?"

"No, but she wouldn't. I was wondering whether everything was all right between them, what with her long stay in hospital, then the pregnancy, now the babies. I know how easily a young husband can feel left out of things at such a time, but I don't think it's that. They seem very happy with each other. But there's definitely something wrong."

"Mother's intuition?"

"I suppose so. I've tried to pose a few delicately phrased questions to him, but you know what he's like at hiding his feelings. It's impossible to see what he's thinking, but I get the impression Katherine's noticed something too. She and he were having a little chat together earlier, which I thought was most odd."

"Perhaps we ought to ask her."

Ilse's face fell. "Karl, I'd rather not."

"No, of course. I'll have a word in a moment."

A shadow fell across them; Sabina had come already to intervene. She looked pointedly at Ilse. "Shall I hold Friedrich for you while you get some food, Ilse?"

Ilse accepted Sabina's forthrightness gracefully. "Thank you, Bina. Seeing your father's food on the plate there has made me quite hungry. Here." She carefully passed over Friedrich and his dribble cloth and retreated to the buffet table, leaving her chair for Bina to occupy.

"It's all right, Bina, I don't need a bodyguard," Karl reproved her gently.

"Sorry, but I thought you needed rescuing."

"She was worried about Siegfried, that's all."

"Siegfried? Because he's drinking too much?"

"Is he?"

"I get that impression, but it may be only when he's got visitors. I don't really know."

"Ilse spotted him talking to Mummy a while ago. Perhaps she's weedled something out of him."

"Are you going to ask her?"

"When I've eaten something. I'm starving. Breakfast was seven hours ago!"

Sabina laughed. "Well, I'll leave you in peace to get on with it and I'll go and ask her. OK?"

"OK," he replied, reaching for his plate.

Sabina returned to Wolf and her mother to make her report. "It's all right. They were only talking about Siegfried. Apparently Ilse's worried about him, although I must say, I am a bit too. He looks so tired."

"She's right to worry," Katherine said. "I think he's haunted by his past. Turning over a new leaf isn't proving easy."

"As I well know," Wolf commented grimly. "But he's got quite a past to be troubled by, has our Siegfried. I can understand he's worried. He must be expecting retribution from our former friends any day."

"Some of them must be here today, surely," Katherine said, her eye falling on the group of people around Sophie's parents. "I wish you'd come and live in England," she added wistfully.

Bina gave her a reassuring smile. "We're settled here, Mummy. Anyway, nothing's happened yet, and nothing's likely to, unless they can find another Siegfried to organise such things." She saw her mother's face fall. "I was only joking. They'll never find another Siegfried," she said, trying to sound convincing.

"I hope not!" Katherine said, managing to raise a smile.

Friedrich gurgled as if in reproof at such talk of his father, then let out a whimper, which caused Freia to stir and wake up with an identical whimper. Both babies rapidly wound themselves up into full-blown wails and Sophie and her mother hurried over to relieve Bina of her burden.

Sabina laughed as her stomach gave a loud rumble. "It's a good thing I don't wail like that when I'm hungry."

"I'd join in," Wolf said. "I'm starving too. Come on. Let's find some food."

They filled their plates at the buffet table near the house, then sat down with Karl, who had already been joined by his father, sister and brother-in law. Karl pulled up more chairs for them all, and as the conversation levels rose, Katherine spoke quietly to him.

"Siegfried was talking to me earlier. I think he's suffering guilt problems from his past, but I'm not absolutely positive."

"Ah." Suddenly Karl lost his appetite. He stared at the food remaining on his plate, not seeing it, only the small boy who had hidden behind his mother's skirts when meeting his father for the first time. Siegfried could have been such a wonderful son. Instead he had been abused, rejected, driven from one home to another and back again. Was it this that had developed him into such a scheming and evil character, or was it solely the later influence of people like Paul Zopf, who encouraged his immoral, neo-Nazi beliefs? Whatever it was, there were clear parallels with Karl's own life. He had not thought to question the teachings of Nazism as a boy. What he had done he had believed to be right, until the day finally dawned in Yugoslavia in the summer of 1943 when he was made to realise Nazi doctrine was totally wrong. Escaping their grasp on him had been a nightmare, one that occasionally haunted him even now. But Siegfried was still in the early throws of escaping from his guilt. It was going to be tough for him. "Perhaps I'd better have a chat with him," he said eventually.

"It might help," Katherine agreed.

"Where is he?" Karl cast his eye about the garden and saw his son posing for a photograph, holding a twin in each arm, every inch the proud father. "He's busy just now. I'll wait for a quiet moment later."

"There won't be one," Katherine pointed out. "Do it now."

She was right as usual. Karl stood up and went over to the group having their photographs taken by Peter Wendt, who waved him into the group.

"Come on, Karl. Stand by Ilse there. Sophie, Liebchen, you move in a bit to make room for me, while I set this up for Heinrich to take."

As Karl made his way past Siegfried, he placed a hand on his shoulder and whispered in his ear: "I want a word."

Siegfried looked at him, puzzled, then gave a brief nod. "After this."

As he took his position by Ilse's side, Karl sensed her moving closer to him, until she was actually leaning against him. It gave him that familiar feeling of being sorry for her, of wanting to help and protect her, such as he had felt in the past when seeing her traumatic first marriage to Erich Röbel. He knew why he was still attracted to her, but whereas she had a husband who seemed to accept her transgression, he had a wife who could not. Yet he did not back away.

Heinrich took several photos then Wolf took some on Karl's camera. It was a few minutes before Karl could escape Ilse's close proximity and steer Siegfried off to a quiet corner of the garden.

"What did you want to speak to me about?" Siegfried asked directly they were alone.

"People have noticed you seem ... worried."

"Katherine, you mean."

"Not just her. Actually it was your mother who mentioned it first to me. Katherine only confirmed it, and said you were troubled by your past. Is that right?"

Siegfried shrugged. "It's a bit tricky at the moment. It's not so easy changing sides, trying to please everyone. I have to watch what I say sometimes, that's all."

Karl's mind was working along more serious lines, however. "Have you had any outright threats from your former colleagues?"

Siegfried laughed. "Ha! Them! They're nothing any more. Wiped out." He grew more serious. "No, it's closer to home than that. Sophie and her parents think I'm just stringing you along."

"Whereas you're actually stringing them along?"

There was a significant pause. Karl began to wonder whether Siegfried would deign to answer, but then he seemed to find the words he was seeking.

"Actually I'm stringing you all along: you, Sophie, my mother and Paul. Everyone."

"That's a dangerous game, Siegfried."

"I know. It's the only one there is. Don't spoil things for me, Father. I'm relying on you. But I know what I'm doing."

Karl looked deep into his son's eyes and saw no trace of guile. In fact he saw an openness which made him doubt he was being strung along at all. So what was the deception, if any? What he could see, however, was sadness. His own eyes at that very same age had held that haunted, martyred look. Katherine had remarked it was partly what had drawn her to him in those post-war days, when he was still a prisoner of war with no near prospect of going home. Now he could see it in his son, a sadness crying out for help, for forgiveness of past atrocities now deeply regretted.

"If there's anything I can do, Siegfried, you only have to ask."

"This is my mess, and I'll sort it out in my own way," Siegfried told him abruptly.

Karl was taken aback by his tone of voice. The sadness had disappeared in an instant, replaced by the old familiar ruthlessness. He sighed. "I still don't understand you, Siegfried. I keep thinking you're like me, but you're not, are you?"

Siegfried shrugged. "Who knows? I don't really know what you're like, so I can't say. I think I'm probably harder than you are. I won't break."

"Not like I did, you mean. That may be true, but it's not necessarily good to be hard. You know the old saying about a reed being bent not broken by the wind. Try bending a little yourself, Siegfried. It might work."

"That's what I'm doing! Bending in every direction. Every direction," he repeated, so quietly Karl almost missed it.

"How do you mean?" Karl asked gently, hoping for a revelation. His hopes were quickly dashed.

"Nothing. I'll explain later, some other time. I'll have to go now. I've got things to do."

Abruptly he walked back towards the house and disappeared inside, leaving Karl watching his back, wondering at his son's inability to share his problems. Perhaps Wolf was the one he would tell, someone of his own age and background.

A moment later Katherine was at his side, followed by Ilse. The two women were keeping their mutual animosity at bay during this more immediate crisis.

"Well?" Katherine asked him.

Karl shrugged at them both. "You're right. There's a serious problem, and he won't tell me what it is." He said it again in German, for Ilse's benefit.

"I think we tackle Sophie outright," Ilse replied. "I've been too circumspect with her up to now. She must have some idea what's troubling him."

"You go and do that, then," Karl suggested, feeling uncomfortable with both his women at his side.

Ilse went to find Sophie but she was busy with her mother attending to the babies. It was some time before Sophie returned with the now sleeping twins and placed them back in the pram. With a heartfelt sigh she sat wearily down in the shade by them. Ilse seized her chance and approached, but just as she was about to broach the subject of Siegfried he reappeared from inside the house, a full glass of wine in one hand, a bottle in the other. As he headed in their direction he made to replenish people's drinks, but most declined. In fact his actions seemed to prompt Tante Hilde and others with long journeys into thinking about leaving, and they began making their farewells. Sophie dragged herself to her feet again to see them off and Karl felt they should also be on their way. It had been a long day for Sophie, and she was visibly flagging.

As Siegfried, Sophie and her parents waved off the first of their departing guests, Ilse made her temporary farewells to her children. She would be seeing them again before she left for Uruguay, but Karl she would not be seeing again. Her goodbye to him could have proved most awkward with his wife standing by, but Katherine, very considerately under the circumstances, disappeared indoors. Ilse reached forward and took hold of Karl's hands before stretching up to kiss his cheek. He met her halfway.

"Goodbye, Karl. Take care. And if you're ever in Uruguay, pop in to see us!" She was trying to be light-hearted to keep the tears at bay. She nearly succeeded.

"Goodbye, Ilse. Safe journey home."

"You too. Drive carefully." Regretfully she let go of his hands and blinked back the tears. "I still love you, Karl," she whispered.

"I know." Despite everything she had done to try to destroy his marriage, he realised he felt the same, yet he could not bring himself to say the words 'I love you too' out loud to her. But he had to say something. "The feeling's mutual."

Ilse smiled. She could live with that. She had a part of his heart still, and the knowledge made her glow. Even Katherine, by slipping away for a few minutes, seemed to have accepted the inevitable and allowed her that part. She was grateful. While Karl got his father settled in the car for the return journey to Medebach, Ilse approached Katherine, who was busy thanking the Wendts for their hospitality.

"Katherine, can we be friends again?" she asked.

Katherine looked Ilse up and down. She had only given Karl space to say goodbye to Ilse because she could not bear to witness their inevitable kiss. She could never forgive Ilse her treachery.

"No, Ilse. I don't think so. Goodbye." She turned her back and headed for the car, accompanied by a jubilant Sabina.

Suitably rebuffed, Ilse watched the Drieslers drive away, then saw Siegfried also getting into his car.

"Hasn't he drunk too much to drive?" she commented to Sophie.

"Who? Karl? I'm not sure."

"No. Siegfried."

"Siegfried?" Sophie suddenly noticed her husband driving off in the opposite direction. "Where's he going?"

Both women watched in astonishment as the car disappeared round the bend in the road.

Sophie turned to her parents. "Did Siegfried say where he was going?"

"No," her mother replied, equally puzzled. "I thought you knew."

"No. I haven't a clue. How odd."

*

Gustav was waiting in the lay-by where Siegfried had instructed. On seeing Siegfried's car pull in, Gustav jumped out of his own car, locked it, then hurriedly climbed in next to Siegfried.

"Been there long?" Siegfried asked.

"Most of the day."

"Most of the day?" Siegfried shouted. "You fool! Whatever for? Someone will have noticed your car."

Gustav made no mention of the Christian incident, merely patting Siegfried reassuringly on the knee. "I'm not that much of an idiot. The car was tucked into the field there most of the time. But since you couldn't be specific about what time you'd arrive, I wanted to be early." He grabbed the door handle as Siegfried took a corner at speed. "Where do you reckon on catching them up?"

"You'll see. It's all planned. I've been over this route and timed it all. I wanted you to witness it, so you'd have no doubts."

Gustav smiled. "Doubts? What doubts could I possibly have about you? This is your forte. This is what we trained you for. I have no doubts. None whatsoever."

Siegfried knew better than to believe him. Why else had they kept records of his previous successes other than to threaten him with disclosure to the police? Approaching a junction he braked hard, judged the distance of an approaching car and pulled out in front of it with a squealing of tyres. Now they were on the main road and heading south, towards the Sauerland and Medebach.

In his rear-view mirror he saw a familiar green Beetle; the one that had tailed him to Iserlohn; the one he had seen parked near Gustav's apartment; the one that most probably belonged to Gustav's current lover.

He decided to make no comment. Gustav probably did not know he was there, and if he did, it would not make any difference to the outcome. Siegfried kept a careful eye on the Beetle as they sped along towards the dark grey towers of the Möhne Dam.

"How do you know they've come this way?" Gustav suddenly asked, gazing at a flotilla of sailing dinghies on the waters of the famous reservoir.

"They always come this way," he replied confidently, noticing the green Beetle creeping closer as the road wound its way through the forested hills. "We should catch up with them very soon."

The traffic had thinned out considerably once past the dam. With an almost open road ahead and behind, Siegfried put his foot down to overtake a busload of pensioners on a Sunday outing and kept it down. This seemed to prove too much for the occupant of the Beetle, who rather than simply keeping up, now seemed intent on catching them up.

"If that's the game you want to play," Siegfried muttered under his breath, "That's what you're going to get!"

"What was that?" Gustav asked, clinging on to the dashboard as they took a bend at high speed.

"Your friend behind us. I think he wants something."

Gustav turned his head and saw Christian's car desperately trying to catch up with them. "Shit! Lose him!"

Siegfried smiled grimly. "Yes, sir. Your wish is my command!"

The Mercedes shot forward, skidding round a sharp bend, its tail swinging dangerously close to the safety barrier. Siegfried controlled the skid and saw the car behind make the same manoeuvre, with the same close shave.

"He can't hope to keep up with us in that car," Gustav said through gritted teeth, his feet braced firmly against the sides of the footwell.

By way of reply, Siegfried made a rapid gear change and overtook the car ahead, nipping back in just before the next bend. Gustav looked over his shoulder and saw Christian make the same manoeuvre the instant he had cleared the bend.

"Next time!" Siegfried promised Gustav.

Gustav clung on tightly, aware of the sudden steep drop on their right hand side down to the valley below. He turned his head as they approached the next sharp bend, willing the troublesome Christian not to make it. He felt the Mercedes begin its turn, heard the screech of tyres, then was flung out of his seat as the car hit the safety barrier.

Christian saw the Mercedes hit the barrier, saw it pass straight through unchecked and disappear over the edge of the road. Slamming his foot on the brake, Christian brought the car to a screeching halt several metres past the impact point. Scrambling out as fast as he could, he was just in time to see the Mercedes finally come to rest in the valley bottom, crushed and almost unrecognisable as it had rolled its way end over end down the steep slope, smashing into trees as it went.

"Oh my God!" he breathed in horror. "What have I done?"

The car they had just overtaken drew up behind him, a young man with his girlfriend climbing out to peer over the edge at the wreck below.

"Any sign of life?" the young man asked Christian.

Christian was in a state of shock. He hadn't meant this to happen, hadn't really had any plans when he set off following Gustav and Driesler. He had been in a jealous rage, had thought of forcing them off the road, denting Driesler's pride and that flashy car of his, but not like this! Nothing like this!

Ignoring the stricken Christian, the young man decided to take control of matters. He turned to his girlfriend. "Drive to the nearest house and call an ambulance, police, everything," he ordered briskly. "It looks serious."

His girlfriend ran back to their car and roared off past the still staring Christian. By now other vehicles were stopping on either side of the carriageway, including the bus-load of pensioners. The authoritative young man delegated another driver to ensure the road was kept clear for the emergency services then grabbed Christian's arm.

"Come on. We've got to get down there. We might be able to help."

It was the last thing Christian wanted: to see Gustav smashed and bleeding, dead even, so he stood firm. The other driver grimaced in despair at his cowardice and, accompanied by a braver driver, followed the trail of smashed trees and flattened shrubs the Mercedes had left in its wake.

*

Siegfried heard silence descend as the wheels stopped spinning and the rain of slithering stones died down. He opened his eyes but was confronted by a lump of twisted metal and broken glass. For a moment he felt nothing, then pain surged through his entire body. He groaned, trying to move, but was held fast by the wreckage, his chest compacted so he could hardly breathe. He lay still, gasping in agony, shallow breaths all he could take, a clammy sweat breaking out on his brow, and something that felt like blood trickling into his eyes and mouth. He licked his lips. Blood.

He listened again. Nothing. Was Gustav dead or thrown clear? He tried calling out but could only manage another groan. But now he could hear the crash of undergrowth as someone slithered down the slope towards him. Now there were voices.

"Can you see anyone inside?"

"Y-yes. Two men."

"I'll come round your side."

Siegfried licked his parched lips again. He wanted to call out to them, but could not take a big enough breath. His vision blurred and he closed his eyes.

"I've found a pulse!"

Siegfried realised someone was holding his wrist. Whoever it was stroked his hand.

"Can you hear me? If you can, squeeze my hand."

Siegfried's fingers twitched slightly, but he had no strength. The pain was overpowering him, taking control. He could no longer think. "Sophie," he gasped.

The man's soothing voice came back to him. "It's all right, help's on its way. You'll soon be out of there." The man kept on talking. "Sophie. Is that your wife?"

"Yes." Siegfried gave another rattling gasp as he tried to draw breath. It was getting harder by the minute. His rescuer sensed talking was too much of an effort but knew he must ask two more questions. "What's your name?"

"Driesler. Sieg...fried."

"And your friend?"

Friend, what friend? Siegfried could not remember who was with him, or why, or what was happening. All he knew was that he could not breathe.

*

Christian watched the emergency services rapidly take control. First to arrive was a police car, closely followed by an ambulance. Shortly after that a fire-tender, another ambulance and two more police cars arrived on the scene. The firemen surveyed the scene and began unloading cutting equipment, which they had to cart down the steep bank a hundred metres to the valley below. Twenty minutes of anxious waiting followed before two ambulance-men assisted by two policemen appeared at the twisted railing with a stretcher. The body was covered over.

Christian gave a whimper but did not dare make a move. He could not get involved. He jumped as a policeman touched his arm.

"I'm told you were first on the scene. Did you see it happen?"

There was no avoiding it. "Y-yes. He took the bend too fast. Just disappeared o-over the edge." Christian was sure his nerves must give him away, but the policeman was used to dealing with shocked witnesses.

As he gave his name and Berlin address, he saw the ambulance with the body driving away. Was it Gustav or Driesler inside? Whichever it was, the firemen seemed to be having trouble getting the other man out of the wreckage. More heavy equipment was sent down and Christian found himself in an agony of ignorance. He could only watch their efforts from above, along with the other onlookers, as finally the side of the car was cut away and a body loaded onto a waiting stretcher before it too was covered over.

The blood drained from Christian's head and he sank to the ground in horror. A minute later he was aware of a policeman in front of him. He looked up. The policeman's fleshy face did not look friendly.

"Would you care to tell me why you were racing with the Mercedes, sir?"

"R-racing? I w-wasn't racing," Christian stammered, standing up awkwardly. "I was just following behind."

"Several witnesses have stated both the Mercedes and your car overtook them at high speed further down the road. They were of the opinion the drivers were racing. Can I see your driving licence?"

Christian fumbled inside his jacket for his wallet, but paused as the stretcher with the second body on it reached the safety barrier and was manhandled up onto the road and into the waiting ambulance. By the longer length of the shrouded body he knew this one was Driesler's.

"Oh God, what have I done?" he groaned softly as the policeman ushered him towards the waiting police car.

EIGHTEEN

Sophie sat watching out of her parents' front window for any sign of Siegfried. She was desperate to get home and the twins settled in bed.

"Where on earth is he?" she asked her mother for the tenth time.

Lisl Wendt and Ilse exchanged worried glances. It was so unlike Siegfried to sneak off like that without a word to anyone, especially on such a day as this. Peter Wendt decided to take matters into his own hands.

"We've waited well over an hour. Why don't I drive you all home, then at least you can get the twins sorted out."

Sophie was reluctant to leave without Siegfried having made an appearance. "What if he turns up here?"

"Then I'll send him straight on home," her mother promised. "Come along, Liebling. Let's get all your things together."

Peter Wendt bundled all the christening presents into the car, while the two older women helped Sophie with the babies.

"Now don't worry, Liebling. He's probably run out of petrol or something. Give us a ring when he turns up, won't you?" Lisl told her daughter.

"I will," Sophie smiled bravely before getting into her father's car, along with Ilse.

It was a short drive home. There was no sign of the Mercedes, but nobody was really expecting to see it. Peter Wendt left as soon as the car was unloaded to get back to his wife, leaving Sophie and Ilse alone with the twins.

"Right! Let's get them ready for bed," Ilse declared, wanting to keep busy and her mind off what Siegfried could possibly be up to.

"I'll go and run their bath," Sophie said wearily.

She was halfway up the stairs, her legs protesting at the strain of the day, when she heard a car pull up outside. Forgetting her pain she ran back down to see if it was Siegfried. Through the hall window she saw a police car.

"Oh no!" she whimpered.

Ilse was at her side in an instant, watching as two policemen got out and approached the house. Ilse reached for Sophie's hand. She felt suddenly sick and light-headed, wanting to sit down, but Sophie was heading for the door. Ilse let go of her hand and leaned against the wall as her knees started to tremble.

"Frau Driesler?" the elder of the policemen asked.

"Yes?"

"May we come in? I'm afraid we have some very bad news for you."

There was a crash behind her and Sophie turned to see Ilse prostrate on the parquet floor.

The younger policemen stepped past Sophie and knelt down by Ilse's side, feeling her pulse. "She's fainted, I think. She'll probably be all right in a minute."

Ilse was indeed already beginning to stir groggily and Sophie went to fetch a cushion from the sitting room to put under her head, grateful to be spared the grim news for a few more seconds. She too knelt down by her mother-in-law and held her hand as Ilse opened her eyes and slowly focused on the faces watching over her. In the background one of the twins began to cry, but Sophie hardly heard as she waited for the policemen to do their job.

When Ilse felt ready they helped her to her feet and escorted her into the sitting room where they sat her on an armchair. Sophie fetched her a glass of water then sat down too in readiness as the elder man perched awkwardly on the sofa nearby while the younger stood by her side. The time had come. Wiping his bristling moustache with the back of his hand the senior man cleared his throat then spoke gently.

"I'm very sorry to have to tell you, Frau Driesler, that your husband was involved in a fatal car crash a short while ago. He died at the scene of the crash. I'm very sorry." He waited a moment to gauge Sophie's response, but she just sat in stunned silence. It was Ilse who reacted most with a loud choking gasp followed by hysterical sobbing.

"His mother," Sophie explained distractedly, then the emotion reached her and her face crumpled up with tears of anguish – and anger. "Where was he? What happened?" she demanded in between sobs.

The moustached policeman put his hand gently on her shoulder and gave her a handkerchief. "I can't tell you much at the moment as to what happened, but it was on the 229 south of the Möhnesee, travelling towards Arnsberg."

Sophie's tears subsided as puzzlement mixed with disbelief. "Are you sure? What on earth was he doing there?"

The policeman could not answer. Instead he embarked on his next bit of bad news. "Did you know his companion, Gustav Halstrup?"

"Gustav? He was with Gustav?" Sophie asked incredulously.

The policeman nodded, while his colleague tried to console the still hysterical Ilse. "Yes. We believe Herr Halstrup was also killed in the crash."

"Believe?"

"We assume it was Herr Halstrup from his driving licence."

Now Sophie felt really confused. There was too much to think about, and she could not cope alone. Ilse was obviously going to be of no comfort.

"I must phone my parents," she whispered, vaguely aware again of both twins crying.

She stood up to go to the phone, but one look at Ilse's distraught face made her reach down and hug her. Part of her longed just to let go and cry like Ilse, but the rational part would not let her. There was too much to do, and too many questions to be answered.

The policemen's jobs were nearly done. There was one last bit of business to organise. "Frau Driesler? We'll need someone to identify the bodies. Is there anyone who could …?"

Ilse stirred in Sophie's arms, regaining some composure at last. Wiping her streaming face with a lace-edged handkerchief she managed to croak: "Karl will. I couldn't. You won't want to, and you have the twins to look after. Karl will do it. I think he would want to."

The policeman looked enquiringly at Sophie, glad to see the two women beginning to cope again.

"My husband's father," she explained. "If you give us the details, we'll contact him."

Five minutes later the two policemen had gone, leaving Sophie and Ilse to make their respective phone calls – Sophie to her parents, Ilse to Karl.

*

Everyone had just sat down to a cup of tea or coffee after the drive home, when the telephone rang in the hall. Anna volunteered to answer it. A moment later she stuck her head around the kitchen door.

"Karl, it's for you." She debated with herself for a moment then decided to tell him who it was so he was prepared. "It's Ilse and she sounds rather upset."

Karl glanced at Katherine. Her expression clearly said: 'What on earth does *she* want?' With a sigh of annoyance he put down his coffee cup and headed for the hall, picking up the receiver from the table where Anna had laid it.

"Ilse? What's the matter? Anna said you sound upset."

Ilse's trembling voice came crackling down the line. "Karl, I can hardly bear to tell you. It's dreadful news. It's Siegfried. He's ..." There was the sound of a choking gulp before Ilse managed to complete the sentence. "He's dead!"

With so little forewarning Karl took a moment to comprehend what Ilse had said. When he did he said nothing, too stunned to respond. Realising this, Ilse carried on talking.

"It was a car crash – I don't know any details except it was on the road south from the Möhnesee. He drove off as soon as you left and none of us knew why or where he was going. All we do know is that Gustav Halstrup was with him when he crashed. I think you know – knew Gustav, didn't you?" This time she waited for him to reply, but still there came no sound down the line. "Karl? Are you there? Are you all right?"

Karl heard her voice but could not react. It was like he had been shot. The pain and realisation would come in a moment, but just now he simply stood, receiver in hand, too stunned to utter a word. His mind could only focus on the name, Gustav Halstrup. The rhythm of its syllables echoed round his head like the ticking of a clock, punctuated by the chimes of the question: What was Siegfried doing with Gustav?

"Karl!"

Her voice finally snapped him out of his trance-like state. "Yes. I heard. I just ..." He swallowed hard. "What do you want me to do?"

Ilse breathed a sigh of relief. She was beginning to lose control again herself and knew she had more information to give. "The police need someone to identify him." She paused and breathed hard. She could not last much longer. "I'll give you a number to contact for details. Have you a pen?"

"Yes." Karl jotted down the number, feeling strangely remote from everything. He sensed Ilse could hardly speak now and knew he should cut short the conversation. "I'll do that. Don't worry. I'll be in touch."

"Thank you, Karl. Goodbye."

The line went dead, leaving Karl holding the buzzing receiver. Slowly he replaced it on its cradle, then made for the front door, still clutching the paper on which he had scribbled the telephone number. Against the front wall of the house was a wooden bench. Karl sat down on it and stared bleakly across the road and meadows beyond to the rolling, forested hills.

Katherine found him five minutes later, still staring out over the hills. His attitude of utter stillness reminded her of his mental breakdown in 1947 when the world had proved too much for him to cope with and he retreated inside himself, unable to respond to human contact of any kind. Cautiously she approached and sat down next to him, sensing something was terribly wrong by the grim set to his face and his remoteness. She reached for his hand and discovered it held a piece of paper.

She spoke softly. "Karl? What's wrong? Has something happened?"

Karl blinked and glanced down at the ground at his feet before looking up at the hills again. He could not face her.

"Now I know what you must have felt when you first heard I was in the SS," he said at last. "Totally betrayed." He showed her the paper in his hand. "That is the telephone number of the police in Arnsberg, near Soest," he explained slowly, his voice leaden. "I must contact them to make arrangements to identify the body of my son, and possibly that of a certain Gustav Halstrup too." He waited for her reaction.

Katherine took her time replying to the stupefying information. "Body? Siegfried, you mean? He's dead?"

Karl nodded.

Katherine sat open-mouthed as the significance began to sink in. "But how? And what's Gustav got to do with it. Do you mean *the* Gustav, the one who gave Siegfried his penknife when he was a little boy?"

Again Karl simply nodded, but finally answered her question. "There was a car crash. What they were doing together, where they were going, nobody knows. But Ilse certainly knew of Gustav. I think he was one of their ... group."

At last Katherine understood Karl's deep sense of betrayal. "You think Siegfried was still a Nazi?"

Karl made no reply, as if to do so would only make his fears come true. Katherine's mind was working along another track, however.

"What about Sophie and the babies? Are they all right?"

"They weren't in the car. They didn't even know where he had gone. He drove off suddenly after we left, not telling her where he was going."

"How odd," Katherine murmured. She followed Karl's gaze, examining the nearby hills, seeing the coppery hint of turning leaves on the stands of beeches amongst the dark conifers. She had not yet grasped Siegfried was dead. Gustav too. Her sister, Sarah, would be interested to hear, having had her husband stolen from her by Gustav. She gave an involuntary gasp as the significance of that last thought dawned on her.

"What is it?" Karl asked, still keeping his eyes from hers.

Katherine hesitated. This was not something she wanted to talk about to Karl, but he had probably already considered it. "I just thought about Gustav and his ... sexual leanings. You don't think he was after –"

"It's possible. Probable," he corrected himself. He gave a deep sigh and finally turned to his wife. "This afternoon Siegfried told me he was deceiving us all – stringing us along rather – even Sophie."

"He told you that?"

"Yes, but I had no idea how until I heard he was with Gustav, then everything clicked into place. Siegfried never intended leaving the Nazis, and Gustav made sure of that, winning his trust, just like he did before when Siegfried was a boy. Siegfried always idolised Gustav. Maybe it was an easy step to take it further than idolising, given sufficient pressure from Gustav."

"But Siegfried's not like that!" Katherine protested.

"We didn't think Gustav was, did we? He was quite a womaniser, I seem to remember."

"Yes, you're right." Katherine recalled Gustav's flattery during his stay on the farm back in the autumn of 1950. Sarah had found him charming enough to end up sleeping with him, then with him and her husband, Perry, at the same time. Somehow Perry and Gustav had begun to spend time together alone and that had been that. No wonder Karl looked devastated. "Does Sophie know, do you think?"

"No," Karl said emphatically. "And she won't, unless she works it out for herself. But I think she'll only see the political side of things. She'll be proud he was still in the fold after all."

Katherine finally realised grief had not come to Karl with the news of his son's death. There was only burning anger at his lies and betrayal. She squeezed his hand. "I'm so sorry, Schatz. I know how much it meant to you having him back.

He withdrew his hand from hers, unable to accept affection while so angry. "I never had him back at all." He slapped the bench seat hard, as though physical pain could drive away his emotional pain. "It was lies, all lies and I believed him. I wanted to believe him, and he knew it. It was so easy for him to convince us all."

Katherine did not like to say she had always had her doubts. It was not the right moment. She had, after all, accepted him in the end. She sat silently beside Karl, wondering how best to comfort him, but it was Anna who came to the rescue.

"Oh, there you are! We were wondering what had happened. Is everything all right?"

"No," Karl said wearily, and explained the news all over again.

Anna turned pale. "Siegfried's dead? Oh, Karl, I'm so sorry. And poor Sophie. She must be devastated. Ilse too. No wonder she sounded upset." Anna's grief took the form of babbling as tears started to flow. "What a thing to happen after such a lovely day, but then he had been drinking rather a lot. It was foolish of him to drive." Rather than being numbed by the news her thoughts went into overdrive. "I suppose you'll have to stay longer for the funeral. Is Sophie organising that, or do they want us to? Perhaps he should be buried here in Medebach in the family plot."

"Anna!" Karl interrupted gently. "One thing at a time. I've got to go and identify his body first." He found his anger subsiding at last in the face of his sister's grief. He looked again at the paper in his hand. "I'd better phone the police and find out where he is."

Leaving Anna and Katherine to inform the rest of the family he returned to the telephone. His enquiries were dealt with sensitively, so much so that he almost felt the resurgence of the grief that had so rapidly been driven out by anger. Entering the kitchen he was met by a host of tear-streaked faces. Even Katherine had succumbed, moved by Dieter's silent, dignified weeping. Stefan looked up from where he was comforting Anna and noticed Karl's dry eyes.

"Do you want me to drive you anywhere, Karl? Anna says you've got to identify the body."

"In the morning. Arnsberg," he replied stiffly, examining his cup of cold coffee. Siegfried's words would not leave his mind. 'I'm stringing you all along: you, Sophie, my mother and Paul. Everyone.' And what was that strange remark about 'bending in every direction'? The mental image this conjured up brought Gustav inextricably to mind. Karl slammed down the cup onto its saucer, making everyone jump. "Sorry."

Stefan moved Anna from his shoulder and stood up. "I think we could all do with something to steady us," he said, heading for the schnapps bottle in the living room. He returned a few moments later with some glasses and the bottle on a tray.

"I'll go and phone Rudi – tell him the news," Karl said, anxious to escape the charged emotion of the room.

"I expect he'll want to come over," Dieter said. "You'd better fetch some more glasses, Stefan."

"Perhaps I should phone home and let Richard and Paul know," Katherine said to Karl as he was opening the door.

"I'll do that while I'm out here," he told her. He needed to keep busy, to keep his mind from the anger and hurt. And shut out his sense of loss.

*

It was easy for Sophie to let her parents take control of things. They came over as soon as she phoned them and happened to mention Ilse was too distraught to be of much assistance. Peter Wendt contacted the police and elicited as many details as he could about the accident and when the body might be released for burial. Lisl sat and hugged her daughter then went out to make cups of soothing hot chocolate for everyone.

Ilse sat and wept inconsolably, longing for someone to throw herself upon, for a shoulder to bury her face in and make wet with tears. But Karl was in Medebach and Paul in Uruguay, and Siegfried was dead. There was always Heinrich and the girls of course. She supposed she ought to let them know what had happened. And Paul too. But not just yet. She could not face another phone call. Karl's response had been so ... She was not sure exactly how he had responded to the news, could hardly remember her call to him now, except that he had not said much until prompted. She wanted to hear his voice again, to hear words of comfort from his lips. Sophie was fine. She had her parents and the twins to keep her busy. Ilse wanted Karl.

She rose from her chair, miming using the telephone to Sophie and Lisl, and went out to the hall, wiping her reddened eyes on her sodden handkerchief. Dialling the familiar Medebach number she breathed deeply, trying to control her shuddering breath. Stefan answered.

"It's Ilse here again, Stefan. Is Karl around?"

"Yes. I'll go and get him." He remembered his manners. "We're all devastated by the news, Ilse. We're thinking of you and Sophie. How is she coping?"

"Oh, well enough, considering. Her parents are over and taking control. I must admit, I feel a bit of a spare part at the moment. I need something to do. I thought I ought to go with Karl to identify ... him."

"He's doing that tomorrow, but I'll fetch him for you. Hold on."

Ilse waited then heard approaching footsteps on the wooden floor of the hall she knew so well. Then his voice came on the line.

"Ilse. It's Karl."

Already she felt comforted. His tone was softer than before, less remote, more caring.

"I'm sorry to trouble you again, Karl," she began, "but I realised I wanted to see him – to identify him too."

"Are you sure, Ilse? It won't be a pleasant experience."

"No. I know. But somehow I've got to accept he's actually gone. I don't think I can unless I see him."

There was a pause as he considered the advisability of bringing her along to such a sordid task, but she knew he could hardly refuse her request.

"Can you get to Arnsberg, or do you want collecting?"

She had not thought that far ahead. "I can get a taxi. You'll have far enough to drive as it is."

"You're sure Sophie doesn't want to do the job instead? Then you can come with her."

Ilse was astonished that Karl would want to palm the deed off onto Sophie of all people.

"No, I don't think she should have to face such a sight. She's got enough to cope with, what with the twins and all. She's quite happy for you to do it."

"Fine, I'll do it. I've arranged to be at the mortuary for ten o'clock."

"I'll be there."

"Are you sure about this, Ilse?"

"Why? Don't you want me there?"

"It's not that –"

"So you don't want me there, is that it?" She knew she was provoking him into declaring his feelings for her, but it was the only thing she wanted to hear at that moment.

"Of course that's not it. You've every right to be there. I just think it will upset you too much."

That's the whole point, Ilse thought. I need to experience the pain, the anguish and the comfort that only you can give me. Out loud she said: "I'm prepared for that. It's just something I feel I have to do."

"I understand." Karl felt the time had come to move on. "How is Sophie?"

"As I was saying to Stefan just now, she's quite stoical at the moment. It probably hasn't really sunk in yet. I think she's just puzzled as to why he disappeared off like that. And with Gustav."

"Yes, I was wondering that too. Had he seen much of Gustav recently?"

Ilse sensed Karl's suspicions. Karl could not possibly know the extent of Gustav's involvement in neo-Nazism, but he might have an inkling, given the fact both she and Sophie were acquainted with him. If Siegfried was in league with Gustav, then it would shatter all Karl's illusions about Siegfried's apparent loss of faith in Nazism, and she didn't want to hurt Karl any more than he was already.

"I've no idea." It had been a mistake to mention Gustav, but Karl would have found out soon enough anyway. She thought quickly. "Perhaps Sophie had invited him to the christening and he got lost, or broke down and rang for help, so Siegfried went to fetch him."

"They were travelling south, away from Soest, and Gustav was very late, even taking breaking down into account. There was something going on between those two, and I'm going to –"

"Karl, it won't help matters now. Just leave it be."

There was no use pressing the point, he decided. Ilse would hear nothing bad about her son. "Sorry. You're right. Now is not the time for recriminations."

The conversation seemed to have died. "I'll see you tomorrow then," Ilse said, realising Karl was in need of comforting as much as she was. "I hope you manage to sleep."

"You too. Goodbye, Ilse."

"Goodbye, Karl."

*

Christian was able to leave the scene of the accident after further questioning. He had gathered from the police that Driesler had given his name before he died but they had had to identify the passenger from his driving licence. Christian did not help them.

His story was that he was in a hurry and had simply followed the Mercedes' lead in overtaking a bunch of slower cars. The police seemed satisfied and did not press charges.

As he returned to his car and drove slowly back to Dortmund, Christian pondered on what would happen to Gustav's body. He knew Gustav had no family. They had all been killed in the war, but there were friends among the acting community in Berlin who would care enough to see him properly buried. He would have to tip them off anonymously as he dared not be linked to Gustav now in any way. It was only too obvious he had driven them off the road while insanely jealous, and now he was guilty of manslaughter, maybe even murder. Those babies had lost their father, the pretty blonde had lost her husband, and he had lost his lover. Tears of self-pity began to flow. Pulling in at the side of the road overlooking the Möhne dam, he began to howl with grief and remorse.

It was while sitting there, his sobs gradually subsiding, that he realised he could not return to Dortmund. He had given up the rental on his tiny flat when his funds grew dangerously low. He had been living off Gustav's largesse and napping in railway stations when not allowed at Gustav's. He had left some clothing there, but nothing vital. He would have to start afresh somewhere if he could – and soon. All his contacts were in Berlin. Gustav's friends were in Berlin. He would have to return there.

He examined his almost empty wallet. If the police stopped him for speeding and he had to pay a fine he would be done for vagrancy. Suddenly he felt very alone, and the tears flowed again.

His stomach growled and he realised he was desperately hungry. He thought of all the food at the christening, how much would be left over and what the parents would do with it all. Then he sat bolt upright. The house was probably empty. They would be with their daughter at a time like this!

Starting the engine again he set off towards the house he had been observing earlier that day. As expected it looked deserted, but he drove past towards the lay-by where Gustav's car still stood. It seemed rather risky leaving his car so close to Gustav's, but his hunger was intense.

He ran down the road to the smart villa and listened intently before creeping up the driveway. He could not see into the garage so did not know if the car was there, but there were no lights on in the house even though evening was drawing in. He paused by the back gate. This was the second house he had snooped around now. He shook his head at the depths he had sunk to then opened the metal gate to the back garden.

They had left the house in a hurry. The kitchen window was still open. Wrapping his hand in his handkerchief, Christian turned the handle and opened the window wide enough to allow him to climb in. He made straight for the refrigerator. It was packed full of leftovers. Not wasting any time, he grabbed a fork from the sink rack and began to tuck in, washing it down with lemonade from a bottle. Once replete, he thought of the day to come and proceeded to shovel more leftover meat, salad and bread into plastic bags he found tucked in a drawer. Leaving the bags on the table he began hunting round the kitchen for a secret hiding place for cash. He was going to need money for petrol and other supplies. Sure enough, after only a few moments' searching, he found a biscuit tin which seemed too light for what was sliding around inside. Opening it he found a wad of twenty mark notes.

"Bingo!" he whispered, stuffing the wad into his jacket pocket.

That was enough, he decided. He could not take anything else which might be traceable to the house. Picking up the bags of food he climbed through the window, closing it to its original position, then set off back up the road to his car.

NINETEEN

Sleep evaded Karl for most of that night, and when it did come he was woken by vivid dreams of a blood-soaked Siegfried acting as though nothing were amiss. Katherine felt him tossing and turning but felt there was little she could do to comfort him. Another dream at four in the morning made him cry out in fright, and Katherine knew things were getting worse. He had not had any nightmares for some months now. When she first knew him, nightmares seemed to be a nightly occurrence. After psychiatric help during his mental breakdown their frequency reduced considerably, but they were still an occasional problem. She gave him a nudge to wake him from his ordeal.

"Do you want to tell me about it?" she asked. Sometimes he did, sometimes he did not. She had no idea why.

He sat up and switched on the bedside light in an effort to clear the terrible images from his mind. "I was dreaming about the twins. Siegfried was holding them and suddenly they were all three of them just bloody messes." He knew she would not understand unless he explained further, although he hated talking about his time as a soldier of the Third Reich. "Like in Yugoslavia, when the little children were shot during my rescue from the Partisans."

Katherine's memory of the incident, as told to her once by Robert Murdoch, was sketchy. "That was the turning point in your loyalty to Nazism, wasn't it? When you realised you were in the wrong."

He made no reply, still consumed by the terrible images in his head, and Katherine knew it would take him a long time to get back to sleep unless she could break into his train of thought.

"Shall I make us a cup of tea?" It was their usual course of action after one of his nightmares.

"Please."

When she returned with the tea he was still sitting up, elbows on knees, head in hands, just as she had left him. She wondered whether to have another word with Robert, himself a psychiatrist, about Karl's nightmares. She could see the sweat drying on his muscular chest and shoulders.

"You'll get cold," she said handing him the cup of tea. "Let me rub you down with a towel."

Her ministering hands and the tea soothed him enough for him to settle back to sleep, but he woke at six feeling bleary-eyed and exhausted. Reluctantly he got out of bed, waking Katherine in the process.

"How are you feeling?" she asked.

"Awful," he replied. "I'll be glad when this morning's over." He reached for his dressing gown from the hook on the door and put it on. With his back to her he said: "You don't have to come, Schatz."

"I want to," she replied, surprised at his change of heart. "As I said, I won't come in with you, but I'd rather be with you on the journey than stuck here twiddling my thumbs, wondering how you are."

"I'll be fine. It's just that Ilse's going to be there. I thought you would rather avoid her." He opened the bedroom door and headed for the bathroom before she could reply. He could hear noises from downstairs already as Anna clattered about in the kitchen setting the breakfast table. His father's bedroom door was ajar. Always an early riser, Dieter was probably out sniffing the morning air. Perhaps he had trouble sleeping too, Karl thought.

Breakfast was a subdued affair, with nobody quite sure what to say. Work matters were the safest conversation topic. Dieter declared he would spend the day with Lothar and Rudi at the sawmill since Stefan would be driving Karl and Katherine to Arnsberg. Anna said she would go to church to pray.

When they eventually set off in Stefan's car for Arnsberg, soberly dressed and in sombre mood, Karl studied the cloud-veiled hilltops and tried to rid his mind of all rancour. Over the years he had tried hard to love Siegfried. When the boy first came to live at Lane Head Farm, aged six, Karl had been fully prepared to love him on equal terms with the two-year-old Sabina. But Siegfried had hated and feared him from their very first meeting, that hatred growing as the boy himself grew. There were times when he concealed the hatred, allowing a semblance of normality, but Karl had always known he could not trust his own son. Sophie's accident had seemed to be the turning point for Siegfried's Nazi beliefs, when Siegfried had found friendship and help where he least expected it, in the form of Judy, the coloured nurse. Siegfried had seemed to reassess his values then and turned to his family for comfort. At long last Karl had been able to love his first-born son, that love being all the stronger for the time and effort it had taken to achieve it. Yet no sooner had that love been achieved then it was brutally destroyed by the discovery it had all been a lie on Siegfried's part.

He sighed deeply, trying to release the anger and tension mounting in him. Brooding would not help matters now, would not help Sophie and the twins, but he could not escape the fact that Siegfried had let him down hard. He was aware of Katherine beside him, her hand wrapped comfortingly around his, but leaving him his thoughts to himself. Stefan too was keeping quiet as the miles passed and the grim task drew ever nearer.

Their arrival at the mortuary coincided almost exactly with Ilse's arrival in a taxi.

"Perfect timing," Stefan remarked.

"You Germans are always punctual," Katherine said to lighten her own spirits as much as anyone else's. The sight of Ilse's tragic face had caused an unexpectedly warm ripple of sympathy, so much so that Katherine decided to get out of the car along with Karl and approach her rival. She sensed Karl's awkwardness and decided that hostility was inappropriate. Both Karl and Ilse were hanging back from each other and Katherine knew that had she not been present they would have embraced each other. That was why Karl had not wanted her to come, she realised. He knew Ilse needed comforting and could not do it in front of her.

Do I really mind seeing him hug her, Katherine asked herself, or am I just being petty-minded and churlish? Yes, I do mind, she decided. But no, I'm not going to be churlish about it – not for something as dreadful as this. Stepping forward she reached for Ilse's hand, leaned forwards and hugged her, murmuring: "I'm so sorry, Ilse. I truly am. If there's anything we can do for you, just say." For once the German words came fluently and easily to her tongue, and Ilse heard her sincerity.

"Thank you, Katherine. You're very kind."

Katherine saw the tears begin to flow down Ilse's powdered cheeks and felt her own eyes moisten in sympathy. If either Richard or Paul had been killed, Katherine knew she would be devastated, but for Ilse it seemed worse. Siegfried had been everything: the outcome of her love for Karl, her pride and joy, her number one son.

Reassured by Katherine's performance, Karl stepped forward and took Ilse gently by the arm. Wanting to spare Ilse's emotions he got straight to the point. "Shall we go in?"

Ilse nodded, checked to make certain the taxi would wait for her, then reached in her bag for a large handkerchief. She dabbed at her face then held onto the handkerchief ready for use.

The air temperature cooled dramatically as they approached the mortuary. Waiting there for them was a heavy-jowled but whey-faced policeman, who was clearly not at ease in such surroundings.

"Herr and Frau Driesler?" he asked rather too loudly to hide his discomfort.

"Frau Zopf," Karl corrected him quietly. "My son's mother. She would like to see him too."

The policeman nodded. "We're all ready if you'd like to come this way."

He led them through a door into a quiet but well-lit room where a shrouded body lay on a trolley. A mortuary attendant waited until they both stood by, then uncovered the head of the body.

Karl looked down at his son's blank face, and felt the blood drain out of his own. It was like looking at his own corpse. It was not just the facial similarity; a part of him had died with Siegfried. Of his four children Siegfried had been brought up most like himself: as a German, indoctrinated with Nazism and taught to kill his fellow man in allegiance to it. They had both suffered physical abuse at some time in their lives, and ultimately had acknowledged guilt for their crimes. Or so he had thought until now. Gustav had a lot to answer for, Karl thought bitterly. His son, the Nazi, lay dead in front of him and he could not grieve for him.

He felt Ilse clinging tightly on to his arm, silently shaking. She had not uttered a sound as yet and he turned to see how she was coping. As their eyes met she dissolved into paroxysms of grief. He held her close, knowing this was what she wanted, why she had come, but it did not matter. Nothing mattered right now.

As he held her there, her face buried in his chest, he looked over her head to the policeman and nodded. The mortuary attendant looked at him enquiringly to see if he could cover up the body again. Karl nodded at him too then laid his head on top of Ilse's.

"Shhh, Schatz," he comforted her the only way he could, his lips brushing against her hair. She stirred in his arms as she raised the handkerchief to her streaming eyes and nose, and he began to lead her to the door. She turned hurriedly but saw Siegfried's body was already covered over again.

"Just one thing, sir," the policeman said uneasily. "We've been unable to find anyone to formally identify the other victim. Did you know Herr Halstrup?"

Karl hesitated, then looked down at Ilse.

She shook her head. "I never met him – only knew his name. Sophie knew him in Berlin."

"We can't ask her to come." He turned back to the policeman. "I met him nearly twenty years ago. I suppose I might recognise him."

"If you could help, we'd be grateful," the policeman replied, giving a thumbs-up to the mortuary assistant. "Frau Zopf might like to wait outside," he continued, giving Karl a meaningful look, which Karl understood. Gustav was not going to be a pretty sight.

"Do you want to go back and wait with Katherine?" he asked her.

Ilse sniffed and nodded. She had no wish to see another body. Karl was about to escort her out, but she put her hand on his arm. "I'll be fine, Karl. You stay here and see about Gustav. Oh yes," she added, suddenly gathering her wits together. "Tell them we'll handle funeral arrangements for Gustav if nobody else comes forward."

It only served to confirm Karl's suspicions about Gustav. He was one of them, and would be taken care of in death by them, as befitted one of their own. He waited impatiently while a second trolley was brought in and the assistant pulled back the sheet covering the body.

Gustav must have died instantly. Bandages covered the worst of the head wound where the right side of his face had been smashed in. Even with the eyes closed, Karl could still identify the left side of the face as Gustav's, even after all those years. He recognised the round, rather boyish features that had endeared him to men and women alike. Gustav had kept himself fit, not putting on much weight or even too many wrinkles. It was a face Karl could never forget.

"It's him," he said confidently.

"Thank you, Herr Driesler. I'm sorry to have troubled you. I'll make a note of what Frau Zopf said about funeral arrangements."

"Contact her, not me," Karl replied shortly and left the room, hurrying back to the warm air outside where he found Ilse and Katherine sitting side by side on a low wall, while Stefan stood anxiously by the car.

"All done," Karl declared, making towards Stefan. "Let's go."

Katherine could not help but contrast Karl's brisk and business-like manner with Ilse's pathetic state. She would have preferred it if had he shown some emotion, but this cold remoteness from the events, along with his renewed nightmares, was worrying. He seemed disconnected from what was going on, while she felt obliged to pander to his and Ilse's needs as parents of the deceased. She could not find it in her heart to spurn Ilse now. Ilse needed Karl as a shoulder to cry on, and with any luck, some of her grief might rub off on him. Instinctively she knew he must not bottle it all up like this.

Reaching for Karl's hand she led him over towards Ilse and put his hand in Ilse's. "Tell us what Sophie wants for the funeral," she said to the bemused Ilse. "If we can help with anything ..."

Ilse looked slowly from Katherine up to Karl and back again, astonished that Katherine had freely loaned Karl to her. She managed a tearful smile at Katherine and Katherine returned it, glad neither Ilse nor Karl seemed aware of how hard she was gritting her teeth.

Karl embraced Ilse. Stooping so his mouth was close to her ear, he said: "Keep in touch and give our love to Sophie. As Katherine said, let us know if there's anything you want doing for the ... arrangements." He kissed her cheek then stepped backwards. He had had two women, two lives divided by a war. He loved them both, but in different ways and for different reasons. And now his main link with Ilse was gone.

It was as if she had read his thoughts. "Friedrich and Freya will need their Opa more than ever now," she told him. "Remember that, Karl."

"I will," he promised, wiping a tear from her face with his hand.

Katherine watched calmly as Karl led Ilse over to her taxi, opening and shutting the door for her. She felt surprisingly comfortable with the way he was treating Ilse, almost as a sister, although she had to acknowledge there was far more to his feelings than that. But strangely enough, things seemed quite different now. With Siegfried dead Ilse was no longer a threat.

Stefan had noticed Katherine's apparent magnanimity and whispered: "Well done. That was very noble of you."

Katherine gave a nonchalant shrug. Sympathy had got the better of her as usual. They watched as Ilse's taxi drove off towards Soest, then Karl returned to Katherine's side. "Thank you, Schatz. You were wonderful."

"Another lost puppy, that's all," she replied under her breath.

"Sorry?"

"Nothing. Let's get going."

They bundled into the car and headed for Medebach, but as they drove, Katherine could not help thinking about the circumstances surrounding Siegfried's death. Were he and Gustav following them back to Medebach? She shuddered and clutched Karl's hand tightly.

*

Wolf looked over his shoulder for the third time as he entered the workshop where a stack of television sets awaited repair. Since hearing of Siegfried's death the day before he had increased his vigilance. Ever conscious of the threat of retribution he now feared an attack on himself could be imminent. The one fact he could not understand was Gustav Halstrup's death. From what he knew of the man, Gustav Halstrup would have been the one most likely to order Siegfried's execution, and was highly unlikely to carry it out himself. So the crash was probably not a drastically botched attempt on Gustav's part to eliminate Siegfried. Wolf reached for a screwdriver and absently began taking the back off the television set on the bench.

There again, what if Gustav had also fallen foul of the party and had also been on a hit list? Two birds with one stone? If that were the case, why was Siegfried with Gustav? Was he persuading him to grass on the Berlin network?

Lifting off the back cover Wolf peered into the workings and spotted the failed valve. He removed it, checked its number then went to the rack on the wall where boxes of valves were stacked. He found the right one and returned to the bench. Sitting back down he knew that was not the answer. If they were together then either Siegfried was still secretly in league with the neo-Nazis or else he was double-crossing Gustav.

He plugged in the television set and switched it on, watching the valves glow as they warmed up. There was a crackling noise and the picture appeared on the screen. He adjusted the contrast and brilliance, turned the volume right down then sat looking at the test card on the screen, deep in thought.

Siegfried could lie through his teeth. Even though they had known each other for years, Wolf could never be certain when Siegfried was telling the truth. His cunning was legendary, his ability to dupe learned from Gustav at a very early age and honed to a fine art over the years. There was no doubt Sophie was still true to her beliefs. There was also no doubt Siegfried loved Sophie. That was about the only thing Wolf was sure of. But now they had children, was it not reasonable for Siegfried to want to be reunited with his whole family by apparently rejecting Nazism? No, he thought, turning off the television set. That could not be it as he had started down that track before he knew Sophie was pregnant.

He wrote out a repair chit, attached it to the set, moved it to another corner of the room and replaced it on the bench with the next one, whose docket declared it had no sound.

Wolf gave up speculating. All he could assume was that he himself was possibly at extra risk. But if they could kill an expert assassin like Siegfried, then what hope did he have of avoiding the same fate? He could only keep his eyes and ears open and watch out for Bina too, without unduly alarming her. He would keep his suspicions to himself.

*

News of Gustav's death had not yet reached Berlin. Christian made a tour of the theatres where they had played and asked for information as to his whereabouts. Nobody informed him of the tragic event. The one good development resulting from his research was the offer of a bed in a flat, so at least he was no longer homeless. With any luck a job would soon come up as well, now contact had been re-established with the theatre world. He strolled along amongst the crowds on the Bismarckstraße heading for the Tiergarten, glad to be back in Berlin on familiar ground after the stress of the past few days.

He dared not pass on the news himself, as it might inextricably link him with the crash. Wracked with guilt, Christian knew he must do something about getting a decent funeral for Gustav, but could hardly organise a collection from theatre friends without broaching the subject and manner of his death. He had to make contact with Gustav's other acquaintances, the ones Gustav had been at pains to keep secret from him, the ones most likely to see to a burial.

A sheet of newspaper whipping by in the wind caught at his feet, a black-bordered box on the page giving him the inspiration he was seeking. He would pay for a death notice, anonymously of course, and hope someone else would take it up from there when they found there were no funeral arrangements.

He breathed easier again, already composing in his head the necessary words in as brief a form as possible. He was able to do something at last, try to make amends for causing Gustav's death. But that thought made him kick out angrily at the paper. It was not his fault! Why was he blaming himself? If that bastard Driesler hadn't been driving so fast ... Christian felt a tear trickle down the side of his nose. He had truly lost Gustav, who was united now in death with his new lover.

"It should be me with him, not you!" he shouted at the newspaper as it fluttered down the pavement only to be caught up by the next obstacle, a rubbish bin. Ignoring the curious glances of passers-by, Christian advanced towards the sheet of newspaper, snatched it up and rammed it into the bin. He felt no better for that small act of defiance. Driesler must pay for Gustav's death – and pay with his reputation. His wife and children would find out how he had betrayed them. His name and memory would be dirt!

Careless now of his own future, Christian strode purposefully to the nearest police station, armed with the courage to tell all. The whole of Berlin would hear of Gustav's death now, but his name would be linked forever with that of Christian Bracht!

TWENTY

Ilse squeezed Sophie's hand. They both knew that what the policeman was telling them was untrue. It was the same moustached one who had informed them of Siegfried's death, and now he was telling them of his apparent treachery, of sexual liaisons with Gustav.

"I thought you would want to hear this first in the privacy of your own home, rather than in open court, Frau Driesler. It's not an easy thing to hear."

"No. Thank you. I appreciate it," Sophie said quietly but evenly, maintaining a calm dignity that impressed the policeman immensely.

It occurred to him that she might have suspected her husband already of having a homosexual affair. That would account for her composure, he realised, shuffling his feet in embarrassment. She was a good-looking woman and it astonished him that her husband should have looked to a man for sex. Not that he wasn't broad-minded. It was his personal opinion that the sooner West Germany caught up with East Germany in legalising homosexuality, the better. It would make his job far less distasteful. Next year most likely, it was rumoured. He turned his thoughts back to the matter in hand.

"We are still of the opinion the accident was caused by your husband's alcohol intake and by the defective safety barrier, rather than any intent on Bracht's part, but obviously it's up to the inquest to determine the facts and rule accordingly. I would imagine arrangements for the funeral will not be delayed unduly. You will be attending the inquest, I trust?"

"Of course," Sophie replied, unable at last to control the tremor in her voice. "Thank you again for your time and concern."

She showed him out and returned to the living room where her mother-in-law still sat on the sofa.

"So Gustav's cover worked for him right to the end," Sophie said, sinking back down next to Ilse. "Who would expect a Nazi to be homosexual?"

"But that's just it, Sophie. He was a homosexual," Ilse explained. "It was cover, but it wasn't deception."

"Actually he was bisexual, but that's beside the point. All I know is, this Christian Bracht fellow has given Siegfried perfect cover too. There's a complete smokescreen over the issue now. No one will see beyond the supposed homosexuality, and everyone who matters will know that Siegfried was with Gustav. There can be no question of his loyalty now. None whatsoever."

"This has really hurt Karl, though," Ilse remarked.

"So what? He was a fool to think Siegfried was so easily turned. He should have known better."

Ilse made no reply. Much as she loved Sophie, there were times when she was a little too harsh in her judgements.

Sophie picked up on her silence. "You won't hear anything said against him now, will you? In fact, I believe you'd marry him tomorrow, if he asked you, wouldn't you? Regardless of Paul."

Ilse looked at her in horror. "Sophie! Really! I hardly think you're qualified to speculate on my emotions like that. Paul and I have a good marriage. He's just very different from Karl, that's all. He treats me like a queen –"

"As a sop to his conscience," Sophie protested, then quickly mollified her tone. "It's all right, Ilse. I'm not condemning you. Siegfried was very much the same." There, she had said his name and talked about him in the past tense. She could do it. "Siegfried learned his attitude to women from Paul. If he'd wanted one, he'd have had one. What I am certain of, is that he would never ever have ... slept with Gustav."

Ilse felt uncomfortable. She had an uneasy feeling that Siegfried would do anything to further his aims. But she would never admit such a thing to Sophie.

*

"And are you sure you can cope for another week or so, until after the inquest and funeral?"

"Yes, quite sure, Mum," Richard told his mother over the telephone. "All the usual arrangements for the apple-pickers are in hand, there's nothing out of the ordinary happening except Paul and I sold all our stock of garden furniture at the Harvest Fair at the weekend. Alf has decided to make more of a beer garden at the Walnut Tree for next year, and snapped up our stuff after I told him we'd be putting up our prices due to demand."

"That's wonderful," she congratulated him. "Now what about funds? Can you manage?"

"Everything's going on account. There's no problem. Oh yes." He paused before tackling a difficult subject. "There's a letter here for Dad. Postmarked Soest the day after Siegfried died."

"How odd! Any idea who it's from?"

"There's no sender's name on the envelope. Could be from anyone."

Ilse perhaps, Katherine thought uneasily. But why would she post it to England? Unless it was put in the box before Siegfried died and was not collected until the following day. That was probably it. And of course she would not write her name on the back. "Well, it will have to wait until we get home," she told Richard, trying to put it out of her mind. "Give us another ring tomorrow after the inquest."

"Rightey-ho. Take care, Mum. I hope Dad copes with it all OK."

"Yes, so do I. Anyway, I'd better go. Take care. Love to Paul."

"Will do. Take care yourself, Mum."

Katherine walked slowly back to the living room to resume her seat in front of the television set alongside Dieter. Karl and Stefan had gone back down to the sawmill to fix a hoist that had jammed late in the day. Lothar was out with a girl somewhere, while Anna was in the cellar doing something with the laundry. Katherine supposed she ought to offer to help, but it was easier just to sit with Dieter than have to discuss Siegfried's foibles in German with Anna. Besides, she needed to think about this letter from Soest and its implications.

She let the light entertainment programme wash over her. James Last and his orchestra were playing their latest hit. Hugely popular in Germany, she could never see them catching on in Britain on such a large scale. Germany was another world, with different culture and tastes. She was surprised every time she visited the country how different in many respects it was from England. Karl gave her a false idea of German identity, having subdued his own for camouflage purposes after the war. Yet here, in his own country, it re-emerged, like he was harking back to the old days, the days when he and Ilse were lovers.

Why had Ilse written to him? What had she got to say to him that she could not say to his face? Surely she knew her letter would not go unnoticed? After everything Katherine had done to ignore Ilse's attraction to Karl, she was being repaid like this. Of course the letter was written before Siegfried died, before Katherine had demonstrated such kindness and forgiveness towards the bereaved Ilse. Nevertheless Katherine felt betrayed yet again by a woman she had once considered as a friend. Ilse would have reckoned that a letter with a Uruguayan stamp would have been obvious, but a letter sent from Soest shortly after their visit there might have passed almost unnoticed by Katherine. It was scheming and underhand and typical of Ilse!

When Karl and Stefan arrived back shortly after nine, grease on their hands and faces, Katherine was still fuming in her armchair. She had almost decided to intercept the letter upon their return before Karl saw it, but realised she could not be so underhand herself. She respected his privacy and his ability to deal with Ilse in his own way. If pressed he might even show her the letter, but she would have to play it by ear. Only if he said nothing at all about it would she start to worry.

*

Ilse sat quietly listening to Christian Bracht's allegations that Siegfried had been having a homosexual affair with Gustav Halstrup. The young man was clearly finding the whole inquest a trial of emotional strength, but his constant glances at Siegfried's family revealed his motive for finally coming forward with his evidence. It was the revenge of the betrayed.

Poor young man, she thought. He had lost his lover to another, so he supposed. They had tended to forget that Gustav had died in the accident too. But with no family to mourn him it had not seemed such a tragedy until Bracht appeared on the scene. Bracht was risking prosecution for his homosexual activity for the sake of bringing shame upon Siegfried's family. She knew just how he felt. They were both spurned lovers. Although, strictly speaking, in

Ilse's case it had been wholly her own fault she had lost Karl to Katherine after the war. Yet what would she do now to rectify the situation? Kill Katherine? No. Never. And she doubted Christian Bracht was the sort to kill anybody either. No. It had been a tragic accident brought about by jealousy.

The inquest verdict was the same. Christian Bracht achieved his ambition to sully Siegfried's name. The press would have a field day, all this coming so soon after Karl's high profile trial earlier in the year. But it would all blow over eventually, and at least Siegfried's own family and friends knew the truth. Or probable truth. Ilse still could not rid herself of the suspicion that there was no smoke without fire. Siegfried would have had a reason for his actions, most certainly, but she had no idea what it might have been.

"Shall we go?" Sophie broke into her reverie. "We can finish making the arrangements for the funeral now. The sooner it's all over, the better."

And the sooner I'll have to go home, Ilse thought sadly. She looked across the slowly emptying room to where Karl and his family were gathering their coats and preparing to leave.

"Hadn't we better let Karl know the provisional arrangements?" Ilse suggested.

Sophie sighed in mock exasperation. "Yes, of course. But please don't be too long, Ilse. I don't like leaving the twins, even with my mother."

"You'll have to find someone else to baby-sit on the day of the funeral. Lisl will want to attend too."

"Yes, I know. Neighbours have offered." She slowly buttoned her black linen jacket. "I'm going to be doubly an object of sympathy after this, aren't I? People will shun me, not knowing what to say. And I won't even be able to defend his name, will I?"

"Siegfried was good at deceiving people. Some of that must have rubbed off on you, surely? Act like you don't care, which you don't, and they'll soon revert to normal."

Sophie managed a bleak smile. "Thanks. I'll see you outside. Don't be too long, remember."

Ilse watched her go out to the car park then sidled over to join Karl. She was surprised by the look Katherine gave her; after all the sympathy of a few days ago it was positively hostile. Feeling emboldened by Christian Bracht's spirit of defiance she took hold of Karl's elbow and turned him slightly to one side.

"We hope to have everything booked for Friday, Karl. It will be at the same church as the christening, hopefully at two p.m., but we've yet to confirm that. Siegfried was not a religious person, as you well know, but we feel a proper send-off is required."

To regain some of his lost respectability no doubt, Karl thought. "Thank you, Ilse. We'll let Bina and Wolf know. They'll have to take time off work, but I'm sure they'll be there. I expect Sophie will be mighty glad when all this is finally over." He paused, remembering concerns he had had earlier, before continuing: "You don't happen to know what provision Siegfried had made for such an eventuality, do you?"

Ilse shuddered at his words. She had been bearing up surprisingly well throughout the inquest, but as usual Karl managed to break through to her emotions. She took a deep breath. "I mentioned it the other day and Sophie said he'd taken out an extra insurance policy when the twins were born. She's got the firm's accountant coming to explain it all to her next week, but I believe she should be quite comfortable."

"Good. That's a relief. I thought that with all the recent financial problems after Paul ... left she might not have been so fortunate. How about funeral expenses?"

"Covered," Ilse said briskly, not wanting to break down in tears again, especially with Katherine watching her so suspiciously. "Don't worry, Karl. She'll be all right. She's a strong girl and she's got her parents and sister close by to help out. She and the twins will be fine." Ilse could not help herself making a final throw of her lifeline to Karl. "Just you make sure you keep in touch!"

"I intend to," he promised gravely, aware of Katherine's censorious eye upon them.

Katherine knew what he was thinking; that he did not want his grandchildren going down the same road as their father. Well, with a mother like Sophie, and grandparents like the Zopfs and the Wendts, it seemed unavoidable. Karl would expect to see plenty of his grandchildren to try to nullify the Nazi influences over them. And no doubt Ilse would make regular appearances for their important life events. Karl would never be free of her.

And what *was* in that letter?

*

Having come out into the open about his relationship with Gustav, Christian was free now to make inquiries about funeral arrangements. He discovered they were already in hand, but he could not find out who had made them. The police had referred him to the mortuary attendant, who referred him to a firm of undertakers in Dortmund, but there the trail went cold. Client confidentiality was quoted, although he was given details of when and where the funeral was to be held. Christian was immensely relieved to hear it was to be local, rather than in Berlin, as he was required to stay in the Dortmund area for his court appearance to answer the charge for his homosexual activity. He would be able to attend Gustav's funeral after all, although he now found himself in a dilemma. Penniless, he had an offer of a room in Berlin and a possible acting job in the pipeline, but he had to stay here, with no job, no roof over his head and no money. Yet Gustav had a flat with the rent paid, a car and no relatives to sort out his estate. He wondered who had been given the keys to Gustav's flat and car. If he could find out who had them, he might be able to persuade that person to let him have access to the flat.

He made another call on the police in Arnsberg, deciding to be totally honest about his impoverished circumstances. "So you see, I'd be on the streets if I can't stay there," he concluded. Then as extra embellishment he added: "I left some money and documents in Herr Halstrup's flat, which I desperately need to get hold of."

To his total amazement it paid off. The police officer dealing with him proved to have a soft heart.

"The keys were handed over to a Herr Wendt."

It took Christian a moment to register the name. Wendt. Of course! Frau Driesler's parents. He had seen the name on an envelope in their kitchen when he had taken the food.

"Why was he given the keys? What right does he have to them?" he demanded, before realising he should not have shown he recognised the name.

"Power of attorney in the event of Herr Halstrup's death," came the officious reply, as the policeman began to regret his good deed. "If you want his address I must telephone him for permission first."

"Thanks, but don't bother!" Christian said angrily, marching out of the police station. Hopefully the policeman would think he had given up on his quest, but Christian was one jump ahead of him. He already knew Wendt's address.

Gustav's car was no longer in the lay-by up the road from the Wendts' home. Christian left his own car there, walked back to the house and discovered the missing vehicle parked in their drive. Wendt must have brought it to the house. A quick scout around revealed no sign of the Wendts, or their car. Christian had no qualms this time about making an entry in through the kitchen window, which once again had been left open. He was astonished people could be so lax about security, but it was his good fortune they were.

Making his way through the darkening kitchen to the hall he spotted what looked like a study through an open door. A carved oak bureau stood facing the doorway, with bookshelves lining the other two walls. A cursory glance showed history and art were the Wendts' main interests.

Using his handkerchief as a glove Christian opened the flap of the bureau, revealing an orderly interior of pigeonholes containing bundles of documents, letters and stationery equipment. Sitting right at the front was a bulky manila envelope marked with the initials GH.

"It couldn't be easier!" Christian murmured, reaching for the envelope. Inside were the keys to the flat as well as a copy of the power of attorney document. Faced with the keys, he realised he could not simply walk off with them. He would be a prime suspect for their theft, after his enquiries at Arnsberg. But he would need to have a key cut, which necessitated borrowing them for a day. Hopefully Wendt would not need them until after the funeral. Pocketing the keys he noticed an envelope bearing a funeral parlour's name as the sender. Carefully withdrawing the contents, Christian could just about read in the gloom the details of Siegfried Driesler's funeral arrangements. To his surprise it was being held at exactly the same time as Gustav's. It seemed most odd, bearing in mind that Wendt was making the arrangements and held power of attorney over his personal life, that he would not be attending the funeral. He remembered the Dortmund undertaker's refusal to reveal the customer's name. If Wendt did not wish to be publicly associated with Gustav, was he a former lover?

Something was beginning to suggest to Christian that there was more to this than sex. Both Wendt and Driesler's involvement, together with the power of attorney document, spoke of something more complex. So why had nobody challenged his claim that Driesler was Gustav's lover? Because they knew it was true, or because it obscured something more sinister?

Car headlights flashed across the window and Christian realised the Wendts had returned home. Stuffing the letter back into the envelope, Christian closed the bureau and hurried back to the kitchen. He was trapped! They were coming in by the back door. Doubling back he made a rush for the front door. In the darkness he fumbled to draw back the bolts but ran out of time. He just made it into the adjacent dining room as Peter Wendt entered the hall, turning on lights as he came.

From behind the door, sweat beginning to pour off him, Christian listened to Wendt's movements.

"Did you want a drink, Liebling?" he heard him call to his wife, who was still in the kitchen.

"An advocaat please," came the distant reply.

To his horror, in the dim light of the room, Christian saw a drinks-trolley laden with bottles standing in the far corner by the window. He dived under the dining table just as Wendt entered the room, switching on the light. The table was covered by a heavy plush cloth, which hung low over the edges. Christian felt hopeful he would not be noticed as long as Wendt did not hear his ragged breathing. There was a clink of glasses and the sound of bottles being opened, but before Wendt could leave the room, his wife had entered.

"So we still don't know where Siegfried and Gustav were going that day," he heard Frau Wendt say with a touch of despair. "I did think someone in Berlin might have the answer, since none of the Dortmund group had any idea."

"If they do know, we're obviously not to be made privy to it," Wendt replied shortly. "You would have thought, under the circumstances, they could have given us some idea."

"Perhaps it was something Siegfried had organised himself."

"Maybe. Or a personal vendetta of Gustav's he wanted Siegfried to deal with. If that's the case then we'll never know, will we."

There was the sound of a bottle being replaced on the trolley. "Here you are, Liebling. *Prost!*"

"*Prost!*"

From under the table Christian heard them leave the room. The light went out and he was left alone with his turbulent thoughts and pounding heart. The words 'personal vendetta' and 'Siegfried to deal with' reverberated in his head. Was Driesler a hired assassin? If so, who was the intended victim? Christian found he was trembling as his thought processes continued to their logical conclusion. None of Driesler's family had disputed Christian's claims he was homosexual because they were covering up his true purpose – to get rid of Gustav's troublesome lover, Christian Bracht!

Under the dining table Christian sat with his knees up to his chin, his head resting on them. He was cramped but the foetal position gave him a slight sense of security as the evils of the world thrust at him. How could Gustav even contemplate such a thing? The idea was monstrous! He clutched his knees even tighter to his chin and began to rock back and forth as he sought to make sense of it all.

It was too monstrous, Christian thought suddenly. Gustav would never do such a thing. He frowned as he re-assessed what he had heard Frau Wendt say. She had mentioned groups in Berlin and Dortmund. What groups could she mean? Who were they, these secret friends Gustav used to meet up with in Berlin and Dortmund? Nothing to do with homosexuals, that was for sure. Frau Wendt and Frau Driesler were both part of whatever it was. Was it criminal? Undoubtedly. They had not told the truth to the police.

The fact that different groups operated in different cities made him doubt it was petty crime. This was either a major criminal operation or nothing of the sort. Could it be religious – or political? Political! Christian sat up abruptly, banging his head on the underside of the table. He curled up again and thought deeply. Political felt right. Gustav was not one to hide his opinions, which leaned to the far side of left. Were they all communist sympathisers? Berlin would be a useful centre of operations if that were the case.

But still it did not feel right. The Wendts, Frau Driesler, Driesler himself all seemed too ... That was it! The name! He cursed himself for not making the connection sooner. Last spring the newspapers had been full of reports about the murdered FDP politician rumoured to be a neo-Nazi. The man eventually acquitted of murder was called Driesler! So Driesler had been hired by Gustav's lot to assassinate a neo-Nazi.

There was still something not quite right in his logic, Christian thought. Then he had it and it blew his theory to pieces. The Driesler mentioned in the newspapers was too old. He had known the politician during the war.

But there was a connection – somehow. Gustav had tried to hide his interest in the trial, as though he knew the participants, Christian now realised. Did assassins pass on the secrets of their trade to their sons? Had Siegfried Driesler taken over from his father in the killing business? If that were the case then all Christian's jealousy was unfounded, and the accident was even more of a tragedy, even if it had possibly prevented someone else from being murdered.

"I'm sorry, Gustav," Christian mouthed through the tears of remorse which streamed down his face. "I'm so, so sorry. You kept telling me there was nothing between you and Driesler and I wouldn't listen. And now I've killed you."

A loud sob escaped his heaving chest and he clamped his hand over his mouth.

The light came on.

"Who's in there? Come out whoever you are!"

Still sobbing, Christian crawled out from under the table. He didn't care if they saw him like this. He didn't care he'd been caught, and he didn't care if they handed him over to the police. Nothing mattered any more.

"Who are you?" Peter Wendt demanded, brandishing a walking stick at the tear-streaked intruder. "Wait a minute. I recognise you now. You're Gustav's ..." It was as though he could not bring himself to say the word 'lover'.

Christian nodded. It was time to grovel.

"I'm sorry. I had nowhere to go. I had to get the keys to his flat. That's all I wanted. Look." He delved in his pocket and produced the bunch of keys.

Now she knew it was safe to do so Lisl Wendt entered the room. "How long have you been there?" she demanded.

Christian realised she was worried he had overheard their earlier conversation. What would they do to him if they thought he knew about their political tendencies? What if they were spies for the Stasi or KGB? Play the innocent lamb, he thought.

"Look, I just wanted the keys," he stammered. "I've nowhere else to stay. Gustav would have wanted me to have them, I know."

Peter Wendt looked at his wife. She shrugged, leaving the decision to him.

"Take them, then. You can sort through all his stuff, save me the trouble. His important documents are at his bank in Berlin so there should be nothing in the flat I need. Any bills that need paying send them on. The new ones are your responsibility from today. I don't know when his tenancy agreement expires but that will be your concern. His car stays here. Understood?"

They were clearly as anxious to be rid of him as he was to get away. "Yes. Can I go?" He began to move towards the door, then paused a moment. "Um, I just want to say thank you for sorting out his funeral. I know you won't be there, but I intend going."

"I'm sure Gustav will appreciate it," Wendt said icily. "Now clear off!"

Christian remembered another small problem. "Um, I'm afraid I don't have any money to buy petrol. Could you possibly lend me a few marks?"

His tear-streaked face was his saving grace. Even though he had accused their son-in-law of being homosexual they still acknowledged he was Gustav's friend.

"Oh very well," Wendt said, reaching for his wallet. He handed over a hundred mark note. "No doubt you'll need some food too. Call it payment for sorting out his flat – that and what you took before. It was you, wasn't it?"

Since there was hardly anything of Gustav's in the flat it was a generous payment. Enough to get him off their hands, but not nearly enough to be called hush money.

"Er, yes. I'm sorry. Thank you. And I'm very sorry about the way things turned out."

He was pushing his luck now, he realised and hastily headed for the front door.

Once he was gone Peter Wendt said to his wife: "Remind me in the morning to let Dortmund group know about him. Although I don't expect they'll do anything until Gustav's replacement's been appointed."

"A nice young man," Lisl commented. "I can see what Gustav saw in him."

TWENTY-ONE

A golden October sun shone down on the funeral party in defiance of the solemnity of the occasion. Feeling the heat in his dark suit, collar and tie, Karl stood poker-faced by his son's grave as the coffin lay poised over its musty depths. He could hear the stifled sobs of the many women mourners gathered around him. Siegfried had been a hugely popular figure in the Zopf and Wendt social circles. Even Sabina had made surreptitious use of a handkerchief during the church service, although she now stood in the open air grimly determined to maintain her composure. Close by his side Katherine stood equally composed, watching over him. For an unsettling moment he was transported back in time, almost a year, to his mother's funeral, when he had stood humiliatingly handcuffed to a prison guard. Karl tried to shake off the unpleasant memories of captivity, but the image of Siegfried strutting boldly around his grandmother's grave, so full of himself and his beautiful fiancée, haunted him. He remembered he had wished Siegfried dead then and there. Now he was dead, the wish fulfilled.

Karl's emotions were trapped in an endless loop of disbelief and anger, with no opening for grief. The son he thought had eventually come to love him had lied and cheated to the end. He felt immense anger at being used by Siegfried to claw-back a semblance of respectability for himself after the revelations about his neo-Nazi involvement. And yet Karl had sincerely believed his son had changed for the better after Sophie's accident. What a fool he had been!

A sharp tap on his elbow brought him back to the present. Katherine was pointing at their joined hands, a pained expression on her face. He realised he was squeezing her hand hard and he instantly released his firm grip. "Sorry," he whispered.

Trying to clear his thoughts of Siegfried he concentrated on the faces of the other mourners. His own family was huddled together, his father looking older than ever today. They had never seen

Siegfried at his most obnoxious self. He had usually behaved impeccably with them in Germany, saving all his malice for his father in England. Siegfried had been a model grandson, nephew and cousin to his German relatives.

His gaze moved round the large circle of mourners gathered around the grave. An utterly distraught Ilse stood supported by her remaining son, Heinrich, and one of her old friends, whom Karl vaguely recognised from Siegfried's twenty-first birthday celebrations. A fellow Nazi, no doubt: one who had escaped the witch-hunt after Wolf's revelations to the police. Ilse could barely keep her sobs under control, and it pained him not to be able to comfort her himself, but Katherine's suddenly resumed antagonism towards her rival deterred him. He wondered what had caused it, whether Ilse had said something to offend Katherine, or whether Katherine had misunderstood something said in German. Katherine was clearly not going to say anything to explain her mood. Forgiveness towards Ilse no longer seemed an option for her, and that was it. He just had to be grateful she still forgave him, and so he dared do nothing to upset her.

Karl moved his gaze on to Sophie, who, compared with Ilse, seemed strangely controlled. Maybe that was not so strange for her. She had always appeared to hold a tight reign on her emotions. Karl reckoned she would quickly make a new life for herself with some other young neo-Nazi approved of by her parents. She would soon find a stepfather for the twins, although heaven forbid they would be abused as Siegfried had been by his first stepfather. Karl shuddered, wishing again that he lived nearer his grandchildren to keep an eye on their welfare. He did not blame them for the sins of their father.

The pastor was saying his final words and the undertakers began to lower the coffin into the ground. Looking every inch the brave widow, Sophie stepped forward to throw a handful of soil onto the coffin. Karl supposed that he would be next in line for that task. He would have rather shown his contempt for his son by refusing, but that would only hurt Ilse's feelings. Dutifully he stepped forward to play his part. As the soil hit the coffin lid he had no last message for the son who had spurned him, but returned swiftly to Katherine's side. Ilse was then helped forward to throw her handful of soil over her son's coffin. She stood, head-bowed over the open grave for some moments before sobbing loudly and shuffling away to be comforted by others.

The official ceremony over other mourners came to stand over the grave or give their condolences to the widow. Karl noticed Sabina and Wolf hanging back, ill at ease in the presence of so many Nazis Wolf had betrayed. Karl moved back amongst the gravestones towards them, Katherine by his side.

"Feeling ostracised?" Karl asked Wolf.

"I don't think they're quite sure what to do about me," Wolf replied unhappily. "But after this I suspect I'm next on the list after Siegfried."

"Surely you don't think they killed him?" Karl exclaimed. "You'd be saying they killed Gustav too! And why would they do that? Besides, we all saw how much Siegfried had been drinking. The inquest proved that."

Wolf shrugged. "It just bore all the hallmarks of one of Siegfried's jobs – as though they'd learned his methods and used them on him. Gustav's presence may have been unforeseen. Or else he had to go because he was homosexual. Such behaviour's not well tolerated."

Although he was quite prepared to believe Wolf, Karl probed for an alternative explanation – a less frightening one. "But they can't have been up to any good driving off secretly like that after the christening," Karl protested. "He and Gustav must have had something planned."

"Perhaps he needed some Dutch courage to do whatever Gustav wanted," Sabina suggested, before blushing deeply as she realised how her words might sound.

An embarrassed silence showed everyone was thinking the same.

"Well I don't think they killed him," Karl said in an effort to dispel their growing anxiety. "Personally I think they're too disorganised at the moment to do anything. They daren't risk harming you, Wolf."

"Want a bet? Come on, Karl! You know them nearly as well as I do. They don't forgive and forget. We'll never be safe, you and I." Wolf glanced back at the funeral party, which was beginning to disperse. Sophie and Ilse were making their way to the cemetery gates, followed by the Wendts and their numerous friends. Karl's

German family stood in a large group in conversation with some of Siegfried's work colleagues, waiting for the pathway to the gates to clear. "I suppose we'd better go and join them all for coffee," Wolf said, "although going into the lions' den is the last thing I want to do at the moment."

"Me too, so let's not," Sabina suggested. "We really ought to be getting back to Dortmund, Wolf. We've got that concert this evening, and I've a hundred and one chores to do in the flat first." She turned to her mother and spoke in English. "I don't suppose we'll see you before you return. You're off tomorrow, are you?"

"Yes. The morning flight. The poor boys must be getting desperate for a decent meal by now, and heaven knows what state the house will be in."

"Gertie will have looked after them. You know that, Mum!" Sabina soothed her. "And you've never been particularly bothered about the state of the house before, have you?" She leaned closer to whisper: "You just want to get away from Ilse, don't you?"

Katherine sighed. "Is it that obvious?"

"I'm afraid so."

If the truth were to be told, Katherine was unsure whether she was anxious to return home. There was that letter waiting there: the letter that was preying on her mind. She put her arm through Karl's. "We can't stand here all day. We'd better follow the others back to Sophie's."

Sabina gave her mother a hug. "We'll give it a miss. You just watch your backs! Have a good journey home and we'll be seeing you at Christmas." She turned to her father. "Take care, Daddy, and don't worry about us. We'll be fine."

Karl hugged his daughter, reluctant to let her go. Christmas was a long way off yet, and Wolf's concerns were very real. "You take care of yourselves," he said stroking her auburn curls. "Don't forget, we're only a phone call away."

"I'll keep in touch," she promised, kissing him on the cheek. She stepped to one side to allow Wolf to bid his farewells, then they were gone.

Katherine reached for Karl's hand. "It's a worry, isn't it?"

"Yes," he replied grimly. "It certainly is."

"Do you still think they might be after you too?"

He shrugged, not wanting to frighten her. "Possibly. But we'd better go and join them anyway."

"Do we have to?" she said in a small voice. "They seem so ... alien to me. Like a bad dream."

"I suppose I'm used to them. Until I was twenty-three I was one of them." He guessed there was more to her reluctance than she was admitting to. "But it's not just Sophie and her lot, is it? It's Ilse, isn't it?"

"Yes," she agreed.

He looked up, giving himself time to think. The cemetery was almost deserted by now. Through the ornamental trees he could see the dark-clad entourage walking past the railings towards their cars. Dieter, Anna and Stefan would be waiting for them, expecting to go back to Sophie's for refreshments.

"I think we have to," he decided. "I don't want to be excluded from anything to do with the twins in future. I need to make my presence felt."

"Fine," she replied, more stiffly than she intended. "Let's go."

They rejoined Karl's father and the others by the car, their tardiness put down to a reluctance to leave the grave.

"All right, Karl?" Anna asked her brother solicitously, with a hand on his back.

"Yes. Are you?"

"So-so. I still can't quite believe what's happened."

She wiped another tear then got into the back of the car. Karl let Katherine sit in the middle then climbed in last. Stefan drove off, following the traffic back to *An der Waldecke*. The cul-de-sac was already full of cars so they had to park on the main road. As they walked down the road a neighbour came out of her house and did a double take when she saw Karl.

"Excuse me, I didn't mean to stare, but you must be Siegfried's father," the young woman said, trying to hide her embarrassment.

"Yes, I am," Karl replied.

The young woman looked flustered. "My sincere condolences to you all," she said. "We hadn't known him long, of course, but I know that everyone in the street who met him liked him and will really miss him. I can promise you, we'll all do what we can for Sophie and the twins."

"Thank you," Karl replied, surprised at the fulsomeness of her praise for his son. They were obviously not acquainted with the real Siegfried, only the projected image.

Having made her speech, the young woman beat a hasty retreat up the road. Karl and the others made their way up the drive, where Siegfried's Mercedes had been replaced by the Wendts'. The house was overflowing with people, although some had already spilled out into the garden, taking advantage of the fine weather. Karl saw Ilse doing her best to look composed again, handing out cups of coffee to a couple of businessmen. He had a strong urge to go over to her, but refrained for the moment as Katherine was stuck closely to him. He understood how Katherine felt, respected her feelings on the matter, but he simply could not ignore his common bond with Ilse at such a distressing time for her. Besides, there were other matters he needed to discuss with her. He turned to Katherine.

"Schatz, I want to talk to Ilse – about Siegfried," he added hastily. "You don't mind, do you?"

"No, of course not. Go ahead." She hoped she sounded sincere. Of course she minded! Reluctantly she attached herself to Anna and Stefan and went with them in search of a drink, leaving Karl to force his way through the throng to Ilse. When he reached her he put a hand on her shoulder, bent down and spoke softly in her ear.

"Ilse, can I have a quiet word alone with you?"

Ilse looked startled by the directness of his approach, before realising that as parents of the deceased they had every right to speak to each other. "Shall we go down to the bottom of the garden? It'll be less crowded there."

She led the way out through the kitchen and into the sunny garden. She carried on across the grass to the far fence by the woods, where only the squirrels would hear them.

"Well, what is it, Karl?"

He stood with his back to the house, obscuring Ilse from the view of any inquisitive onlookers. "This is very difficult for me, Ilse. No," he quickly added, as he saw her face show a spark of interest. "Don't think this is about us. It's not. It's about politics."

"Oh," she said, disappointment flooding her face.

"Look," he said gently. "Wolf and I are very concerned for our safety. We wondered whether you had ever heard anything at all to justify our concern. It's been over a year since ... Goslar's death. Admittedly I was in custody for half that time, but surely if there were going to be reprisals they would have happened by now?"

Ilse looked horrified. "Karl, you can't expect me to be told anything like that. Everyone knows what you mean to me. They'd never breathe a word of anything in front of me."

"Couldn't you find out? Surely Sophie would be in the know?"

Ilse's horror became terror. "Karl, please, you can't ask such things of me."

"Not even to save my life?" he pleaded.

"But it wouldn't, would it? If they had something planned and I scuppered it, they'd just plan something else with me on the list too."

"What about Wolf?" Karl persisted. "You might hear something about him."

"Hardly likely. I'm an acknowledged security risk because of you. I'm not a part of anything any more, just an honoured guest at social functions."

"But you could try to find out something? Just knowing if we're in danger or not would be a start."

She was weakening, he could see that, and for Wolf and Sabina's safety he had to try to enlist her help. He reached for her hand. "Please, Ilse. Find out for sure whether Wolf and I are in any danger."

She squeezed his hand hard, hating what she was about to say. "They don't forgive and they don't forget, Karl. But you know that already."

"So why haven't they done anything yet?" Ilse's hand froze in his. "Or have they already tried?"

Tears began to pour down Ilse's cheeks. She snatched her hand from his and grabbed an already sodden handkerchief from her bag. Dabbing at her cheeks and eyes she gulped down her tears and managed to speak.

"You suspect Siegfried, don't you, Karl? I've noticed how aloof you've been about his death. You think he and Gustav were involved in something, don't you? Only that stupid lover of Gustav's managed to get in the way."

"The thought had crossed my mind," Karl admitted.

"You were convinced!" she exploded. "I can see now why you haven't shed a tear over his death. You thought he was back in league with Gustav."

"Well he was, wasn't he?" Karl replied sharply.

"I ..." Ilse's anger deflated as suddenly as it had arisen. "I don't know," she continued more quietly. "I honestly don't know what he was doing with Gustav."

Karl decided to be brutal. "Well just remember, Ilse. Wolf and I must watch our backs every second of every day. If you hear anything that might warn us, our lives could be in your hands. Remember that!"

He turned abruptly away, but then halted in his tracks. He could not leave her like that. Turning back to her he softened his expression again. "I still love you, Ilse. I think Katherine knows it, and of course finds it very hard to accept that I can love two women. So I won't kiss you again, or show anything other than normal politeness to you. But you'll know my heart is part yours."

"And part Katherine's," she finished for him. "I know, Karl. It's very much the same with Paul and me. I love him too. My life's with him, yours is with Katherine. I wish you a long and happy one."

"That may be up to you and your influence."

"I have none, Karl."

"Well, even so, will you do your best for us?"

She bit her lip, nodded then burst into fresh tears; tears which, on the day of her son's funeral, could not be contained.

Despite his recent words Karl found himself hugging her, holding her until at last her shaking body calmed and she struggled once more to dry her eyes. He knew curious eyes, including Katherine's, would be upon them, but it could not be helped. This was a funeral, after all.

His fingers stroked the soft curve of her jaw, lingering longer than was wise. He had to leave her now but he delayed too long.

"Karl, I've lost everything," she whispered. "You, Siegfried, my homeland, my family. Don't leave me now. I couldn't bear it. We can make a life together here in Germany, just like we should have done from the start." Her voice picked up in volume as her enthusiasm mounted. "You would be nearer your family and –"

His fingers moved across to her lips to still them. "No, Ilse. You can't ask that of me."

She pushed his fingers away and grabbed the lapels of his jacket, drawing him closer in her desperation. "Why not, if it's what you want? What's to stop you, Schatz?"

"Everything," he said firmly. "Katherine, your Paul, my life in England. You forget, Ilse, I have a life beyond you." He peeled her fingers from his jacket, but gently, unwilling to cause her more hurt. Behind his back he sensed Katherine was near, watching every move, but he had to do this right for Ilse's sake. "You too have a life, Ilse," he reminded her. "Paul needs you, the twins will need you, Margit, Roslinde, Edeltraud and Heinrich all need you and love you. You still have them. Go to them."

"It's you I want, Karl."

"You can't have me." He realised he was still holding her hands. Bringing them both up to his lips he kissed her knuckles tenderly, lowered his hands and let go.

"We'll meet again some time, Ilse."

She blinked a tear away. "Of course, Schatz."

He smiled then turned his back on her. Katherine was watching him from the patio. She was not the only one. His father stood by her side. He walked briskly over to them, aware of his father's censorious eyes and Katherine's barely concealed anger. "She was upset," he explained. "I had to do something."

Katherine and Dieter looked at each other but neither said a word.

*

A few members of the acting fraternity had made it to Gustav's funeral. Christian did not recognise all of them, but several had come up to him to acknowledge his particular loss as Gustav's rumoured-now-confirmed lover.

Christian studied the wreaths laid against the wall outside the crematorium. The flowers were already wilting in the surprisingly hot sunshine. He moved along the line, reading the cards until he came to one comprising red roses, white carnations and a deep purple, almost black foliage plant. The card on it simply read: *In memory of a trusted and loyal colleague*. There was nothing to indicate who sent it. The acting fraternity would have blatantly put their names to it. Most likely it was from the Wendts or Gustav's secret friends from Berlin. Perhaps he could find out from the florist's concerned, under the pretext of wanting to thank them for the floral tribute. He was beginning to realise Gustav's secret life was far more complex than he had realised, and he needed to know more.

"Are you coming back to Berlin with us, Christian?" an elderly actress asked, her fleshy face almost concealed by a swathe of black tulle scarf.

"No, not yet, Edith. I've got this court appearance in Dortmund first."

"Oh yes, of course, darling. You and Gustav had a thing going, didn't you? Well, I hope they're sympathetic and we'll see you back soon. Detleff says he's got a role that's just right for you."

"Yes, I know. He mentioned it recently when I was there." Christian suddenly realised he could use the famous actress' help and gave her his most charming smile. "Edith, darling, could you do me the hugest favour before you go back to Berlin?"

"Of course, my sweet boy. What is it?"

"Use your charm to find out from a florist here who sent that wreath."

Edith Horn frowned. "Why?" She reached for the glasses suspended by a chain round her ample neck and peered through them at the card on the wreath. "Is it important?"

"It might be. But be discreet. I don't want them to know it's me asking."

"Of course, darling. I'll do my best."

Christian fished in his jacket for pen and paper and jotted down his telephone number as he explained: "I'm still in Gustav's apartment, although heaven knows how long for. I might be in jail soon, for all I know."

"I'll come and visit you," Edith glibly promised him, quickly turning away to find her escort for the day.

With nothing left to stay for, Christian returned to the empty apartment. He had already boxed up all Gustav's belongings and had arranged with the local Red Cross to collect them. One or two items he had kept as mementos, but for the most part there seemed very little to show for Gustav's entire life.

Later that evening as he was carrying the boxes one by one down the communal stairs to the entrance hall the telephone rang. He put down a box by the open front door and ran back in to answer the phone. Edith Horn's deep contralto voice greeted him.

"I'm sorry, darling, it was no-go at the florist's. Couldn't get a thing out of them. The woman there turned quite nasty when I tried to insist."

"Not to worry, Edith. Thanks for trying. Whoever it was obviously doesn't want to be traced."

"You will come back to us in Berlin, won't you, darling, once all your business in Dortmund is sorted out?"

"Yes, of course. There's nothing to keep me here now."

"Well, good luck then and bye-bye."

"Goodbye, Edith." As he put down the receiver he felt the hairs on the back of his neck rise but his sixth sense had warned him too late. A gloved hand clamped itself over his mouth, an arm went round his chest then he was dragged rapidly backwards through the open doorway to the stairs. Christian struggled frantically, guessing he was fighting for his life, his mind racing: Why? Why? Arched sharply backwards, his arms hung uselessly behind him and he could do nothing to prevent his momentum towards the stairwell. As the balcony rail pressed into his thigh he made a frantic lunge for the uprights, but a second assailant grabbed his ankles and raised them over the rail. Christian screamed in terror as he hurtled into space.

*

Sabina yawned widely and settled herself at the breakfast table. The pop concert had been loud and exuberant, and her ears still rang from the volume of music. She and Wolf had managed to enjoy themselves, putting aside all thoughts of Siegfried's funeral, but this morning her thoughts returned to the half-brother she would see no more. In the end she had grown to almost like him. She wondered how Sophie felt now, with rumours rife about his sexuality. Poor Sophie. Her married life had been blighted from the outset, and now her memories of Siegfried might be tainted. Still, she would be too busy with the twins to dwell on matters during the day. It would be alone at night it would hit her hardest.

Sabina poured herself a strong cup of coffee and reached for the newspaper Wolf had bought along with the bread rolls while out on his morning run. As she leafed through to the local news her eye was caught by several familiar names. She read the relevant article carefully.

Suspicious Death of Dead Actor's Lover

A fortnight after the death of Berlin actor, Gustav Halstrup, the body of his 28 year-old lover, Christian Bracht, was found last night in Halstrup's Dortmund flat. A police spokesman said Bracht had apparently fallen over the stairwell railing, but he refused to comment on speculation that Bracht may have committed suicide.

Bracht's homosexual relationship with Gustav Halstrup came to light at Halstrup's inquest. Bracht admitted he had been following the car in which Halstrup was a passenger when it came off the road near Arnsberg. Halstrup and the driver, Siegfried Driesler, were both killed in the incident. An inquest on Bracht's death will be opened next week.

A chill ran through Sabina as she read the article. Another death. She remembered the young man from Gustav's inquest. He had seemed a pleasant, sensitive person, obviously shattered by the loss of his friend. She showed the article to Wolf when he emerged from the shower.

Wolf's face went white. "My God! They got him too!"

TWENTY-TWO

There was the pile of post waiting for them on the kitchen table: two weeks' worth of it. Katherine tried to ignore its menacing presence as she put the kettle on and began checking the state of the fridge and larder. Some urgent shopping was necessary, but on the whole the boys had managed to keep the house in order during her absence. They were out with Karl now, giving him an update on the farm and livestock, and would probably be out for a good half-hour yet.

She looked back at the pile of post. She could no longer ignore it. With an anxious glance through the kitchen window, she gave in to temptation. Sorting through the pile she separated personal letters from farm business, but the letter she was hunting for was right at the bottom of the pile. She picked it up, examined the handwriting and turned it over. Apart from the German stamp and Soest postmark, there were no clues as to who had sent it. She sniffed it to see if she could detect Ilse's perfume, but it had lain too long amongst the other post and general kitchen smells.

The kettle began to boil and she looked at the steam pouring from its spout, tempting her to steam the envelope open. She moved slowly over to the range.

Could she do it? Should she do it? She stood irresolute, envelope in hand, trying to decide whether to spy on her own husband. She had never opened someone else's post before and she felt like a traitor to him for even considering it. There was always the chance she would not understand it, perhaps would not even be able to read the writing, then her treachery would be pointless. And so what if Ilse had written a love-letter? She would soon be back in Uruguay and out of the way. Nothing could come of it.

Or so she had thought before. But Ilse and Karl's love for each other seemed to lie dormant then burst out afresh whenever they met up again, even years later. They were old friends, happy in each other's company, and nothing would ever change that. The real test of Karl's loyalty would be whether he told her about the letter. But then she remembered what she had decided when Richard first told her about the letter. She should stick with that decision and leave it up to Karl to tell her.

She hesitated a moment longer; too long. It was no good. She had to open it. Her hand trembling with anxiety and self-loathing, she held the letter up to the steaming kettle. Deceit was alien to her nature and came hard, but if she needed to shield Karl from the predatory Ilse, then it was a necessary evil. With a final surge of determination she held the back of the envelope over the emerging steam and waited in a turmoil of impatience and guilt lest Karl or one of the boys should suddenly walk in.

The kitchen clock ticked, a log crackled loudly in the range right by her, making her jump, but still the envelope remained firmly stuck down. She stepped back from the range and picked gently at the seal. Her fingernail slipped underneath the flap, bending it back slightly. Progress at last. She held it back over the steam and repeated her picking and steaming several times until, finally, the flap lifted cleanly and she could open the envelope.

Now the moment had come, guilt nearly overwhelmed her, but she gritted her teeth and carefully extracted the folded sheet of paper. Rooted to the spot by the range, she unfolded the letter and, breath held, looked to the bottom of the page for the signature.

She gasped in surprise. Should she read it? She glanced furtively towards the back door. Two weeks ago she would never have done such a thing, but circumstances had radically changed. Now the compulsion to read the letter was overwhelming. Shocked by her actions and the letter's signature, she sat in the rocking chair, breathed deeply and began to read.

By the time she reached the end she was scarcely breathing. With her hand over her mouth in horror, she read it through again, more quickly this time now she had the gist of the German. Despicable as her actions were, she was glad she had read it. Her knowledge could make a big difference.

Casting a quick glance at the clock, she carefully folded the letter and replaced it in the envelope. She went to the tallboy and rummaged in the bottom drawer for a bottle of gum. As usual the rubber spreader had sealed itself over and she had to find a knife to insert into the slit. At any moment Karl might come in and she would be caught red-handed. In her hurry the gum smeared slightly when she pressed the flap closed, and she had to wipe away the excess. She peered at her handiwork. Would Karl notice the envelope had been tampered with?

Carefully she placed it back in the middle of Karl's pile of mail with the two other German letters. She recognised the Berlin postmark of Ernst Winter and the official prison stationery from Auer; both men were regular correspondents now. Yet more people for Karl to inform of the tragedy. Turning her back on the letters, she used the steaming kettle to make a pot of tea then sat down at her own pile prior to preparing dinner.

All through the meal Karl's post kept catching her eye, but it was not until much later in the evening that he picked up the stack of correspondence left on the table for him and disappeared into the little study to deal with it.

There were the usual bills and circulars, which he dealt with and filed appropriately. One envelope contained a cheque from one of his tree surgery customers, along with an invitation to attend a harvest supper. The date had already passed, however, so Karl would have to send his apologies for not replying. He decided to leave that until after he had opened the three letters with German stamps. When he saw one was postmarked Soest, it immediately took priority. As he turned it over, he noticed a small tear on the flap, which was slightly creased. He frowned and ran his finger over the seal. It was damp. When he squeezed the seal a tiny quantity of glue seeped out. Surely Katherine had not opened it? Perhaps she had simply opened it in error. But why the subterfuge in sealing it down again?

Reaching for the letter-knife he sliced through the top and pulled out the letter. He frowned and anger welled in his chest as he saw Siegfried's signature. No doubt the letter contained more lies and deception. If Siegfried had not died, Karl might have discarded it unread. But it was his last communication from his son, so he gave him the right to be heard.

2.9.68

My beloved Father,
Please read this alone and make sure nobody else sees this letter. If everything has gone to plan, then I will be dead when you read it. God knows, I've had enough practice arranging these accidents for others. It would be a poor show if I couldn't succeed with my own.

You are the only person who needs to know all this. It has to be so to ensure Sophie gets my life insurance and the reputation of Zopf Construction remains unsullied. I have done all this for the sake of Sophie and the twins. If there had been any other way, believe me, I would have avoided this, but I have thought long and hard ever since Gustav Halstrup first approached me back in April with his ultimatum, and this was my only solution. To prove I was still loyal to the Nazis and that my apparent reconciliation with you was only a sham, I was ordered to kill you. If I did not, then Sophie and the twins would be in grave danger and my previous killings would be made known to the police. I would have ended up in jail for life, with my wife and children dead.

I admit I was tempted to kill you as the easy way out. At Bina's wedding I could have done it, until Judy reminded me of my new values in life and, for the first time, made me feel remorse for the people I killed before. I now also feel deep remorse about the pain and grief I've caused you and your family over the years. And just when we were reconciled and I could look forward to many years of your love and wisdom, I have had to end it all, and even take Gustav with me. Yet another murder on my hands! I know that with Gustav's death, the threat on your life will not diminish. Although he was a prime mover for revenge on you and Wolf, others may take over his quest unless his and my deaths divert their attention. I sincerely hope so.

I am paying now for my violent and misguided past. If there is an after-life I doubt I'll make it into heaven as a murderer and suicide, so I won't even have the chance of spending eternity with you, but I wish it could have been so.

I thank you with all my heart for the love you showed me at Bina's wedding. How I envied Richard and Paul their lives with you. My final requests are that you destroy this letter immediately, remember me with love and forgiveness, and be my children's inspiration and guide as I can never be.

Your loving son
Siegfried.

"Oh God, no!" Karl whispered. A tear fell onto the page, blurring the signature. Hastily he wiped his eyes with the back of his hand. He sat looking blankly at the letter, seeing again Siegfried's face at the christening, smiling but troubled. His guilt had proved too much for him to handle and he had killed himself, unable to confide in anyone until it was too late. Karl was the only person who knew what Siegfried had done for the sake of his wife and children. His death had secured their safety, had put an end to his deeply troubled conscience and, by means of this letter, had brought him ever closer to his father.

Head bowed in grief, Karl sat silently contemplating the son he had not understood until now, the son who had passed on the burden he could no longer carry. Now Karl held the knowledge, and it lay heavily on his shoulders. Siegfried had asked him to look after his children. How on earth could he do that?

A slither and a clatter outside the study door made him look round. Katherine stood there, a mug of tea in her hand.

"I thought you might like this," she said very gently.

Their eyes met and he knew at once that she must have read the letter. His reaction surprised him. Springing to his feet, he held up the letter in front of her.

"You read this!" he accused her. "Why? It was clearly addressed to me."

Startled by his sudden outburst, Katherine stepped backwards, spilling hot tea on her hand. Hastily she put down the mug on a pile of box files. "It was a mistake!" she stammered. "I thought it was from someone else and when I discovered who it was from I –"

"But you still read it, didn't you!" he shouted at her, dimly aware his emotions were spiralling out of control. "Who *did* you think it was from? Ilse? Is that why you opened it, so you could spy on me?" His voice had begun to break with emotion, whether anger or grief he did not know or care. "That was *my* letter, addressed to *me*. You had no right to –" His voice choked and he stopped his tirade. He looked away from her, his breath ragged and his hands clenched, but it was disappointment in her he felt most keenly.

Katherine was desperate to reassure him. "Karl, I'm truly sorry. I admit, I did read it. But don't you think it's just as well that I know too, so I can share in your grief and you don't have to bear this alone?" She saw his stern expression soften slightly, his mouth twitched as he tried to control his conflicting emotions. She saw his determination not to lose control, either of his anger or his tears.

The latter she could handle, but not the former. "Schatz," she said gently, approaching him with hands outstretched in supplication. "Isn't it better that I know? I can help you deal with this."

He looked down at her, holding his distance and his emotions tightly in. Suddenly the tiny study felt claustrophobic. He had to escape this situation. Clutching the letter tightly in his fist he pushed past her and strode to the back door, donned his sheepskin jacket and boots and cleared off.

Katherine let him go. She had intruded too much upon his privacy and he resented it. She must give him time and space to calm down. Then he would come to her and accept her words of comfort. That was her hope. But Karl was in a strange, unpredictable mood.

Picking up the mug of tea, she followed his path to the kitchen. As she put the mug down on the table, Richard came in from outside.

"What's up with Dad? He just stormed past me."

"Oh, he just had some letters about ... everything which rather upset him. He'll be all right," she said, adding as nonchalantly as she could: "Which way did he go, did you see?"

"Up to the woods, I think." Satisfied by his mother's explanation his thoughts turned back to the matter in hand – his stomach. "Is there any of that fruit cake left?"

"But you've only just eaten."

"That was nearly an hour ago and I've been busy sawing. It's hard work."

Katherine sighed and gave in. "In the tin, but leave some for Paul, won't you?"

She stood at the back door as Richard rummaged in the larder for the cake tin. There was no sign of Karl. It was quite dark outside, with no moon to speak of. A few clouds drifted across the thin crescent of light in an otherwise black sky. Should she go after him? He wouldn't be long out, surely? Wrapping her cardigan more tightly around her, she stepped outside and round to the front of the house where the narrow track continued up from the lane to the brow of the hill. She could see nothing at all in the darkness. She tilted her head and listened hard. No sound broke the air except the creaking and rustling of branches in the wind.

Perhaps she ought to go looking for him. In his present mood he might resent further intrusion, but she was beginning to grow concerned. She shivered and her decision was made. Hurrying back to the kitchen she grabbed her own sheepskin jacket, donned a headscarf and Wellington boots and grabbed a torch from the tallboy before setting off up to the woods. Richard was all set to accompany her, but she waved him back. This was none of his business.

*

He had not been inside the cavern of old-man's-beard since the children were small, when he had been held captive by them in it during a game of cowboys and Indians. But before that it had been Siegfried's domain, his sanctuary. Karl sat down on the dry leaves and, in the almost total darkness, felt its womb-like quality. He drew his knees up to his chin and tried to imagine what the lonely little boy had felt here.

It was all my fault, Karl thought bitterly. I was stupid to bring him to England against his will. It blighted our relationship from the start and he could never forgive me.

He let his mind wander on, over the years, to the culmination of Siegfried's hatred for him. It was a shadowy memory, but there nevertheless, of Siegfried using his penknife to nick a vein in Karl's arm where Garisch's dog had bitten him. Karl could remember little of the events subsequent to him shooting Garisch, but Siegfried's ominous presence at his side, as he lay in a rapidly enlarging pool of blood, was clear in his mind. Siegfried had meant him to die.

Karl shivered, despite his sheepskin jacket, and clutched his knees closer to his chest. The crumpled letter crackled in his hand, bringing his thoughts back to his son's recent predicament. Sitting here, where Siegfried had sat as a boy and lately as a man, Karl opened his mind to let in his son's anguish and dilemma, his newly found love and, above all, his newly recognised guilt. Karl knew that guilt, had suffered himself from its vice-like, suffocating grip. There was no escape. It had followed him everywhere, especially into his dreams, until he could no longer cope with it. Help had come after his mental breakdown, but even so, the memory of that guilt lingered. He still could not escape what he had done, which was so bound up with his nationality. The British, the rest of the world quite rightly would not forget, and nor would he. Now Siegfried had found the worm that burrowed deep into the heart, eating away at the soul. He had no one to help him deal with it – had not been able to disclose his anguish to anyone, least of all the father he had been ordered to kill. He had found no answer, no hope of salvation except in the ultimate sacrifice.

The vice tightened in Karl's chest as guilt and grief boiled together inside him until he could contain them no longer. He drew a deep, shuddering breath then threw back his head and gave vent to an animal howl of despair.

*

From the track Katherine heard his cry. She started to hurry forwards, the torch beam lurching over the uneven ground in front of her. As she neared the summit of the wooded hill, she realised he must be in Siegfried's old lair. She slowed her pace then stopped, listening to the awful sound of his raw grief finally being voiced.

He had come up here for a reason. He needed to let this out, in private, unobserved. He wanted no sympathy or comforting, just to be alone with his son.

Reluctantly Katherine turned round and headed back down the track, his cries echoing in her ears long after she was out of earshot.

The light from the kitchen window was a welcoming beacon as she stepped back into the warmth and removed her jacket. Richard and Paul were both there, waiting anxiously. She put the torch back in its drawer and tried to act normally.

"Right! Who wants some hot chocolate?"

The boys both looked quizzically at her, wanting answers, but she had none for the moment. "He needs to be alone now," was all she could say.

She could see they were worried by their father's strange behaviour, but it was not so strange to her. In times of stress he retreated into himself, seeking solitude. She had always been on the alert for warning signs since his mental breakdown, and this was the closest she had seen him come to the brink, but she could do nothing. She was certain he would push her away if she intruded on his time now with Siegfried.

"Let's have a drink and give him some time. I expect he'll appear soon, and we won't pester him about what he's been doing, OK?"

Paul glanced towards the door as though he expected his father to walk in. Katherine followed his glance but there was nothing. Richard got up from his chair and reached for a saucepan from the rack.

"Paul, get the milk out," he said briskly. "Let's make Mum some hot chocolate."

Katherine looked gratefully at her elder son. He seemed to understand what this was all about, but Paul looked frightened. Despite having seen Karl so ill in hospital last year, to Paul he was a tower of strength. Paul knew some of his father's history but had not seen for himself the devastating effect it had had on Karl. She sat down wearily and felt Richard grip her shoulders reassuringly before busying himself at the range.

They sat in near silence drinking their chocolate, each listening out for the sound of footsteps outside, but none came. After half an hour of sitting, waiting, listening to the ticking clock, Paul said: "Do you know where he is, Mum? Do you think we ought to find him now?"

For the first time she felt irresolute. She really did not know what to do: whether to leave him be or go and find him. She looked yet again at the clock. He had been up there over an hour. Surely that was long enough? He would start to feel the cold soon. Her chair scraped the flagstones as she stood up.

"All right. I'll go and look for him."

"Shouldn't we come too?" Paul asked.

"No. I know where he is. He's probably just lost track of time. You get ready for bed. You two boys can do all the chores in the morning. We'll give Dad a chance to sleep in for once. I think he might need it."

As she spoke she was pulling the torch out once again and donning her warm clothing. Setting off back up the track, she knew she was right not to bring the boys.

All was quiet now as she neared the old-man's-beard. Not wanting to frighten him she called out softly: "Karl?" There was no reply. Perhaps he had not heard her. She called again, flashing the torch onto the thicket. Still there came no reply. She searched for the way in and poked the torch in to light up the interior. She saw Karl's huddled shape sitting there, quite still, his forehead on his knees, his right hand still clutching Siegfried's letter. Scared now, she stepped over the strands of creeper and squeezed inside, brushing against him as she did so.

Startled he looked up, and Katherine felt the relief flood through her that he was all right, that he had not closed off his mind as he had once before.

She laid a hand gently on his arm. "Are you all right, Schatz?"

He looked at her face, illuminated faintly by the torchlight, and was glad she had come. "No," he croaked.

Katherine saw a shudder run through him and she put down the torch to hug him to her breast. As his arms went round her, she heard the crackle of the letter. She let him hug her for a few minutes, not speaking, not intruding any more than she had to. But after what seemed an age she felt her knees cramping and had to move. She shifted to sit beside him and held his right hand, the one with the letter. She decided to take control now, as he seemed incapable of doing anything.

"We need to deal with the letter, don't we, Schatz?"

Her calm, reassuring voice soothed him and he sighed deeply. "Yes." He slipped his hand from hers and opened out the creased letter. Reaching for the torch he read it through once again. "So precious and yet I must destroy it. I don't want to, Schatz. I really don't."

"I know."

He sighed again as though breathing had become a necessity once more. "I think I'll bury it here, with him, where I can think of him, I mean."

"This is where he is for you, isn't it, Schatz? Here, in his old lair."

He made no move, however, so Katherine shifted to leave a clear space on the ground. "How about here?" she prompted.

Without looking up, Karl began to scrape out a hollow in the leaf mould. Then he folded the letter carefully into four and placed it in the depression. His fingers lingered a moment on it. "Goodbye, Siegfried," he silently mouthed before slowly heaping the leaf litter over his last memory of his son.

Katherine reached again for his hand. "You're cold. Come back down to the house and I'll make you some hot chocolate."

She began to edge backwards out of the thicket, torch in one hand, Karl's icy fingers in the other. Once they were both out in the open again she put her arm around him and guided him back down the track by the light of the torch. He said nothing, stumbling more than once as though he was not watching the ground. Katherine directed the torch beam more in front of his feet, increasingly concerned by his remoteness.

At last they reached the back door and she steered him inside. He seemed unaware of his surroundings as she pulled out a kitchen chair and made him sit down. Fortunately, Richard and Paul were upstairs, but she knew they would be listening out.

"Take off your coat, Schatz," she said loudly, letting them know of their father's return.

Slowly he did as he was told, but instead of hanging it up, he left it dumped over the back of a chair. In the light she could see his red-rimmed and puffy eyes. He had been doing a lot of crying, but they were dry now. She bustled about putting milk on to boil, hung up his coat, put mugs on the table and found the remains of the fruit cake in the larder. Richard had left a small piece.

"Here, drink this" she said, putting the mug of chocolate on the table in front of him and wrapping his cold, work-roughened hands round the outside.

He sat there, head bowed, holding the mug until the heat penetrated the china and became too hot to hold. Letting go the mug he looked up at her, his eyes full of abject misery.

"Oh, Karl," she whispered and stood by him, cradling his head against her breast. "I'm so sorry, but I am glad I know."

His hands squeezed her hips in agreement. "But no one else, Schatz. Absolutely no one else must ever know. Promise me."

Dared she ask? "Not even Robert?"

His head came abruptly off her breast and his hands pushed her hips away. He looked up harshly. "No one, I said. Not even him." He lowered his gaze. "And I know what you're thinking: I'm not handling this well. I know. I'm sorry."

"Don't be sorry. It's not your fault."

"But it *is* my fault!" he exploded, banging the table with his fist. "It's *all* my fault."

"That's ridiculous," she reasoned calmly. "How can it be? If it's anyone's, it's Ilse's for turning him against you and bringing him up a Nazi. You mustn't blame yourself."

He made no reply, but she could tell he did not believe her. At last he picked up the mug and began to drink, but when he had finished he was as grim-faced as ever.

*

The weapon sat like an old friend in his grasp. The bolt-action Gewehr 98 had seen him through military training, through the campaigns in Norway and Russia. He had killed many men with it. Its range was 800 metres, but Siegfried stood only a few paces away in a dead end, up against a wall with nowhere to run. Siegfried was looking directly at him, pleading with him, begging him not to shoot. Karl raised the rifle to his shoulder, looked down the barrel and aimed. Without hesitation, he squeezed the trigger.

Karl sat up in bed with a gasp as Siegfried's blood-soaked body fell to the ground. He knew he was awake but the ghastly images were still playing in his head. He was still watching Siegfried lying on the ground, the blood seeping into his shirt from the neat hole in his chest.

He was dimly aware of Katherine fumbling for the bedside lamp. As she switched it on, Karl looked at her to wipe the image of Siegfried from his mind.

"I shot him," he told her.

"Who? Who did you shoot?" she asked gently.

"Siegfried."

Katherine's heart sank. Karl had been right. He was not coping well with this. His sense of guilt was overwhelming him as he blamed himself for Siegfried's death. She saw the nightmare images gradually fading from his eyes as he came to his senses again.

"Karl?"

"What?"

"I really think you ought to talk to Robert about this. Before it goes too far and gets out of control."

"No. There's no need."

"Maybe not yet. But bear it in mind."

Angrily he turned his back on her and turned on his own bedside light. He knew he should not blame her for caring about him, but she did not need to question his sanity quite so obviously. He picked up a farming journal lying on the floor and began to flick through it.

Katherine left him to it. She had said her piece. What more could she do?

TWENTY-THREE

Karl woke to find the bed empty. Daylight filtered through the curtains.

"*Scheiße*! What time is it?" he muttered, grabbing his watch off the bedside table. Half past nine!

Throwing back the bedclothes he went to the window and drew the curtains. It was a fine day. What was Katherine doing, letting him sleep in like that?

Ten minutes later he was down in the deserted kitchen. He grabbed a glass of milk and a slice of bread and butter then realised he was not sure what day it was. Had they all gone off to church? He tried to work it out, but found his brain curiously befuddled. They had travelled back from Germany on Saturday, stayed overnight in London and taken the train home on Sunday. So today was Monday. Paul would be at school, Richard would be ... somewhere, he supposed, and Katherine would be doing what he should be doing – organising the apple pickers. He hurried to the back door, stepped into his overalls and boots and headed across the yard.

He strode towards Steps Meadow from where he could see the pickers already in the orchards, but he could also see Katherine and Molly puffing back up the hill.

"Morning, sleepyhead!" she called cheerily. "Don't worry. They're hard at work."

The sight of her smile did little to banish his residual anger. "Why didn't you wake me?" He was feeling like a spare part in a well-oiled machine. They had all got on with life while he was in prison and now they were doing it again. Katherine had slipped back into her old role in charge of the farm, leaving him to feel like a paid hand.

Katherine saw his hackles rise and guessed the reason. "What had you got planned for today then?" She leaned on the meadow gate and looked west towards the distant escarpment of Hay Bluff.

"Nothing yet," he admitted.

Katherine noticed that, unusually for him, he was leaning with his back to the gate and the meadow full of sheep, almost as though he had lost interest in them. His mind was clearly not on the farm after yesterday's shocking discovery. "How about going into town then and doing some shopping?" she suggested. "I need to get some food in and you could have a good browse in the hardware shop – stock up on nails and things. When Richard gets back from the sawmill," she added to explain his absence.

Karl nodded vaguely. She was right. He needed something to distract him today. A trip to Hereford would be good, even if he had been away from the farm for two weeks already. Richard and Paul had coped with everything, and there was nothing urgent that needed doing.

Katherine stood erect. "I don't suppose you've had a proper breakfast yet, have you?"

"No." He levered himself off the gate and set off back to the farmhouse. Molly shot past him, chasing a rat into the hedge. "Useless dog," he remarked. "All she does is try to round them up."

"No killer instinct," Katherine joked.

Karl froze, reminded of a remark made by Ernst Winter. He had referred to Karl as a 'natural killer', and his dream last night had proved it.

"Karl? Are you coming?"

He could feel the weight of the rifle in his hands. Four kilos of wood and metal that had become a part of him, an extension of his arms, doling out death as he chose. He had been awarded sniper's badges for shooting the enemy, was a natural killer indeed, who could kill without compunction. Except he had killed Siegfried last night and hated himself for it.

"Karl, are you all right?"

"Yes. Fine." He strode past her, shocked again by his dream and the crystal-clear brutality of it. Reaching the house, he hurled the back door open and collapsed onto a chair, muddy boots still on his feet. The image of Siegfried in his sights would not leave him; he could feel his finger curling round the trigger and the gentle squeeze sending the bullet on its terrible course.

Katherine's voice finally broke through to him. " ... Robert."

"What?"

"I'm going to phone Robert," she repeated quickly. "You're not well, Karl. I think you ought to speak to him."

"No! I'm fine. Just hungry."

"Karl, you were miles away just then. You didn't seem to hear me at all. Surely, after everything that's happened, a quick word with him would be helpful?"

"No. There's really no need. It's just shock from yesterday. I don't want Robert to know about that. He's not to know. We agreed!"

"I know," she pleaded, "but surely just Robert could be told?"

"First you, then Robert. How many other people will end up knowing? Eventually someone will let slip, and then what?" he demanded angrily. "At best Sophie has to repay the life insurance, at worst ..." He raised his eyes to her in despair. "At worst, revenge for Gustav's death."

Katherine knelt down in front of him and pulled off his boots, then rested her hands on his knees in supplication. "Please speak to Robert. Don't tell if you don't want to, just let him know you're having trouble coping with Siegfried's death."

"What good is that," he growled, "if he doesn't know the facts?"

"Then tell him!"

"No!" Abruptly Karl stood up, brushing Katherine aside, irritated by her meddling.

As he made for the door to the hall Katherine tried to stop him from leaving in such a mood. "Let's have some breakfast. You said you were hungry." As he paused, she added, "Richard will be back soon, hungry too, no doubt. You go and get changed for town, Schatz, while I put the bacon on."

He snorted, startling her. "I don't think bacon would suit you," he said in deadly seriousness as he headed for the hall.

She stared after him in disbelief. Was that a joke? If so, it was most unexpected. Confused by his behaviour she frowned then turned her attention to the frying pan.

*

He was surprised at how much he had bought in Price's hardware shop. Once he started browsing he began picking up all manner of useful items: replacement blades for his Stanley knife, Evostick glue, a bolt for the gate into the tree nursery, a selection of grades of sandpaper and a large bag of fencing staples. Karl loaded his purchases into the Land Rover, glad that Mr Price, unaware of recent events, had chatted normally to him.

He had arranged to meet Katherine outside the Butter Market and found he was early. As he stood waiting, watching the shoppers bustling by, he sensed someone watching him. He turned and came face to face with Andrew Kellett. He swore under his breath as his old adversary engaged him in conversation.

"Sorry to hear about your sad news, old boy," Andrew said breezily, his tone of voice belying his words. "Now you know how it feels to lose a son."

It was a blow below the belt. "Back off, Kellett. I don't need your sympathy."

"I'm only being friendly, old thing. Don't knock a man when he's down and all that. Mind you, there's many round here would say good riddance, especially after that little episode in the livestock market. You lost a few friends that day, I think."

"Kellett."

"What?"

"Shut up!"

"Before you hit me, you mean? That would be typical of your lot, wouldn't it, resorting to violence." He glanced over Karl's shoulder. "Ah, here comes your charming wife to the rescue, as usual. At least she knows how to be friendly." He threw in his parting shot. "Watch how you go, old boy. Don't take your friends for granted. You might be disappointed."

He broke into a smile as Katherine arrived, slightly out of breath after hurrying when she saw who was with Karl.

"How do, Katherine?" Andrew greeted her cheerfully, with a tip of his trilby. "I was just commiserating with Karl here over the loss of his son. Tragic. Well, must get on. Nice to meet you." He tipped his hat to her again and moved on, quickly disappearing amongst the shoppers.

"Was he commiserating?" Katherine asked doubtfully.

"No. He was ..." Karl, still fuming, could not think of the word. "It doesn't matter." He noticed her full shopping bags and took them off her before they headed back to the car park. "Did you get everything you wanted?"

"Yes, I think so. Oh! I saw Mrs Walker in the chemist's and she said to give you her condolences. I don't know how she knew, but word has certainly got round. Gertie probably."

"Or Vera."

Katherine smiled. "Ah yes. Could be her." Her mind rapidly connected Vera to her husband Werner and thence on to Ernst Winter. "I noticed a letter from Ernst on your pile. How is he?"

"I didn't get around to opening it, or Auer's. I'll do that this evening. I'll have to write back and tell them what's happened, if they haven't heard it all on the news already."

"I doubt it. It wasn't an important story. For the national news, I mean."

"It's the name, Schatz. We're infamous in Germany now."

She noticed how depressed he sounded. When they reached the car park and had put the shopping in the Land Rover she suggested to him: "Let's go and have lunch somewhere nice. I feel in that sort of mood."

"Feeling reckless with our money, are you?" he smiled.

That's better, Katherine thought.

*

Andrew Kellett stepped out from behind a parked car, his hat shielding his face, but Karl knew who it was. The street was packed with shoppers, mostly women laden with bags and small children. Karl stood in a shop doorway, assessing the range – a mere fifty metres. An easy target. He could not miss. Raising his rifle to his shoulder he followed Kellett's progress towards him, dodging pedestrians and traffic. An opening presented itself between a delivery van and a bus. Now, Karl thought, and squeezed the trigger.

He woke up.

This time it had been no nightmare. He had not woken Katherine. He even felt satisfied with the dream, which worried him. Did he really want to kill Kellett? Of course he did, after what the brute had done to Katherine.

Perhaps I ought to go and shoot some rabbits tomorrow, he thought as he rolled over and prepared himself for sleep again.

Then I can satisfy my killing urge on those vermin instead of Kellett.

He snuggled closer to Katherine's warm body and put his arm over her breast, trying to think of more pleasant things to fall asleep to.

On waking early he told Katherine of his intentions, then went to stick his head round Richard's door.

"Do you want to shoot some rabbits?"

Instantly awake, Richard replied: "OK. I'll be ready in a tick."

From his room Paul called: "Can I come?"

"No. You've got school. Perhaps at the weekend."

They set off as soon as it was light, shotguns crooked over arms. The air was raw with huge clouds piled up in the west, although, with luck, the rain might pass them by.

Settling behind the hedge adjacent to the tree nursery, they loaded their shotguns and waited patiently until half a dozen rabbits were contentedly grazing nearby. Karl tensed, knew Richard was ready too, lined up on the rabbit furthest to the right then whispered: "Fire!"

He did not see the rabbit fall. Instead he saw Siegfried clutch at his chest as blood poured through his fingers. He saw him stagger back, stumble and fall to the ground. There was no doubting he was dead.

Richard wondered why his father had not fired his second barrel. It was too late now. The rabbits had bolted off into their hedgerow burrows in a flash of white tails. He lowered his shotgun and turned to his father who stood stock-still, shotgun still raised to his shoulder, his face frozen in horror.

"Dad? What's up?"

Karl blinked. Slowly he lowered the gun and automatically broke it open, pocketing the unused cartridge.

"What happened? Why didn't you shoot again?" Richard repeated anxiously. His father's face had turned deathly pale in the early morning gloom.

Karl felt himself begin to shake, his legs trembling beneath him. He couldn't move. He took a few deep breaths to try to steady himself. Suddenly he felt sick with shock.

"Are you all right, Dad?"

Karl felt terribly confused. He could not work out what was happening, but knew he must try to behave normally and ignore what he had seen. "Not really," he replied. "Must be something I ate. Let's get back to the house."

As they walked across the meadow up to the farmhouse, Richard clutching the three dead rabbits by the ears, Karl struggled to forget what he had seen and put his mind to other things.

"Will you take the tractor down to the orchards later on and see to the apple crates? Then we can tackle the fence along the road, now that I've got the staples, or else those sheep will be out again."

"Are you sure you feel up to it, Dad? You don't look very well."

Karl shrugged. "We'll see."

Leaving Richard to hang up the rabbits in the outhouse, Karl went to return the shotguns to the study. Katherine was busy at the range stirring porridge as he passed through the kitchen.

"Any luck?" she asked.

"Three for the pot," he replied.

Richard must have missed his second shot, she thought. "Not so lucky today?" she asked him when he came in.

"Eh? Oh! No. Dad was ill suddenly and didn't manage his second shot."

"Ill?"

"Yes. Didn't he say? He went awfully pale."

Katherine rested the spoon against the rim of the porridge pan and went out to the study. Karl was sitting at the desk, head in his hands. She stood behind him and gently rubbed his shoulders.

"Richard said you were ill. Are you feeling any better?"

His shoulders lifted under her hands in a shrug.

"Do you want any breakfast?"

He shook his head slowly.

"Perhaps you'd be better off back in bed, Schatz. I'll bring you up a cup of tea."

"No. I'll go for a walk. Fresh air's what I need."

He stood up, his face still pale under its tan, and went out leaving a worried Katherine alone in the study.

*

Richard tackled the jobs his father had set and, as he hammered in fence staples, he found himself thinking ahead to the time when the farm would be his. He had taken to heart his father's advice to learn more about farming and to continue diversifying so both Paul and he could have an income, as well as provide some extra support for Mum and Dad in retirement. Not that that would be for many years yet, he hoped fervently, but Dad had been through an awful lot in his life. He had nearly died last year, and was ill today. Perhaps the SS experiments on him at Dachau might still be affecting his health? Mum had certainly always feared possible lasting effects. If only Dad could talk about it more! But he never did. It was his private nightmare of utter humiliation, torture, shame and guilt. No wonder Dad still had a few crazy moments.

His melancholy mood continued throughout the morning, but finally lifted as thoughts of food made him head back up to the house for lunch. His mother was anxiously watching out for him from the back door.

"I'm not late, am I?"

"No, no. It's just that I haven't seen Dad since before breakfast. He said he was going for a walk, but I didn't think he'd be gone this long."

"Do you want me to go and look for him?"

A strange expression crossed his mother's face, like she had a premonition of disaster. "We'll both go. Lunch can wait. I fancy a bit of fresh air myself. Wait while I get my coat on."

As Richard stood by the back door, he noticed Molly was not about. He gave a long, loud whistle of summons. A moment later he heard a distant bark from up in the woods. By the time his mother emerged, buttoning her coat, Molly had come hurtling round the corner of the house.

"Come on, Molly! Let's find Dad!" he urged the excited dog.

They set off at a gentle pace up the grassy track, expecting to meet Karl on his way down, having heard Richard's whistle, but the track stretched up the hill before them with no sign of life save Molly's trotting figure some yards ahead.

"I think I know where he is," Katherine muttered.

In a few moments Molly confirmed her guess by flopping down by the old-man's-beard thicket.

"He's in there?" Richard asked incredulously. "Why?"

"Siegfried's old haunt," she replied, increasing her pace up the hill. She called out as they approached the overgrown bird's nest of creeper. "Karl? Are you in there?"

There was no reply. Richard began to step forward but Katherine held him back.

"Let me," she said and pulled aside the creeper over the entrance to the hideaway. She peered in. Just like the day before, Karl sat there, head on knees. He had not looked up or seemed to notice her intrusion. Her heart pounding with fear, she put a hand on his arm. He did not stir.

"Karl, can you hear me?" she murmured as her heart filled with dread lest this was a repeat of his previous breakdown. He still did not move so she tried again. "Schatz!" It was the word that had broken through his isolation before.

Slowly he raised his head and looked at her with sorrowful eyes. "It's all right," he said with a leaden voice. "I can hear you."

She felt like saying, 'So why didn't you answer?' but prudently held her tongue. Instead she said: "You can't sit here all day. Come back now and have something to eat."

"I'm not hungry."

"Well come back anyway. There's no point sitting here –"

"You don't understand!" he snapped angrily. "I shot Siegfried! How can I come back?"

His words came like a slap in the face to Katherine. "What?" she stammered. "What are saying?" He was obviously confused. "No. That was only a dream. It was Goslar you really shot."

"I shot Siegfried," he repeated bleakly. "This morning."

Katherine kneeled in the soft leaf litter and tilted his chin so he would look at her. "Listen to me, Schatz," she said gently but firmly. "Siegfried died in a car crash." She remembered Richard outside. He would hear everything. "It was a rabbit you shot this morning," she explained, as suddenly all became clear to her.

"I shot Siegfried," he repeated dully.

Katherine sat back on her heels in despair, wondering what to do. First she must get him out of the thicket. She held both his hands in hers and gently pulled him towards her. "Come here, Karl. Let's go home. Richard's out there. He wants his lunch. Let's not keep him waiting, shall we?" As she spoke she got to her feet, applying gentle pressure to his hands to encourage him upwards. To her immense relief he obliged, crouching in the confined space. She stepped sideways through the gap in the creepers, holding onto him with one hand, and drew him outside. Richard stood there in horrified silence, having heard everything.

"Richard," Katherine addressed him briskly, "take Dad's arm and let's get him home."

Between them they guided Karl slowly down the track, his progress reluctant and sloth-slow. He said nothing the whole way back to the house. Once inside they sat him on a kitchen chair and Katherine tested communications.

"Are you going to take your jacket and boots off, Karl?" she suggested.

He looked at her, then slowly did as he was told. Katherine breathed a sigh of relief and removed her own outdoor clothing.

"You stay there, Richard. I'm going to phone Donald."

"OK, Mum."

Poor Richard sounded terrified, Katherine thought as she headed for the hall table where the telephone stood. At least she had seen Karl worse than this, and seen him come through it, but it was frightening nevertheless. Her fingers shook as she dialled the Murdochs' number. To her relief, Donald answered.

"Donald, it's Katherine here. I've got a problem," she hastily said to forestall any pleasantries.

"Oh? What's that, lass?" he replied, his professional manner instantly engaged.

"It's Karl. He's not so good. I think we might need Robert's help," she explained, knowing Donald would understand. "I'd have called Dr Granger, but you know Karl's history better ... and everything."

"I'll be straight up," Donald told her. "Don't you worry, lass. He'll be fine."

The grandfather clock at her side chimed the half-hour and it had chimed the hour before Donald, accompanied by Gertie, arrived at the farm. Katherine took their coats then led her godparents through to the kitchen where Karl sat in front of his untouched soup.

"Karl, it's Donald and Gertie come to see us," Katherine said breezily, watching for his reaction.

He looked up, looked at the visitors then looked down again without a word.

"Shall we leave you, Donald?" Katherine asked.

"No, no. All stay. We just need a chat," Donald said, sitting down at the table opposite Karl. Katherine pulled up the rocking chair for Gertie.

Donald began his assessment, while Richard stood by the range anxiously looking on.

"So, Karl. How are things?"

Karl turned to face him, rested his hands on the table and studied them for a while before meeting Donald's gaze.

"I know why you're here, Donald," he said flatly. "I know Katherine's worried about me. I'm worried too."

"Well, that's a good sign – that you're worried," Donald comforted him. "What is it that's troubling you?"

"I shot Siegfried."

It came again, that totally absurd statement. Katherine and Richard were half prepared for it, but Gertie gasped audibly. Donald, however, kept his face impassive, his voice measured.

"Why did you do that?"

"I don't know. I just shot him."

"When?"

"This morning."

"So where is he?"

"I buried him in the old-man's-beard thicket."

It was starting to make sense to Katherine, but she could not tell Donald what Karl had really buried there. Donald looked round at her, his face now grim.

"I think you're right, lass. Robert needs to deal with this. Can I use your telephone to see if he can come down?"

"Go ahead. I'll come out with you in case he wants to ask me anything."

In the hall, Katherine waited anxiously as Donald dialled the Edinburgh hospital where Robert worked as a psychiatrist. It took a few minutes before he came to the phone, but then Donald rapidly explained the situation.

"Is there any chance of you coming down to see him?"

"Not a hope, Dad. I've got a court appearance the day after tomorrow, then Alice is going in for a minor op on Thursday and I don't want to leave her on her own with the boys. I might manage it next week, if I can juggle a few –"

"Don't worry, Robbie. I've got another idea. How about if Gertie and I come up with Karl to see you? Then we'll be around to help Alice and see the boys, and you won't have to take any time off work."

There was a significant pause. "Is Karl well enough, Dad? It might be a tricky journey for you and Mum."

"We'll cope, I'm sure, as long as Karl agrees to come, which I think he will. He knows he has a problem," Donald pressed on, seeing Katherine's nod of agreement. "Don't trouble Alice with beds for your mother and me. Karl can have your spare room and we'll stay in that hotel down the road. We want to look into something while we're up there."

"Fine, if you bear in mind Alice won't be around, so you might need to ... keep Karl company while I'm at work. When will you be up?"

"I'll give you another ring when we know. Some time tomorrow, I expect."

"Right. Look, I'll have to go now. Let me know at once if there's any change in his condition."

"Of course. Cheerio for now." Donald put down the receiver and turned to Katherine. "Right! That's settled. Let's go and see what Karl has to say about it."

Please don't let him make a fuss, Katherine prayed as they returned to the kitchen. Gertie had made a pot of tea in their absence, and Katherine was pleased to see Karl was drinking his. She went over to him and kissed him on the forehead.

"How do you fancy a trip up to Edinburgh on the train with Donald and Gertie?"

"We'd be glad of your company, Karl." Donald butted in. "We're not as young as we were and we've been looking for the chance to go up there soon." He looked at Gertie, who nodded, before continuing: "The truth is, we've been thinking about selling up here and going back to our roots; finding a wee bungalow near Robert so he can keep an eye on us, and we can see more of him and Alice and the boys."

"Yes," Gertie broke in. "We decided that if we don't up and move now, it will be too late."

Karl suddenly spoke to nobody in particular, heedless of the Murdochs' news. "I'll go and see Robert, if you think it best."

His uncharacteristic rudeness was understandable. He was the reason the Murdochs were here, after all.

Katherine squeezed his shoulders. "I think you could do with a good heart-to-heart with him."

Suddenly the room felt oppressively overcrowded. Karl stood up from under her hands and went outside without another word. Katherine made to follow him but Donald stopped her.

"Let him go, lass. He'll be all right, I reckon. He's said he'll go and I believe him. He may just be embarrassed that he's having some problems. Leave him for a bit."

Katherine looked uncertainly towards the back door, then accepted Donald's advice. "You're right. And that was very clever of you, the way you offered to go with Karl. I don't think he was fooled, but it helped him agree to go, I'm sure."

"Well, it's true," Gertie said. "We had been planning on moving, and this little trip has come at an opportune moment."

Katherine sat down on Karl's vacated chair and sighed. "The village won't be the same without you both. Who's going to run the Women's Institute and organise jumble sales? Who am I going to call on for a chat when I'm down shopping?" She suddenly realised how much she would miss this dear old couple who had so readily taken the place of her own, long-dead parents.

"You'll just have to inherit my various hats," Gertie suggested chirpily. "That way you'll find you've more than enough people to call in on."

Katherine had to laugh. "Perhaps you're right. Now the boys are virtually grown up, it's time I spread my wings a bit and did more outside the farm."

"There you see?" Gertie smiled. "I knew some good would come of it." She looked towards her husband, who was finishing his tea. "Well, Donald. Time to go, I think. We've got a lot to organise if we're to be away tomorrow."

"I'll run you to the station, of course," Katherine said as she led them out to the front door. "Just let me know what time the train is."

"Will do, lass," Donald said, kissing her lightly on the cheek. "Keep your chin up. He'll be all right. It's not as bad as last time."

"Not yet," Katherine said quietly.

He gave her a comforting squeeze. "Robert will sort him out, you'll see."

Katherine nodded, then hung her head to hide the tear that had slipped out.

As she waved them off, Richard moved quietly to her side. "Don't cry, Mum. I'm here for you."

She hugged him thankfully to her. The farm would be safe in his capable hands. Whatever happened.

*

The rolling countryside of the Midlands sped past the train window: hedgerows, sheep, brick houses. All so very English. Later, the greyer tones of Scottish stone would dominate the landscape and the buildings. In all the years Karl had lived as a free man in Britain he had never travelled beyond the Midlands, London and Harwich. Holidays, when taken, were always to Germany. He should never have left the place.

Why had he suddenly thought that? He frowned, then caught sight of Donald's reflection in the window, observing him. He looked across at Donald. They had hardly spoken all morning. Gertie was deep into her book, Sir Walter Scott's *Ivanhoe*, no doubt getting herself into the Scottish frame of mind, but Donald was playing caretaker, or guard, keeping watch over Karl's mood. They were alone in the compartment, so could speak freely if they wished.

Karl opened the conversation. "Back to your roots, you said, Donald,"

So he had been listening, Donald noted with interest. He waited expectantly for Karl to say more, but that seemed to be it. He smiled. "Aye. There comes a time in your life when you think about where you want your headstone. Sounds morbid, I know, but Gertie and I both want to lie in Scottish soil."

"And be near your descendants so they can tend your grave," Karl suggested.

"Well, there's that of course, but that was never in our minds," Donald laughed. "No, we want to have the benefit of our descendants while we're still alive. Douglas and Stewart are growing up and we haven't seen all that much of them. It would be nice to get to know them better now they are a wee bit less noisy."

Karl had to smile. Douglas and Stewart were certainly boisterous, lively lads. His own children had always had great fun playing with them on their visits to Herefordshire. Cowboys and Indians was a particular favourite. His smile vanished as he remembered their use of the old-man's-beard as a wigwam. He swallowed hard.

Donald spotted the sudden mood change. "All right, Karl?"

"I'm going to stretch my legs," he declared, standing up.

Sliding open the compartment door, he stepped out into the corridor. Turning left he moved a few paces on until he was out of the Murdochs' sight. As he stopped by a window, the carriage's interconnecting door opened with a crash and a loud clattering of train wheels. A bulky man lurched through the doorway and Karl's hackles rose. Kellett! Karl's fists balled, but he hastily stifled his instinct to punch his enemy as he realised it was not Kellett staggering past him with a sandwich from the buffet car, but some innocent man who had been within a whisker of receiving a bloody nose. Karl gripped the window strap, shocked at what he had nearly done.

I can't go on like this, he thought bitterly. I've got to do something to stop myself killing people!

He stood there a long time, vaguely aware of passengers passing by from time to time. He even sensed Donald step out of their compartment to see where he had got to, but he did not look round and Donald returned without comment. As the miles raced by outside, his own mind raced through his turbulent history; sifting, sorting, analysing, trying to find an answer to what he was seeking. Siegfried's death had knocked the ground from under his feet. He felt lost again, as he had when Katherine had rejected him so many years ago now. What had he wanted then? To return to Germany. He had felt the same just this morning when that thought had flashed through his mind. Why had he not gone back home after the war? He should have done, then none of this would have happened. Siegfried would have been more willing to live with him in Germany. They would have bonded as father and son eventually. Everything would have been all right.

*

Donald was shuffling with tiredness and Gertie's joints were stiff from the long journey as Alice and Karl helped them out of the car and into the smoke-blackened town-house Robert and Alice had bought as newly-weds sixteen years previously. Over the intervening years Alice had impressed her own vibrant personality on the interior décor, with bold print curtains and brightly coloured carpets. To her in-laws' eyes it looked garish and verging on the psychedelic, but Karl noticed little as he carried his bag in from the car.

"Douglas!" Alice called loudly. "Stewart! We're home."

The two lads appeared from the lounge where the television blared out a children's programme. Fourteen-year-old Douglas approached sedately but his younger brother, Stewart, rushed out to greet his grandparents. Douglas was growing into a miniature version of Alice in looks, with his mouse-brown, wavy hair, but Stewart had his father's dark hair, inherited in turn from Gertie. Both were slightly built and shorter than Karl's strapping family at that age.

Alice took immediate charge of her brood. "Turn that television off, Douggie, and take Uncle Karl's bag up to the spare room for him. Stewart, stop pulling Gramps over and help Nan with her coat while I get the kettle on." She grinned at Karl. "They've been like five-year-olds since they heard you were coming up. They seem to think you're going to want to play football with them all day."

Karl smiled, glad Alice was treating him perfectly normally. He followed the family into the living room and sank into a rather grubby, lilac-coloured armchair that clashed spectacularly with the orange carpet. He was the odd-one-out here, not a member of the family, but he felt strangely at ease for once, away from all the recent events at home. The room was warm, the armchair enveloped him and he quickly found his eyelids drooping. Donald and Gertie were interrogating the boys, so he gave up the struggle to stay awake.

He woke to find the boys gone and Robert sitting quietly chatting to his parents, glass of whisky in hand.

"Oh! I'm sorry," he yawned, blinking the sleep from his eyes.

"Don't worry, Karl," Robert grinned, stepping over from the sofa to greet his old friend. "It's great to see you at last."

Karl stood up and they shook hands then embraced each other. Each had worked a miracle in the past for the other and they were like brothers now.

"Let me get you a wee dram," Robert said. "You're behind us."

Karl noticed both Donald and Gertie had tumblers by them, while Alice's stood ready for her when she returned from the kitchen. He assumed the boys were busy with homework, as all seemed quiet.

"You're looking well," Karl said as Robert handed him his drink.

"Overworked and underpaid, but otherwise not too bad, considering." The last word referred to Robert's period of captivity by the Japanese during the war. It had been their shared status as prisoners of war that had helped forge the bonds of friendship between them initially. "And you, Karl," Robert commented. "You're not looking so bad yourself."

"Considering," Karl said pointedly.

"Aye, there's that."

Gertie waved her glass at Karl. "You are looking better, dear. That sleep must have done you some good."

Karl nodded but made no comment as Alice appeared, oven-glove in hand to snatch a sip from her glass.

"Cheers! I'll be back in a moment. Just putting the tatties on."

Gertie struggled to her feet. "I'll come and help you, dear."

Alice was about to refuse her help, then realised her mother-in-law probably wanted to hear all about her impending operation. Glass in hand, she escorted Gertie out to the kitchen, leaving the men to themselves.

Nothing serious was discussed, however, until after dinner when Robert had driven his parents to their hotel for the night and

Alice had retired to the bathroom for a self-indulgent soak out of the way.

With the coal fire banked up and the whisky bottle at the ready, Robert was all set to quiz Karl about his problems, but Karl needed no prompting.

"Do you remember when Siegfried was eight and he ran away?" he began the moment Robert sat down. "You came with me to Gloucester to fetch him back."

"I remember," Robert said slowly. "Go on."

"On the way back home I told him he could go back to Germany. I felt that would solve everything – if he went back to Germany. Well, now I feel the same about myself. I think I need to go home."

"Any reason in particular?"

Karl took a sip of whisky and let it slide down his throat as he contemplated his answer. "Many reasons – all selfish. I haven't considered Katherine's feelings at all in this."

"That's not the point. I want to hear what *you* need at the moment."

Karl raised his eyes to the ceiling and gave a deep sigh, then looked directly at Robert. "I need to be near my grandchildren to keep an eye on them. I need to be near Siegfried's grave to put flowers on it. I need to be away from Andrew Kellett so I don't kill him, and ..."

Robert waited patiently, knowing this last item was perhaps the least important but the hardest to acknowledge.

Karl bit his lip. "And that's it."

"No it isn't, Karl. You were going to say something else just then. If I'm to help you I need to know everything, even what you consider private. I know it's difficult me being your friend as well as psychiatrist, but I promise you that it's professional advice I have to give, not just that of a mate. Trust me like you did when we first met."

"I didn't know you then. Now I do and I'm too ashamed to tell you."

"But you want to. You nearly told me just then. You just need me to press you a bit harder and that's what I'm doing. There's something you want to discuss and you can only discuss it with me. So come on, Karl," Robert urged gently. "Out with it."

Karl knew he was right. He *did* need to talk over this with someone, more to get it off his chest than anything else. If he had still been a practising Roman Catholic he could have taken it to the confessional, but Robert was his confessor now. He drained his glass, needing the courage the whisky would give him to open up, then put the glass down on the table beside him. He could sense Robert expectantly waiting, but wanted to prolong the moment before he might lose Robert's friendship.

"Right," he said at last. "Robert my friend, close your ears and Robert my counsellor, open them." Karl paused again, more to steel his nerves than for dramatic effect. "Another reason I want to live in Germany is that I have more chance of seeing Ilse again there."

Robert's heart leapt. This was worse than he had thought, but he gave no outward sign of shock. He sat silently, waiting for Karl to explain, noting his friend's inability to look him in the eye, with all the signs of a guilty conscience. Damn, Robert thought. Poor Katherine.

"I've seen quite a lot of her recently, what with one thing and another. Too much, as you may have guessed." Here Karl finally looked up at Robert and saw his nod. "I slept with her – just the once – or rather she slept with me. She made all the advances, but I know that is no excuse. Katherine knows about it, unfortunately. I know she has found it very difficult to ... forgive me." He looked down again, hiding his guilty eyes from his friend, but continued his confession. "I could have let Ilse out of my life again, but when Siegfried died everything was too much. She needed me and I had to comfort her. I realised I feel too much for her still to never see her again. But I love Katherine too and I don't want to hurt her again. The trouble is, I want them both. I want to be able to see Ilse, even if nothing else ever happens again. Which it won't."

"How can you be sure?"

Karl raised his head and looked Robert honestly in the eye. "I hurt Katherine badly. I won't do that again."

"You would be putting temptation in your path, seeing Ilse," Robert told him sharply. "She wants you back in her bed. Who's to say you wouldn't lose control again? She can be a very forceful woman, I imagine," he added, but with a smile to show Karl he understood and did not condemn him outright.

Karl returned the smile. "Yes, she can be, especially when she's upset. I feel I have to comfort her." His smile abruptly faded. "I've messed up so much, Robert. I wish I could turn back the clock."

"How far? To your time in Yugoslavia? If you'd obeyed Goslar's order to torture that woman again you might have finished the war still a hero in Ilse's eyes. She would have waited for you. You would have got married, settled down in Germany, had more children. Is that what you really wanted all along? To be a happy torturer?"

Karl made no reply, his eyes fixed on the orange swirls in the carpet.

Robert, thinking he had struck gold, continued his diatribe. "Could you have lived happily with that on your conscience? I think not, for the simple reason that you weren't able to obey his order a second time. Your life would have turned sour. You couldn't have lived with yourself."

Karl blanched. Had Katherine told him about Siegfried, despite her promises? No. Robert simply had superb intuition. The parallel with Siegfried was just that. Siegfried had finally turned out for the good, like his father.

"Think what you have got from marrying Katherine," Robert persevered. "A whole new way of life, love and respect from your former enemies –"

"No!" Karl burst out angrily. "The British treat me and my race like dirt. They'll never forgive us for what we did, and until I turn my back on them and go and live with my own kind again I won't be happy!"

"Ah!" Robert said, stretching out his legs in satisfaction. "Now we're at the real crux of the matter! I would have said you were talking nonsense if I didn't know this is Andrew Kellett we're talking about really, isn't it? You said you were afraid of killing him."

"I would never plan to kill him," Karl hastened to explain. "Not like in my dreams when I'm hunting him down." He ran his fingers through his hair, deciding just how much to tell Robert. It had to be everything. "It's serious, Robert. He raped Katherine – twice – and there's nothing I can do about it! He can make trouble for me or the boys and he knows that he can get away with it every time. Short of killing him, I feel helpless. He's British establishment, I'm German interloper. He wins every time."

Robert was horrified at the turn the conversation had taken. Ilse he could handle. That was love. But this was pure, unadulterated hatred. And to make matters worse, he was beginning to feel the same as Karl. Katherine was like a sister to him. "He raped Katherine? When?"

"A few months ago, when she tried to dissuade him from pressing charges about Richard punching him. The first time was before we were married," he added, "and Kellett's quite convinced it wasn't rape."

"But Katherine says it was."

"Maybe just mixed messages. I don't know. But the second time I'm sure was rape, despite what Katherine maintains. Perhaps she could have protested more but she had to 'allow' it to keep him from pressing charges on Richard, as I explained. He's a clever swine. Knows just how far he can go."

"And you want to kill him."

"I dream about it. In the heat of the moment it might happen. I've killed many men in the past."

"That was war, Karl."

"So is this. And I killed Goslar."

"We don't know that for certain."

"I think now I did."

"I see." Robert needed time to dwell on what Karl was telling him, so he shifted the conversation slightly. "But you've also been dreaming about killing Siegfried. What's all that about then? You didn't want him dead, surely?"

Karl thought for a moment. "I was acknowledging that I killed him indirectly. I should have let him stay in Germany as a child, then none of this would ever have happened. It was all my fault. My family, even Katherine, said at the time Siegfried should stay with them in Medebach, but no, I knew better. I dragged him kicking and screaming to England. And so I dream I am killing him, because I did."

"But his death was an accident, Karl."

"He was with Gustav," Karl said shortly, avoiding the truth.

Robert nodded, making the connection with Nazism. "And by going to live in Germany, near his grave, you think you will be doing the right thing by him?"

"By keeping an eye on his children there, I will be. That is what he wa- would have wanted."

"Then perhaps you should go, Karl."

Karl looked up in surprise. "And Katherine?"

"If that's what you really want, I'm sure she'll go willingly. Why don't you ask her?"

It was almost too much to hope for. Karl brushed aside the suggestion for the moment. "You don't think I'm going mad again then?"

"You seem perfectly rational now. Do you know what happened the other day? Why you seemed convinced you *had* shot Siegfried?"

Karl gripped the arm of the chair as he remembered the events in question. "It was real, Robert. As real as I'm talking to you now. I know now I shot a rabbit, but then ..." He licked his lips. "I can't explain it. Siegfried was there, in the flesh. I shot him. There was blood. It was real. Who's to say it won't happen again, only next time I'll shoot Kellett because I'll think he's a rabbit?"

"It wouldn't work like that, Karl."

"No? How can you be sure?"

Robert took a careful sip of his whisky. "Is that what you were thinking about on the train coming up? Dad said you'd spent a long time alone in the corridor."

"Yes." Karl gazed into the glowing coals of the hearth, ashamed of his mental frailty. "I can see it happening. I'll shoot Kellett – unintentionally – and then the whole thing will start all over again with psychiatric assessments, trial. This time they'll put me away for good. Could my family even stay in the village after that? Probably not. I can't put myself or Katherine through that. It's easier not to risk it, and go back to live in Germany."

"Leaving Richard and Paul to run the farm? Aren't they a bit young still?"

Karl's head jerked back from the hearth to stare at his friend. "You agree with me, don't you? You do think there's a risk I might kill Kellett!"

Robert steepled his fingers in front of him and looked at Karl over his fingertips. "You're a very complex person, Karl. You've just given me three cogent reasons to return to Germany. All very sound, from your perspective. I can't argue with your reasoning.

We can possibly blame those doctors at Dachau for some of your troubles – your hallucinations, depression, emotional outbursts – but losing Ilse and Siegfried was your own responsibility."

"No it wasn't. It was Goslar's. Without his interfering, I'd have married Ilse, if we'd both survived."

"Without Hitler you'd never have met Ilse! Come on, Karl! You can't blame everyone else. The chain of 'what ifs' is indefinite." He lowered his voice again. "What I'm saying is, you obviously feel a deep need to maintain your connections with both Ilse and Siegfried in whatever form you can. Which simply means, living in Germany. But then what of your responsibilities to your English family? You can't ignore them."

Karl slumped in his armchair. "I can't wait until Richard and Paul are older. This business with Kellett won't go away."

Robert reached for the whisky bottle and leaned forward to refill Karl's glass. "Do you want me to have a word with Katherine about going to Germany?"

It was as if the dungeon door had suddenly been flung wide open, letting in light and hope again. "Would you? I think it would help a lot."

"On one condition."

"Which is?"

"That I warn her about Ilse."

Karl smiled ruefully. "There's no need. She won't let me out of her sight again, where Ilse is concerned."

"Good." Robert sat back in his chair. "Now, the next question is: who's going to tell Katherine first? You or me?"

"Tell? Don't you mean ask?"

Robert shrugged. "It strikes me, your mind is made up on this, Karl. Unfortunately for Katherine, I don't think she'll have much say in this. But knowing her, she'll want what's best for you."

"I hope so, but I still think I should at least ask. You can tell her, if necessary."

"If necessary, but I doubt it will be. She's always considered your needs first."

"I know. I can't believe how lucky I was to get her. And thanks to you too, Robert, for playing go-between."

"That awful winter of 1947 helped," Robert chuckled, already heading back in time. "Do you remember how readily my parents agreed to you staying up at the farm that night?"

Their reminiscing lasted late into the evening and Karl finally went to bed feeling far happier about the future.

*

Throughout the return journey Karl tried to plan his approach to Katherine. Donald and Gertie, satisfied he was no longer in any danger of going mad on them, spent the entire journey discussing the bungalow they had found and all the plans they would have to make to sell and move out of Yew Tree Lodge. Karl shut his ears to their animated voices and mused upon his own future. What work would he do in Germany? In the sawmill? Where exactly would they live? Somewhere in Medebach or in Haus Fichtenblick itself, now that Anna and Stefan's children were beginning to leave home? The latter hopefully. He wanted to be part of his own family again, and at least Katherine would not be among strangers there. He felt radiantly happy at the prospect of moving. Penchurch held nothing for him any more. Richard and Paul would manage somehow. At Richard's age he had become a soldier, ready to kill people. He had grown up rapidly. Richard would too.

But Paul. What would Paul do? Somehow nothing seemed as simple now as it had up in Edinburgh.

He kissed Katherine warmly when she met them at Hereford station to drive them back to Penchurch.

"All right now?" she asked him tentatively.

"For the moment," he replied, shoving the luggage into the back of the Land Rover. "But I'll tell you all about it later. Robert and Alice sent their love, by the way."

After they had dropped off Donald and Gertie at Yew Tree Lodge, Katherine suddenly said: "Richard's got himself a new girlfriend. Met her at a party he went to while you were away. He seems very smitten with her."

Karl was driving so kept his eyes on the road. He did not want Katherine to see his keen interest. "Oh really? Who is she?"

"One of the Turner crowd from Ledbury. You know them. There's hundreds of them. Vanessa's got three older brothers who're all into farming, as well as loads of uncles and aunts. John Turner, who you met at the County Show last year, is an uncle."

"Was he the one demonstrating archery, who wanted shafts for arrows?"

"That's the one. He's into this historical re-enactment lark. Goes off to fight the Civil War or whatever at weekends."

Karl remembered John Turner well now. A friendly man, passionate about his hobby and keen to introduce Karl into the joys of reconstructed battle should he ever have time. Perhaps his niece, Vanessa, was equally friendly and passionate. He hoped so for Richard's sake. Farming stock too. She should know how to work hard.

As he pulled into the farmyard all was quiet. Karl already felt detached from the place, as though he no longer lived there, his heart already left for Germany. Richard would be all right with a competent woman at his side. That just left Paul.

And Katherine.

"I feel like stretching my legs after that long journey," he told her after he had put his bag in the kitchen. "Do you fancy a walk down to the river?"

She was glad he had not suggested up to the woods and Siegfried's lair. "Yes, all right then. Let's get our boots on."

He held her hand as they strolled down through the meadows, past the neat rows of apple trees in the orchards where the pickers were still hard at work, and along the valley to the lowest meadow by the river. Despite drainage schemes over the years it was still rather boggy in places and prone to flooding, so was only grazed in summer. It was empty of sheep now. Karl led Katherine to the riverbank and leaned against a pollarded willow. They stood a few moments in silence, watching the muddy water with its swirling eddies and calmer patches under the overhanging bank.

"Like life," Karl said, breaking their silence. "And I'm in a whirlpool at the moment."

"I rather thought you had something to say," Katherine said, leaning against him to shelter from the brisk wind.

Her close proximity comforted him and he held her shoulders gently as he bent to kiss her. "I love you, Schatz. You are so wise and so calm. You protect me even when I ... hurt you."

Katherine tensed. Something important was coming. He rarely opened up so freely.

Karl held down a lock of her wayward hair, both hands cradling her face. "I need you now, Schatz. I need you to do something you won't want to do, but for my sake you must. I want you to come with me to live in Germany."

He felt her go rigid. Then her eyes slid away and he knew it would not be so easy, as she stepped back out of his embrace.

She looked back up at him, her eyes cool. "Why now, Karl? After all these years here, why now?"

"I'm in danger here."

"In danger here? But I thought you were worried the neo-Nazis were still after you. They're more likely to get you in Germany, aren't they?"

"If they really want me dead it won't matter where I am. Siegfried came over, so did Ernst Winter. It makes no difference where I am. But what I meant was, I'm in danger from myself here. Mentally. Robert agrees."

"Does he indeed? And what does he know that I don't?"

He had shaken her. She was becoming unusually aggressive, but he was threatening her home, her whole way of life. He had to be careful.

"What about the boys and the farm?" Katherine was working up a fine head of steam now. "Do we simply abandon them? They're not old enough to cope on their own just yet."

"And I might not cope if I stay here," Karl retorted more sharply than he intended.

Katherine stepped back a pace, her pale face fixed in determination. "Are you asking me to choose between you and the boys?"

"Ilse left her children to follow Paul to Uruguay."

Mention of Ilse proved too much after all the stresses and strains of the past year. For the first time in her life she lost control. "How dare you bring *her* into this!" she screamed, raising her hand.

Karl saw the slap coming but let her hit him. It hurt and he deserved it. It was a stupid thing to say.

"Go on," she screamed at him again. "Go to your precious Germany! I won't protect you any more. I've had enough!" She was in tears now, tears of rage, disappointment and shock at her own behaviour. Turning her back on him she hurried away.

The sight was too much for Karl to bear. He leapt after her, grabbing her by the wrist. "I'm sorry, Schatz. Forgive me!" he begged. "I shouldn't have said that. You were right to hit me."

Katherine turned to face him, trembling with the shock of what she had just done. She saw his desperate need of her. She could never desert him. But nor could she leave the boys just yet.

"Please reconsider, Karl. Stay here. At least until Richard's twenty-one. You'll be all right, I promise. It wasn't too bad this time was it? Robert seems to have sorted you out quite quickly."

Karl swept her into his arms and held her close to him, not wanting to let her go. He had thought she would come readily, but it was not to be. He had taken her love for granted too often and now he had to repay that commitment. He would stay for the time being. But he would have to be very, very careful.

TWENTY-FOUR

Andrew's blue jaguar was following Katherine down the valley. She drove faster, trying to show she wanted nothing to do with him, but he kept up. When she stopped outside the Post Office in Penchurch, he pulled in too. She hesitated to get out of the Land Rover, but decided she could not sit there all day.

At the counter there was a short queue. Everybody was buying Christmas stamps, Andrew included.

"Morning, Katherine," he greeted her, standing in line behind her.

"Good morning," she replied coolly.

He nodded at the bundle of envelopes in her hand, with the destination 'West Germany' clearly written in capital letters on the uppermost. "Not seeing his family this Christmas?"

"No, we never do, but Sabina and Wolf are coming over for a week." Katherine struggled to sound friendly, but her innate politeness overcame her desire to rebuff him. "And you? Have you many visitors this Christmas?" She stepped forward a pace as the queue moved up.

Andrew shrugged. "The usual crowd, I suppose. I leave all that up to Audrey. That's her department." He dropped his voice and leant forward to whisper in her ear: "Not so good in bed these days, though." It was a hint he would be calling on her soon, confirmed when he added out loud: "Is your husband keeping himself busy?"

"He's always busy about the farm," Katherine declared, looking him meaningfully in the eye. "He'll be there if you drop by." She knew it was not what Andrew wanted to hear, but it gave him a clear message, she hoped, to leave her alone.

"Right." Undeterred he changed tack. "If you're ever going Christmas shopping, I'm sure Audrey would love to share a trip to Hereford with you. You could drop by first for a coffee."

"Oh, I'm sure Audrey would rather shop by herself," Katherine told him. "There's always so much to think about, a companion can be distracting."

"Maybe, but give us a ring, anyway," he told her, adding as if to emphasise his point: "Is Richard all right? Not been in any more fights, recently?"

Katherine scowled, but the queue had moved up again and it was her turn at the counter. She asked the postmistress for six stamps to West Germany and twenty of the fourpenny Christmas stamps, then stood to one side to stick all the stamps on. Andrew joined her a few moments later.

"I'll expect you to call soon, or there'll be trouble!" he whispered, then marched out of the Post Office.

Katherine continued licking stamps, the thump of her fist as she stuck them down the only outward sign of her rage.

*

It was hot in the sitting room with so many bodies gathered for the Christmas Day festivities. Sabina sought a moment's refuge in the kitchen to replenish her and Wolf's drinks. She was thinking how well Richard's girlfriend, Vanessa, had thrown herself into the thick of things. She was a nice girl: very sensible and capable, very Richard.

Her Aunt Sarah was already out in the kitchen doing a spot of washing up, trying to keep pace with the constant demands on the crockery.

"Phew!" Sabina sighed, wiping her brow. "There are too many people in there."

"I know. That's why I'm out here," Sarah replied. "Do you want to wipe up a few of those glasses for me? I'm running out of room to put them."

"Sure." Sabina added the two glasses she was carrying to the dirty pile then grabbed a tea towel from the rail by the range. She had not seen her aunt since her wedding and was glad to have the chance of a few quiet words with her. She thought carefully about her choice of words then broached the subject of her father.

"Does Daddy seem a bit quiet to you?"

"Ah. So you've noticed it too."

"Yes. It's since Siegfried died. Richard was telling me he doesn't go out much these days. Hardly at all, in fact."

"Really? I didn't know that."

"No. He doesn't even go to market now. Leaves all that to Richard. It's almost like he's frightened of going out." Sabina found a tray to stack clean glasses on. "I'm wondering whether he thinks the neo-Nazis are on his back again. Wolf's certainly got the jitters, especially since the police think that Gustav's lover didn't commit suicide after all, but was murdered."

Sarah frowned. "When did you hear that?"

"Shortly after it happened. Apparently this Christian Bracht bloke had been on the phone to an actress friend only minutes before he died. She said he sounded quite normal and was talking about returning to Berlin."

"Doesn't mean a thing," Sarah declared. "I saw an acquaintance of mine the day she committed suicide. She was returning something she'd borrowed before supposedly moving back up north. Next thing I heard was she'd taken an overdose."

"Poor thing," Sabina murmured, but her sympathy for the unknown woman was short-lived. "No, there's more to it than that," Sabina continued. "Once the police started looking into it, a witness said she saw two men leaving the apartment block at about the time it happened. Wolf said their description matched that of two men who had followed him and Siegfried some time before that."

Sarah was anxious now. "And you think that's why Karl's hiding himself away?"

"Could be."

"But does he know about this Christian Bracht thing?"

"Yes, of course. We told him." Sabina looked around the kitchen for any more dirty crockery for washing. They seemed to have got to grips with it for the time being. "Well, I'd better get back in there before Wolf expires of thirst. Did you want a glass of anything?"

"Cider would be nice, please, Bina."

Sarah accompanied her niece back to the family in the sitting room. Donald and Gertie were there too, making the most of their last few weeks in Herefordshire prior to their move after New Year. She found a space on the sofa next to Vanessa and sat back to observe the latest developments in the family, paying particular attention to Karl. This time last year he had been in prison for assaulting Siegfried, but nobody had wanted to put a damper on the day by mentioning the fact. He seemed jovial enough today, she decided, with his paper hat perched jauntily on his head. He was trying to remember the list of items purchased in Hereford market. The list was up to a dozen items now and he rattled them off with no problem. She was momentarily concerned when his own addition to the shopping list turned out to be a dozen arrows, but then she remembered Vanessa's uncle's interest. Even so, it showed Karl's thoughts lay with weapons.

Katherine dropped out of the game on the next round, having forgotten Donald's item, a box of matches. As she took the chance to go out to the kitchen Sarah followed her out.

"Oh! All the washing up's been done," Katherine exclaimed, surveying her tidier kitchen.

"Bina helped. We had a bit of a chat while we were at it," Sarah said, pointing to a chair for Katherine to sit on. Katherine took the hint and sat down next to her sister.

"Well?" she asked. "What was the chat about?"

"Mostly about Karl not going out any more. Is he that worried about the neo-Nazis?"

Katherine shuffled uneasily on her chair, but decided she could do with someone to confide in. "It's not the neo-Nazis, Sarah. It's Andrew."

"Andrew! In heaven's name why?"

"Because he's got it in for Karl. And Richard. Ever since that stupid episode last summer when Richard punched him, Andrew has realised he can needle Karl, and Karl daren't do anything lest he lose his temper with Andrew and seriously hurt him. You know how it is between the pair of them. Andrew's never forgiven Karl for stealing me away from him, and he feels confident enough in his position to bait and taunt Karl at every opportunity to regain the upper hand. You know what Andrew's like: spoilt, authoritarian, a bully. He also won't leave me alone, so Karl hangs around the farm not just to keep him away, but also to avoid chance meetings elsewhere with him."

"So he's a virtual prisoner here on the farm? But that's stupid!"

Katherine lowered her voice. "Sarah, you don't realise how terrified Karl is of accidentally killing Andrew. He's had nightmares about it. He even had to go up to see Robert. He wants us to move to Germany because of it, but I said we can't until the boys are that little bit older and we can leave them here."

"My oh my, that's serious!" Sarah thought for a moment. "I don't suppose Audrey can do anything to help?"

"She and Andrew hardly speak to each other these days. Live separate lives. That's partly why Andrew was hassling me so much."

It took a moment to register. "Do you mean he wants you for sex?" Sarah asked slowly.

Katherine drew a deep breath. "Yes. Though why he can't find some young floozy, I don't know. He probably can and has, but it's really this whole business with Karl. If he can have me, he's got one over on Karl."

"Yes, I can see he would think that. But why does he think he stands a chance with you?"

Katherine lowered her eyes. "I had to let him once, to keep him from pressing charges against Richard. Now he appears every so often wanting more payment for his largesse."

"And do you give it to him?" Sarah asked in horror.

"I didn't at first. But then came Siegfried's death. Karl took it so badly and his nightmares started up again. I couldn't afford a confrontation between them. I make Andrew stay away from Karl by agreeing to his demands, but it's getting harder to find the opportunity now Karl doesn't go out very often. He makes Richard and Paul do the tree surgery work, while he looks after things here."

Sarah could not believe what she was hearing. Katherine was prostituting herself to protect Karl. "Does he know what's going on between you and Andrew?"

"Only that first occasion."

"I'm surprised he didn't kill Andrew then!"

"So was I, but I made out I was more willing than I actually was, so Karl couldn't blame Andrew too much. Besides, he was more in control then. I don't think he is now. He's slipping back into himself."

"But what if he finds out?" Sarah whispered, not daring to speak louder. To her horror tears began to fill her sister's eyes.

"I dread to think."

"Don't you think what you're doing is far riskier than a chance encounter between them?"

"You don't understand, Sarah. Andrew is driving this. He wants to keep needling Karl. Conflict is inevitable unless I keep him happy."

Sarah found herself momentarily speechless. "I would suggest going to the police," she eventually said, "but I don't see that it would help."

"No. It wouldn't."

"God, what a mess. Bina thinks it's the neo-Nazis, but it's worse. It must be awful for you having to be at Andrew's beck and call."

Katherine dried her eyes on her hanky. "It is, but it's better than Karl being arrested for attacking him – or worse." She looked up at her sister. "When Karl went up to see Robert he was bordering on the delusional, thinking he had shot Siegfried. Apparently on the train he nearly attacked a man he thought was Andrew. He wasn't making sense but Robert sorted him out, although he encouraged Karl to move to Germany. He obviously considers Karl's in danger here."

"Perhaps you ought to go then."

"I can't leave the boys just yet, Sarah, they're –"

Paul burst into the kitchen. "Mum, where are the bingo cards?"

"In the bottom drawer of the chest in the hall."

Paul hurried out on his mission leaving Katherine and Sarah alone briefly once more. Sarah stood up. "I think we'd better rejoin the party before we're missed. Just one thing though, Katherine. Don't let Andrew near you again. He'll get greedy and it will get worse, trust me."

It was all very well for Sarah, Katherine thought as she took a bingo card and stack of counters from Paul and sat down on the arm of Karl's chair. She didn't have to turn Andrew away. Andrew would have her, willing or unwilling. It was easier to be willing.

"You've got the fifteen," Karl nudged her. He was calling the numbers so had no card of his own to worry about.

"Oh, so I have." She put a counter over the relevant square and tried to concentrate on the game but her thoughts kept drifting to the next encounter with Andrew. How could she make him leave her alone?

Katherine had little opportunity to think over her dilemma during the next few weeks. Once her visitors had gone, she was busy helping Donald and Gertie sort out and pack up their home, ready for the move on the 24th January. Karl accompanied her several times to Yew Tree Lodge to shift heavy items and take a load of rubbish to the dump, but he still seemed ill at ease away from the comparative safety of the farm.

His policy of not leaving the farm seemed to be working, as Andrew had not attempted to drop by. It did not stop her from seeing him at church on Sundays, where his indifference to her was striking in its contrast to when they were alone.

After yet another trip to the Murdochs' to shift boxes of books out for a jumble sale, Katherine persuaded Karl to stop off at the Walnut Tree. It was a raw January evening and she felt they could both do with some cheering up after seeing the Murdochs' home gradually emptying.

"I don't mind driving back," she offered. "You just sink a few jars with whoever's in there and relax a bit. You can't stay at home forever, Schatz."

The suggestion certainly appealed to him. Kellett was hardly likely to be there and he could certainly do with seeing some different faces. Katherine was right. He must get over this Kellett business and start living again. Christmas had been a turning point. He had managed to enjoy it, despite everything. Bina and Wolf's visit had helped a lot, taking his mind off himself at last. The news about Bracht's possible murder was not good, but still nothing had happened to show there was any threat to themselves. Siegfried's links with Gustav seemed to have confused the neo-Nazis sufficiently to create a breathing space for Wolf. His own fate was still in the balance, but he would just have to live with that. Hopefully, thoughts of revenge for Garisch's death were now far down their agenda.

He parked the Land Rover outside the pub and ducked under the lintel behind Katherine. The warmth of the log fire hit them and Alf Butler's cheery wave from behind the bar welcomed them in. Other locals raised glasses in greeting and once he had been served, he joined Katherine at a table with several members of the Penchurch Players, who had just finished a performance of this year's pantomime, 'Cinderella'.

"We could have done with some extra adult members this year," Vic Threadgold, the producer, told him as he sat down and gave Katherine her half of cider. "I was just saying to Katherine, you should join us again, Karl. We're always short of men. Our next play in March has a part that could have been written for you. It's –"

"Lambing, Vic. Sorry."

Vic looked rueful. "I know. That's the trouble with you farmers – always working. You ought to get a nine to five job like me, or else stick to your tree surgery. That's more sociable hours, isn't it? Come to think of it," he added after a swig of beer, "I've been meaning to get in touch about a job I've got for you. I'd be grateful if you could come and have a look at a tree in my garden. It's shading out everything else and I want it lopped or something. Could you take a look?"

Karl saw Katherine's anxious face. It really was time he pulled himself together. "OK. When had you in mind?"

"Erm, it'll have to be a lunch-time. Let's say one o'clock on Monday? Is that all right?"

"Fine. It's Richard who'll be doing the estimate. I'm training him up in that side of the business."

"I'd better be nice to him, then," Vic laughed, then remembered the latest gossip. "I hear he's found himself a nice girl in that Vanessa Turner."

"Yes, we like her."

Katherine sipped her cider, glad to see Karl so much better. Perhaps she and Karl could get out a bit more. The last eighteen months had been truly ghastly, apart from Bina's wedding. Surely now they could look forward to better times ahead: another wedding, christenings in time. She saw Karl's easy manner with Vic and the others, and smiled. The shock of Siegfried's suicide was gradually fading. Karl would get over it and she could begin to relax her protective watch over him.

*

The day of the move came and went. They watched the removal van drive off at four o'clock on Friday afternoon, then Katherine drove Donald and Gertie up to Lane Head Farm for a last night together, before putting them on the train to Edinburgh the next morning. Robert and Alice would help supervise the unpacking on

Monday, while Karl would find a buyer for the car Donald had decided to sell rather than drive all the way to Scotland. Buses and shanks's pony would serve them in their new home.

They were all tired after the hectic day and retired to bed early, apart from Richard and Paul who were out at a dance. The bleary-eyed boys surfaced at seven next morning to get the chores done and see off their surrogate grandparents. Katherine found the goodbyes at the station particularly hard, as Donald and Gertie had been like parents to her since her own died.

"Take care, both of you, and thank you for everything you've ever done for Karl and me," she said hugging them in turn, trying to hold back the tears. "We'd never have survived without you. Enjoy your new life in Edinburgh, and make lots of new friends."

Karl hugged the diminutive Gertie then shook Donald's hand. "Thank you," he said simply, still grasping Donald's hand.

Donald put his left hand over Karl's in a rare gesture of warmth. "Take care of yourself and all your family, Karl. And remember, we're only a phone call away if you ever need us, or Robert."

"I will. Thank you again, Donald. I wouldn't be here without your family. You mean a lot to me." Suddenly a handshake was not good enough. Karl embraced the man who had shown such tolerance towards a former enemy and had helped and stood by him over the years. "We'll miss you."

"And we'll miss you all," Donald replied. "Just you make sure you send us an invitation to the next wedding!"

"We will," Katherine and Karl said in unison.

They were both quiet as Karl drove back from Hereford, each reflecting on the dear friends who had just left, then Karl suddenly tensed. Driving behind them was a car he recognised – Kellett's blue Jaguar – and it was right up his bumper.

"Damn him!"

Katherine looked across in surprise. "Who?"

Karl nodded to their rear. Katherine turned and saw Andrew's face through the Jaguar's windscreen. Andrew grinned then pulled back, having made his presence felt. Katherine felt a chill of alarm sweep through her. Karl and Richard would be out most of Tuesday working at Vic's. Did Andrew know that already? It was possible. One of the estate workers could have overheard the conversation in the pub a week ago and reported it to Andrew. How else did Andrew get to know when Karl would be out? She clasped her hands tightly to stop them trembling. If he did turn up, this time she would say no and mean it. Sarah was right. He would constantly pester her unless she became forceful with him. But Karl mustn't have the slightest inkling she was expecting trouble. She must deal with this herself.

TWENTY-FIVE

"Just watch out or Vic will be after you to audition for a part in the next play," Karl light-heartedly warned Richard, as they packed up the Land Rover with tools for their tree-lopping job. "He's already tackled me but I managed to come up with an excuse."

"Well I've got a good one," Richard laughed. "Vanessa. My spare time's spent with her."

"Don't I know it! You're never around of an evening these days." He flung the coil of rope onto the pile of tools and shut the back of the Land Rover. "You enjoy yourselves while you can," he added more gently. "Your mother and I never had the chance to go out at first."

"It isn't easy now, is it, Dad?"

Karl looked at his perceptive son. "I'm going to have to get over this, aren't I? Kellett be damned. If I kill him, I kill him."

"It won't come to that, Dad. He's as frightened of you as you are of him."

"I don't think so."

"Besides, it's only in your dreams you kill him. People do all sorts of things in their dreams. Hell, I can even fly!"

Karl laughed. "And I can shear sheep." He looked at his watch. "It's ten o'clock already. Let's be away. We've a job to do."

With a wave to Katherine through the kitchen window, they set off out of the yard and down the narrow lane to join the valley road where they turned left towards Penchurch. A hundred yards down the road a flash of blue in the rear-view mirror caught Karl's eye.

"*Scheiße!*" he swore, slamming on the brakes.

"What is it?" Richard asked, bracing himself as his father rapidly turned the vehicle in a gateway and headed back the way they had just come.

"Kellett's driving up the lane! He must have known we were going out."

"Why would he be calling if he knew ... Oh!" Richard gasped as he worked things out for himself. "It's Mum, isn't it?" He saw his father's grim expression, the clenched teeth and white knuckles. "Easy does it, Dad. Perhaps we should give Mum a chance to get rid of him herself."

"He won't let her. He knows what he wants and he won't take no for an answer." Karl was driving fast up the lane now, but he slowed down as they approached the house, cutting the engine to roll into the yard. There was to be no warning to Kellett of their arrival. Karl wanted to see for himself what the man was up to. He got out, avoiding slamming the door. Richard followed closely after his father through the back door.

As he entered the house, Karl was telling himself to keep calm. Violence must not be an outcome otherwise Kellett would have won. But when he saw Kellett in the hall, with Katherine forced up against the wall by the grandfather clock angrily trying to fend off his kisses and his intruding hands, he nearly forgot his resolution.

"What are you doing to my wife?" Karl growled, barely restraining himself from grabbing Kellett by the windpipe.

Kellett turned at the sound of his voice and instantly released his grip on Katherine. Seeing he was outnumbered he began to bluster his way out. "I thought you said he would be out, Katherine!" he hissed at her, sidling past her towards the front door. "Now your damn husband's found out about our little affair. A pity, but no matter. We'll just have to get together some other time." He glanced at his foe. Karl's silence in response to Katherine's frantic signals gave him confidence. The German and his son clearly did not dare attack him; the risk to their freedom was far too great. Kellett's relief made him cocky.

"Well, Driesler, I can see why your wife is fed up with a wimp like you." His hand was on the front door latch now, starting to open it, but he had reckoned without Katherine's fury. She slammed her shoulder against the door and stood herself between him and his means of escape, wanting to leave him in no doubt as to her feelings.

"You're done for, Andrew!" she threatened him, launching herself into a vitriolic tirade. "You've gone too far. You think you're above the law and that we daren't touch you. But you're wrong. I've had enough of your cavalier attitude. I'm going to report you to the police and nothing you say will prevent them charging you with attempted rape."

Andrew snorted in derision. "Rape? How many times have I had you now, and you're only just yelling rape? You wanted it, Katherine, and you damn well know it!"

"No I didn't!" she screamed, her temper wholly unleashed. She could see Karl wanted to intervene, but she had to keep him out of this. It was time to show Andrew Kellett that she meant what she said. Grabbing an umbrella from the stand by the door she brandished it in his face. "Get out!" she yelled.

He only grinned in disbelief that she would actually hit him, but his cockiness proved the last straw for Katherine and she lunged at him with the umbrella. He raised his left arm, deflecting the umbrella aside and sending it smashing through the little window to the right of the door. Katherine tugged the umbrella from the gaping hole in her haste to renew her assault. Seeing her furious advance on him again, Andrew grabbed hold of the umbrella and swung her briskly away from the door, sending her hurtling headfirst towards the broken window.

Karl had kept out of the fight until he saw Kellett shoving Katherine so forcibly aside. His anger boiled over. "Bastard!" he shouted, but Kellett already had the door open and was making his escape. Neither man had heard the sound of more glass breaking from behind the open door.

Karl chased after him up the front path to the lane. He was stretching out his hand to grab Kellett's collar when he heard Richard's bloodcurdling shriek of alarm.

"Dad! Help!"

The utter terror in Richard's cry broke through Karl's rage. His arm dropped and he skidded to a halt, leaving Kellett to make a run for it. He turned round and looked back to see what had alarmed Richard so. He staggered at the nightmare sight that met him. Blood was cascading from the broken window down the whitewashed wall. Above the scarlet cascade were Katherine's auburn curls. He could not see her face, but her head stuck far enough out of the window for him to realise her throat was impaled on the broken glass.

For a few seconds Karl froze, and in that instant he knew she could not be saved. There was too much blood.

"Dad! Help!" Richard called again, panic-stricken.

Karl ran up to the window, bent down to get a closer look but could see little past Katherine's chin except gushing blood. She was gripping the frame in terror but she was already weakening, her body slumping back, tearing open the hole in her throat.

"Support her, Richard!" Karl yelled, trying to assess the desperate situation. Stepping in a growing pool of blood, he tried to soothe his stricken wife. "It's all right, Schatz. We'll get you out." A few seconds of careful probing around her neck told a different story. "Damn! The glass is deep in her throat," he told Richard. "It's also stuck in the frame. I can't break it off."

"Sh-shall I call an ambulance?" Richard asked.

"In a moment. Let's get her off this glass first, so I can see better." Karl knew that if there was any chance at all, however remote, of saving her, he had to get her out of the window. She would otherwise bleed to death long before an ambulance could arrive. "Keep her supported while I try to free her," he told Richard. He could see she was barely conscious now. Easing both hands around her neck he raised it up, feeling the shard slip out of her throat. Once she was free, Richard pulled her head back through the window and Karl stepped through the open door to take her from him.

"Get a towel then ring for an ambulance!" he barked, sinking slowly to the floor with Katherine's head against his chest. She was struggling for breath, drowning in her own blood, her eyes flickering open and closed as she tried to remain conscious. The kitchen towel fell to the floor beside him. He grabbed it, holding it firmly on her throat, but she was fading fast.

He had a sudden recollection of her father dying in his arms. Now she would do the same. He bent down and whispered in her ear: "I love you, Katherine. I love you so much." Her eyelids fluttered. She had heard him.

The towel was already soaked. He moved it away, trying to locate the severed blood vessels while the area was comparatively dry, but there were too many to control, the gash too wide. Bubbling noises came from her windpipe and he knew she did not have long.

Richard finished calling for the ambulance and skidded down beside him, crying freely as he saw the colour draining from her skin. "Mum! Mum! Don't die. Please don't die!" He looked up at his father and saw the hopelessness in his face.

Karl held Katherine tight in his arms. From her throat blood still oozed, but less so now as her pulse faded away. He knew she was going, maybe even gone already, peacefully slipping away, oblivious to pain and to his presence. He would never see those soft green eyes again, never hear her gentle voice nor feel her soothing hands. He had lost his Treasure, his Schatz. He was destitute once more.

Richard laid his head on his mother's blood-sodden breast to listen for a heartbeat. Nothing. He looked up at his father, huge tears welling from his eyes, and shook his head.

The blood had stopped flowing now. Katherine's face looked white, her lips red with her blood. Karl sat with her still lying across his lap and felt his own throat constricting in grief. Unable to speak, he bent his head and kissed her lips, his tears running down her face, mingling with her blood. He closed his eyes, overwhelmed by the blackness and sat there, cradling her in his arms, dimly aware of Richard's sobs beside him.

It was Richard who heard the ambulance eventually draw up outside. He stood up and went out to tell the crew the situation. Karl, blood-soaked and ashen, was also on his feet by the time they came in to check over Katherine's body. They took over matters, consoling Karl and Richard, advising that, under the circumstances, a doctor had to confirm death and the police notified before the body could be removed. With nothing else to be done, the ambulance returned to base.

Father and son watched it leave, too shocked to move until they could no longer hear its engine, then Karl took a shuddering breath and laid a hand on Richard's shoulder.

"We must let Paul know. And call the police. That bastard's not going to get away with this."

Richard stirred himself. He must be strong and help his father through all this. "Shall I do the phoning?"

"No. I need something to do. You go and get cleaned up."

Richard nodded. His father was remarkably calm now, considering. His composure helped Richard. "We'll be all right, Dad. We'll cope."

"Yes, we'll cope," Karl said grimly, leaving a trail of blood as he headed for the hall table and picked up the telephone.

The police told him they would be there soon. The headmaster of Paul's school said he would drive him home personally. Sarah was away at a meeting but would be given the message. Alice broke down in tears and promised to let the rest of the Murdochs know immediately. Werner and Vera were coming straight up to help in any way they could.

Karl sank to the floor by the phone, still covered in blood, his eyes closed. The phone calls to Germany could wait until later. He needed to shut off for a while.

The police arrived first. Richard let them in, rousing his father to speak to them. They took detailed statements while the police surgeon examined Katherine's body, confirming her death. By the time the police photographer had come and gone and the body had been taken away for autopsy, the house had filled with people. A reporter turned up, managing to snap the bloodstained front wall before being hustled away by Werner, who fed him information about Kellett's part in events. With the police's permission, Vera donned rubber gloves and wielded a mop to try to clean up the hall. Werner cleared away the fragments of bloodstained glass from the window and covered the frame with board until the window could be mended.

Finally Karl washed Katherine's blood off him, changed his clothes then sat in the kitchen staring at the sink where Katherine had stood that morning and waved them off. Paul and Richard sat with him, silent in grief.

Rev. Williams arrived at three thirty to offer comfort. He took the cup of tea Vera handed him then sat down at the kitchen table by Karl's side, laying a gentle hand on his shoulder. After offering his sympathies he went on: "Knowing your feelings on religion, Karl, I don't want to force anything on you, but just remember you have the whole of Penchurch to turn to. Make use of us. We're here. Katherine was much loved and respected here and we will all do anything we can to help you through this dreadful time."

"Thank you," Karl said. "She loved it here. Now she doesn't have to leave." He turned to Richard and Paul. "I'll leave it up to you to decide with Reverend Williams about the funeral service. I'm not competent at that."

"We'd still like your approval of our choices, Karl," Rev. Williams told him. "You need to be involved. It helps."

Karl shrugged. "Whatever." He sat and listened to the Reverend's words of solace for another twenty minutes before seeing him out by the back door.

Werner and Vera stayed until eight that evening, tending to Molly and the farm animals then making sure Karl and his sons had eaten something, before reluctantly going home. The threesome sat on in the kitchen, listening to but not hearing the radio, going outside to use the toilet in the yard as none of them wanted to enter the hall. At ten they knew they had to turn in some time. Karl locked up and together they progressed through the hall, not looking at the boarded-over window. Karl laid a comforting hand on his sons' shoulders and they climbed the stairs, but as Richard headed for the bathroom, Paul stopped, shrugged off his father's hand and looked up at him with swollen, red eyes

"Why did you let it happen, Dad?" he demanded angrily. "Why didn't you stop him?" With a loud sob he fled to his room, slamming the door behind him.

Karl could hear Paul's heart-rending crying but decided to leave him be. Hopefully he would cry out his anger and be more amenable in the morning. Richard came out of the bathroom, toothbrush in hand.

"Don't worry, Dad. I'll speak to him. It wasn't your fault. He just wasn't there to see what happened."

"He's right, though," Karl muttered. "I should have stopped him."

"We both should have," Richard said firmly. "But we didn't foresee what would happen. Don't blame yourself, Dad."

Karl squeezed his son's shoulder as if in agreement, but as he opened his bedroom door and stepped inside, he could not delude himself. He was a coward, frightened of getting embroiled. Now Katherine was dead because of him.

The emptiness of the dark room hit him like a battering ram and he slumped face down on the bed, fully clothed, and wept until he could weep no more.

*

The police came back the next morning at nine o'clock. Richard opened the front door to the two men, Detective Inspector Groves and Detective Sergeant Hutchinson.

"Richard Driesler, isn't it?" Groves asked briskly.

"Yes."

"We'd like another word with you and your father."

Richard did not like the tone of his voice. The appropriate sympathy seemed to be lacking. He beckoned them inside. "My father's outside. I'll go and get him. Do you want to wait in the kitchen? It's warmer there." He led them through the hall to the rear of the house and left them nosing around while he went out the back door and across the yard. He found his father leaning on the gate to Steps Meadow, looking out over Hay Bluff.

"Dad, the police are here again. They want to ask us more questions."

Karl stood up, drawing his hand across his bristly face. He had not shaved that morning, unable to tackle such a mundane task, while his eyes were dark-rimmed from lack of sleep. He looked a right mess, although Richard did not look much better. "Come on then," he muttered, leading the way back to the house.

The two detectives stood by the kitchen window, watching them approach. Karl nodded in greeting then signalled them to sit down at the table.

"I'll get straight down to matters, Mr Driesler," Groves began briskly, one eyebrow raised. "Did you know your wife was having an affair with Mr Kellett?"

Richard gasped at the suddenness of the onslaught but Karl did not react except to quietly ask: "Who says?"

"I'd be grateful if you just answered my questions, Mr Driesler," Groves reprimanded. "We'll get through this quicker that way."

Karl knew which way the wind was blowing. "You've spoken to Kellett, haven't you? And he's blaming me somehow for Katherine's death."

"I didn't suggest anything of the sort, Mr Driesler. But since you have brought up the subject, then yes, he is denying any part in her death. He says that when he left here yesterday on your sudden return home, he could hear you shouting at your wife."

"That's not true!" Richard stormed.

"I'll ask for your comments when I'm ready, young man. Until then, hold your tongue!" Groves snapped.

The kitchen door opened and a rumpled-looking Paul appeared in his dressing gown. "What's going on?" he asked his father.

"The police," Karl told him gently. "Just sit down and stay quiet, no matter what you hear."

Groves seemed put out by Paul's entrance, as though he needed to moderate his approach now. "How about answering my first question, Mr Driesler? Did you know your wife was having an affair?"

Karl flinched. "She wasn't having an affair."

"So why was Kellett here yesterday? And why should he say he was, even though it could ruin his marriage."

"It's ruined already and now he's ruined mine."

"So he and your wife were having an affair."

"No!" Karl shouted, jumping to his feet and sending his chair flying. He strode to the sink and leaned on it, looking out at the scene Katherine had spent so many hours in front of. He realised Groves was waiting for him to come up with an explanation for Kellett's presence yesterday. Slowly he turned round to face the room.

"He was forcing her to ..." His gaze fell on Paul, not wanting to be explicit in front of him.

Groves understood. "He said she was willing."

"No! He was attacking her. He forced himself on her once before when Richard was in trouble for punching him." He paused uncomfortably. "No doubt you know all about that?"

Groves nodded. "Of course. And about your attacks on Mr Kellett shortly after the war. You have a history of violence, Mr Driesler."

"Never against my wife," he muttered, knowing it made no difference.

Groves stood up. "I think, Mr Driesler, it might be better all round if you and your elder son came with us to answer further questions."

"Are you suggesting Richard had anything to do with it? That's ridiculous! It was Kellett who pushed her through the window. It's him you should be questioning, not us!"

"You're not being very helpful, Mr Driesler," Hutchinson warned, putting away his notepad and pen.

Karl slammed his palm down on the draining board, rattling the crockery stacked there. "Helpful! You expect me to be helpful at a time like this?" He felt close to tears, overloaded by his emotions. Catching sight of Paul's anxious face, he took a firm grip on himself.

"Paul, phone Werner. Get him to help you out up here. God knows how long we'll be. You might phone your Aunty Sarah too. Let her know what these fools are thinking. It might turn out to be a long haul." He turned to the two detectives. "It seems it's Kellett's word against mine and Richard's, and we all know what that means, don't we?"

Neither Groves nor Hutchinson made any comment, simply escorting them out to the car. Karl slumped into the back seat, unable to believe this could be happening to him all over again. The shock of Katherine's death was starting to bite. Yesterday he had got through the day helped by adrenalin then Robert's self-hypnosis technique. Today he was faced by an abyss, with no Katherine to cling on to. She had died protecting him, as she had always protected him. Now he had to try to cope without her. He turned his face to the car window. Beside him he heard a sniff from Richard. He could offer him no comfort.

By lunchtime Karl had stopped answering their questions. The police clearly still suspected him of killing Katherine in a jealous rage, and nothing he had said so far seemed to change their minds. He was given a sandwich for lunch but not allowed to see Richard, then the rigorous questioning resumed at two o'clock. Glover and Hutchinson were as fresh as before lunch, but Karl felt shattered, unable to concentrate on what they were asking him.

"If Mr Kellett was attacking your wife, as you make out," he vaguely heard Groves say, "why did you stand back and leave her to hit him? A man like you would protect his wife, surely? Unless she wasn't actually being attacked!" Groves' own attack picked up pace. "You caught your wife making love to another man and it was her you hit, wasn't it!"

Karl shook his head slowly. This can't be happening, he thought. It's all too ridiculous – a dream. Am I imagining this too?

There was a knock at the door. The desk sergeant came in and whispered in Groves' ear. Groves looked momentarily nonplussed then spoke to Hutchinson.

"Stay here with him. I'll be back."

Karl shut his eyes. He needed a break. He heard Hutchinson light a cigarette before he shut out all noise for a few minutes, resting his mind and allowing calm to envelope him.

Groves' return fifteen minutes later brought a change of atmosphere. Karl roused himself and saw in him a more sympathetic demeanour.

"I've just been speaking to your sister-in-law, Mr Driesler," Groves began, sitting down opposite him. "She's just driven up from London after your son phoned this morning. She's corroborated your claim that Kellett had been molesting your wife. She also said that she had advised your wife to be more firm with him in future and not let it happen again. It seems your wife was trying to do just that when you returned." He smiled ruefully. "I'm sorry, Mr Driesler. It seems probable Kellett was attempting to rape your wife, there was a struggle and she fell through the broken window as you said. We can charge Kellett with attempted rape, if you want?"

The prospect of yet more court appearances filled Karl with dread. He couldn't face any of that any more. He'd had enough. "No. I just want to go home."

"There'll have to be an inquest, of course," Groves told him. "Any action we take with regard to Kellett will depend on that."

"I see." Karl felt the crushing weight of despair. This whole business could drag on and on.

"I'm sorry," Groves said quietly, standing up to usher Karl out.

Sarah and Richard were waiting for him in the foyer of the police station. Sarah stood up when she saw him. "Oh, Karl. Isn't this awful." She approached him slowly, saw his stubble, his dull eyes, his utter exhaustion, and reached out her arms to hug him. He stood quietly, accepting her embrace.

"I'll drive us home," she murmured into his ear. Releasing her hold, she beckoned to Richard. "Come on. Let's go." She held both of them by the hand as they left the police station, leading them to her car parked nearby.

"I've taken a week's compassionate leave," she told Karl as she drove. "I hope you don't mind me staying with you. I just thought you could do with some help, especially now Donald and Gertie have gone."

"I don't mind at all," Karl said. "Lane Head's your old home. You're always welcome." He yawned, felt his stubble as he put his hand over his mouth. What a wreck! But he was glad she had come. The boys would appreciate her company too.

*

Robert also took time off work to give Karl moral support during the inquest. The whole situation was taking its toll on Karl, and Robert watched anxiously as he gave his evidence. Having argued his case with the police already, Karl managed to get through the ordeal of describing the events leading up to Katherine's death without succumbing to his emotions. He steadfastly ignored Kellett throughout the proceedings, not once making eye contact, blanking him out as though he did not exist. When the coroner delivered a verdict of accidental death, Robert heard Karl utter a sigh of relief.

"You really didn't want Andrew charged, did you, Karl?" he said, once outside the coroner's court. "I would have thought you'd have wanted him arrested and put away. Then you could relax."

Karl walked briskly back to the Land Rover, anxious to avoid Kellett and the local news reporters who had surrounded him. Sarah was taking Richard and Paul back in her car, so he and Robert could talk freely. "Let's just say I'm getting phobic about court rooms. Besides," he added, unlocking the passenger door for Robert, "I can't entirely blame him for wanting Katherine. I am guilty of stealing her from him. He always wanted her back."

"That's extraordinarily generous of you!"

"I can understand how he felt, that's all."

"Why's that?"

Karl gave him a meaningful look, as though he ought to know. Robert cursed himself, remembering what Karl had told him on his visit to Edinburgh. Ilse! Seeing the light had dawned on his friend, Karl started the engine, saying nothing. Robert did likewise. It was not an appropriate time to comment on Ilse, nor did Robert think it was warranted, but eventually the silence became unnerving. As they approached Penchurch Robert could bear it no longer.

"So, now we can have the funeral," he said. "That will be a relief."

"Yes."

"Will your folks be coming?"

"Sabina said she would organise a coach to bring everybody. They can stay in a hotel. Easier that way."

"Good. I'll stay on here until then. Silly to go all the way home and back down again."

"Can you leave your patients that long?"

"I've taken a week's leave. I'm due it and I'd like to stay."

"To keep an eye on me, you mean."

"If you like."

"Thanks. I appreciate it."

Robert felt reassured. Karl's acceptance of help was a good sign. He was not trying to deny his grief this time, as he seemed to have done with Siegfried. They were driving out of the village now and up the valley road towards the farm. There was not much time left for discussion so he pressed on with his ministrations. "What about the boys? How are they coping?"

"Richard's OK. Despite seeing her die, or maybe because of it, he's handling it better than Paul. It came as more of a shock to him. She waved him off to school and he never saw her again."

"Do you want me to talk to him?"

"If you like."

"I'll do that then." Robert sat back in his seat, satisfied with Karl's responses. The extraordinary behaviour brought about by Siegfried's death seemed to be over. Karl was grieving appropriately for his beloved wife.

*

Karl stood pale-faced but dignified as Katherine was buried beside her father in the churchyard of St Michael and All Angels. Even Audrey Kellett was there, Robert noticed, defying her husband and local opinion. Socially Andrew was finished and Audrey knew it. It was widely rumoured divorce proceedings were well under way.

The numerous mourners gathered afterwards at the Walnut Tree where Alf Butler had laid on refreshments. Along with Katherine's relatives, the whole village wanted to offer their condolences to Karl and his family. Vanessa and her parents had turned out too. So many people had loved Katherine and wanted to help her grieving family.

Karl began to feel overwhelmed by kindness and found himself withdrawing into the heart of his German family until Robert appeared at his side.

"All right, Karl?"

"So far." He paused to see if they would be overheard, but everyone was tactfully giving him and Robert space. "I've decided I'm definitely going back to Germany as soon as I can."

"I wondered whether you would," Robert said. "There's not a lot to keep you here now, is there?"

"No," Karl agreed. "I only ever stayed because Katherine loved it here and I did too, but without her ..." He swallowed hard. "Richard will be making a life for himself here soon. I don't want to get in his way. He'll have all Vanessa's family for help and advice if he needs it. What Paul will do, I don't know, but I have more family in Germany now. Bina and Wolf are there, the twins too. I'll easily slot into life in Medebach. I won't be so alone there."

"I understand, Karl. I think you're right. You need your family now."

"The only problem is Richard is still very young. He and Vanessa are getting on fine, but I don't want to force their relationship along too fast in case it comes unstuck."

Robert shrugged. "Compromise. Give them and yourself six months or so. That'll get him through the busiest part of the year on the farm. By mid-summer he should have a clearer idea of how things stand between them, and it will give him time to get used to the idea of running the farm by himself. Paul will have the chance to think about what he wants too – whether he stays to help Richard or goes to Germany with you."

"What you're really saying is that it also gives me the chance not to rush into a decision, isn't it?"

"Yes, well, there's always that."

"I won't change my mind, Robert."

"No, I don't suppose you will. But for the sake of the boys ..."

"All right. I'll wait."

Robert slapped him on the back. "Good for you."

TWENTY-SIX

In the pre-dawn darkness the comforting sound of bleating greeted Karl from the lambing sheds. Ducking under the corrugated iron roof, he cast his eyes around the flock, at the newborn lambs in separate pens with their mothers, at the still-pregnant ewes sitting placidly waiting their time or restlessly wandering. Their sour ovine smell was as familiar to him now as that of the sawdust and resin of his youth.

He ran his fingers over the back of a swollen-bellied ewe, her warmth and softness a reminder of what he had lost only a month ago. Katherine was here in the lambing sheds, around the farm. His visits to her grave in the churchyard had been pointless. He had felt nothing there; here was the connection. Every moment he was reminded of her: picking up something she had touched, doing a chore that had always been hers. She haunted his life; she was still here for him. What would it be like when she was a more distant memory?

A ewe bleated in agitation and Karl spotted her, turning round and round in the straw like a dog before lying down, neck stretched forward, bleating pitifully. She would be the next. He leaned against the shed wall, keeping an eye on her progress, glad when she safely produced her lamb. He gave her a few minutes to lick it clean and get to know its bleating, before moving them into a side pen where they could bond in peace.

Richard approached bearing a welcome cup of coffee as he emerged from the pen.

"Anything happening?" Richard asked.

"Not at the moment." Karl took a quick sip from the steaming mug. "I could do with an hour or two's more shut-eye. I feel knackered."

Richard did not need to be told his father was exhausted. The strain of the previous eighteen months, especially the last, was clearly written on his face. "I can do the shopping this afternoon, if you want to stay here and rest."

"You've had less sleep than I have, Richard."

"Yes, but I'm younger."

Karl sighed. It was a tempting suggestion but he couldn't expect Richard to do everything. "No, I'll go. It'll do me good to get away for an hour."

"OK, but get some sleep first," Richard told him.

Karl nodded. "Same applies to you. Isn't it about time you went to bed?"

"Just going. Give me a shout at midday."

"Will do." Left alone with the sheep once more, Karl contemplated what other jobs he ought to be doing that morning while keeping an eye on the ewes. Logs always needed chopping but he just couldn't summon the energy today. It was warm and cosy in the sheepsheds. He might as well stay here.

Shortly after midday he washed the blood off his hands after assisting a sheep deliver twins, then went inside the house to rouse Richard. He then went straight to his own bedroom, flopped under the covers and was asleep in an instant. Two hours later Richard woke him.

Karl stood up with the weakness of sleep still upon him and looked out of the window. It was raining hard. He stretched, trying to work some strength back into his tired body, but he still felt limp and feeble. Running a comb through his hair he could not avoid catching sight of himself in the dressing table mirror. He looked awful.

Downstairs Richard had warmed up some tinned soup. They sat and ate in silence, listening to the rain drumming on the kitchen window, the yard already awash. Karl mopped up the last of the soup from his bowl with another chunk of bread then reached for the keys to the Land Rover, which were lying on the dresser behind him.

"Anything you can think of we need?" he asked Richard.

"Aunty Sarah said we needed some more washing powder, and she was planning on cooking treacle sponge on Saturday so make sure we've got enough golden syrup."

Karl stood up and went across to the larder. He lifted the green and gold tin of syrup. It felt almost empty. He cast his eye over the shelves of provisions and saw the ketchup sauce bottle was also on its last legs.

"Razor blades," Richard called out as he dumped their bowls in the sink and ran the tap over them.

Karl decided he had better make a list. Sarah's weekend visits were proving a godsend, not least because she did the more mundane chores for them, but also her company in the male household was a pleasant change. Vanessa was also a regular weekend visitor, and Karl had let it pass that last weekend, after a night spent on duty in the sheepshed together, she had slept with Richard in his room. He was glad that Richard had someone to share the long and lonely nights with him.

He gathered up the letters for posting, put them in the shopping bag, donned his coat and dashed through the rain across the yard to the Land Rover. As he wiped the windows clear of mist, his thoughts turned again to his sons. Richard was coping well with his mother's death, but Paul was another matter. He had clammed up, become uncommunicative and sullen, although his schoolwork seemed not to be suffering too much. Karl had spoken recently to the headmaster and been reassured on that count, but at home he seemed resentful, still blaming his father for what had happened.

He's right. I am to blame, Karl told himself for the hundredth time. I should have stepped in sooner, but I was too much of a coward, trying to avoid more trouble.

He slammed the Land Rover into gear, drove out of the yard and down the lane. He hated shopping trips to the village store, having to endure the sympathetic enquiries of everyone he met. He craved anonymity but it was impossible here.

Penchurch's Post Office-cum-General Store had expanded recently, having been taken over by a small supermarket chain. The range of items on offer would have amazed old Mrs Tucker, who had run the store during the war and who had been so kind to him in his early days in the village. Now it was run by a newcomer, who had modern ideas, modern lines and modern manners. Karl slunk in, picked up a basket by the door and began browsing the shelves. As he stood upright after picking up a tin of golden syrup from the bottom shelf, a wave of giddiness flooded over him. He staggered, knocking tins of custard powder over and sending them rolling up the aisle. He put down his basket to lower his head but the giddiness would not pass. A helping hand steadied him as other customers retrieved the errant tins and he was guided to a chair by the post office counter.

"It's Mr Driesler," he heard the woman who had steadied him tell the post office clerk. "He's not well. Perhaps we should call an ambulance."

"No, it's not necessary," Karl told them, not wanting the fuss. "I'll just sit here a moment. It's just a giddy spell."

A figure pushed her way through the small crowd. To Karl's dismay he recognised Kellett's estranged wife, Audrey. Why did *she* have to be here now, of all people? As he expected, she took instant control of the situation.

"Karl, you look dreadful!"

"I'm just a bit tired, Audrey."

"Tired! You're exhausted by the look of you." She picked up his shopping basket. "Give me your list and let me get the rest for you, then I'll drive you home."

"Really, Audrey, I'll be –"

"Rubbish! You'll likely drive off the road and kill yourself the way you look. You're lucky it didn't happen on your way down here."

Her words brought awful images of Siegfried's shattered body to mind. Meekly he handed her the list and sat quietly while she dealt with it.

She insisted on carrying his shopping to her car – not the blue Jaguar he was glad to see. Andrew must have kept that.

"How are you feeling now?" she asked as she drove him back up the valley road.

"Better," he replied untruthfully. "It's very good of you, Audrey, to come out of your way."

"Least I could do, after what Andrew did," she muttered.

Karl kept silent. He did not want to discuss Katherine's death, but Audrey had other ideas. If Karl did not want to talk, she did.

"Things had been bad between Andrew and me before," she said, "but when the police said he had attempted to rape Katherine before pushing her through the window, I knew that was it. I've moved out to a small house in Hereford, but I was just calling back here to get a few more belongings." She omitted to say she had seen Karl's Land Rover parked outside the Post Office and had come in the shop deliberately to see him.

"What about your children?" Karl asked.

"They're staying with Andrew. Boarding school takes care of them the rest of the time. Angela's going off to secretarial college soon, and Alan will probably join the army. Off my hands now, both of them."

"And you?" he asked politely. "Have you any plans?"

"I'll get a job. Maybe go back to being a legal secretary. Who knows?" She smiled. "Perhaps I'll even find a nice man eventually."

"No doubt," Karl said dryly.

She was silent a moment, then put a hand on his thigh. "Karl, I know now's not the time, but if you ever need a bit of ... well ... you know, I'd be only too pleased to help you out – no complications. Just like before."

He smiled at her forwardness. Audrey had not changed a bit. "Thank you. I'll bear it in mind."

"I'll give you my phone number. Next time you're in Hereford, look me up. I'd be pleased to see you, even if just for a chat and a glass of something."

They had arrived at the farm. Before getting out of the car, Audrey scribbled down her phone number and handed it to him. He folded the scrap of paper and put it in his pocket.

"Is Richard about?" she asked him as she took his shopping out of the car. "I could run him back down to the village to fetch your Land Rover."

"He's probably in the lambing sheds. I'll take a look."

"Are you sure you're OK?"

"Much steadier now, thanks." It was true. He did feel better as he wandered into the dim shed and found Richard bending down by a heaving ewe. Richard was shocked when he heard what had happened, but since the ewe chose that moment to successfully eject her lamb, he was able to take up Audrey's offer of a lift.

"Keys?"

Karl handed them to his son and followed him out to where Audrey stood waiting by her car.

"Now you take more care of yourself, Karl. And don't forget what I said," she winked, after Richard had got in and shut the door.

"I won't. Thank you for your help today, Audrey."

"My pleasure," she beamed getting into the car.

*

When she arrived at the weekend, Sarah was dismayed to hear about Karl's giddy turn. Richard knew his father would not mention it, so he told her himself in private.

"Mrs Kellett had to drive him home," he concluded.

"Audrey? I thought she lived in Hereford now."

"She was passing by," Richard explained.

Sarah decided to tackle Karl on the subject, finding him down in the lower orchards. She had been giving a lot of thought to the Driesler household in recent weeks and Richard's news seemed to have brought matters to a head. Paul was busy taking his turn in the lambing sheds, so she would have Karl to herself. She spotted him hauling broken branches down to the gateway, where there was already a large pile.

"Storm damage?" she asked by way of announcing her arrival.

"Some." He threw the branches down on the pile and wiped his palms on his thighs to get rid of the green algae.

"Couldn't Paul or Richard do this? You're supposed to be taking things easy."

"So Richard told you. I guessed he would." He began walking back up the row of apple trees to find the next piece of storm detritus. "I can't sit doing nothing, Sarah. You know me."

"You've got to, Karl," she said, stooping to pick up a small branch.

"Then I've got to get away." He stopped suddenly, deciding to confide in his sister-in-law. "Before all this, before she died, I'd told her I wanted to go back to Germany. She didn't want to go until the boys were older, but at the funeral Robert agreed with me that I needed to go ... home." He looked at her and saw she understood. "You still feel this is your home, even after all these years, don't you?"

She nodded. "I've really enjoyed coming back here. Everything's so familiar, and I love being around family."

Karl examined his palms and wiped them again. "Nearly everyone I was close to here has gone. I feel an outsider again without Katherine. Now I just want to be with my family in Medebach, see Bina and Wolf, visit my grandchildren. Even call on my old cellmate, Auer, in prison or relive the good old, bad old days with Ernst Winter in Berlin. There's so much for me in Germany now. Here I feel ..." He shook his head, unable to find the right word.

"Confined?" Sarah guessed.

"Exactly. Confined." He gazed at the orchards stretching away up the hillside, their rows of trunks like prison bars. "Richard has Vanessa and her family, but Paul ... Paul doesn't like me anymore."

Sarah touched his arm in sympathy. "I'd noticed he was a bit cool towards you. Maybe it's just the teenage years, nothing to do with you."

"Maybe, I don't know. He won't talk."

"I shouldn't take it to heart, Karl. He'll come round, I know he will. He's quite friendly to me."

"Mother-substitute."

"Yes, I suppose so," Sarah said softly. She looked round the orchard and felt her heart lift. This *was* home. It was also the right time to mention what had been growing in her mind recently. "Karl, if you need to go home, then go. Don't worry about the farm or the boys. I can keep an eye on them."

"From London?"

"No, from here." She smiled. "I love it here, Karl. I've got fed up with my aimless existence in London. Sure, I've got friends and a good job there, but I miss this place so much. I always hate returning to London. Maybe I'm just getting middle-aged and wanting a bit of peace and quiet finally in my life. London's just got too hectic these days. Give me a month and I can be here." She saw the relief in his eyes, the realisation that the prison door was opening and he could leave. In case he was still in doubt, she added: "The boys will miss you, and Werner will, but they'll manage."

"They can always visit – you too."

She grinned. "I'd like that. I've never been to Germany."

"Shame on you! You don't know what you're missing." Suddenly the world was a rosier place for Karl. He reached for Sarah's hands. "Thank you, Sarah. You've given me a life back again. I can start afresh."

She squeezed his hands. "It seems it's all change for everyone, not just Gertie and Donald. The village will never be the same again."

"You'll have to take on Gertie's good deeds. Katherine was going to ..." He broke off, releasing her hands, as raw grief threatened to overwhelm him. Swallowing hard he shut out the pain. "Audrey will be pleased to have you nearby again."

"We can get up to all sorts of mischief together! We'll both come and visit you! Medebach won't know what's hit it."

His mind now fixed on the future, Karl cast a last glance around the orchard. "I'm through here. Let's get back to the house."

"Just one thing, Karl," Sarah needed to point out as they headed back up the hill. "You can't take more than fifty pounds out of the country now. You know that, don't you?"

"Yes, I had heard, but it doesn't matter. I'm sure my family can help me out until I've earned some. But what about you? You're earning good money. Won't you miss it?"

Sarah smiled. "I've managed to save up quite a bit over the years. Plus there's my flat. I could rent that out easily enough and get a tidy income. No, it seems you and I have both hit our mid-life crises. I want a change ... and to be needed."

"Why didn't you ever get married again after Perry?" Karl asked, holding open a gate for her.

"Too busy enjoying my independence, though I regret not having children of my own now. I'll just have to take on yours and be a full-time aunt."

"They'll appreciate you, I know."

"Let's hope so."

*

The battered suitcase on the bed was a history of his recent turbulent past. It had come with him and Sabina on that fateful trip to Germany when he had shot Goslar. Katherine had learned of his adultery when Ilse had returned the suitcase to her. He had been using it when Siegfried died. Now it would accompany him on his return to Germany to a new life, a new beginning. He had no regrets about his decision. He was moving on.

Sarah interrupted his musing with a brisk knock on his open bedroom door before entering with an armful of clean laundry. "Here's the last of it," she said, laying the shirts flat on the bed. She peered at the contents of the suitcase. "Is that really all you're taking with you?"

"I can buy any clothes I need. I only want a few mementos, photos that sort of thing."

Sarah nodded. "Got your passport and tickets?"

He patted his jacket. "Yep." He packed the shirts he had been waiting for, closed the suitcase and locked it. "That's it then. I'm ready."

He cast a last glance around the bedroom that had been Katherine's parents', then his and Katherine's. Soon it would be Richard and Vanessa's, now that their engagement had been announced. His gaze fell on the painting of the bluebell wood that hung over the bed head. It had been Katherine's favourite picture, and was the only thing he regretted having to leave behind.

"It's her, isn't it?" Sarah said, pointing at the picture.

"Yes. It's her. So it stays. She didn't want to move to Germany."

Sarah smiled. "I'll make sure the boys look after it."

"Thank you. I'll expect to see it when I'm next over." Karl picked up the suitcase and his overcoat and left the room without another glance. That was it. He would be back. There was no need for wholesale farewells. He paused briefly at the foot of the stairs and cast a glance towards the front door. That was a memory he could do without. He turned his back on it and headed towards the kitchen where Richard and Paul sat waiting. They stood up when they saw him.

"Right, I'm ready. Let's be off."

Karl drove, Richard acted as navigator, while Sarah sat with Paul in the back. She did not want to usurp Katherine's place next to Karl, even though she had taken on the role of Paul's mother. Originally Paul had not wanted to come to the airport with them, but Sarah had persuaded him. Now she looked at the fair-haired lad and saw his pain and confusion. He had cut himself off from his father since Katherine's death, blaming him for allowing it to happen. Now she saw his realisation that the father he had once adored was leaving too, with a gulf still between them.

Sarah ferreted in her handbag for her diary and a pencil, found a blank page and wrote: *Tell your father it wasn't his fault. Tell him you still love him.* She showed it to him but he only glanced at it and looked away.

Nobody spoke much on the journey to Heathrow. Karl was glad to concentrate on driving, while the others all seemed wrapped in their own thoughts. He was relieved when they arrived at the airport and had found a parking place. He lifted out his suitcase, then handed the car keys to Richard. It was like handing over the baton in a relay race. It was all up to him now. Richard sensed the importance of the moment and looked into his father's eyes briefly before pocketing the keys.

They trooped into the departure hall, got Karl checked in then had half an hour to say goodbye. Sarah knew the time must not be wasted. She took Richard's elbow and whispered in his ear: "Disappear for a few minutes. Go and buy a newspaper or something for your dad to read on the journey. I want to leave him alone with Paul. I think they've got to talk."

She let go of his arm, saw Karl had not noticed their conversation, then said out loud: "Excuse me while I nip to the Ladies'."

When Richard also disappeared on his errand, Karl sat down on a nearby seat in the busy departure area to await their return. Paul realised this was his moment and sat down next to him. He stared at the floor between his feet, wishing he knew what he felt, what he should say. He just knew he must say something before Richard and Aunty Sarah returned.

"Dad?"

"Yes?"

Paul paused. He had to be grown up about this. He must stop thinking about himself, see matters from his father's perspective and say the right thing. He gave it a try. "Don't worry about us. We'll be fine. I'm happy to stay here and finish school. I'll miss you, of course, but it'll be like when you were ..." He lowered his voice. "... in prison." He looked sideways at his father and smiled at him for the first time since his mother's death. "You need to get away from here, though. I can see that now. You'll have all the family over there to help you cope. Richard and I aren't very good at that sort of thing. Bina is. She'll be like Mum, worrying about you. It's best you're near her."

A businessman sat down by them and began sorting through his briefcase. Paul noticed documents in English so switched to speaking in German. "You won't forget about Mum will you?"

"Of course not. Why, do you think I would?"

"No, but ..." Paul's eyes slipped away from his father's. He suddenly knew what was troubling him and now was the moment to say it. "You'll probably find someone else, and I couldn't bear that," he mumbled.

Karl put his arm around Paul and drew him close. "Who knows what the future will bring? I may find someone in due course, but you wouldn't want me to be a lonely old man, would you?" He felt Paul shrug. "Mum will always remain with me in my heart," he continued, "but people move on. I know that well. In fact, talking to you like this is helping me realise that. I don't want to be alone, Paul. I need someone to help me through life, and I can't ask you or Richard to do that."

Paul clammed up, his thoughts too mutinous to risk opening his mouth. He turned his head away and looked for Richard. He spotted him loitering by the departures board, newspaper in hand.

Richard saw things had turned awkward for Paul and hurried over, joined a few moments later by Sarah. Karl and Paul stood up, as there were no spare seats for the others.

"It was silly to drag you all this way," Karl said, seeing their anxious faces. "I should have caught the train and been done with it. Goodbyes are so difficult."

"Nonsense," Sarah said brightly. "They're important, and seeing you leave from here helps us come to terms with it better. Doesn't it, Paul?" She looked at him hopefully.

Paul knew what she was asking. He had to let his father go and find a new life and happiness. "Yes." It dawned on him he meant it. "Yes," he said again with more conviction. He turned to his father. "I hope you find what you're looking for, Dad."

"Thank you, Paul. I knew you would understand."

EPILOGUE

Ilse had been thinking about the letter all day. Now she sat in the winter sunshine on the balcony watching the ships as she had so many times before, wishing she were on one going home. It was not just her children and grandchildren she missed, it was the whole German way of life: having places and people to visit, being able to converse easily, having summer in July and August and crisp, cold winters in December. Life in Uruguay held no attraction for her – not even Ricardo. She wanted her old life back.

Now this letter from Sophie had come and it changed everything. She had not let the letter out of her sight all day, had read it three times already and wanted to read it again now just to convince herself it was true. She unfolded the sheet of paper again and read:

20th *August 1969*

Dearest Ilse,
Here are the latest photos of the twins for you. Don't they look sweet in the birthday outfits you sent them! They were both on their best behaviour, luckily, as we had quite a few friends and relations round for the party. Freia charmed everyone – typical girl! – and was busy saying all the words she knows already. She's added 'cat' and 'drink' to the list now. Friedrich is biding his time, but makes up for lack of words with volume. I can't decide yet whether he looks like Siegfried or me most. Maybe you can tell from the photos.
I'm glad Karl managed to come up from Medebach for their birthday. After what happened I feel more of a bond with him. He was a lot quieter than in the past, and I think he's finding it difficult adjusting to life without Katherine. I know just how he feels, wanting to be near his family at such a time. I'm so grateful I had everyone around me when Siegfried died. I'm gradually finding it easier to talk about him and look at photos of him but I miss him terribly. I'm sure you do too.

My parents are just terrific and enable me to get out on my own occasionally. I went to the cinema with a girlfriend recently, and I finally managed a very gentle game of tennis last week. My legs will never be brilliant, but at least I can get about, which is the main thing. I don't think I'll ever wear a miniskirt, and I felt very self-conscious in a tennis skirt, but there was only my friend Eva there to see the scars.

My parents send their love and best wishes to you, as do I, and I hope it won't be too long before we see you again.

With our fondest love,
Sophie and the Twins

Ilse put the letter down again, satisfied she was correct in her assumption that Katherine was dead. She wondered why nobody had told her. Most likely everyone thought somebody else had. For the first time since opening the letter, she wondered how Katherine had died. She hoped she had not suffered unduly, but her thoughts did not dwell on the subject for long. More important was the fact that Karl was all alone and back in Germany. And she was stuck here in Uruguay with a life she was beginning to hate. Karl needed her. Perhaps not just yet, but in a few months he might turn to her again. She must be there for him.

She heard Paul come in from work and went inside to greet him. He sensed her excitement immediately.

"You're all of a twitter today. What's got into you since I left this morning?" he asked with a grin. "Has Ricardo paid a visit?"

"Not today," she replied, helping him off with his jacket and pouring him a beer. She handed him the glass then sat down on the sofa beside him. "Have you been seeing Maria today, then?" she asked slyly.

"Ah well, that would be telling, wouldn't it. I try to keep my indiscretions quiet, even if you do know about her."

"About her and Lucinda and Brigitte and Rosa! I know them all, Paul." She smiled indulgently and kissed him. "Or have I left any out?"

"Well ... maybe one or two, but who's counting?" He took a sip of beer, then asked: "So what *has* got into you today? You haven't told me yet."

Slowly she drew out the envelope containing Sophie's letter from the pocket of her cardigan and passed it to him. Paul read it quickly, then again more slowly, then he put it down on his lap and looked at her intently.

"Is Katherine dead?"

"I think she must be. Karl wouldn't stay in Germany otherwise."

Paul at last understood Ilse's mood and recognised the inevitable. Ilse had always been Karl's and always would be. There was little point trying to fight it. She would never rest easy here now. "So you'll be leaving, then?" he asked softly.

Ilse let go her held breath and smiled her gratitude. "Yes, Paul. I'm sorry it's ended like this."

"I knew you weren't happy here."

"And at least you've got Maria," she pointed out.

"And the others."

She kissed him. "Thank you, Paul. I knew you would understand."

Shades of Grey by Caron Harrison

In October 1946 who is truly free?

Katherine Carter believes she is. With all her life spent on her father's Herefordshire farm, her future seems mapped out – until she meets Karl.

Karl Driesler has little freedom. His future is bleak. Still a prisoner of war eighteen months after Germany's surrender, he suffers nightmares and his fiancée has just married another man.

Robert Murdoch, the village doctor's son, also suffers nightmares. A former prisoner of the Japanese, he finds freedom unexpectedly hard to cope with – until he meets Karl.

These three find their growing bonds of friendship and love tested to the full as Karl's dark secret is revealed by Katherine's jilted fiancé. Katherine withdraws her love, shattering Karl's hopes of a future with her. Suffering a mental breakdown, he is helpless as his British friends rally round to assist, while his rival for Katherine's love does his utmost to break him entirely.

Divided Loyalties by Caron Harrison

The horrors of war are receding for former prisoner of war, Karl Driesler, now happily married and living with Katherine on their Herefordshire farm. But a new war is about to begin.

Ilse Brünninghaus has taught her illegitimate son, Siegfried, to hate his father, Karl, as a traitor to Nazism. But when she is forced by her brutal husband to find a new home for Siegfried, she has only Karl to whom she can turn. As Ilse hands over her son to her former lover, she realises she still loves Karl, and Siegfried is her access to him.

All too soon Karl discovers the extent of his son's hatred, as Siegfried's aggression leads to an increasingly bloody chain of events.

But love can prove an equally disruptive force.